KU-691-969

STRING OF PEARLS

Madge Swindells

severn
House

This first world edition published 2009
in Great Britain and in the USA by
SEVERN HOUSE PUBLISHERS LTD of
9–15 High Street, Sutton, Surrey, England, SM1 1DF.
Trade paperback edition published
in Great Britain and the USA 2009 by
SEVERN HOUSE PUBLISHERS LTD

Copyright © 2009 by Madge Swindells.

All rights reserved.
The moral right of the author has been asserted.

British Library Cataloguing in Publication Data

Swindells, Madge
    String of Pearls
    1. World War, 1939–1945 - England - Dorset - Fiction
    2. World War, 1939–1945 - Evacuation of civilians - Great
    Britain - Fiction 3. War brides - Fiction 4. Love stories
    I. Title
    823.9'14[F]

ISBN-13: 978-0-7278-6663-9   (cased)
ISBN-13: 978-1-84751-144-7   (trade paper)

Except where actual historical events and characters are being
described for the storyline of this novel, all situations in this
publication are fictitious and any resemblance to living persons
is purely coincidental.

All Severn House titles are printed on acid-free paper.

Typeset by Palim
Grangemouth, St
Printed and boun
MPG Books Ltd.

HAMPSHIRE COUNTY
LIBRARY

C014786704	
HJ	30-Mar-2010
AF	£10.99
9781847511447	

With grateful thanks to my daughter, Jenni, for her valuable plotting ideas, and to Peter for his help with the research, to Shelley for her editorial assistance and Anna Telfer for her meticulous copy-editing.

'If we are together nothing is impossible. If we are divided all will fail.'

Winston Churchill

One

On a sunny August afternoon, Helen Conroy, housewife, mother, riding teacher and war worker was halfway home when she stopped cycling to watch a skylark singing its heart out as it hovered over a field, then swooped and rose, trilling loud and shrill. She had just completed her five-hour morning stint packing explosives at an armaments factory, a tense and tiring job. Cycling home along a narrow country lane, bordered by oak and elm trees, between fields of ripening wheat and barley, brought her joy and the chance to unwind.

The air was hot and sultry under a hazy sky. The buzz of insects reverberated in her ears, midges swarmed, rooks circled and squabbled. How wonderful to have escaped that noisy, stuffy factory where she'd been stooped over a bench, her clothes sticking to her, never relaxing for a moment for fear of blowing herself and others to smithereens. It was lovely here. She was tempted to sit on the bank and enjoy the morning. She could scent honeysuckle, wet grass and warm, damp earth, reminding her of their last summer holiday in Devon. *Damn! Why did she think of that?* Her eyes burned as she remembered.

Eric is lying on his back, almost hidden by dried grass and wild fennel, with the sun shining on his face, his eyes glinting with fun. 'Come on. Don't be a baby. There's no one around for miles.'

'There are the cows.' She is trying to make light of her reluctance. She stares down at Brixham's tiny fishing harbour and the rows of houses straggling uphill. The sea is a translucent blue, but she can see the dark shadow of the wreck her husband is salvaging. Today the sea is deceptively calm, but sometimes it terrifies her: when Eric is down in the smashed hold.

'What's the good of coming here for a holiday if we don't enjoy ourselves? I haven't seen you for months.'

She takes off her coat awkwardly and kneels amongst the fennel, the strong, acidic scent wafts around her. She presses her hand flat on the ground, feels the dew that will penetrate the only coat she has with her and maybe stain it. She turns her coat inside out and rolls it up. Sitting on the grass, she feels the dampness penetrate her skirt and then her panties.

'Oh, for fuck's sake. Just look at your expression!' Eric jumps up and brushes the burrs off his trousers in sharp, angry gestures, his face sullen and disappointed. 'You hate sex.' He walks away.

'I do not. It's just that the grass is damp,' she calls after him. Hadn't they made love for hours last night and briefly this morning? But by now Eric is almost out of sight, striding towards the lane. She climbs to her feet and picks up her coat. As she expected, there is mud on the hem. It is all she has to wear to dinner tonight. She will sponge it lightly when she reaches their hotel. He'll get over it, she tells herself, unaware of the approaching danger.

Helen frowned, regretting her lack of control. That was over a year ago. She had promised herself not to keep going over the past. She had taken the children to join Eric for the summer holidays. Miro and Daisy were turning sixteen and they loved it at Brixham. Until the last evening she had happily imagined that they were having fun. Since then she had fought to protect her marriage.

Suddenly she wanted to get home. She cycled faster, skidding around the corners. The sight of her father's rambling Victorian home, with the ivy creeping over the red brick walls to the eaves, always comforted her. It stood well back from a broad, gravel lane and at the back of the garden it overlooked the sea. They had always enjoyed their private bay, which wasn't theirs at all, but there was no way to get down to the sea except by boat or else from the zigzag path which her great grandfather had constructed, leading from the bottom of their garden. Their eight acres were spread around the bay, which was enclosed at both ends by cliffs jutting out to sea. It was low tide and she could see the ragged bows of a wreck breaking the calm surface of the sea. This was a fairly recent addition to the bay: a Greek owned, Liberian registered freighter, carrying a cargo of copper from Zaire, which had foundered on the rocks one foggy night in 1939, just after war was declared. The crew had been saved by the local lifeboat from Poole, which set out as soon as her father had called them.

They shared their lane with three houses and all the gardens were substantial, but since the war began only parts of them were cultivated. Hardly anyone had time to tend the gardens. Most of the lawns had become meadows where wild flowers were sprouting while the flower beds were covered in weeds and the hedges were running to wood. Their garden looked better than most because Helen's father was an enthusiastic gardener and his war work consisted of only three nights a week in the ARP – the Air Raid Precaution service.

Cooper House stood three miles from Mowbray village and only a short drive away from the New Forest, if you had petrol to waste. Three generations of Coopers had lived here. This was where she had been born and brought up until she left home at seventeen to study dress designing in London. She'd met her husband at a party in London. He had fascinated her with his tales of underwater daring in the world of salvage, his travels around the world, his wavy black hair and blue eyes and he had danced her off her feet. Oh God! Now she was back to Eric again, but it was only three months since he'd left her and her wounds still hurt.

She found her father working in the stables. 'Hi Dad.' She forced a smile.

'Ah, there you are Helen.' Bent over a sack of feed, John Cooper peered over his shoulder before grabbing hold of a strap to pull himself up. When he stood straight, which wasn't often, he was six foot tall, a strong, wiry man with no excess fat. His hair was grey, but his grey eyes were as youthful as a young man's so that you didn't notice his wrinkled skin or his arthritic hands. She knew that he was too old to take on all this work. She had been selfish to start their riding school, but her father had been keen and the additional income came in handy. Dad had offered them his home and himself as cook, stable hand, char, adviser, gardener and odd-job-man. He was seventy-five and very fit, but lately his back was acting up with the strain. Once the financial director of a ceramics plant and later, when her grandfather died, the proprietor, he had retired seven years ago, but he still retained an air of command which worked well with the children. Her father's kindness and dependability had helped Helen through all her problems, but even he was unable to help her now.

'You do too much,' she said.

'Nonsense. Exercise keeps me young.'

He turned and looked towards their fields where their twelve horses had been put out to graze. Daunty, their black stallion, had been Eric's. He had insisted on having him even though she and

Dad had wanted a gelding. A stallion in a riding school didn't make any sense, particularly since they kept six quiet mares for their younger pupils.

John seemed to read her thoughts. 'We should sell Daunty; don't you think so?'

'Maybe later.'

John didn't argue. He never gave unwanted advice. That was one of the great things about him. He understood that she was not yet able to let go.

'Helen,' John called after her. 'You're running out of time.'

'Heavens!' She hurried to change into her jodhpurs and a T-shirt. Glancing out of the window she saw a few children arriving. Most of the youngsters in her class came from the local farms. Today they were going to have their first lesson in jumping. They were smart, unafraid and easy to teach. She enjoyed the lessons and it took her mind off her hurt. The afternoon went faster and better than she had expected.

Later, Helen bathed and changed into her old corduroys and a blouse, which she wore for her evening stint at the NAAFI canteen. She hurried to the kitchen to prepare the family supper.

Miro came home first. 'Where's Daisy?' he called from the hall.

'She said she might be late. Extra gym practice.'

'Perhaps I should go and fetch her.'

'Why? She's all right. It's light and safe.'

Sometimes Helen worried about Miro's excessive concern for Daisy, but when you thought about what he'd been through it was understandable that he should find the world such an unsafe place. He was exactly the same age as Daisy and sometimes people took them for twins. Whereas Daisy had ash-blonde hair like hers, and the same blue eyes and milky white skin, Miro had startling dark eyes, light brown hair and a sturdy, square face that was vaguely Russian in appearance. She had a sudden memory of seeing him for the first time on a rainy morning at Dover station. He had been so thin and gangly and his features seemed too large for the rest of him, but now everything fitted together perfectly and he was becoming a very good looking boy.

She felt a hand on her shoulder. 'That smells great.'

'Oh, Miro. You made me jump.' She turned round for her customary kiss on either cheek. This had never been a family habit, but they were learning from Miro. 'There's a big bowl of jelly in the larder, Miro. The stew will be ready by seven, although it's a tough old bird. I swopped it for—'

'Don't tell me,' Miro said. 'Your precious clothing coupons. You should have taken Cocky.'

'Eat Cocky!' She gaped at him in astonishment, but saw from Miro's grin that he was teasing her.

'Cocky wakes me every morning at dawn when I want to sleep,' he grumbled.

'It's a great way to start the day. Don't you think so?'

Miro shrugged. 'If it makes you happy. I'm going to study.'

By six p.m., Helen was sitting in the lounge with John listening to the news. It was all bad: the German army had encircled Smolensk, capturing 300,000 Russian soldiers, and over 3,000 tanks, a shattering defeat for the Red Army; Churchill had accused the Nazis of 'merciless butchery' in Soviet territories where whole districts were being exterminated; there was growing unease over Japanese expansion in Indochina; and Pétain had imposed fascist rule on France.

It was a relief when the news finished and they could listen to ITMA (*It's That Man Again*) with Tommy Handley, on the radio. As usual, Mona Lot was complaining, this time about the colour of their bread.

'Of course, she's right.' Helen laughed. 'The bread's a dirty beige colour nowadays. That's why I always toast our sandwiches.' Helen sipped her tea and munched her toast. Margarine was entirely out until they started on the next page of ration coupons on Monday. The jam was insipid, mainly flavoured gelatin without much fruit or sugar, but that was all she could get. No one complained. The enemy's U-boats were trying to starve them into submission, too many supply ships were torpedoed and their merchant navy boys were dying in order to bring them food. They were truly grateful for whatever they had.

The doorbell rang, startling her. 'Damn!'

'I'll go,' John said.

'No, no. You stay there. You need a rest.' Helen hurried to the front door as Enid Warrington rang again. Flushed and sweating, she leaned against the wall. Enid had joined the council last year and she was doing the job of two men who had been called up.

'Have you come to check the meter, Enid?'

'Not this time. I have to find billets for soldiers and it's urgent.

We've had a memo from the War Office. Rooms are needed as of now. I need to look around.'

'Help yourself.' Helen went back to ITMA, leaving Enid to tramp through the house and the grounds.

Ten minutes later Enid knocked on the door. 'Are all those fields behind the stables yours?'

'Yes. And the wood. You look exhausted. Come in and have some coffee.'

'Thanks, but I haven't time. I reckon they'll want the fields.'

'I hope not. We run stables here with twelve horses. We need the grazing.'

'I'll mention that.' She scribbled in her notebook.

'So, the Yanks are coming at last,' John said. 'Just in time, I might add.'

'What makes you think so?' Enid looked up nervously. Perhaps this was classified information.

'The War Office has enough land for all its needs. The Yanks will have to set up camps and they'll want space for training and stockpiling their equipment.'

'I might as well break the bad news, Mr Cooper. You're bound to get one of them billeted on you. The War Office insists on a bedroom, a bed, linen, towels, a table, a wardrobe and a chair. Your place is 'officer class'. You'll probably have to find alternative grazing for your horses because they're bound to want those fields.'

'Do we have to provide food?' Helen asked her.

'No.'

'Well, thank heavens for that.'

Enid looked around enviously. 'I bet you'll get one of those sexy Yanks who look as if they're straight out of Hollywood.'

'I'm sure he'll be a pain whatever he looks like,' Helen said, as she showed Enid out.

Daisy was coming up the driveway. 'Hi darling. Where were you?'

Daisy shrugged and tried to push past her, but Helen stood firm. 'What is it with you, Daisy? For goodness sake lose this antagonism. Where were you?'

'Studying with a friend,' she muttered. Pushing Helen's hand aside, she walked into the lounge and made a point of hugging her grandfather.

'But where will the horses graze all day?' Daisy wailed when her grandfather told her about the probable loss of their fields.

'I guess we'll have to give them the run of the garden,' John replied.

Daisy looked horrified. 'They'll ruin the lawn.'

'For goodness sake, Daisy.' Miro sounded agitated. 'Have you ever considered what our lives would be like if we lost this war?'

Then the bleak look they knew so well came into his eyes again. It was like pulling down the shutters. 'Sorry.' He stood up ready to flee.

'Miro!' Helen's voice was sharper than usual. 'You're entitled to your say, like the rest of us and what you said was very much to the point. Please don't go.'

He sat down looking guilty. Helen hated him to look like that. All the love she had lavished on him had not been able to erase that expression.

'We'll have to grow our own vegetables in the front, and the horses can have the back. Lawns will be a thing of the past and we might as well get used to it. Plus, we must sort out the bedrooms,' John said.

Chaos erupted as no one wanted to give up an inch of their space.

Two

Swaying to the tango, in an exclusive nightclub in Buenos Aires, with the best looking girl in the room in his arms, Captain Simon Johnson should have felt great.

This was a nightly ritual and Uncle Sam was picking up his tabs, so why wasn't he laughing? The truth was he felt a heel. He'd been tiptoeing around every proffered friendship since he arrived and in the process he'd become an accomplished liar. But the focus of his guilt was the woman in his arms. He hadn't actually lied to Maria, he argued with himself. He'd merely omitted to tell the truth. He'd learned to get by with the magic word 'maybe'. Compassion surged as he imagined her distress when she found he had gone. He had used her, but he had never imagined that she would fall in love with him.

Unable to bear looking at her, Simon glanced around. Dimmed lights reflected on the gilt walls and pillars gave a distinct impression of a golden cave: cosy, rich and decadent, where wayward, well-heeled civil servants danced and drank until dawn. The faces of the males exactly matched the decor, but the women were beautiful, clinging, overanxious, fearing they would soon be dumped.

The music changed to a slow foxtrot and Maria nestled closer. He could feel the warmth of her breasts pressing against his chest, her legs against his. Her body, so warm and supple, created an illusion of oneness. As her perfume wafted over him, Simon experienced a brief moment of regret. He sensed that he was becoming as decadent as the other regulars. He should have left long ago, but he was under orders.

The past six months had been packed with danger, guile and a hectic social life and Maria had proved invaluable. She worked for one of the ministers and she had been very useful in bringing home files and chattering about her bosses. Due to her indiscretions, he had located three homes with enemy agents and transmitters. All their messages were being successfully intercepted by CIA spooks. He was leaving for good in the early hours of the morning and he would never see her again, but how could he tell her this? He had warned her not to fall in love. He'd said he was a rolling stone, but she, with her dark beauty, her allure, her costly penthouse, her sports car and her amazing talent for dancing, had felt sure that she could hold him. She believed in his alias – that he was a disbarred American lawyer currently employed as a cheap legal clerk for the Ministry of Foreign Affairs. It was partly true. He gave them top legal advice for next to nothing, they provided him with the information he had been sent to uncover. Everyone was satisfied with the arrangement.

Simon had volunteered for the army a day after Pearl Harbour, abandoning a highly paid legal career in Manhattan. He longed to fight his way through Europe and help to rid the world of the scourge of Nazism, but he'd soon realized that he had picked a bad time. A prominent Chicago lawyer, Alfred McCormack had been called upon by the Secretary of War to set up and deal with the processing of communications intelligence. McCormack drew heavily on lawyers from elite firms. They were nabbed as fast as they volunteered, given reserve commissions, sent for minimum training and drafted into Military Intelligence. Simon had fallen into his lap.

Since then Simon had sent three urgent applications to the head of the Special Branch requesting a transfer to active service. He'd received his transfer, but not to where he wanted to go. He was sent to a special branch of the newly-established Military Intelligence Service (MIS), dealing with Axis penetration and subversion in Latin America. After a brief training, he was sent to Argentina where he had spent the past six months. He had been uniquely successful and his sudden recall spelled a reprieve. He hoped this was his chance to join a fighting unit. He was aching to go.

Maria raised her sexy arm to pull his head towards her. Her lips brushed his cheek. 'Let's go home,' she murmured. When she laughed and pressed against him, Simon felt a startling rekindling of desire.

'I can't go home yet. Sorry. I have a meeting. It's something I can't avoid.'

'I'll stay awake. See you after the meeting. I don't mind how late you are.' Suspicion clouded her face, making her look older. She pursed her lips, removed her arms from the back of his neck and smoothed her long black hair, a provocative gesture, but behind her brave attempt at coquetry, he sensed her desperation. She had honed in on his elation, but he had not shared the reason for it.

Compassion surged, and then his guilt. He had no wish to harm her. He felt depressed, too, because he had no regrets at leaving her. He suspected he was lacking in some vital emotion. At forty-one he had never been in love. He had married young and their ensuing separation had been terrible and inevitable. What was love anyway? A load of hype dreamed up by advertising agents and romantic writers.

'Maybe,' he told her, avoiding her gaze. But this was not to be. By midnight he was on a plane to the States and by ten a.m. the following morning he was reporting for duty to his commanding officer in Miami.

'You've done exceptionally well, Johnson,' Major Norris told him. 'It seems you lawyers have a talent for spying.' He looked at him with distaste as he picked up his file. 'I'm sending you to our newest Military Intelligence Training Center at Camp Ritchie, Maryland.' Norris was a regular army guy, top on discipline, but lacking in charm. He was as solid and strong as a buffalo, his complexion, seared by years in the sun, had turned a russet brown, contrasting with his thin, ginger hair and pale grey eyes. Taking in an all round view of him, he was a bastard, Simon had decided.

'Sir, I have repeatedly requested a transfer to active service,' Simon said.

'Forget it, captain.' Norris barked his reply, splattering Simon in saliva. 'You're in a special branch of the army's intelligence which is about to expand into some very unusual areas. You're going to the Counter Intelligence Corps. These guys have set up new training facilities. You'll study psychological warfare, propaganda and counter intelligence of the enemy's propaganda. Crowd of odd balls, but you'll probably fit in. After that you'll go on to a new training facility at Camp Sharpe, Pennsylvania, for combat training underwater, using techniques which the Brits learned from the French. I hope you can swim.'

'Yes, sir.'

'Good. When you've completed this training, you're going to Britain. On your arrival in London you'll be met and taken to Lieutenant General Walters, part of the hierarchy of the European Theatre of Operations, US Army, known as ETOUSA.' Norris broke off as his sergeant came in and pushed a file in front of him.

'This is urgent. Take a look at the brochure they sent me, Johnson. Tells you all about the so-called SCUBA system.'

Simon skipped through the details. SCUBA was an acronym for Self Contained Underwater Breathing Apparatus, he read, which meant that divers carried their own supply of air. Mankind had been trying to find means of breathing underwater since 500 BC, when Xerxes cut the Persian fleet from their moorings by using a hollow reed as a snorkel. Simon flipped through the pages, stopping to read again that in 1936 Dr Christian Lambertsen, in the USA, had designed an underwater oxygen breathing apparatus for the US military, developed from recent French designs. It was a rebreather and the first device to be called SCUBA. This, the brochure read, was the system taught for combat training at Camp Sharpe. Its main disadvantage was that oxygen toxicity made it unsafe for depths greater than fifteen meters.

Norris meanwhile signed a paper, handed it to the sergeant, and leaned forward inquiringly. 'Now where was I? You'll be attached to the 29th Infantry Division, which is about to be sent over to Britain. Set up your base with the Reconnaissance Unit and choose a lieutenant and a sergeant to serve under you. You'll also need to pick a special group and teach them these new techniques, which *will* be needed, I've been told.'

It was getting hot and stuffy. Norris wiped his forehead 'God, I hate Miami. You'll be invading Europe with the 29th right at the start of the invasion and you'll accompany them on their fight through France to Germany. This is not going to be a picnic, Captain. You'll be responsible for rooting out the SS and Nazi sympathizers wherever we go. They'll go to ground all over Europe. If it's action you want you're guaranteed to get it.'

But hardly the kind of action he'd been hoping for, Simon reminded himself.

'In the meantime we have a vital job for you in Britain. Axis propaganda is trying to spread distrust between the Allies, specifically between us and the Brits. This must be countered. It's vital. Nazi sympathizers – they call them Fifth Columnists over there – and spies must be hunted out and handed to the British authorities. They hang them pretty smartly. You with me, Captain?'

Simon nodded politely.

'Now listen carefully. You'll need all the skills you're about to learn at Camp Ritchie to bring about closer ties between our GIs and the British population. These skills will be vital to us in newly-occupied territories after we invade. It will make all the difference to our fighting power and our boys' safety.'

'But, sir . . .'

'Listen, Johnson. After the war you can pick and choose what you want to do, but right now you're under military command.

MacMillan here will sort out all the details. Your first call is to Chicago for quick basic army training. From now on you will be in uniform, but you will remain in MIS throughout the war, so for God's sake stop sending me applications for a transfer. Good luck, Captain.'

He might as well have stayed in Manhattan. Simon pursed his lips sullenly as he went in search of the canteen for a late breakfast.

Simon was met at Croydon Airport and driven to ETOUSA's head-quarters near Marble Arch. He had not come unprepared since he had studied all the statistics: 23,000 people killed by bombing in London alone, more than a million houses destroyed or damaged locally, a million civilians injured. The blitz on London had begun with widespread bombing for fifty-seven nights in a row. It was mainly over by now, but signs of the catastrophic bombing were all around. A similar story had unfolded over most of Britain's cities. The good news was that the blitz had not affected Britain's war effort and the civilian population had not been cowed. On the contrary, their determination to stick it out and eventually destroy the Nazis had hardened.

However, reading and seeing are quite different and Simon was saddened to see a city that he loved so much lying wrecked and bleeding. The depressed and shabby pedestrians, mainly female and old men, upset him, too. Lost dogs scurried around, white-faced children played amongst the ruins. Christ! He'd had no idea, despite knowing the statistics.

The building that housed ETOUSA's top brass was half-smothered in sandbags, with sticky paper strips over the windows, smog-smudged walls that could do with a coat of paint and a general air of austerity. There was a strong smell of smoke and dust all around. Looking along the street he saw that several buildings were flattened towards the end. He'd get used to it, he guessed. He went inside and endured the stench as he waited in the hall for his appointment. An attractive, blonde lieutenant with a New York accent, showed him to Lieutenant General Walters' office. It was a large room and it smelled as bad as the street. Simon couldn't help thinking that he'd take the stench with him when he left London.

Walters stood up and glared at him long and hard before pushing his hand forward. 'At ease, Captain. I haven't got long. I have a meeting upstairs. Eventually you'll be based with the 29th Infantry

Division in Dorset. You probably know that Major General Charles Purnell is running the show, but they haven't settled in yet. Meanwhile, I've detailed a driver to take you to Inverness, where you are to teach a group of Brits the underwater techniques you learned at Camp Sharpe in Pennsylvania. The equipment will go up with you and it's due to arrive tomorrow morning, so you have the rest of the day off.

'It's quite a pretty place, I've heard, but maybe not as great as you're used to,' he added belligerently. 'I hear you've been having a ball in Buenos Aires. Well, do your job, whatever it's supposed to be, Captain. For my part, I'm more interested in your underwater training, so don't waste too much time on Counter Intelligence, that's my advice.

'I'm counting on you to set up adequate training facilities around the coast. We need teams of men willing and able to conduct underwater fighting and sabotage. Good luck.' They shook hands again and that was that.

Simon spent a lonely day mooching around London and an even lonelier evening in the Strand Palace Hotel where he was served a meagre dinner of Woolton Pie, consisting of carrots, turnips, parsnips and potatoes in an oatmeal stock, crowned by a pastry crust and served with brown gravy, but at least the wine was good.

At seven a.m. the following morning, a driver picked him up and drove him to Scotland. The journey took two days as they meandered along a maze of winding country roads, between fields and woods and funny little stone houses, and spent an uncomfortable night in a country inn. By the time they reached a hotel overlooking the sea, where he would be staying, it was dusk and a thick mist had fallen over the landscape. An old man, gnarled and bent, with eyes that looked fiercely in opposite directions, attempted to carry his gear, but Simon fended him off and followed him to his room. He dumped his gear on the bed and stared out of the window.

'What's the temperature of the water around these parts?' he asked.

'Close to freezing, sir,' the old man replied, wheezing from the effort of walking and talking. 'The current comes down from Iceland.'

'I guessed as much.'

'I believe you'll be training in the loch, sir.'

'Is that warmer?'

'Not much, sir, but there's a pub nearby.'

'Well, that's something,' Simon said, trying to keep his spirits up.

He dined alone, but not unobserved. He assumed he was the first American soldier seen around these parts, for twenty pairs of eyes watched him surreptitiously. Eventually a man at the table by the door stood up and walked towards him. He seemed a little unsteady and Simon guessed he'd had too much to drink. 'You guys took your bloody time,' he growled, swaying precariously over him.

'But now we're here and we're Allies,' Simon answered smoothly, trying to remember something appropriate from his Counter Intelligence training.

The woman who had been sitting with the man hurried over and took his arm. She said something that sounded like an attempt to placate, but her strong, local accent prevented Simon from understanding her. He only caught the words 'son' and 'Dunkirk'.

'I'm sorry . . .'

'You're sorry!' The man's growl turned to a bellow. 'Sorry is not good enough. Go to hell.' He wrapped his dignity around him like a cloak and stalked out.

The diners kept their eyes fixed on their plates. For a few minutes there was absolute silence. Then a girl of about eleven stood up and approached timidly. She paused, trying to pluck up courage to speak and Simon didn't know whether to flee or to smile encouragingly. He chose the latter.

'My dad . . .' she began. She paused and swayed onto her toes and back again. 'My dad says we'll win now you Yanks are coming over. He says you've got the men and the guns to flatten the Huns.'

'We'll flatten them together,' Simon assured her.

'Here, here,' called the little girl's father. A slow clapping began around the tables.

Simon stood up, ready to flee. 'Well then, would anyone like to join me in the bar?' he suggested, wondering if this was appropriate. Evidently it was, because everyone came, even the little girl, her eyes alight with excitement as she clasped her mother's hand.

There were four Dunkirk veterans present from an infantry battalion, part of the King's Own Scottish Borderers. At first they were reluctant to talk, but after a while, one of them, called Ian Haig, began to reminisce and the others joined in. Simon pieced together their stories and what he came up with stayed with him in his dreams for months. All four of them were gunners in the Dundee Battery, which was ordered to hold the line, until the troops of the British Expeditionary Force were taken off the beaches at Dunkirk. When the Germans advanced on Dunkirk, the gunners drove them back three miles, but again they were ordered only to hold the line.

Retreating behind the main troops, they eventually arrived at the outskirts of Dunkirk. Again they were ordered to hold the line. 'Heavy shelling hit us all day and the night and well into the next day, with huge explosions all around,' Haig explained. 'Only thirty of us made it to the beach.'

Haig shuddered. 'Come on boys,' he called. 'This is supposed to be a birthday party. Let's forget about the war.'

Simon slipped off to bed as soon as he could. He had to get up early, but he lay awake for a while. He'd read enough books about Dunkirk, but hearing eyewitness accounts had made it much more real.

Tonight, he thought, I've glimpsed the grit that will save this nation.

Three

'What's wrong with you, Miro?' Daisy asked. She had waylaid him in the cycle shed and he was trapped.

'There's nothing wrong,' he lied. 'Why should there be? I'm late, that's all. Please mind out of the way.'

'We've always been good friends,' she said, hanging on to his handlebars. She leaned over the bike and scowled in mock accusation. 'It's like you're someone else these past few days. You're in a world of your own and it's not a very nice one. Tell me what's wrong.'

Miro tried to hide his alarm. He could not afford to let his foster sister read his mind and he would rather die than let her get involved. 'It's just . . . I'm behind with my work,' he mumbled.

'Oh, nonsense. You're always top of everything and you never do any work. There is something wrong and now you're lying to cover up. Look at your hands. They're shaking. Why can't you trust me? You know I'll help you.' She leaned forward impulsively and put one hand over his and he saw her breasts in naked detail, smelled her scent: a beguiling mixture of lavender water, toothpaste and the lanolin soap Helen, his foster mother bought for Daisy's over-sensitive skin.

'Leave me alone, Daisy. You'll get grease on your clean dress.' He flushed at the thought of grappling with Daisy, yet he longed to touch her. She was so beautiful with her white skin, ash-blonde hair and eyes so blue you could get lost gazing at them. Impelled by his defensive pride, he pushed past her, very aware of his red cheeks and hoarse voice.

'I'll tell Mum.' She voiced a silly threat.

'Of course you won't. You never do. This has nothing to do with you . . . it's something I have to sort out for myself. Truly, Daisy, it's not your business.'

Looking deeply offended, Daisy flounced back to the house while Miro set off for school, but his mind kept going over his alternatives. He only had two and both were unendurable. He felt weakened by his guilt. Seeing an open gate, he dismounted and pushed his bike into the field. The hedge was tall and thick. No one would see him here, so he collapsed on to a patch of dried grass.

Lying back in the warm sunshine, surrounded by bird song and the dense, vibrant hum of thousands of insects, his life seemed so pleasantly humdrum, but a worm had crawled into his psyche and it was eating him from the inside out, like a maggot in a rotten plum. Why had it happened to him?

The funny thing was, he had never felt particularly Jewish despite his orthodox upbringing. He'd always preferred to be at his friends' homes. Their lives were so uncomplicated. None of them bothered much about religion. They didn't have to practice on the clarinet, or compose a melody each week, or read the right books, or bother with extra-mural studies and he found their free and easy lifestyle to be very relaxing.

Whilst studying for his Bar Mitzvah he had suddenly been made aware of their differences. He was a Jew and therefore required to learn and obey God's laws. There were over six hundred of them. He still did not know them all, but he felt sure that there must be a law of loyalty: thou shalt not aid and abet thine enemies, particularly those bent on killing every Jew. Thou shalt protect thine own people and save them from genocide.

But he wasn't a Jew, was he? Not after that fateful day in May, 1939, when he had sworn to serve the enemy. He had fallen into a trap and there was no escape. If only Papa had taken the Nazi threat seriously they could have fled Czechoslovakia while it was still possible, but he was an optimist and not the least bit interested in politics, nor business. He was simply a wonderful musician and his life was music. He looked the part, too, with his soft features, large, expressive eyes and his brown hair always tumbling over his forehead. God knows, Mama had nagged enough. Towards the end even Miro had become alarmed.

They'd lived in Volary, a quaint old town in Sudetenland, eight miles from the German border, but this was not a good place for them after the Germans walked in and took over.

His father played the violin in the Czech State orchestra and returned home only for weekends, so Mama closed their house and moved them to Papa's small furnished apartment on the outskirts of Prague, where a synagogue, a Jewish school and a kosher butcher shop lay within walking distance. In the weeks that followed, news from home, conveyed to them by anxious friends and relatives, terrified them: German-speaking Sudetenlanders, anxious to show their solidarity with Germany, were rounding up the Jews.

Within days, Mama made up her mind that they must leave Czechoslovakia and she set about persuading his father to see reason, but Father was eviscerated by his state of denial.

'I'm not a religious person, Rachel,' he told Mama. 'I'm a musician. That's all I am. Are they going to lock up half of Prague's orchestra?' he joked.

Despite Papa's reluctance to leave, Miro's mother spent her days plaguing foreign embassies in Prague for visas. In the evenings she sat, remote and shocked, in her chair by the fire staring into space at nothing in particular. She had always been smart and fashionably dressed, loving to entertain, never happier than when the house was filled with friends, but after the Munich Pact, Mama was too frightened to care about anything, other than finding a country that would take them.

In March, 1939, the Germans marched into Prague and not a shot was fired. They came in lorries, cars, bicycles and some even on donkey carts. Watching from the window of their sixth floor apartment, Miro witnessed the entire catastrophe. Mama's search for a haven intensified: to the Jewish Board of Deputies, to the Red Cross headquarters, to embassies of countries she had scarcely heard of. The school holidays came and since Miro was at home, his mother took him with her on her rounds.

As they hurried along the pavement Miro kept his eyes straight ahead. Like a horse with blinkers on, he never looked to either side. He did not want to see the many signs in offices, restaurants, theatres and even benches in the park and public toilets stating: *Jews forbidden.* His stomach was knotted with painful lumps, as it always was then, for he lived in a permanent state of terror and tension.

By a new ruling they had to wear a yellow Star of David on their arms. The penalty for breaking this new law was immediate removal to a concentration camp. His mother could not take this chance, since she could be asked for her papers at any time, but wearing the yellow armband invited every lout to abuse them. Miro could not stand being singled out for contempt. He trailed along behind his mother wishing the earth could swallow him.

At last they reached their destination, the Bolivian embassy. Mama hurried through the gates with a sigh of relief, but Miro was so worried he hardly noticed where he was going. Had their application been successful? Bolivia was the very last country left for his mother to try.

He lost sight of her in the noisy, crowded room, but minutes later he found her standing at the end of a long queue of anxious people, most of them Jewish and elderly. An hour passed and then another. It was noon before his mother reached the desk, where a dark-skinned woman with large hazel eyes and a kind expression said in German: 'Your name and reference number, please.'

'Mrs Rachel Levy.' She passed her number through the slot and stood there unashamedly praying.

Miro tried to relax, but the woman was gone for a long time.

'It will be all right,' he told himself. 'They will take us. It has to be . . . they are desperate for settlers.'

This was their last chance. No one wanted unskilled, penniless Jews, as they were classified.

When the clerk returned, she avoided looking at his mother, which Miro knew heralded bad news.

'Unfortunately our government cannot accept responsibility for your maintenance. You are too old to be useful for immigration. We need strong young people who can work the fields and turn the land into profitable farms. Your son could reapply as soon as he reaches seventeen.'

'He should live so long,' Mama retorted. 'But forgive me. I did explain,' she argued tearfully. 'I would be able to support them. I am a very good machinist, almost a qualified tailor. You must understand that you are our last chance.'

The woman looked sadly at them. 'Perhaps you know someone in Bolivia. If you could find sponsorship from a family or a prospective employer, then perhaps . . .'

Upset by his mother's reaction, the clerk looked stricken. 'Perhaps the bank could help you. If you could raise enough capital you would be acceptable immigrants.'

Mama wiped her forehead with a handkerchief 'Forgive me,' she said quickly. 'It is not your fault.' They had received several offers for their house, but at a fraction of its true worth. Not enough to provide them with escape permits.

Obsessed with their problems, they hurried home and stumbled into a group of louts who were rounding up Jews to clean the pavements. Before Miro knew what was happening, Mama was forced down on her knees and given a pail of water and a brush to scrub the gutter. The boys jeered. Bitter tears of humiliation scalded her cheeks.

Miro felt paralysed with indecision. He longed to confront the thugs, but he was afraid. How could he, a mere boy, take on six fully grown louts armed with batons? He wanted to cry out for help to the passers-by, but they were averting their eyes and crossing the road. His cowardice made him feel sick. His mother, whom he idolized, was crying and he stood there watching. Why her? Why not him? He lurched towards her with a sudden spurt of bravery. 'Don't cry, Mama. Give me the brush.' He tried to wrench it away from her.

'Don't cause a disturbance,' she whispered. 'They will kill us both. Run home, Miro. Go! I beg you. Do as I say.'

He could not. He wanted to pull her to her feet, but he was too afraid. Instead he backed away to the corner of a building and hung around there. He longed to dash forward and say, 'She's my mother. Why are you picking on her? She's done you no harm,' but his fear made him feel unreal, it was as if he were watching the scene unfold at the cinema. He had an overpowering impulse to lie down on the pavement and let it all drift away. It was too macabre to be real.

People stopped to watch the women. Mama became wet and muddy. Dirty water ran in the gutter and someone kicked it over her. She was terrified and so was he. At last the punishment came to an end. Mama stumbled to her feet, dizzy with fright and blinded by tears. As he ran towards her, a police van pulled up at the roadside and the women were bundled into the back of it. Miro ran towards Mama, but the doors slammed in his face. He pounded his fists on the van, shouting, 'Mama! Mama! Let her out.'

A baton struck his shoulder and sent him reeling across the pavement. The van took off. Miro raced after it, but it turned out of sight at the end of the road.

Breathless and guilty, he ran to the concert hall to tell Papa. Wide-eyed and dishevelled, he created panic amongst the musicians, many of whom were Jewish. Papa and he hurried to the police station and then to the town hall and the Jewish Board of Deputies. Despite his father's efforts to find his wife, Miro never saw his mother again.

Three months later, he and his father were summoned to the town hall. Crowds of Jews had been brought there. After waiting four hours they were taken by trucks to Dachau Concentration Camp. Tired and thirsty, they arrived at dusk to find the yard lined with armed soldiers. Miro was shaking with fright. His father put his arm around him and whispered, 'My boy, we might be separated. I want you to remember what I'm telling you now. Hang on to goodness. There's always a choice, you see. Choose the moral path and never forget that you are a Jew.'

If only he could replay the scene. In the terrible days and nights that followed he relived his mother's humiliation over and over again, but each time he was there at her side, refusing to move away, comforting her and sheltering her from the Blackshirts, forcing them to let her go.

Miro could never get to grips with his new life in England. It seemed unreal. He often thought he would wake, as if from a dream, and find himself back in Czechoslovakia. He worked hard, studied English assiduously, came top in his exams, loved his foster family and dreamed about lovely Daisy, but his true reality was back inside the barbed wire with the dogs, the guards and the pockmarked gypsy woman who ran the children's camp. She was ugly and inarticulate, but the few words at her disposal had been powerful enough.

'They tell me they want you. Do what they want. If not, you all die . . . all your family,' she told him one morning, when he had been in the camp for six months. To prove her point she took him to see an execution of a young Jewish girl by garroting. They had a special machine for this, which took pride of place in front of the gallows in the main square. As they watched the girl screaming, then gasping and choking, and finally dying in agony, while her face became mottled and her eyes bulged, a tear gathered in the corner of the gypsy woman's eye and slithered down the crevices of her eroded cheek. This surprised him. Behind the bullying voice, the coarseness and her cruelty, a small spark of compassion had survived. As for him, only guilt surfaced. He had not tried to rescue the victim. He had stood watching again like a dumb beast.

Later that day he was taken to the office of the camp comman-dant, but the man waiting to see him was a civilian. He was plump and white like a maggot. His ring, his gold-rimmed spectacles and his bald head glistened in the harsh light, but it was his eyes that frightened Miro. There was no gleam of humanity there – it was like looking at a wild animal.

'Miroslav Levy,' he began in a soft, high-pitched voice. 'I am going to tell you something that may surprise you. We are not cruel people, but we don't feel obliged to feed and clothe those of you who cannot help yourselves. Take your mother, for instance, she is working here, but she is getting thin and tired. She is not a strong woman and she is not used to hard work. You, as her son, should support her, and I am sure you would be willing to do that. After all, why should we? You look to me like a well brought up young boy who would be pleased to do his best for his parents. Irwin Levy, your father, may be able to cope with the hard work we expect from our labourers, but who knows. We don't have a position for a musician right now.' He laughed softly. 'However, if you were to work for us, both your parents would be well looked after. Dachau Camp is the best we have. There are many inmates living out their retirement here in relative comfort and absolute safety. They are parents of those who help the Third Reich. On the other hand, if you fail to obey your orders, your parents will suffer. So what's it to be?'

'I'll do whatever you want,' Miro mumbled. 'Why don't you let them go, since you have my word?'

'Let them go? But Miro, no Jew is safe in Czechoslovakia. You saw what happened to your mother before we brought her here.'

'So you are keeping them as hostages.' As soon as the words escaped he regretted them. Now those eyes blazed with hatred.

'Put it whatever way you like. Work for us and your parents live. Otherwise . . .' He smiled. 'It's a simple choice, Miro.'

Refuse. Tell him to go to hell. Tell him you'd rather die. But the memory of the humiliation and hurt in his mother's eyes when they forced her into the gutter was stronger than his desire to refuse. He loved his parents.

'Yes, of course I will work. I am quite strong,' he said.

The man smiled. 'We don't want your brawn, Miroslav, but your brains. You will keep your eyes open and send information to us as and when we contact you.'

He felt the slow anger of the conned. A spy? he wondered. 'I agree to whatever you want, but what proof will I get that my parents are still alive?'

'We will send pictures occasionally. I have a Jewish bible here. Put your hand on it and swear to obey any orders you are given by representatives of the Third Reich.'

Trembling, he pushed his hand on the book and swore.

'You will be contacted when you are old enough to be useful,' he was told.

This was the great evil which lay like a foul smell in his memory, contaminating his life. He had sworn to obey these people in order to keep his parents alive and no amount of rationalizing could ever diminish his guilt.

He was released the same day and driven to an orphanage in Prague. Two days later, he was collected by a Swiss nurse who liaised with *Kindertransport* and taken to the station. After an anxious six-hour wait, he was put on a sealed *Kindertransport* train with other children. The train crossed Germany into Holland where they disembarked at the Hook of Holland and from there they travelled by ferry to Southampton.

Glancing around the field, Miro reached for the envelope, which had been pushed into his pocket by a stranger at cricket practice ten days ago. In it was a small picture of his mother. As he gazed at it, tears came to his eyes. She was much thinner, her hair had turned white and her eyes seemed larger. They conveyed the vivid intensity of her hatred. He had never seen his mother look like that. He knew at once what she would say to him, if she could, 'Tell them to go to hell, Miro.' There was no picture of his father and that sent spasms of fear through his stomach. Had he died? Or been murdered in the camp?

The message was brief: *It's time.*

'Love surmounts politics, patriotism and all other allegiances,' he whispered to comfort himself. But did it surmount his duty to God? He had been given the choice of good or evil, but his only concern had been to keep his parents alive.

Three years had passed since the day he had sworn to help the Nazis and no one had contacted him, but he never stopped despising himself as a coward and a traitor, to his parents, to all Jews, to his foster family and the Allied cause. Now he had been called. Obviously 'they' knew that the Yanks were coming. 'I can't do it,' he whispered. 'I can't.' But what choice did he have?

Four

One morning, early in September, Daisy was woken at dawn by Cocky's strident cries. As she lay half-awake gazing at the ceiling, pondering on her mother's affection for this noisy bird, she heard other strange sounds. Pushing back the eiderdown, she rushed to the window and saw that their fields were jam-packed with camouflaged tents which had been erected during the night. How on earth they had managed to do all that in the dark amazed her. It was something. It really was. Loudspeakers blared as a convoy of troop carriers moved ponderously along the country lane from the direction of the main road from London. As each vehicle reached the gate it slowed, never stopping, and GIs tumbled out, each one carrying a large backpack, a rifle and assorted paraphernalia dangling from his belt. The superb organization of this sudden occupation left Daisy breathless. A self-contained village had been created out of canvas, right on their doorstep. She rifled in her drawer for her binoculars and studied some of the guys. Good looking, she thought. Hmm! Not bad at all. The Yanks had been piling into southern England for weeks. She and her friends had seen them jiving with local girls on the newsreels at the cinema. Nice girls weren't supposed to be seen with GIs. Mum would have something to say about it if Daisy tried her luck.

She scowled at her reflection in the mirror. What she saw displeased her. Her breasts were growing and she hated them, hated the whole distasteful business of becoming a woman. The onset of her periods had been . . . well, yuck! Words failed her. She'd like to bind her breasts like nuns did. Even worse was the feeling of self-disgust allied to a strange restlessness. She tried to analyze her problem and she came to the conclusion that her depression stemmed from missing her father whom she loved. Dad had left because of her mother's temper. She had heard her mother blasting him for days before he left. Yes, it was all Mum's fault. If only she could find Dad, but even Gramps hadn't been able to trace him.

A sudden idea hit her and she wondered why she hadn't thought of it before: Dad's mother would know where he was, even if she hadn't told Mum. They usually visited their grandmother on their rare visits to London. She was always pleasant, although a little forgetful. If she went to her grandmother, Dad would come and fetch her and perhaps he'd let her stay with him sometimes. They had never even said goodbye. The last time she saw Dad was in June, when he took her riding on the day before her birthday. He'd said, 'See you next week, love,' but she had not seen him since.

Having made up her mind to go, she started planning. What to take was a major problem. Money was another. Her savings would just about get her there. She would leave very early on Monday morning while everyone was sleeping, she decided.

Come Monday morning, stylishly dressed in bits and pieces begged and borrowed from friends, Daisy rapped her knuckles on the ticket clerk's counter.

'Excuse me,' she voiced loud and clear. 'I've been waiting here quite long enough.'

'Oh yes, and where d'you think you're going?' The ticket clerk turned, looking pompous, frowning, king of his small patch. 'Is your journey really necessary, miss? There's a war on, you know.'

'I know there's a war on because of rationing, blitzes, blackout and interfering busybodies like you trying to take over our lives.'

'None of your lip then. Where're you off to and when are you returning?'

'Victoria, London. I'm going to see my grandmother. I'll stay a few days.'

He shrugged. 'It's likely to be a rough journey. For starters the train's late. God knows when it will arrive. Platform one. Don't say I didn't warn you.' He pushed the ticket and her change under the glass.

'Whereabouts exactly?' Now he was looking genuinely concerned. 'They still get blitzed, mainly around the dock and city areas.'

Gran lived in Clapham, but Daisy had no idea where that was. She shrugged, bit her lip and looked away.

Low clouds hung over the grey chimneys compressing the moist September heatwave. Life had become a monochrome canvas, but one solitary, dark green tree stood alone and defiant in front of the pub across the road. The scene was well-balanced, she decided. Funny how nature always provided a good composition no matter where your stance happened to be. But on second thoughts.

'Move along there, miss, you're blocking the queue.'

Flushing at her stupidity, Daisy grabbed her ticket and left. She lugged her suitcase to platform one, failed to find a seat and leaned against the wall, still composing her canvas in her mind's eye. Passing men eyed her curiously. There were plenty of pretty blondes around, but her lovely face and her fierce expression caught their attention. She was something special, regal and stacked, too.

Seeing their predatory stares, Daisy imagined that she was too fat, or her hair was wrong, or maybe they could sense that she was homeless, as from this morning. Almost all the reasonable clothes she possessed were crushed into her one large suitcase and her handbag. She'd had enough. She and Mum had been at loggerheads the past three months. As for Miro . . . he used to be her best friend, but he'd retreated into his shell and was acting even more remote than when first joined the family. She could not bear either of them a m ient longer.

A loudspeaker startled her out of her misery.

'The train about to depart from platform two is the seven-thirty a.m. service to London, Victoria.'

Platform two! But that idiot had said one. Daisy grabbed her suitcase and ran . . . along the platform . . . up the steps . . . across the bridge . . . and down the steps, her heavy suitcase bruising her legs. She just made it.

'Idiot . . . idiot . . .' she muttered, trying to catch her breath as she pushed her way along the corridor. She managed to squeeze on to half a seat, next to a fat lady who'd had garlic for breakfast. The carriage was dirty, dust coated the windows and the air stank.

At Basingstoke the train was held up for four hours by an electricity failure. Something to do with last night's blitz, she gathered, although she only heard half of the announcement. She tried not to worry. Soon her thoughts returned to her father.

Dad was the bravest man imaginable, he had a chest full of medals to prove it. He was known to be the best salvage expert in Britain. If she closed her eyes she could see her father clearly, his black hair slightly sprinkled with grey, his eyes as blue as forget-me-nots. Dad was lovely. Even her school friends said so. Once they'd set eyes on him, they were hooked, making silly excuses to pop round to the house. Squeezing her eyes tightly shut, she imagined Dad galloping back from a morning ride, his cheeks glowing and Daunty, his magnificent black stallion, covered in foam. She always helped her father rub down Daunty. Her mother had wanted him to buy a gelding to save future trouble with their mares, all newly purchased for the riding school, but Dad was adamant. 'Why do women want everything castrated,' he'd shouted loud enough for Daisy to hear. And they were off again. She had never known her parents to fight, but this summer they had hardly ever stopped.

The train shuddered and seconds later they were moving forward.

On the outskirts of London the train stopped for another two hours while workers battled to remove debris from the lines after another air raid. Daisy stood in the corridor watching the passing scene. She could never have imagined such desolation – like a Russian painting from the First World War she'd seen at the Tate, miles of rubble with a solitary, jagged ruin pointing accusingly at the sky. It was half past three by the time she reached Victoria Station, only to find that the underground to Clapham was closed. She stood in the taxi queue for half an hour, wondering if she had enough cash to pay for the ride. Eventually her turn came and she had just enough. Would Granny be there? she wondered for the first time as the driver took numerous detours to avoid roads blocked by debris. The air smelled of dust and smoke and her eyes burned. They passed children playing in ruined buildings, flowers bursting through rubble, cats perched on broken walls and birds in shattered trees. Life goes on, she thought wonderingly as she filed the scenes in her memory bank. She would paint them one day.

The driver pulled up in a blitzed street. Gran's house was still standing, but the windows were shattered and boarded up, the door padlocked, several tiles were missing on the roof and the tiny front garden was buried in dust and rubble, probably from the ruins further along. Only a few houses were left standing. Asking the driver to wait, she ran to the first house still intact. A woman was sweeping debris from the front passage.

'I came to see my gran, Mrs Conroy who lived just down there. Is she all right?'

'Don't fret love. She was fine last time I saw her . . . three days before our raid. She had a premonition, she said. She took her cat and went to Wales. She's got friends there.'

Dazed and confused, Daisy hurried back to the cab. What a fool she had been, but how could she possibly have known?

'Sorry about this, love,' the driver said when she told him what had happened. 'This bloody war has turned every family upside down. I've got one daughter and her kids in Scotland, another in Wales, and the wife's at home pining. I can't leave you here. Where d'you want to go?'

Daisy looked in her purse. 'Thanks, but I'll walk,' she said.

'Listen. I'll drop you anywhere you want to go that's on my way home. It won't cost you a penny. I live near the station.'

Her concern about her grandmother's whereabouts had brought a lump to her throat. She couldn't think straight. 'I'll hitch home. Take me some place where I can get a lift . . . if that's all right with you.'

'Where d'you live then?'

'Near the New Forest.'

'OK, I know a cafe near my home. Lorry drivers use it because it's just off the main road.'

The cafe was a friendly place with an enticing smell of fish and chips with vinegar and noisy music in the background. Daisy was too broke to eat. She ordered a pot of tea and waited. When drivers walked in, she asked them if they were going to Dorset, but she was unlucky.

Two hours passed while Daisy sat and worried about the changes at home. Why hadn't Dad come to see them? Why hadn't Gran told them she was going away? Why was Mum so different? She used to be such fun until Dad left, but since then she'd acted like she had stomach ache, all drawn into herself and unable to think of anything but her pain.

'We're closing in half an hour, miss,' the waitress said, looking sorry. 'You'd stand a better chance of getting a lift up at the main road.'

Daisy glanced at her watch. It was after seven p.m. Tired and forlorn, dragging her heavy suitcase, she trudged up the steep slope to the main road, still hanging on to hope. Someone must surely give her a lift. Dusk was spreading over the land. Birds twittered as they gathered in the trees, a plane droned overhead and in the distance a dog barked. Clouds were gathering fast. Then came a spatter of rain. *Oh God! What a bloody awful day. What a fool I've been.*

It started to pour and in next to no time she was soaked. How was she going to get home? What if she was still waiting when it got dark? Her entire life had gone wrong, culminating in this frightful moment.

A jeep drew up beside her with screeching brakes and a spray of water, but who cares, she was already drenched. A young GI jumped out and ran towards her.

'Hop in, ma'am?'

'Oh, thank goodness,' she said, and then she sneezed.

'Sounds to me like you've caught a bad cold. No wonder, standing around here in the rain. You're wet through. Where're do you want to go?'

'To Mowbray, it's a village five miles from Christchurch, past the New Forest.'

'I'm heading that way. Let's go.'

Stiff with cold, Daisy swayed and found herself being caught by one elbow and pushed towards the jeep. The Yank picked up her bag as if it weighed next to nothing and tossed it in the back.

'Jesus, you're shivering badly.' He put one hand on her arm. 'And freezing. Hang on a minute.' He rifled in the back and produced a khaki jersey and a cape. 'Put these on.'

'I can't wear your clothes, I'll make them wet. I have a coat in my suitcase. I'm all right. Don't bother about me. It's just that everything has gone wrong today and I wouldn't care if I did die of cold.'

He looked at her and laughed. 'That bad, huh? Just put them on. Who cares if they get wet.' He switched on the engine. For a while they drove in silence. The clouds moved away and the sun came out.

'When I see a sunset like this, it reminds me of home. I get pretty homesick most of the time, although when I was there I was dying to get off the place and see a bit of the world.'

He had a lovely voice, deep and musical. His profile was OK. Not many people had a good profile. His was quite regular. His neck was muscular, his nose a bit too blunt, his lips a bit too full, otherwise he might have modelled for the Grecian statues in her book on ancient art. He looked strong and dependable.

'Off the "place"?' she queried.

'Our family owns a ranch eighty miles west of Denver. Mainly cattle. Except for the equipment suppliers, almost everyone around has a ranch. We meet up in groups for horse shows and barbecues and there are all kinds of fetes and fairs at the weekends. During the week it can be pretty lonely, but it's always beautiful.'

With his black hair and blue eyes he looked a bit like her father. Not too much, but there were certain similarities: his thick black eyebrows, for instance and his wide cheek bones, but she would not tell him that.

She said, 'Thanks for picking me up. I was silly to be so upset, but I thought I'd never get a lift. I've had an unlucky day. Everything went wrong. It hasn't rained for two weeks, but finally, when I got to the side of the road to hitch a lift, there was a deluge.'

'A deluge, was it!' He was laughing at her, she realized. 'Back home when it rains you know all about it.' The Yank groped in the cubbyhole for his sunglasses and put them on.

'Sunglasses spoil the colours. Look! It's lovely. All those pale greens and violets and that wonderful creamy shade higher up,' she exclaimed. The light was muted and the trees ahead were darkly silhouetted against the western sky which was a kaleidoscope of subtle shades changing as she watched.

'I have to look at the road, not the sky. We have beautiful skies and sunsets, too, especially when it's windy. They say it's caused by pollution, but I'm not sure I believe that. The sky's OK here, but for the rest . . . let's just say it's not my kind of nature. All this green . . .' He shrugged apologetically.

Daisy was warming up and feeling safe in the knowledge that she was on the way home. 'So tell me about your home,' she said, since that seemed to be uppermost in his mind.

'It's about as different from England as you could possibly imagine. Space. It's all about space . . . just as far as you can see . . . not cluttered up with trees and houses.' He broke off. 'You must think I'm crazy, all this talk about home.'

After a while he said, 'I'm looking straight into the sun . . . it's resting bang on the road. Are you in a hurry? There's a pub I found half a mile further on. I came this way a week back and stopped there for lunch. The food isn't bad by your English standards, although they don't give you much. How about it?'

Daisy smirked and cleared her throat. She had never been in a pub, but she longed to go. The trouble was, she didn't have enough cash to pay for her meal. She said, 'You go ahead, I'm not in a hurry. I'll wait in the jeep.'

'No, please come. I won't go in without you.'

'The truth is, I don't have any money,' she said shyly.

'Who asked you for money? I only asked you to supper. I've got plenty. Uncle Sam is pretty good to us.'

Daisy puzzled over Uncle Sam, but then the penny dropped. 'Yes, I've heard you're much better off than our boys, so if you mean that, then thanks, I accept.' Calling the soldiers 'boys', as her mother and grandfather did, made her feel more adult. Her confidence was seeping back and she was ravenously hungry.

He drove into the half-empty car park, drew to a halt beside an oak tree and jumped out. Frowning, he scanned the cars. 'Our commander has a mission in life to make sure we and you Brits remain apart, but I reckon no one will see us here.'

'I can't go in like this. I'll get my coat out,' Daisy said. Her beautiful, blue, cashmere coat had taken most of her mother's clothing coupons for the past year. It was the first non-school coat she had ever owned. It had cost the earth and it was a reward from Gramps and Mum for winning a scholarship to a London art school where she would go next year. At least she hoped she would. Mum wanted her to take off a year for a boring secretarial course because she was considered too young to live away from home.

Daisy leaned over the seat, rummaged in the suitcase for her coat and put it on. Taking a comb out of her handbag, she ran it through her hair and draped her long, damp curls over one shoulder. Should she risk using Mum's discarded lipstick? Why not? She gazed into her hand mirror and smoothed it over her lips.

'Hey, you're beautiful,' he told her, seeming surprised. It was more of a remark than a compliment. 'I guess everyone tells you that.'

'No. Actually no one has. My friends go way back. They're not likely to say such a thing to me. I'm just Daisy.'

'Daisy! That's nice. Daisy who?'

'Conroy.'

'Mike Lawson,' he said, shaking her hand.

The crow in the branch overhead let out a piercing, raucous cry. Daisy looked up and laughed. 'He's introduced us.'

Mike grinned. 'I could do with a drink. How about you?'

Daisy hesitated. She didn't want to look a fool. 'I'm thirsty, too,' she said. Mike shot her a doubtful glance and Daisy frowned. Had she said the wrong thing? But what harm could it do? She'd probably never see him again and no one would ever know.

'Let's go,' she said, squaring her shoulders.

Five

The long summer evenings were over and lately it was dark by nine. From his window Miro could not see the driveway because of the trees, but he could see the road. He had been trying to concentrate on his studies all evening, but without much success. Everyone was confused and upset by Daisy's sudden flight and no one knew what to think, but they all had their own theories. Miro's theory was a GI. It was too much of a coincidence that Daisy should go off a week after the American troops arrived on their doorstep. There had to be a connection. His suspicions had brought with them a dozen different tension symptoms, worst of which were stomach cramps.

Early that morning, Helen had found Daisy's note propped against the kettle telling them she had gone to London to see her grand-mother and to get news of her father. John had criticized Helen for not telling Daisy the truth, and he had listened in unashamedly. 'She blames you for the break and that's absurd.'

'You're right.'

Helen cancelled her war work and spent the day scrubbing and polishing, her face screwed with tension, shoulders hunched, listening for the sound of a taxi, or Daisy's footsteps in the driveway. Gramps had been on the telephone most of the day. The Metropolitan police had called on Daisy's grandmother, they told him eventually, only to find that the house was boarded up. Mrs Conroy had gone to Wales, a neighbour claimed. Daisy had already been there, but she had left in a taxi. 'Presumably she is on the way home,' the police suggested. 'If she's not back by midnight call us again and we'll open a missing person's file.'

So she had been to her grandmother's after all. That surprised Miro and lessened his pain, but he was convinced that a Yank was involved. He was aware of the GIs' athletic appearance, set off by their superbly casual uniforms and he longed to possess a fraction of their easy self-confidence.

At ten that evening he saw headlights flashing as a vehicle turned the corner. A jeep turned into their road and drew up at the gate. The driver jumped out and ran around to the other side to open the door, but Daisy pushed him away. 'I can manage, thanks,' she said clearly, sounding hurt and angry. He lifted out her suitcase, but she caught hold of it and a tug of war ensued. 'Leave it. Please . . . go . . . I can manage.'

The driver got back into the jeep and drove to the entrance of the camp. The bar lifted and the jeep drove into the parking zone, but Daisy was still outside. Miro raced downstairs and went out, shutting the door quietly behind him. Daisy, a mess of wet cheeks and swollen eyes, was standing under the trees. He would kill that guy when he found out who he was, Miro promised himself.

'What's going on?' he whispered. 'What the hell have you been doing?'

'Nothing is *going on*. I hitched a lift home, but really, Miro, it has nothing to do with you.' Daisy made for the door, but Miro caught hold of her arm.

'Ow! That hurts. Let go of me.' She looked angry and this upset him.

'Mum's been worried all day and Gramps has been on the phone to the police.'

'Oh, heavens. I left a note.' As she spoke a strong smell of wine enveloped him.

'You've been drinking. You stink of wine.'

'We stopped for dinner on the way back.'

'Gramps will have something to say about that. Better look out. There are some peppermints in the top drawer of my desk. Clean your teeth.' They went inside and shut the door. Miro pulled the blackout curtain across the doorway and switched on the light. 'Look at the bruises on your wrist. He hurt you.'

'Oh nonsense. That's from hockey practice.'

'You're lying.'

The conversation terminated as Daisy fled upstairs.

At that moment, Helen opened the living-room door.

'Daisy's back. She's fine.' Miro gave her his very best smile.

'Oh, thank heavens, but where is she?'

'In the bathroom.'

Helen sank on to the monk's bench. 'Is she all right? Are you sure?' She looked distraught. Helen's love was sometimes hard to cope with.

'She's fine, Mum. You can stop worrying. She hitched home.'

'Thank heavens she's all right. Come in the lounge, Miro. It's so cold here. I have to talk to you both.'

Five minutes later, Daisy walked in, safe in her aura of toothpaste, peppermint and *Eau de Cologne*. As usual, she was playing the injured party, her shoulders squared and her bruised arm hidden by a cardigan.

'How could you, Daisy? How could you worry us so? To go off like that without telling anyone.' Mum was close to tears.

'What about my feelings?' Daisy countered. Her eyes narrowed and her hand went on her hips – a familiar pose when Daisy was on the defensive. 'You know how much I miss my father. He should have come to see us. I'm sure he would have if you two hadn't fought so much. We don't know where he is. That's all right for you maybe, you can marry again, but I'll never have another dad.'

Helen gasped and looked hurt.

'So I went up to Gran's . . .' Now she faltered. 'Oh Mum. It's terrible. Half of London is blitzed and around Gran's home just about every second house has been destroyed. Her house is boarded up, the windows smashed, tiles knocked off the roof . . .' She went on at length and Miro could not help admiring her strategy.

'But what did you do when you found that Gran had left? Why didn't you call us? Surely you realized how worried we would be.'

'I ran out of cash because the taxi cost far more than I'd expected, so I decided to hitch back. The taxi driver gave me a free lift to a cafe by the main road to the south-west, but I waited for hours. Then I walked up to the main road and a young GI brought me back here. He's stationed at the camp next door.'

Daisy sneezed and that seemed to shake her poise. Suddenly she was crying. Mum caught hold of her and hugged her.

John was looking cross. 'Tell them now,' he insisted. He walked out, closing the door behind him.

Helen looked uncertain. She gazed from one to the other as if waiting for someone to prompt her. 'It's time I told you both the truth. I didn't want to hurt you. Especially you, Daisy. I know how much you love your father and how close you both are . . . were. I don't know where to start.' She forced a smile which didn't work. 'When Eric left hospital and came here, he was depressed and difficult. I'm sure you both noticed that he wasn't himself. Eventually he told me why. He'd fallen in love with his secretary.'

'What?' Daisy exploded. 'That simpering, insipid, absurd woman? How could he?'

'He explained that his chances of reaching the war's end were slim, so whatever time he had left he wanted to spend with her. He said he owed it to her, since she'd stood by him. He didn't seem to think he owed us anything. He wanted a divorce so he could marry her.' A pent-up sob emerged like a hiccup. 'He said she's pregnant and that she makes him feel young.'

Mum's voice had risen an octave, so Miro sat on the other side and held her hand. 'Eric said he didn't want to waste any more time. That was what hurt the most.'

'Sh!' Miro said. 'We get the picture. You don't have to spell out every word. Would you like some coffee? I'll make some.'

'Yes,' she said forlornly. 'I would. Thank you, Miro. Worst still was losing you two because you blamed me.'

'You never lost us, Mum,' Miro said. 'No matter what happens . . . even when I find my parents. I'll always love you. Daisy was just upset at not seeing her father, which is understandable. She'll always love you, too.'

'Of course I will, Mum. I didn't understand. I'm so sorry. How could Dad do this to us?' Daisy was trying to be brave. '"A waste of time . . ." he said that? Another child! Well, fuck him!'

'Daisy!' Despite her sadness, Helen was shocked. 'Don't ever . . .'

Miro paused in the doorway and looked back at the two women he loved so, clasped in each other's arms. Daisy hadn't told the truth about stopping for dinner on the way home. Helen had been side-tracked, as usual. Besides, she judged the world by herself and since she was entirely trustworthy and kind everyone else must be, too. He'd like to kill Eric, but he guessed that he was ancient history. They'd never liked each other. Eric was an arrogant, self-assured, selfish bastard. Gramps, on the other hand, was a regular guy. Miro could hear him in the hall sounding thoroughly exasperated as he tried to get through to the police to tell them Daisy was back.

'Coffee, Gramps?' Miro asked as he passed.

'No, not for me, thank you.'

'Real GI coffee with real sugar.'

'Where did that come from?'

'A sergeant brought a box around this morning. He said it was a neighbourly gift from their captain.'

'Good God! Oh yes, I'll have a cup, my boy. Many thanks.'

Gramps was looking happier. Daisy was back and they had real coffee in the house.

There are too many secrets in this family, Miro thought as he spooned the coffee into the percolator. Even Gramps had a secret, although Miro didn't know what it was, only that he went out alone some nights and stayed out until just before dawn.

Miro had known about Eric's girlfriend. By chance he'd stumbled across them together in the village. She was very young and very pretty and Eric was a fool to meet her in Mowbray, but no one else had seen them. Now Daisy had a secret, but his own secret was the worst of all.

Once there was a young Jewish boy called Miroslav Levy. He had a father, Irwin Levy, who played the violin in Prague's state orchestra and composed great works, destined never to be heard. Miro's face twisted in anguish as he remembered Papa's efforts to get his compositions played. Father wasn't a strong man, being subject to every virus that passed their way, but he was handsome, according to Mama, with his large brown eyes and curly brown hair. He was tall, but thin and rather stooped. Mama was always nagging him to stand up straight. But all that was in the past.

'I'm not your son, Papa,' he murmured. 'I'm someone else . . . a Nazi spy.'

'Miro, where's the coffee?' Gramps called.

'Coming.' He put some of the GI's biscuits on a plate and carried in the tray.

Miro is late. John has left the house. Helen and Daisy took forever to go to bed. It is warm, but overcast, there is no moon as Miro pedals behind a slit of golden light from his headlight. He has a comforting feeling of being completely alone. A soft wind brings the scent of grass and damp earth and something quite fragrant although he can't think what it is. He can smell smoke, too, and a drift of ozone. He brakes, p s his feet down and leans forward to flick off his lamp, enjoying the peace and security of the darkness. He can hear shouts and laughter from the GI camp and he envies them all. He longs to be free of his burden of guilt. He has only to turn back. No one can force him to do what is so abhorrent to him. He has learned to love this comfortable country and the kindly people. They don't say much, but they mean what they say. They seem slow and old-fashioned at times, but you can depend upon the strong streak of morality that runs through the core of the people. So why help their enemies? He turns and crosses the narrow road, about to head for home. 'I can't do it. How can anyone expect me to,' he mutters.

A high-pitched scream came from behind the hedge, troubling in its intensity. A rabbit has been caught by a fox, perhaps, or in a trap. He feels the pain, remembering. 'No . . .' He pushes the hated memory away, but it never goes far. It's always hanging around in the back of his mind. His parents are locked in that hell. There is no escape for them. He turns again and pedals fearfully towards his destination.

Six

There were plenty of pillboxes scattered along the beaches around Mowbray: ugly squat structures, tall enough for a man to stand upright in, with low slits running parallel to the ground for half a dozen rifles to protrude. Last year, at the first sign of danger, they would have been manned within minutes by the members of Home Guard who were always on hand. Now that the threat of invasion was over, they were lying idle: ugly monuments to the dogged perseverance of the retired locals, who had been prepared to halt the enemy advance for as long as they lived.

Miro knew this place well. Hotels and shops stood opposite, but it was too dark to see them. He flicked his torch on to find the way down to the beach. The wooden steps were slippery and he was glad to reach the sand. Shouldering his bicycle, so as not to leave tracks, he made his way to where he thought the pillbox stood. At first he could see nothing at all. As his eyes adjusted, the ugly concrete structure was silhouetted against the glittering sea. His shoes became wet, the damp air sank into his skin. His hands felt sticky and he was trembling. He stopped to wipe his sleeve over his forehead. Reaching the blockhouse, he leaned the bike against it so softly that he made no sound at all – but someone heard.

'Put it inside, boyo, and sit here beside me.'

An Irish accent, a light tenor voice, a man in his thirties, he deduced, knowing that he would remember that voice for the rest of his life. Lifting the bike into the entrance, he recoiled with disgust. Someone, kids perhaps, had been using it as a lavatory, there was a stench of urine and excrement mingled with the sea mist. It was as dark as pitch in there. He felt disorientated and bumped into the wall grazing his hand as he stumbled to find fresh air.

'Get a move on, Levy.' The voice, so soft and intrusive, gave him the shivers, with its soft, lilting cadence, the rounded vowels, the slight trill of the 'r's. Not just Irish, but something else, something closer to home. German parents, perhaps. He stowed this into the back of his mind. The stench of decayed seaweed and wet cement stayed with him as he trudged around the corner to the sea side of the structure. A glow of a cigarette led him to a figure crouched on the sand.

'Sit down, boyo.'

Now they were sitting side by side on the sea-drenched sand. The wetness penetrated his pants and brought on a fit of shivering. Or was it fright? His backside began to itch with the sticky dampness. The stench of rotten seaweed and ozone made him feel sick, but at least it was better than inside the pillbox.

'Next time, padlock your bike to the rails along the pavement. Right now you've left tyre tracks in the sand. You must think, boyo. Think of your own safety. It's all right once, although someone might see them in the morning.'

Miro didn't bother to answer.

'Now what have you got for me?'

'Nothing . . . that is, I don't know what you want.'

'What do you think I want? Troop movements, numbers of vehicles, just how many Americans are housed in the camp next door to you. Pick on a GI near your age, make friends, find out what they know. When and where. You grasp my meaning. They might have some ideas. Do you have anyone billeted on you?'

'We were told that we would, but no one has come.'

'They will. Reckon your home is officer status. You fell with your arse in the butter, but don't forget who sent you. You might have been shut up in that camp, but you volunteered to work for the Third Reich to support your parents.'

'I'm still at school. I work to a timetable. Even at night I have sport and homework. How do you expect me to find out anything useful?'

'I don't suppose you know what's useful and what's not useful, but I'll help you.'

The man drew a small photograph from his pocket. He flashed a torch on to it for Miro's inspection. He saw a soft-eyed woman in her forties. She looked sadder than he remembered and much thinner. New lines had appeared on his mother's face and she had lost that soft, friendly expression. She looked fierce. Miro was glad. Her innate strength would help her to survive. Miro struggled not to cry out as he reached for the picture, but the man withdrew his hand.

'Yes,' Miro said.

'Yes what?'

'Yes, that is my mother, but how is my father? Give me the picture.'

'Not so fast. We work quid pro quo. You've heard of that, I expect. You give me what I need and I tell you what you want to know. I might even give you the picture. It's a workable system.'

Miro wanted nothing more than to grasp him round the neck and squeeze the life out of him, but that would cause reprisals too horrible to think about. Besides, he could sense his bulk. He was taller and stronger and probably a trained fighter, but he was in training, too, Miro reminded himself. One day!

'What do I call you?' he asked.

'I'm surprised you ask such a stupid question. I was told you'd been picked for your intelligence. You don't need to call me anything.'

Then 'Paddy' will do, Miro thought to himself.

'You don't want to know me. If you did it might prove dangerous for you, if you get my meaning.'

'Of course.' He cursed himself for his stupidity.

'We have a job to do . . . it's called Counter Intelligence. We sow the seeds of discontent between the Allies. Have any of your foster family had any contact with the camp?'

Miro tried to work out the implications of his words. The man was tiptoeing around his brief, but it didn't take long to get his meaning.

'So think, Miro,' he was saying. 'If I send back a blank report on your behalf your mum will be starved, or beaten, until you bring us some news.'

A surge of fury almost sent him groping for the man's throat, but Paddy was only a messenger, the SS would still have his parents. 'I don't understand,' he said, playing for time while he tried to make up something.

'We want to set the locals against the Yanks. See what I mean?'

Thoughts were buzzing through his head. What possible harm could it do to Daisy? Or to anyone? Perhaps her boyfriend might be sent to another camp. If so, that would be the end of the romance. He guessed that she had been necking with the Yank. Perhaps the guy had tried to go all the way. Daisy could look eighteen when she tried.

'My foster sister went up to London today, but she was short of cash so she hitched back, which was crazy. She was picked up by a GI, but when he dropped her at the gate, she looked upset. She'd been crying and I noticed her wrist was bruised. She's only sixteen.'

'So she had to fight him off.'

'Perhaps.'

'Where's he staying?'

'At one of the local camps. That's all I know.'

'Did you see him? Could you recognize him?'

'No. It was dark.'

'Wait a minute! Are you making this up?'

'No, I'm not.'

'So how did you come to see the jeep?'

'I was looking out of the window.'

'Sweet on her, are you? What does she look like?'

'Blonde, tall for her age. She looks older than she is. She's beautiful,' he added and then wished he hadn't.

'Well that will do for starters. Keep going like this and your parents will see the war's end.'

Bastard! I'll get you one day.

When Paddy stood up Miro became aware of the sheer bulk of the man, six foot and squarish, he reckoned. A real bruiser. Trembling with fear, he said, 'If you want me to work for you, bring pictures of both of them regularly.'

'Whose side are you on, Miro? You swore to help the Third Reich, but maybe you didn't mean what you said. Maybe you just pretended to get out of the camp. They are tough on Jews. I sympathize, but you have to work to keep your parents alive. You're in no position to lay down terms.'

'But I have to know that they *are* alive.'

'You've got a nerve, I'll say that for you.'

Miro shivered and stared out across the Channel. Out there, not far away, the Nazis were strutting around, doing their best to convince themselves and others of their superiority. He wasn't the only victim. He tried to turn his mind away from thoughts of rebellion. He had a mission and he wasn't aiming to abandon his parents. Not ever. He shuddered.

'I didn't come empty-handed either, Miro. Your parents have been moved to Terezin, it's the old fortress of Theresienstadt which has been converted to a concentration camp.' Miro had heard the rumours. It was supposed to be a model ghetto for Red Cross inspectors to examine. 'They tell me your father plays the violin. He's been invited to join the camp orchestra. A cushy job if ever there was one.'

Joy coursed through Miro in uncontrollable shudders. His relief was clearly obvious.

'They mean a lot to you, don't they? If you work hard, they'll be all right. I'd say you're one of the lucky ones. How many Yanks do you reckon are around Mowbray and Claremont? Their equipment is stowed around. For instance, you could take a square mile as an example. Easy enough on your bicycle.'

Miro listened and said nothing. If Paddy disappeared someone else would take his place and maybe his parents would suffer.

'I get the picture. I must go. I said I was going to help a friend with his homework. My foster mother might phone them. She's waiting up for me.'

'Go then. I'll be in touch.'

Drenched with remorse over his guilt and his mad jealousy, Miro retrieved his bike from the foul pillbox and set off for home. He was very aware that Paddy might embroider his story and this might have consequences, but there was no possibility that the story could lead back to Daisy. She was his guardian angel. She always had been, right from their very first glimpse of each other. He, in his half-mast trousers and shirt sleeves, red-nosed, shivering with cold, scared . . . a lost boy, had found himself gazing at a vision of loveliness and kindliness and he had loved her ever since.

The sun is shining and Dover's legendary cliffs look dazzling white as the train approaches Dover. Passing through a narrow track between the cliffs and the sea, Miro glimpses a castle set amongst green hills and forested slopes. The train stops with a series of shudders. He and the social worker from Southampton, step on to the smoky platform. They look anxiously around and see a woman hurrying towards them. He has been told that an English woman has promised to look after him for the duration of the war, but it can't be her. She is too lovely to be a foster mother. Miro has very firm views on foster mothers: they are middle-aged, fat and bossy, like those in the orphanage. She glances at him and then looks away, trying not to show her shock.

Miro saw his reflection in the lavatory mirror on the train – the first glimpse in months and it was a shock. He is skinny from his time in Dachau, red-eyed from weeping, with the worse haircut in the world, the work of his Gypsy supervisor and he is wearing someone else's clothes. He hasn't had a shower for over a week, so he probably stinks. When he breathes in, a sharp pain between his shoulder blades brings on a fit of coughing. Forlorn and wretched, he waits while the woman argues with his carer. He is convinced that she won't take him. 'It's disgraceful,' she says loudly. Miro makes a point of remembering this word so he can find out the meaning later. Finally she shrugs, takes his hand and leads him through the station to her car, a three-year-old Alfa Romeo, which impresses him. The woman is angry, he can see that.

Miro longs for his mother. By now she would have pushed him into bed and she would be fussing around with a thermometer, hot compresses and sore throat sweets, blackcurrant and eucalyptus, the kind he loves. He blinks his tears away. As they drive past small shops and wretched rows of tiny houses, he longs to be back in Prague, which is beautiful, but those days are forever gone. All he knows is that somehow he must keep alive, so he can work to protect his parents.

Soon they are in a leafy suburb, which gives way to fields with horses, cows and sheep. His foster mother speaks to him – an ongoing string of words, but he has no English so he merely shrugs. After a long drive they turn into a steep lane running between fields and woods. Right at the top is a bungalow, set in front of a wood. The woman swings into the gate and parks in the driveway.

'Daisy, Daisy,' she calls. A dog rushes towards them. 'Johnny,' she says, pointing at the dog who is leaping up and down, long ears flapping. 'Home,' she says, pointing at the house. 'Daisy,' she says, pointing at a vision of loveliness running towards him. Is she real? Her long hair floats like threads of spun silver. Her skin is tanned, eyes of deep violet are smiling at him. He feels bewitched by the warmth in her eyes and the way she takes his arm and tugs him along the driveway.

She calls to her mother and they argue, but in a friendly way. He understands that Daisy wants to take him to the stables, where he can see two horses watching them. Her mother wants him in the house. Daisy wins. He has the feeling that she always does. She shows him the garden, the fish pond, the horses and shows him how Johnny can sit or walk or come at her command. She is talking in words of one syllable as if he is an idiot. He wants to explain that he speaks Czech, German, Hebrew, Yiddish and French, but not English, but he will learn this language as fast as he possibly can. He says this to her in all five languages and she does her best to reply in her school French. Now he is excited. They can communicate. He sprawls on the grass excitedly and writes the words he wants to know in the earth in French, and in turn helps her to pronounce the French words properly.

That is how Helen finds them ten minutes later after she has called the doctor and the village chemist. They are lying full length on the grass, swopping words with the help of the flower bed. Belle? 'Beautiful,' she says. Cheveux? 'Hair.' 'Beautiful hair,' he manages in English, pointing at hers and she flushes and looks pleased. Helen lets them stay there until the doctor comes. A hot bath follows, medicine and a two-week stay in bed, because

Miro has bronchitis. By the time he recovers, his wardrobe is full of new clothes, he has gained eight pounds in weight, he has a smattering of English, enough to get by at an English school, and Daisy's French is vastly improved.

A car was approaching, filling the lane and driving too fast. Miro swerved to the side and thrust his feet down. *Can't they see him? They seemed to be coming right at him.* He jumped up the bank into nettles, hauling his bike after him. *Phew! That was a close shave. Idiots!*

'Damned Yanks,' he said, rubbing his ankles from the stings. Dazzled by the bright lights in pitch dark it was impossible to know what kind of vehicle had driven him off the road, but then he remembered to switch on his headlight. All he knew was that the coming of the GIs had changed his life irrevocably. He and Daisy had always been inseparable. 'But what was, was,' Miro whispered bitterly, remembering a phrase of his mother's.

Seven

It was a sunny, humid day, with thunder clouds on the horizon. Helen was hanging out the washing, hoping that it would not rain before she got home. She tried not to stare at the Yanks loitering on the other side of the fence, but she found them interesting. They looked so casual, shirts hanging loose, hands in pockets, slouching, but they were friendly and extroverted. What touched her the most was their youth. How could they send kids like this into battle? Some time had passed since the Yanks arrived. To Helen it seemed like weeks, but when she worked it out, it was only eight days, which surprised her.

A tempting aroma of food was drifting across the garden. It must be coming from the GIs' kitchens. Who else could produce such tantalizing smells in wartime? She could smell bacon. Oh my God! Imagine having bacon and eggs with toast and butter – oodles of butter – and marmalade and maybe porridge to start with. And would they have fruit, too? She couldn't stop envying them.

'Breakfast is ready,' Dad said from right behind her. 'How are you doing?'

· She was drooling for bacon, but she kept this to herself. 'Famished.' Helen hurried inside to gobble her porridge and toast. Daisy and Miro had an egg and a beef sausage each because they were growing and they needed the protein, not that there was much protein in the sausages they bought nowadays.

Helen was late for work. She rushed outside, fetched her bicycle and moments later she was cycling towards the factory at breakneck speed. All along her route tents had been erected on every grassy verge, even on circles at crossroads. Every available space was filled with tents or parked vehicles covered in tarpaulin. All the side roads that weren't vital for motor traffic were roped off to store all kinds of war vehicles. The village green, the park, the green belts bordering the river, and the gardens in front of civic buildings were full of tents and the streets were crowded with GIs wandering around, examining the bomb damage, going into shops and trying to make friends. Every day there seemed to be more and still more of them. She smiled to herself. Real hope was spread around her. It was the first time she had felt confident of winning the war. But what of the future?

Everything's changing, nothing will be left of our old lives. Will we forget who we were? But who was I? Not a real wife, not since Eric was having an affair with a woman half my age and I never suspected him. I won't be a mother for long either. Daisy will grow up and leave and Miro will go home at the end of the war. I'm thirty-seven, but I feel no different, exactly the same as I felt when Daisy was young. Do we ever get old, I wonder? Or is it our bodies that age and we, trapped inside them, have to adjust and pretend, just as we are adjusting to the war, and our losses, more each day, she told herself feverishly. But what's all this gloom and doom, Helen? Get a grip on yourself. Be positive. You'll find another role to play.

She stopped beside a group of GIs and said, 'Thank you for coming.'

They looked startled and a little embarrassed. Perhaps they thought she was a bit gaga and to tell the truth she was this morning, sensing that she had reached a watershed. Soon she caught sight of the factory roof through the trees. Padlocking her bike in the shelter, she hurried inside.

The explosives factory was set at the edge of a farm near a copse and it was camouflaged with dark green and khaki stripes on the roof. Inside, the walls were whitewashed and covered with posters depicting lovely young girls with super hairdos and make-up, smiling as they did their stint for Britain's war effort. It was half-true. The girls in her group smiled a lot and sometimes they sang and some of them were young and a few were pretty. They wore brown overalls, which disguised their figures, scarves over their heads and large goggles. Helen's place was at the end of the work bench, beside the wall. She had been warned against this position. If there was an explosion, due to someone's carelessness, the blast would be worse where she stood, but she enjoyed the semi-privacy and she liked her neighbour. May was a cheerful woman of forty-five who had married young and never had a job, rearing six children instead. Her husband, Reg, had owned a small haulage company, but now he was fighting in North Africa and the family was hard-up. May was a rough diamond with enough courage for three men, and a loyalty to her mates that was legendary. She was a true survivor, keeping her would-be boyfriends at arms' length and enjoying extra meat and groceries because the shopkeepers loved her. She always had a joke to tell, and she was overly generous, sharing her largess with anyone in need.

'I'm glad you're OK. I was worried because you're never late,' May said.

'It's silly, I know, but I'm scared to leave before I see Daisy in case she takes off again. I dawdle a bit so we can meet at breakfast.'

'You got your Yankee yet?' she asked cheerily.

'Not yet. I think they've forgotten us.'

'No such luck, but perhaps he'll be dishy.'

'Some hopes. But we're ready for him. I'd like to say that we gritted our teeth and got on with yet another austerity in true British style, but the truth is we bickered and fought and tried to hang on to our space. Neither of the kids wanted to relinquish their bedrooms. Daisy played the martyr. Then my father decided to quit his downstairs study with the French windows leading into the garden which, I must tell you, he loves so much, and move his desk, bookcase and clutter to his upstairs bedroom. The family is stuck with only one bathroom now. It's such a nuisance, but Daisy and I are still using ours until our lodger actually arrives. I hope this fellow is civilized and that he doesn't chase Daisy.'

May, who had never seen Daisy, laughed at her. 'She's only sixteen, isn't she? Did you notice how crowded the camps are getting? Hundreds more moved in during the night. I hope we don't have any more trouble. You heard about the attempted rape, I suppose. The locals are good and mad.'

'I haven't had time to read the papers lately. We listen to the radio at night to get the war news.'

'One of the Yanks attempted to rape a girl of sixteen. She got home bruised and crying. This'll have repercussions, you'll see. I was in our local cafe when the pint-sized owner tried to chuck a Yank out. He's a little runt and the Yank was a big, burly black guy. He just stood there while this little guy punched him time and again. He didn't move a muscle, but he looked upset. When the guy stopped, he shook his head and said, "I'm the 29th Division's boxing champion – that's why I didn't fight back. One punch would have floored you. One of these days you folks will be glad we came."

'We felt terrible. The local girls are kicking up a fuss because the Yanks have been barred from the local Palais. They are crazy about jiving.'

The morning wore on slowly for Helen as she listened to the

girls chatter: how to make face cream when there wasn't any, how to tan your legs without sun, how to mend your own shoes now the shoemaker had joined up, a million makeshift do-it-yourself remedies. Some of them even made coffee by roasting dandelion roots.

By the time she rode home, the weather was hot and sultry, but the rain was holding off. Helen wondered why she never felt tension from the danger all the time she was working. It was only later, once she'd left, that she began to feel like a puppet with the string pulled too tightly.

She needed a swim, but were the GIs training in the bay? Hurrying to the end of the garden, she peered down. The bay twinkled and winked at her, bringing back childhood memories of picnics and later midnight barbecues on the sand. It all looked deserted. Ten minutes later she was picking her way down the badly eroded, zigzag path to the beach, riding her mare, Leila, who was well-schooled and used to the cliffs. At the end of the beach was a fresh water spring, almost hidden amongst the grass and shrubs. Wearing her modest, skirt-fronted, one-piece bathing suit she pushed her clothes into a bush and walked barefooted on the sand, leaving Leila to munch the grass around the spring. The delicious feeling of sun and wind on her bare limbs and sand between her toes was strangely thrilling.

She swam out in a fast crawl and returned through the breaking surf, diving under the rollers, avoiding the rocky areas. Her mouth and eyes stung with salt and her skin tingled. Setting off in a lazy crawl to deeper water, she paused for a rest and lay floating on the surface, enjoying the solitude as she rose and fell over the gentle waves, hearing the soft splashes of water against her cheeks. Clouds drifted past, gulls swooped and soared, and she caught snatches of jazz from the GIs' camp. Slowly, lethargically, she began to swim backstroke.

Turning over, she flinched at the sight of a large black lump floating under the surface of the water only a few metres away. Don't panic, she told herself urgently. There are no man-eating sharks in British waters. Could it be a lost whale? Or a dolphin? But as she watched, it sank rapidly down into the depths. One moment it was there and then there was nothing. Thrusts of fear pierced her stomach. What could it be? The thought of that black thing swimming beneath her was frightening. She was far from the shore and she had never seen anything like it. If she had to guess she would choose a giant squid. But of course they didn't exist. Or did they?

Fighting back her fear she took a deep breath and dived into the water, finding herself too buoyant to get further down than a few feet below the surface. Suddenly it was zooming towards her. Magnified by the water's refraction, it looked huge, something out of science fiction. Displaced water splashed around her like a fountain as the *thing* caught hold of her arm.

'Are you all right, Ma'am?' She heard. So the beast was human! Anger replaced fear.

'Let go.' She kicked him hard.

He pushed back his mask. 'I'm sorry. Truly I'm so sorry. I'll get you back to the shore. Just relax. I'm a lifesaver.'

'I'm not panicking and I don't need help. Let go of me.' She set off for the shore, annoyed that he had seen her fear.

Lifesaver! Huh! Tortoise would be more like it. She reached the beach, mounted Leila and set off for home, grabbing her clothes from the bushes as she passed. Halfway up, she paused to look back and saw him staggering up the beach with a large oval container like a boiler, strapped to his back. No wonder he was so slow. She watched him crouch on the sand to undo the harness strapped around his chest. Once free of the tank, he stretched and rubbed his shoulders before retrieving a trailer from the bushes. She was so busy watching, she let Leila step too close to the edge, which crumbled. As one leg slipped over the cliff, Helen jumped down fast and pulled the mare back onto the path. That's enough scares for one day, she said to herself. She walked the rest of the way, but when she passed the Hawthorn copse, on top of the cliff, she paused. Smacking Leila on the rump to send her galloping home, she peered through the thorny branches and watched the GI strip off his black rubber suit and stand naked on the sand. He was suntanned and strong. All muscle and no fat, she noticed and despite his broad, lean shape, there was a delicacy of movement in everything he did. She admired his black hair rippling in the sunlight. When he turned away, she noticed that his buttocks were solid and his legs shapely. The effect of his beautiful naked body on her psyche was devastating. Feeling deeply ashamed she walked back to unsaddle Leila.

Later that evening, when they had finished dinner and washed up, the family sat in the lounge listening to *No Place to Hide*, on the radio, Miro's favourite serial. The anticipated storm had not materialized and it was a lovely evening. Shadows were gathering and they could hardly see, but switching on the lights meant drawing the blackout and that would be a shame. The windows were open and they could hear birdsong and the repetitive boom of waves on the shore. They could scent the tobacco flowers John always grew beneath the windows. By a unanimous decision they decided to wait until the last possible moment before shutting the windows and drawing the curtains.

The programme finished and Miro stood up. 'I'd better go and study.' He bounded upstairs. Then the doorbell rang.

'I'll go,' Daisy said. Helen heard her talking. The deeper, male reply which sounded all too familiar, brought spasms of nervousness to her stomach.

'I'd like to see your father, or your mother, if it's convenient.'

Helen panicked. The urge to flee sent adrenaline flooding through her. Unable to sit still she jumped up, but there was nowhere to go, the only door led to the hall and *he* was there. She had hoped never to see him again. She hated him for his innate power to send her body into sexual longing. She had intended that this would never happen again. She was a mature woman even if she did still feel like a young girl, but she had been caught unaware. Trying to compose herself, she sat down.

Helen was not proud of the absurd fear she'd felt earlier out at sea so she had kept their strange encounter to herself. Now it would all come out. Moments later, Daisy came into the room, her eyes bright with excitement. She bent over Helen.

'Listen, Mum. He's straight out of Hollywood. Or he should be. Talk about dreamy. He wants to see you or my *father*,' she said with heavy irony.

'He can see Dad, can't he?' She looked at John apologetically. 'You don't mind, do you?'

'Of course not.' He raised one eyebrow and smiled enigmatically as he went out.

'John Cooper. Great to meet you,' she heard.

'Captain Simon Johnson from the camp,' *he* replied. 'I'm a scuba diving instructor, among other duties. I came over to see if Mrs Cooper had recovered from her swim. I'm afraid I frightened her.'

The lounge door was open and Simon glanced around, hoping that he did not look too curious. The decor contrasted with the Victorian house. It looked Scandinavian: bright handmade rugs on polished wooden floors, ultra modern furniture, the paintings were modern, too. One in particular caught his eye: a modern rendering of the bay below the house in varying shades of grey.

'My wife's work,' John said, catching his interest.

Why had she married someone so old? Simon wondered, guessing Cooper to be in his mid-seventies. An old husband might account for her lurking in the shrubbery. He'd had a feeling he was being watched and he'd checked the footprints and seen exactly where the horse and woman had parted company and where she had waited. In his youth he'd been a skilled hunter, but later he became sickened by the sport, so nowadays he hunted with a camera, or nothing. He said, 'I hope your wife is all right.'

'Well, I guess you must be talking about Helen, my daughter,' John said. 'My wife died several years ago.'

'Oh, I'm sorry . . . The War Office commandeered your fields for us, but I want to assure you we shall leave them exactly as we found them. In the meantime, with your permission, we aim to fix the fencing and improve the path down to the bay. Your daughter had a dangerous incident there on her horse this afternoon.'

'Good heavens. Come inside. I've heard nothing about this.' The old man ushered him into the lounge. He followed Cooper, automatically stooping as he did so. It was an old house and the doorways were little over six foot high. Cooper just made it without scalping himself, Simon noticed.

'This is my daughter, Helen Conroy and my granddaughter, Daisy.'

They shook hands and murmured, 'How do you do,' English style, which always struck Simon as ridiculous, so he said, 'Hello there,' to both of them.

'So was it you or Daisy?' Dad asked Helen.

'Me,' Helen said shortly. 'Leila's back foot slipped over the edge. It was my fault. I wasn't paying enough attention. It certainly wasn't dangerous. Captain Johnson is exaggerating.'

'I hope you didn't scratch yourself too badly on the cliff top,' Simon said. 'Hawthorns are nasty critters.' Watching her cheeks burn crimson, Simon wished he hadn't teased her.

'So what happened, Captain?' John asked.

'I was testing some new gear. I apologize for frightening you, Mrs Conroy. I should have let you know that I'd be there. I'm sorry.'

'Startled would be nearer the truth,' Helen snapped. 'For a few insane moments I thought you were a giant squid.'

'First impressions are usually on the ball.' Now he was openly laughing at her.

'Why be sorry. It's your bay now, isn't it? It was never really ours, but we were the only ones who could get there. Now you can. Unfortunately!'

How bitter, she sounded. Despite his attraction Simon did a double-take. Looks weren't everything. He exhaled slowly. Helen was mean, but stunning. He had caught sight of her a few times since he'd arrived. He'd watched her teaching riding and admired her proficiency. He'd seen her in her modest swimming costume and admired her sexy shoulders and her trim waist and long slender legs. She had a good backside, too. He'd had a good demonstration of her cool courage when he startled her, and when her horse almost slipped down the cliff face, but look at her now, hiding her beauty behind her scowls and frumpish clothes, her hair scraped back in a bun. She seemed to be wearing a man's shirt over a bulky jersey. Without either make-up or any attempt to look pretty, one could be forgiven for believing she was butch, if she hadn't watched him stripping from her vantage point deep in the prickly hawthorn.

'Let's share the bay, shall we?' Simon said.

Now Simon seemed on his guard and wounded. Helen was glad. Handsome men were out as far as she was concerned. Or any men, come to that. She scowled at him, resenting his suave manner, his close-cropped dark hair and his arresting eyes. It was absurd the way Hollywood had entered their lives, imposing standards that no one could reach. Anyone normal came off second-best, but not him. Why did he annoy her so? Perhaps because she knew what she looked like dressed in the old clothes she wore for the canteen job.

'Would you like a drink, Captain?' John asked, trying to offset her rudeness.

'One of your famous English beers would be perfect.'

'We have cold lager in the cellar.'

'Ah, even better.' He settled down as if for a long stay and Helen scowled at her father.

'Homework,' Helen murmured to Daisy, who got up reluctantly and paused in the doorway. 'So what exactly were you doing out there, Captain? Or is it classified?' Daisy asked.

'It's a new skill called SCUBA and that is an acronym for "Self Contained Underwater Breathing Apparatus", which means we can stay underwater, to blow up bridges, or fight, or attach bombs to the hulls of ships, but first we have to learn how it's done. I'm here to train a team, but I'm still practising myself.'

Daisy was watching him with cow's eyes, obviously very taken by his good looks, Helen noticed. Suddenly Daisy flushed and ran upstairs.

'Would your husband object if we patronize your riding school, ma'am?'

So he's curious to know if I have one, but why should he care? Helen wondered. And why should I answer? She looked away without answering.

'My daughter and her husband have separated,' John answered for her. 'Perhaps you'd like to come and see the horses, but I'm sure they are too tame for you. Most of our pupils are children.'

It was only when they had gone out to look at the stables that Helen realized they had been sitting in the dark. 'Phew!' she exhaled. 'He must think we're mad sitting here like that.' She slammed the windows and fastened the blackout. First came the thin black, Government-issue blind, that was prone to tear and crackle and never worked properly. Then the proscribed blackout curtains, which were not sufficient either, and lastly their own lined, velvet curtains, old-fashioned, but effective. After this she pulled the lined curtain over the front door and only then could she put on the light. Just let one beam escape and the police would come knocking on their door to threaten them with a hefty fine.

Not long afterwards the men returned via the back door. Simon shook her hand formally. 'You have an exceptionally beautiful daughter, Mrs Conroy,' he said, offering her his very best smile.

'She's only sixteen,' Helen said flatly.

'I guessed as much. It must be delightful to have a child who is the image of you.'

She was startled. It was years since she had received a compliment, even one as roundabout as this. Oh, he was just too smooth for words. She wanted to put him in his place, but she couldn't think how. How dare he try to butter her up this way. She knew very well what she looked like, particularly right now, past her prime and getting frumpish. That's exactly how Eric had described her when they fought over the coming split. Why should he be interested in her? She scowled at him.

Damn all lying, cheating men, she muttered to herself.

Back in his tent, Simon made a note that the cliff path should be considered top priority and put it in his 'out' basket. While showing him the horses, Cooper had tried to excuse his daughter's bad manners by explaining that she was overworked: she packed explosives for four-, five-hour stints a week, and most nights she worked in the troops' canteen. But Simon felt that he understood her mood better than John. He guessed that her broken marriage had left her with a poor self-image. She was bitter and angry at being dumped. So was he, but he had managed to handle it better than she had. He found her very attractive and he admired her courage, but he decided that he would steer clear of her in future. It wasn't often that Simon lied to himself.

Eight

The moment the first unconfirmed reports began to surface Simon knew that war had begun. His war! And he had to fight it his way. The allegation of attempted rape of a young girl made major headlines in local and national newspapers. Next came whispers that spread like wildfire from pub to pub: a pensioner hurt his ankle when a GI jostled him off the pavement; a housewife had her purse snatched; a girl was accosted on her way to school; a woman carrying a child was knocked down the steps of the public shelter when the air-raid siren sounded; and so on. Each incident was trivial, but together they created a furore. Over the following weeks tension between the Yanks and locals heightened. GIs complained that they were booed when they appeared in the village, the local dancehall banned them, shopkeepers were loathe to serve them and one restaurant put a notice on the door saying: *Civilians Only*.

Simon used a carrot and stick approach to woo newspaper editors, radio personnel, shop keepers and businessmen. 'Prove it or publicly apologize', was his pithy message over many excellent lunches in the relaxed venue of the local yacht club, which he had joined. He and the local detective inspector, Rob McGuire, planned a radio interview highlighting this successful Axis whispering campaign. McGuire was a man likely to inspire confidence with his kindly expression, his candour and engaging grin. The inspector's talk was based on a circular Simon was distributing:

America and Britain are allies. Hitler knows that we are both powerful countries, tough and resourceful. He knows that we, with the other united Allied nations, mean his crushing defeat in the end. So it is only common sense to understand that the first and major duty Hitler has given his propaganda chiefs and spies is to separate Britain and America and spread distrust between us. If he can do that, his chance of winning might return. I'm not saying we Yankees are all angels, but many of us have volunteered, leaving our homes and families for the express purpose of beating the Nazis. So if anyone comes to you with a rumour, get to the bottom of it and if there's any truth in it, go to the police at once.

'So far we have received no complaints,' the DI told Simon, 'and there has been no report of an attempted rape. I checked with the hospital and local doctors.'

The only exception was an old lady who reported that the Yanks had stolen her dog. Simon investigated and found that Rover, a cross Airedale-Irish Terrier, was prone to wander. The neighbours told him that Rover did the rounds in the early mornings, raiding the doorsteps for the families' eggs and cheese left by the milkman. A month ago he had even smashed a bottle of milk when he knocked over a bicycle to get at the owner's meat ration. Now Rover had found unlimited scraps around the GI canteen where he had taken up permanent residence. Simon set up a rota of youngsters to take the dog home whenever he turned up, with a parcel of scraps.

Slowly the two men worked hard to squash all anti-American feelings amongst the locals, but they were both aware that a network of agents were masterminding a skilled, Axis counter intelligence campaign. They could be German spies, or Nazi sympathizers.

Simon's next task was to warn the troops, which he completed over the next few days with a series of informal talks in the canteen. 'We are moving towards a joint invasion,' he told them, 'but while we're waiting we have to be on our guard. On the day we storm the beaches we want to know we are surrounded by friends. Only idiots would fall out with their allies.' He left it at that.

Later that day, Simon had a surprise visit from Sergeant Mike Lawson.

'Sir, I wondered if I could talk about the rape allegation. You asked for news of any incident that might have been misconstrued. I have something to tell you . . . that is, I certainly didn't try to rape someone, but the bruised wrists . . . well, it got me wondering . . .'

'Carry on,' Simon prodded gently.

'Well, this girl I gave a lift to kind of fits the bill, sir. Sixteen, but looking eighteen. Funny thing is, I didn't even notice what she looked like until she dried out a bit. I was coming back from London about five weeks ago. It was almost dark and raining and there was this girl . . . she looked half-drowned sitting on a suitcase by the roadside with her head in her hands. I stopped and offered her a lift and as it happened she was on her way here, because she lives next door to the camp and her family owns this land we're camped on.'

It was going to be a long story. 'Why don't you sit down?' Simon said. 'Better still, let's have a drink in the mess. I have to finish some work. I'll meet you there in half an hour.'

'Yes, sir.'

The break gave Simon a chance to finish his report and examine Lawson's record. He had volunteered right after Pearl Harbour, although he'd just completed his studies in order to run the family's ranch. He was a first-class recruit, tipped for rapid promotion, capable, hard working and reliable. He also noticed that he was the captain of his school's swimming team, and he'd got a few guys together to make up a water polo team in the camp. They might be just the men he needed for the scuba training.

Sergeant Lawson was clearly ill at ease. He jumped to his feet when Simon arrived and stammered as he launched into his story before they'd even sat down. 'You have to understand, sir, that I feel a bit of an ass. She looked eighteen.'

'Relax, Lawson. Start at the beginning when we've ordered. I've been reading about your water polo team. I'm interested.'

By the time they'd finished their first lager, Lawson was visibly relaxed and he'd been talked into volunteering for Simon's under-water training. Simon said, 'Well, I guess we'd better get on with the alleged attempted rape, Lawson.'

'Yeah. As I said, I picked her up, but as for the rape . . . well, it wasn't like that at all. She was . . . no, she *is* a very nice girl. She went up to London to trace her grannie, but she found the house boarded up and badly damaged. She didn't have enough cash for the return trip, so she hitched, but no one picked her up until I came along. I must admit it was great to talk to a girl. It was the first time for months, so I suggested we have dinner on the way home and she agreed.

'To start with I felt a bit of a country lout, I mean, she seemed sophisticated and she was talking about winning a scholarship to a top London art school. Later, I decided she was putting on an act to seem grown up, but by that time the damage was done.'

Damage, Simon thought to himself, trying to hide his dis-appointment. Maybe there was some truth in the rumour. 'Carry on then,' he said amiably enough.

Mike tried for total recall, but whatever he said, and he tried to be truthful, could never recapture the sweet sense of belonging that began on that magical evening.

Mike had a bitter sweet memory of Daisy framed by a potted palm, her eyes wide open and as blue as the summer sea. You could dive into them and lose yourself in the depths. The evening began awkwardly. He'd ordered a bottle of semi-sweet white wine because he'd learned at the barbecues back home that most girls like that best.

'Where does it come from, this amazing hair of yours?' he'd asked, feeling like a country idiot, tongue-tied and shy for the first time in his life.

'My grandmother was Danish. Gramps says I'm exactly like her, but I'm also like my mum.'

'Danish,' he had repeated oafishly, savouring the word. Daisy would never wait for him. He'd be fighting his way through Europe while she was at art school amongst the sophisticates. She'd be the loveliest girl there.

'How is it that you are a sergeant? You're so young.' She smiled warmly and he felt encouraged to tell her more about himself.

'This is war, don't forget. They need men. All kinds of men. As soon as I finished my degree, I volunteered.'

'Go on,' she said encouragingly.

What did he know apart from farming? Precious little. He was acutely aware of his sheltered upbringing and the probable short-comings of his conversation.

'When I was fifteen my mum died of cancer,' he told her. 'From then on Dad and I have gotten along as best we can without a woman in the house. We're close friends and we both work hard.'

Mike loved ranching and he was glad of a chance to spend his days doing the work he loved so much. They were prospering and Mike's half share of the profits were increasing, but he had no particu-lar love of money: he drove a modest 4 x 4 and invested most of his profits back into the ranch. He enjoyed the smell and the sight of the land, he had youth and strength, good friends who often dropped by, and a great sense of humour. He worked hard and he was a good rider, competing and usually winning the dressage and jumping competitions. He even scored at rodeo events, all of which would be of little interest to this lovely girl who was sitting across the table from him. He'd seen beautiful women on the screen, but never in the flesh and here was Daisy hanging on his every word.

What was he to say? Just how should he treat her? He had his first experience of real panic, fearing that he might do or say the wrong thing and lose her.

'It was a problem for my dad when I volunteered, but I knew he was proud of me. He took on a couple of hands and he's coping well enough.'

Daisy was gulping the wine down like lemonade. She became talkative.

'London was awful,' she confided. 'The sight of all those poor kids playing in ruined homes, and the stray cats crying, and the dust . . . I just couldn't stand it.' When her eyes clouded with tears he reached across the table and held her hand.

Mike was a good listener and intuitively he sensed her world: people are good or bad. Life is heavenly or disastrous and everything she sees is either beautiful or ugly, but mainly the former. Lately life had gone horribly wrong for her and she listed all the horrors in date order. Eventually she recounted their move back home to her grandfather's house, on the cliff, overlooking the bay and how they were forced to paddock the horses in their beautiful garden. That was when Mike realized that they were neighbours.

'Well, how about that.' He leaned across the table and took both of her hands in his. 'I don't want you to hate me, Daisy. Promise me you won't. How can I make amends? I'm good with horses. I can even shoe them for you. That and ranching are about all I can do. I get time off. How about if I give you a hand?'

'What are you talking about?' She frowned.

'I'm with the Reconnaissance Unit of the 29th Division and we're parked right on your fields.'

She shrieked with astonishment and too much wine. A few heads turned, but the place was almost empty.

'I don't blame you. Good heavens. You're here to fight a war. That's vital for all of us.' She giggled and squeezed his hands tightly.

'Well, I would be sore if someone put their troops on our grazing, but of course it would take an army to fill it up.'

Daisy's joy at their new status as neighbours stayed with her through supper as she plied him with questions. By the time they left the pub Mike felt that he knew all there was to know about Daisy and for some reason he wanted Daisy to know everything about him. He helped her into the jeep and climbed in beside her.

'Can I kiss you?' he asked.

'Yes, all right,' she whispered after a pause.

Their teeth clashed and he felt her lips hard and taut under his. That should have warned him. She'd never been kissed, so he gave her a few lessons. 'Listen, keep your lips very soft and relaxed and slightly open. Let's try again.'

'What's my score?' she asked, pulling back giggling.

'Four stars. Let's go for five-star status.'

After a few more lessons he felt tormented with desire. He imagined driving somewhere lonely and lying naked in the back of the jeep with her beside him. His hand strayed to her breast and he felt her taut nipples grow harder beneath his probing fingers.

'Oh . . . oh . . .' she gasped. Her arms pressed tighter on the back of his neck, pulling him closer. One knee came sliding over his thighs and somehow she slithered over him and sat astride his lap. Mike managed to start the jeep and move slowly forward, peering over her shoulder. He'd noticed a turn off into the woods on a previous trip, so he drove slowly towards it, with Daisy chattering away on his lap. This was a cinch. He was going to get lucky, but why was she talking about her teddy bear and why did her school friends figure so strongly in her conversation?

He pulled his mouth away, but he was still as horny as a spring hare as he hung on to hope. 'So, how old are you, Daisy?'

'I'm sixteen,' she murmured, trying to fit every part of herself into every small cavity between them.

A hot wave of embarrassment surged through Mike. Jesus! He'd fallen for a kid. She was the same age as his friend's young sister in plaits and bobby socks.

'Were you supposed to be drinking in a pub?' he asked.

'No . . . Shh . . .' She put her finger to her lips. 'That's our secret. Mustn't tell.'

Captain Johnson was yawning. Mike realized that he was taking too long and being too descriptive.

'I told her to shift off. She didn't want to, so I told her that it's dangerous driving this way and it was time we got home.

'She felt miserably rejected . . . I sensed that it wasn't just me, but somehow I was coupled with her father leaving, making one massive rebuff. She sat stiff and upright, gazing ahead, but I could see the tears running down her cheeks.

'"What's wrong with me?" she asked. "Why have you changed? Why hasn't my father come to see me? Why am I being rejected all the time? I wish I were dead." Honest to God I tried to calm her down, sir. I remember I said, "You must take better care of yourself, Daisy. Don't drink with strange men. Don't kiss like that. It's too provocative. You were asking for trouble."'

'She lost her temper and said she wanted to walk home. Next minute she'd pushed open the door to jump out. I caught her wrist and hung on hard, but she fought me off. I said, "Jesus! You're mad. You're going home to mother in double quick time . . ." and that's how we got back. I was relieved when we stopped at her gate, but that was when I saw that I'd bruised her wrist quite badly. She looked furious as she got out of the jeep. She wouldn't let me carry her suitcase, or meet her family. I was feeling pretty miserable myself as I drove into the camp. So you see, sir, it wasn't a case of attempted rape, quite honestly it was the other way round, but hell . . . what a looker. I can't stop thinking about her.'

'Raped by a sixteen-year-old virgin. I doubt anyone would believe you. Listen, Mike. Safeguard yourself in case this goes further. Write it down and hand your statement to the commander. I'll vouch for you.'

'Thank you, sir.'

Simon sat up late writing a report to their commanding officer pointing out that Mike had been very truthful and he was not connected in any way to the rumour of alleged rape. He had done no wrong and in fact he was about to choose him as his PA, with the CO's approval.

Then he sat back and considered the facts. How did he know that Mike's escapade was not connected to the rape rumour? It was easy enough to turn the bruised wrist and the tears into an attempted rape. But who else besides Mike and Daisy could possibly know about it? He must look into it, but how? He puzzled about this for a while before falling asleep.

Nine

On a windswept October morning, Captain Simon Johnson left his draughty tent on the Dorset coast and ordered a jeep and a driver to take him to London. Although he was wearing his fur-lined parka over his uniform, he still felt cold. Winter officially began in mid-December, so there were six weeks to go. If this was Autumn, what would winter would be like? The prospect of four cold, damp, winter months spent under canvas was appalling. His driver was exceeding the speed limit, but Simon said nothing. The sooner they passed these gloomy vistas of soggy fields and swirling leaves, made damper by the mist, the better.

They stopped near Canterbury for a late breakfast in a roadhouse where powdered eggs scrambled to a mush with soya sausages was the only dish available. They ate quickly. Swilling down the ersatz coffee, they moved on. Simon gave up trying to start a conversation with his driver and leaned back to consider the war.

The news of the massacre of Warsaw's Jews, plus the failure of the Allied raid on Tobruk, had depressed the hell out of him. The city of Stalingrad had just been hit by a new German offensive of 60,000 troops and two tank divisions and it seemed that the city would fall. Some of the bravest fighters of the battle for Stalingrad, he had read, were the female pilots of the flimsy Russian P-2 biplanes, which were flying through the shells to bomb the German lines. In America, too, women were doing their bit by taking on dramatically different tasks to replace the men at war. Training had just begun to teach women welding and armature winding. Over a thousand woman had been hired to work in the steel plants and were making and assembling aircraft parts and accessories.

There was some good news, too. In North Africa, Lieutenant-General Montgomery had launched the El Alamein offensive and US-made M4 Sherman tanks were being delivered to British brigades fighting in the desert.

London was more battered than on Simon's previous visit. There had been a daylight raid an hour back, they were told. Firemen played their hoses on blitzed houses, ambulances raced through the streets and bug-eyed kids hung around watching the Heavy Rescue personnel, all past their prime, searching for signs of life in the rubble.

Simon was not looking forward to another session with Lieutenant General Walters. At their last meeting, the general had been openly antagonistic towards intelligence agents whom, he considered, were highfalutin weirdoes. This time he could add incompetent to his view. Simon's arrival in Dorset had coincided with the very worst confrontation yet seen between US forces and the locals. It had happened right under his nose and he would take the blame for letting it get out of hand. He felt as if he was up on the high wire without a net.

At last an American army sergeant, young, female and very pretty, came to fetch him from the corridor outside Walters' office. He felt he had scored and he decided to ask her out if he saw her again. He was shown into Walters' office, a room as functional and dour as the man was.

'At ease, captain. Sit down,' Walters barked. 'Have you heard the news? Earlier today the Germans succeeded with their rocket launch at Peenemunde. The A4 free-flight rocket has made its first successful flight. Wernher von Braun will no doubt convince Germany's Armaments Minister that it should go into full-scale production. And guess where they'll land? Right here in London.'

'I expect so, sir. There was a bad raid last night.'

'Now this is highly classified, captain,' Walters went on smoothly. 'Despite talk that a Continental invasion might come as early as 1942, Allied leaders have finally decided not to make the assault for quite a while, to give the US time for its build up of equipment. During 1942 and '43, Allied forces will concentrate on wearing down Germany's resistance through air attacks. Off the record, this delay is a matter of some friction. Eisenhower wants to push right in, but the Brits have more experience in fighting the Huns. Bearing in mind the German victory at Dieppe, it seems that an invasion of the Continent will require far more meticulous preparation, more men and much more equipment.'

This was bad news, but Simon's job was to listen, not to interrupt.

'So you can take it that we are here for up to eighteen months. By the time we invade we will have one and a half million trained men in Britain. The southern counties will be bulging at the seams and the locals will have to endure a good many sacrifices.'

'They already have,' he murmured.

'Yes, of course. That's where you come in, captain. I've been going through your report on the Mowbray incidents and I think congratulations are in order.'

Simon found himself fraught by feelings he had never experienced since his school days: elation, pride, but mainly relief. He struggled to conceal his surprise.

'So what are your plans for combating these rumours in future? I must be honest. This kind of warfare is completely abhorrent to me.'

Simon caught the undertone, but decided to ignore it. After all, they were sharing a mutual problem.

'Better liaisons, better contacts. Communication is the key. Misunderstandings are the Axis tools. Of course there are going to be incidents in the future. Every regiment has its bad eggs, but that's life. The English will understand this. The good impressions set by others will more than offset any future problems. It's those "good impressions" we have to work for. I should add that most of my ground work would have been far less effective without the excellent cooperation of the British police. In particular, DI Rob McGuire has bent over backwards to help.'

'Liaise and communicate . . . well, yes, you seem to have the right ideas.'

'That's something I wanted to bring up with you, sir. The local commander is doing his best to prevent his troops from forming any contact with the locals. I consider that a mistake. We need to bring the locals into our camps, have parties, hold dances, help out with all manner of problems. Local GIs should be encouraged to attend social functions.'

'I'll have a word with him. I heard your broadcast on the BBC two nights ago. It was repeated this morning. That's exactly what we need. Putting it into the words of their own police chief was an excellent idea. Now listen, captain. The speed at which the Brits took umbrage is alarming. It could happen anywhere, at any time and it probably will.'

'It's similar to what took place in Brazil. Enemy sympathizers work to a pattern.'

'Yes. You seem to have quite a record, captain. You scored in South America. Tell me something. Is there any truth in any of these Mowbray media reports?'

'None that we've been able to find so far—'

'And the attempted rape? I presume you've caught the Axis agent who spread the rumours?' Walters interrupted him.

The force with which Walters asked the question in his cold, impersonal voice, jolted Simon back into a state of unease.

'Negative, sir.'

'Catch whoever is responsible and hand him over to the police. They hang spies in wartime. Make it your top priority, Johnson.'

'Yes, sir.'

'I've decided that you deserve the flexibility of procuring your own counter intelligence personnel. You're in charge of keeping Anglo-American relations in tip-top condition until the invasion. I want you to recruit and train your own agents to operate around the coast. Three or more in every camp. Thinking ahead, it might be sensible to choose from those with som language abilities. German and French will be needed when we get over there. Set up a counter subversive programme, give it guidelines, pass on all that you've learned on the subject. At present, you're the only one around who knows the first thing about this new kind of warfare. Reckon you can cope? I read that you ran a pretty big law firm in Manhattan.'

'Yes, sir. I have some men in mind.'

'Good. I'm opening up the files for your perusal. I've been told that lawyers have particular aptitude for this kind of work. My sergeant has a file of enlisted lawyers and linguists ready for you. Transfer these men to wherever you need them. Perhaps you should shift your base to London.'

'I would prefer to remain in Dorset, sir. The southern coast is where our troops are and where the action will be. But in the meantime, if I could have a desk somewhere here. It would be easier to have the men come to London for interviews and lectures, since they'll be gathered from around the coast.'

'My PA will organize whatever you need, a temporary secretary, and of course our files.' Walters stood up. 'Well, that just about covers everything, but captain, don't neglect the underwater teams. They could be needed at any time.'

They shook hands. 'These incidents have taught me the value of the work you do, Johnson. I don't mind telling you that some of the placards I've been shown hurt: Yanks Go Home, for instance. What the hell do they think we're here for? Two years in tents in the Brits' foul weather is no picnic for our guys. So I'm sending my views to the various commanders, hoping that this will ensure you better treatment than you had with me.'

Walters pressed his buzzer and the pretty female sergeant came in.

'This is Sergeant Lucas. I'll hand you over to her. Good luck, captain. Keep in touch please.'

Six hours later, Simon left headquarters feeling unusually elated. His hard work had paid off, he had a list of good men to contact, three of whom he knew, a date for dinner and dancing with June, the pretty sergeant, and she had booked him into a top London hotel for the forseeable future.

Despite a great evening of dinner and dancing at the Savoy, Simon could not sleep that night. His mind was too active. He was remembering the details of the attempted rape story. There were too many coincidences, and Simon distrusted coincidences. The victim of the attempted rape was said to be at a private school and only sixteen, she had a badly bruised wrist, she was tall and blonde and lovely.

Was there a link between the rumour and Daisy's scuffle in the jeep with Sergeant Lawson? Had someone heard about it and embroidered the story? Perhaps it was like the game of Whispers, where the original message bore little resemblance to the final one. Who could have started the rumour in the family? How about John Cooper? Perhaps he'd had one too many at the pub. He'd have to keep an eye on him. Or could it be Daisy? She might have exaggerated the story at school, yet it seemed to him she was a lot like her mother and she'd be unlikely to tell anyone. Nor would Helen gossip at the canteen or the factory where she worked. Then there was Miro. The boy was a whole new ball game. Was he really Jewish? Or was he the Nazi replacement of a boy who had died in a concentration camp? It was too early to point a finger at anyone, but all this would be checked out as soon as he could find the time.

His first priority was to set up and train cells of counter intelligence men in every camp. Two weeks would only get him started. He'd have to spend the next six weeks in London. At least he'd be out of that damned tent on the soggy ground.

Simon returned to Mowbray to pick up his gear and his lecture notes. He decided to rope in Sergeant Lawson as his Mowbray assistant. He needed someone reliable to carry on his work while he was moving around the various camps. It took two weeks to pick and interview a team of thirty men and another month to train them in London. They were linguists and lawyers and they had no difficulties with the course. None of them were regular army guys.

Simon didn't need discipline, he was looking for original thinkers. On the last night they had a party at the Savoy.

Simon went alone. He had taken June Lucas out a few times, but he was still suffering pangs of guilt from dumping Maria in Buenos Aires. He didn't need another attachment and he could see that June was getting too fond of him.

The course had gone well, he considered. With the communication network they had set up, they'd be able to hone in on any future Axis disinformation and deal with it promptly, or so he said in a farewell speech to a room full of newly created military agents. Behind his confident manner he was aware that he had not yet found the agent responsible for creating mayhem in Mowbray. 'Never forget the other side of the coin, which is to forge close ties with our local communities,' he said to round off his speech. 'You've all come up with brilliant ideas, some of which I shall crib, but now you have to put these ideas into practice.'

Back in Mowbray again, it was cold and raining and the fields were a quagmire. After a night spent under canvas, Simon made up his mind to call on the local council and see if there were any billets still available. As it happened there were plenty. Most of his compatriots preferred to be with their pals in the camps. When he saw Cooper House on the list he made up his mind at once. 'This will do,' he said to the young woman who was running the office. She marked it off, made a note of his name and number and he drove back to get his gear.

Ten

John was mucking out the stables and swearing quietly as the fierce wind gusted into whirlpools and played havoc with the straw. It was chilly, even for December, and if the weather didn't improve they might have a white Christmas. That would please the kids, but no one else. The camouflaged US army tents were fluttering noisily, and the mares were startled enough to race around, churning up what was left of the lawn. Daunty was jostling the mares, showing them who was boss. Absurd to have a stallion in a small riding school, but Eric insisted on having him. He always had to have his way.

John had never liked Helen's husband. Like his horse, he was stuffed full of testosterone. Eric was a womanizer and this was tough on Helen. She had loved him since meeting him at only eighteen. Both John and his wife had fought the idea of Helen marrying so young, but she had always been headstrong and she had her way. After their marriage, they travelled the world together as Eric moved from one salvage contract to the next. Like everyone else, the war disrupted their lives. Eric's salvage business was taken over by the Admiralty and Eric found himself in uniform with the honorary rank of commander. From then on he moved from one sunken ship to the next. His work had taken them to most of the blitz areas: Dover, Southampton and Plymouth. Two of their homes had been destroyed, two beloved dogs killed, although she and the kids were in municipal shelters at the time. Even Daisy's school had been blitzed, supposedly in a safe area, but thank God she was home for the weekend at the time.

Then came the night of the worst raid on Plymouth's docks. Seven bombs were seen to have sunk the cruiser Eric was salvaging, but only six exploded. Eric had called his crew and rushed to the sunken vessel to assess the damage. The final explosion released a concrete block that pinned him in the hold. Eventually his linesman had dived down and brought him up unconscious. On that same night Helen and her children had been burned out of the Farley Hotel, where they were staying. He went looking for them when he heard the news and found them in a Red Cross shelter. He brought them home and when Eric left hospital, a month later, he too had returned here to recuperate. And this was where he had broken Helen's heart.

John stopped raking and leaned the rake against the wall, panting more than he should. Sitting on an oak stump, he lit a cigarette and thought about his family. If only he were younger. The children needed him and so did Helen, but at seventy-five he was past his prime, unable to do the hard work that had to be done. The stables and the estate were the worse for it.

He hated the Yanks having his fields, mainly because it made them neighbours. John had a fear of losing his family and he worried about Daisy. She was still a kid at heart. Her looks and her sensuality bewildered her, but lately he had seen her using her guile on anyone who called, savouring her unexpected power. She reminded him so much of his late wife, Mia.

John was twenty-seven when he met his wife. As the newly-appointed marketing director of his father's pottery company, it was his plan to widen their exports by a series of marketing drives through the Scandinavian countries, but business was forgotten the moment they met. He could still remember the thrill when he set eyes on her. He took her out every night and a month later he proposed.

'When you want me for myself and not for my looks, perhaps, who knows,' she had teased him. He could still remember the sexual lather he was in. She had to be his or his life would be ruined

On his return to Poole he told his father he was going to stay in Copenhagen until Mia married him. They argued and his father threatened to disinherit him. John lost his temper and threw back his shares. He scribbled a note of resignation which his father tore up. Their fight became louder and harsher and when they came to blows, his stepmother called the police. Dad had bailed him out at midnight and given him two hundred pounds. 'Don't come back until you're ready for hard work and then you'll get your shares back,' he had told him.

He knew all about the need to possess such beauty. He had set off for Copenhagen on his yacht and stayed there until Mia married him. It took over a year, while he scraped a meagre living giving sailing lessons and working shifts in a local boatyard. The marriage had turned out well and they been very happy until she'd died ten years ago.

He longed for Helen to be as happy as they had been. She was

still lovely and young enough to marry again, or even have more
children, if she wanted to, but not to a GI. America was a bit too
far away for him to be there if she needed him. The less he saw of
the Yanks around here the better.

Feeling irritable, he began stuffing the soiled straw into sacks.
'Speak of the devil,' he muttered under his breath when he saw that
damned Captain Johnson striding around the house towards him.
How smart the bastard looked in his off-duty, tailored jacket and
brilliantly creased trousers. He couldn't help comparing him with
their own officers who had no off-duty gear.

'Hello John. Hard at work as usual I see.' Simon held out his
hand which John ignored.

'Good morning, Captain Johnson.' He looked away, hating their
easy familiarity and American habit of calling mere acquaintances
by their first names. 'I won't shake your hand since I'm on a filthy
job,' he said, remembering his manners.

'The sun's come out at last.'

'Windy!' John scowled, unwilling to swop inanities.

'I've been thinking of volunteering to help with the horses.'

'Thank you, but that won't be necessary.' Irritation surged again,
but he fought it down.

'But we have your fields. Fair do's. Come on, give it a break.'

Johnson reached for his pitch fork and John, in a rare moment
of spite, let him have it. Hah! In that outfit, he laughed to himself.
Convinced that the offer was not genuine, he sat on a tree stump,
moodily scraping the muck off his shoes with a stick and let Simon
get on with it.

Johnson had a determined look in his astute brown eyes. He hung
his jacket on a peg, rolled up his trousers, and had the last three
stables cleaned out a good deal faster than he could have managed,
to give the fellow his due. He washed his hands at the outside tap.
'Does Miro help you with this job?'

'Of course. Miro loves the horses. He probably does more than
the rest of us, but we all take turns with everything.'

'That's a sound, democratic, process.'

Why is the bugger being so patronizing? It occurred to John that
this was the captain's way of trying to be pleasant. He's definitely
after Helen, he decided, but he's not getting round me.

'I'd love a cup of coffee,' the Yank said. 'That's if you'd sit and
chat with me. I've saved you time here,' he added, when he saw
how reluctant John was.

'We only have instant . . . made out of chicory . . . ghastly stuff.'

'I brought coffee along . . . instant and filter coffee.'

'Real coffee?' John's mouth was watering.

'Sure. Costa Rica and Kenya. It's a nice mix.'

'Used to be. I haven't seen it for a couple of years.' John followed him to the jeep which was parked outside their front door.

'You going somewhere?' he asked, noting two suitcases in the back and feeling uneasy.

Johnson didn't answer immediately, but took a box from the seat.

Beware of GIs bearing gifts, John thought to himself, seeing at least twelve packs of coffee inside. He led the way to the kitchen.

'Perhaps you'd better sit down, John. The fact is I've been billeted on you.'

John felt his cheeks flushing. The damned Yank was infiltrating his family and there was nothing at all he could do about it. He'd seen the bugger's shock when he set eyes on Helen. He'd bet his last penny that she was the best-looking woman he'd seen in a long while. He'd heard the clumsy compliment he paid her. How the hell had he swung this one? John tried to hide his chagrin. Evidently he didn't succeed because Johnson flushed and began apologizing.

'I'm sorry, Mr Cooper. I promise you I'll do my share of the chores when I'm around, whenever I can, that is. I have a heavy work schedule at the camp and I spend half my time in London at present, but of course we get time off. I'm tidy about the house, and I'm a lawyer, or I was, in case you need any legal advice.'

'I can't see that happening,' John said. 'Would you like a sandwich . . . I mean since you're living here. We have some cold chicken. The fact is, we knew we'd get someone billeted on us. It was arranged some time ago.'

'Thank you, sir, but I'll eat at the canteen. Where is everyone?'

John gave him a scathing look. 'If you mean Helen . . .' He glanced at his watch. 'Right now she should be sleeping. She works at a factory packing explosives for five mornings a week and runs a canteen for servicemen and women four evenings a week. She gives riding lessons to kids three afternoons a week, although not today. She's exhausted most of the time, so I've persuaded her to sleep when she gets a break, which isn't often.'

While he listened, the captain was spooning the coffee into the percolator.

'Where shall I put this stuff?' he asked, touching the box.

John pointed to the larder. The bastard is taking over and he hasn't got his foot in the door yet.

'And Daisy?'

'Daisy is out painting somewhere. She's finished school and she has her matric. She won a scholarship to an art school in London but Helen feels she's too young to go. She'll start the year after next.'

'Miro is not part of your family, is he?'

'In a way he is. We think of him as ours. He's billeted on us for the duration of the war, rather like you, but you'll be gone sooner.'

The captain grinned and said nothing.

'We don't know if Miro has a family to go to. He lives in a world of his own. He doesn't make many friends and he won't talk about the past, but we were told that his parents are in a concentration camp in Czechoslovakia.'

'Is he Jewish?'

'So they told us. He never talks about it.'

'My grandfather was Jewish. I learned a bit about Judaism from him. I loved him, but he died a couple of years back.' He looked around, found some mugs and the sugar and poured the coffee. 'Where's the milk.'

'In the fridge behind you.'

'I see the milkman with his horse and wagon every morning. Magnificent cart horse. I've never seen such a beauty.'

'He's a Shire carthorse. Frank, the milkman, is very proud of him.'

'Is milk rationed? Do you get plenty?'

'From today our milk allowance is cut to two and a half pints a week per adult. It's quite enough, to tell the truth. Another cut is expected soon, but we don't use a lot of milk. All sorts of cuts take effect from today, for instance, confectioners will be allowed to add only one layer of jam or chocolate to cakes after baking. We don't eat many cakes so that won't be much of a problem, either.'

They discussed the rationing and the war effort and refilled their mugs, and soon John couldn't help thinking that under any other circumstances he might get to like the guy. Eventually he said, 'I'll show you to your room. You have a French window that leads to the garden, but your bathroom is upstairs on the right.'

'Thank you, sir.'

'Better call me John. How long will you guys be staying in England?'

'That's the best kept secret of the war, John. I'm just a humble scuba diving instructor. And I'm Simon.' He tried not to grin at this sudden capitulation.

'Well, there we are. On first name terms already. You guys are going to change Britain out of all recognition.'

He gave him a key, pointed to the door and left Johnson to take in his suitcases and unpack. As John went out into the garden, he was more uneasy than he'd been for years.

Simon took the key and ran upstairs to the bathroom, his mind going over the different responses he could have given to John's question. 'Maybe we'll stay long enough to toss your nation out of the Victorian age, John, but I doubt you'll ever lose your xeno-phobia.' To Simon, the Brits were victims of their repressed feelings, resulting from their hypocritical class consciousness in a society hide-bound by tradition. Only time might change them.

He pushed open the bathroom door and stood gaping as time came to a dead halt. Each moment seemed to last forever as his body reacted to the unexpected sensuality of Helen standing naked in the bath, holding a bar of soap in one hand and a long brush in the other. Her elbow was tilted towards the ceiling, her right breast had risen and her hand holding the brush was out of sight behind her back. His blood raced, his mind panicked, his phallus roared up to meet the challenge, his skin prickled and lust almost propelled him to walk forward and touch her . . . grab her . . . any damn thing. But he, too, was a victim of repressed feelings and he backed out stammering, 'Sorry,' and slammed the door.

But what incredible loveliness! He sat on the top stair, his hands over his face, trying to memorize the scene. No, more than that, he wanted it engraved in his consciousness: the creamy whiteness of her skin so invitingly touchable, her gorgeous honey blonde hair tumbling out of the shower cap to her shoulders, her lips perfectly formed, such sensual lips when they weren't forced into a hard, thin line, to match her mood. All that loveliness should never be hidden behind her frumpish clothes, her ugly head scarf and her cold exterior. He felt he had seen the real woman: trembling, defence-less and utterly desirable, but he guessed she would never forgive him for what he had seen.

'Shit!' he exclaimed, but at that moment the bathroom door opened and she came out of the bathroom, her hair now hidden under a towel, and her lovely body, with the full breasts, the narrow, brave waist, swelling to perfect hips, disguised by a tatty man's dressing gown.

Simon stood up fast. They spoke at the same time, and they both said the same word, 'Sorry!'

'Have you been billeted on us?' Helen took a step forward and leaned towards him as she scanned his face. A wave of perfume, soap and the softest scent engulfed him.

'Afraid so.'

'Afraid?' She mused at the use of that word and frowned. 'But you're a captain, so presumably you had a choice.'

'Yes . . . that is so . . . yes. I checked and saw which billets were available.'

'It was my bathroom and I had no idea . . . no idea at all.'

'John said you were sleeping.'

'Yes, that's right. I was. Are you here permanently?'

'Yes, but I'm in London a great deal, too. I'll be here tonight, but tomorrow I must go back to London. I'll be there for a few days, maybe longer.'

'See you later perhaps.'

'Yes, but I'll eat at the mess most of the time. Wait . . . just a minute . . . I want to say something.'

She paused impatiently, her door half open.

'I don't have to be here. There are a couple of other places available. I haven't yet unpacked . . .'

'You must not try to make others take responsibility for your decisions, captain,' she said mockingly. She went into her bedroom closing the door behind her. He heard the key turn in the lock and that offended him, although he knew he was being absurd.

That night an almost physical sense of guilt ruined his sleep. He used to be truthful until he became a spy. No wonder they shoot spies or hang them, he pondered. It is the most despicable of all professions. All too soon deception becomes a way of life. He had allowed Helen to think that he was here because of her, but he was here to investigate Miro. That was what he had told himself, but what was the real reason? Was it ever possible to have one's motives cut and dried and laid out on a plate? he questioned. All he knew was that the sight of Cooper House on the list of available billets had inspired him to book it instantly. For Miro? For Helen? More likely for a dry mattress, on a sprung bed, under a substantial roof that didn't buckle and crack in gale force winds.

In the first grey light of dawn he stood at the window gazing out to sea wondering how cold the water would be when he began his scuba training. It was about five hundred metres to the wreck. There should be plenty of fish around the rocks out there. It was a good place to begin. He could see the dark shadow of the bows which were only visible at low tide. He reached for his binoculars and focused on the wreck. It was then that he saw a boat surging away from the ship and moving westward in the direction of the next bay. A dinghy with an outboard engine, he decided. He could just make out four figures huddled under oilskin capes with hoods. Fishermen perhaps, but he couldn't see their gear. Strange, but there was probably a perfectly innocent reason for them being there. As soon as his London classes were over and done with, scuba lessons would be his first priority.

He showered and dressed and crept downstairs, scenting coffee as he neared the kitchen door.

'Coffee's ready.' Helen called. 'Help yourself. It's yours after all.'

She flushed prettily when he walked into the kitchen.

'Not mine. Uncle Sam's,' he said automatically.

'It's a pity my husband isn't here right now,' she began, and something about the way she said this made him realize that she had rehearsed her speech. 'He's a salvage expert and a deep-sea diver, so you and he would have a lot in common. He left us, as you know, but I think he was having a breakdown. He was badly injured earlier this year in a wreck he was repairing in Plymouth docks. We've tried to trace him . . . John tried for weeks and the police are still searching for him.' She bit her lip and stared fixedly at the percolator she was holding. 'I expect he will come home soon.'

There, that was it. That was what she had been rehearsing. She was still married, and with divorce being extraordinarily difficult in Britain, she was likely to stay married. She was warning him off. He was getting to know her a little better.

'I'm in the throes of a divorce myself,' he told her. 'It's much easier on the other side of the Atlantic. It's a straightforward affair.'

'I'm sorry to hear that,' she said.

No more questions? How very English. Maybe she just didn't give a damn. Why should she? Two lies in two days. I will never lie to this woman again, he said to himself, but his promise was futile.

'What exactly do you do in London?' Helen was asking. 'It's hardly the place for a scuba diving expert I would have thought.'

'I help out on legal matters. ' He thought how easily lying came to him nowadays. He gulped his coffee and left. When the war is over, he told himself solemnly on the drive to London, I'll go on a six-month rehabilitation course. It will be tough, but I'll survive and I'll be truthful.

Eleven

It was a small Anglican church dating back three hundred years, but the well-heeled citizens of Mowbray had kept it in good nick. Miro particularly liked the stained glass windows, the vague scent of incense, and the highly polished wood, all of which was very different to the synagogue back home. They were reciting the twenty-third psalm which had always been his favourite ever since he could remember. *'Surely goodness and mercy shall follow me all the days of my life: and I will dwell in the house of the Lord forever.'*

When he first arrived in England and Helen had persuaded him to accompany them to the Sunday morning church services, Miro had been shocked by the similarities between Christianity and Judaism. The ethics and even the words they used in the services were the same. Amen was a Hebrew word which meant 'so be it'. Likewise Hosanna, which was Hebrew for 'God save', and Hallelujah, which meant 'Praise be to God'. So many of the prayers, hymns and all the psalms were from Judaism. He had always been taught that Jews were chosen by God to spread his word, in other words, the Bible. Jesus had done that and he was a Jew. So why did everyone think that they were so different? He would never understand this.

At last they traipsed out into the fresh air. A brisk east wind had cleared away the morning's heavy mist, revealing a hazy blue sky and pale December sunshine. Soon, the family had collected their bicycles and they were strung out along the winding country lane which provided a shortcut to their home. As winter morning's go it was superb, the air was sparkling and there was a smell of wood smoke drifting over the fields.

'Aren't the trees lovely even though they're bare,' Helen called.

'Yes.' Daisy answered, as if in a muse. Miro guessed that she was dreaming about Mike Lawson. Lately *he* was all she thought about. Gazing rapturously at nothing in particular she cycled straight into the ditch and momentarily disappeared.

'Ouch!' Miro ran to haul her out of nettles and brambles. 'Idiot! Will you never look where you're going? Just look at your face.' He felt furious as he pulled her up on to the bank.

'I'm not hurt. Really I'm not. I was looking at the silver birch
. . . so lovely.' She looked upset, but surely not because he was cross
with her.

'Just look at your blisters and scratches,' he scolded.

'Hang on,' Gramps said. 'Dock leaves always grow around
nettles.'

'Here's a few clumps,' Miro called, breaking off the leaves.

'Give me a leaf, I'll do her face,' Gramps said.

'Push your arms out, Daisy,' Miro ordered.

Helen was on her knees, rubbing her daughter's legs.

'If you had only worn stockings, like I told you to, instead of
ankle socks, you wouldn't be so blistered.'

'They're school stockings and I hate them.'

'How many times must I tell you to look where you're going.
One day you'll kill yourself,' Miro snarled.

'Oh Miro, don't say that,' Helen called. 'We'll have to hurry. I
promised we wouldn't be late.'

'Promised who?' Daisy asked.

'Yes, who?' Gramps sounded furious.

'It's a surprise. I said I wouldn't tell you.'

'It's Dad. It's Dad,' Daisy cried out. 'I knew he'd come. I knew
it!'

'Oh. God! No! It's not. I'm so sorry, darling. It's Captain Johnson.
I promised not to tell. He called last night from London. His plan
was to drive back early and arrive shortly after we left for church.
He's bringing a turkey. It's an early Christmas affair – a surprise. I
said I wouldn't tell you. Oh Daisy!' She fumbled for a tissue and
handed it to her daughter to wipe away the tears that were rolling
down her cheeks. 'Sorry, darling.' Moments later they were clasped
in each other's arms.

'Fancy crying for joy over a turkey,' Daisy sniffed, trying to make
a joke out of her tears.

'Is he a cook?' Miro asked.

'He's a scuba diving instructor,' Helen told them.

'Let's get going.' Daisy got on her bicycle. 'These stings will
probably hurt all day. Serves me right.'

'What about vegetables and gravy?' John sounded dour.

'He's probably waiting for us to do that,' Helen said.

John glared at Helen. 'I don't know how you could leave a stranger
alone in your kitchen . . . or the house.'

'Anyone who brings a whole turkey can feel free in our kitchen.

The captain says it will help him to feel at home and start him off on a favourable footing.'

'Do we want him to feel at home?' John asked cautiously.

'We're stuck with him, like we're stuck with the horses on the lawn, rationing, blitzes, blackout . . .' Helen broke off.

The truth was she resented Captain Johnson because he made her feel down at heel. As the former managing partner in a Manhattan firm of lawyers, as he had explained to her, he was surely used to sophisticated, fashionable women who had never had to endure blitzed houses, no clothing coupons to replace the things they'd lost, no time to put on make-up, working until you could drop with exhaustion. 'It's just that he's spoiled,' she grumbled. 'Otherwise he's all right.'

'But handsome,' Daisy added.

'To you everything's fine as long as it looks OK,' Miro said bitterly.

'You're very handsome, Miro,' Daisy teased.

'You're too impressionable. Handsome covers a multitude of sins,' Helen lectured her daughter.

'That's because she's an artist,' Miro interjected. He always jumped to Daisy's defence.

'For goodness sake, let's get going. Are you feeling a little better?'

'I'm fine,' Daisy said, but Miro knew she was lying. She was badly stung, she'd hurt her neck and she was bitterly disappointed.

'A turkey deserves some wine.' Gramps was looking a little happier. 'I have a few bottles stowed away for a special occasion. I think I'll retrieve two of them.'

'Bet he hasn't stuffed it,' Helen muttered.

'I bet he has,' Daisy challenged her. 'Some exotic Mexican stuffing.'

'I like sage and onion,' Gramps said.

'Just look at us,' Helen said. 'We can't talk about anything but the turkey. Just shows how starved we are.'

'Perhaps we should keep a few turkeys,' Gramps suggested.

'Why bother?' Miro retorted. 'Mum wouldn't let you slaughter them. They'd all become family pets . . . like Cocky.'

'Here we are. Please stop talking about the turkey, act civilized and try to look surprised. I wasn't supposed to tell you. You have five minutes maximum to wash and get downstairs.'

Five minutes later they were gathered around the kitchen table smiling with pleasure at the sight of dishes of sweet potato, roast potato, yellow rice, peas, butternut, broccoli, a steaming, crispy turkey and a bowl of gravy. The kitchen smelled wonderful, a scent of spices, vegetables and turkey mixed together in the steaming atmosphere.

Their chef was wearing khaki trousers and a white cotton sweater. He looked pleased with himself, but anxious. 'I thought we could help ourselves from the kitchen table. I couldn't see a warmer.'

'Bombed!' Daisy said. 'First one, then another.'

'We gave up after that.' Helen told him. 'Besides the wood stove is perfect, but I didn't light it. I couldn't expect you to keep it stoked as well as cooking.'

'What's this then?' Daisy asked pointing at the stuffing in the turkey which had burst out of the turkey breast. 'It smells wonderful.'

'Dried apricots and sultanas mixed with minced giblets and a few spices. A Mexican recipe.'

'I told you so,' Daisy gloated.

'You're psychic,' Miro laughed.

'Oh my! This takes me back to prewar days.' Helen sighed.

'Would you carve, John?' Simon asked.

'Your treat,' John said. 'But let's see you whip up something tasty when we're clean out of coupons. You had it easy today.' He sounded churlish, almost jealous. Miro noticed that Helen was glancing anxiously at him.

'OK, sir. I'll carve now. Could someone lay the table? We don't want to let it get cold, do we?'

John went to fetch the wine, Daisy started laying the table, leaving Helen in the kitchen. 'You must excuse my father,' Helen said. 'He's had a bad time and he worries about us. He took us in after we were bombed out three times, and he tries to solve all our problems.'

'Oh, Miro. I didn't see you there, but it's true, isn't it?'

'I expect he felt I was being praised for doing very little and he was right,' the captain said. 'I told the chef to pack me a hamper. As easy as that. Don't worry, Mrs Conroy. I admire your father. I'll try not to throw my weight around again.'

'Oh Lord. You have taken it the wrong way. Please don't. Look, just forget an old man's envy. He's very kind. I think you should call me Helen . . .' She broke off and shrugged. 'Let's get going, shall we?'

A few minutes later they were gathered around the dining-room table.

'Do you say grace?' Simon asked.

'Sometimes on Sunday. Not often.' John frowned. 'We don't always get the chance to eat together.'

'Why don't you say grace?' Daisy said to Simon. 'It's your treat.'

'I only know one that my grandfather taught me. He was Jewish.'

'A Jewish grace for a Christmas lunch?' Miro laughed cynically.

'Miro!' Helen said.

'For what we are about to receive may the Lord make us truly thankful,' Daisy gabbled fast and furious. She sat down and the others followed her example.

'Tell us about your grandfather,' Daisy prompted Simon.

'His story is a bit of a cliché. He left Poland as a young man, having sold everything he owned to pay his steerage passage to the States. He hitched all over the States until he found where he wanted to stay, which was San Francisco. His name was Mendel Mazinter. He turned his back on Judaism and married a Polish dressmaker. Together they built his small tailoring workshop into a cut, make and trim workshop and then they branched out with their own brand of men's shirts. Finally they scored. He had two sons and a daughter, the sons went into the business, but my mother married an English lawyer from an old Bostonian family. After he retired, my grandfather began to hanker after the old ways. He went to synagogue and he taught me many of the old traditions, but of course, I'm not Jewish.' He paused. 'So where did you have your Bar Mitzvah, Miro?' Simon asked.

'In Volary, a quaint old town in Sudetenland, Czechoslovakia, eight miles from the German border, but I've put all that behind me. I am no longer Jewish.'

'Really. Is it a matter of choice then?' Helen asked, looking puzzled.

'Everything in life is a choice, Mum. We are free to choose, but we don't always make the right choices.'

'But you have a Jewish background,' Simon persisted. 'So why have you made the choice to turn your back on Judaism?'

Miro stared at him, but he could see no malice in his expression, so why did he have the feeling that he was being interrogated? 'One of our greatest rabbis of all time, Rabbi Hillel, was asked to define the essence of Judaism while standing on one foot. He said: "What is hateful to you, don't do to your neighbour. The rest is commentary. Now go and study." I guess he knew that it is not always clear which is the ethical way, hence the need to study. Judaism has hundreds of laws on ethics and they all have to be studied, but life throws up new calamities all the time. You can't always find the answers in an old book. For instance, how would one make a choice between two great evils, if there were no other way? The answer to your question is, it's all too complicated for me, so I opted out.'

There was an awkward silence. Miro sensed that they were feeling embarrassed. The English didn't talk about love or feelings, especially not religion that easily. He wished he'd kept his mouth shut. He had never intended to voice his dilemma. He must be mad to blurt it all out. It must be the wine.

'You're talking in riddles, Miro,' Daisy said. 'Let's talk about riding. Do you ride, Captain Johnson?'

'Oh, please call me Simon. Of course I ride. I'm hoping you'll let me ride that magnificent black stallion I've seen around the beach.'

'Wear the bugger out . . . any time.' Gramps was delighted. It was the first time he'd looked pleased with Simon. The conversation seemed to stick to horses after that, which was a safe topic. Simon arranged to take Daunty for an early morning ride whenever he was there.

They were eating their Christmas pudding when the doorbell rang. John was getting up when Daisy put her hand on his shoulder. 'I'll go,' she said.

Picking up his empty plate for a second helping, John went through to the kitchen.

'This is from our brigade commander,' John heard a voice at the door say quite plainly. 'It's an invitation to our Christmas Dance for your family. It's on the twenty-third. It starts at eight and goes on until there's no one left.'

'Oh, Mike. What fun. Will you be there?'

'Of course I'll be there. Please come? I would have been over before, but I've been ordered not to see you.'

'So have I. We're a modern day Romeo and Juliet.'

'Hang in there, Daisy. We'll have a happy ending. Promise.'

'Yes, we must. Mike . . .?'

'Yes . . .'

'I'm sorry. That evening . . . I drank too much wine.'

'That was my fault. I let you drink it like lemonade. I didn't realize that you're just a silly kid. I'm sorry, too, Daisy. I was upset when I found out how young you were. Of course, you'll grow up fast. I'd better go. Is the captain there?'

'Yes, we're having lunch. He cooked it.'

'Wow!' He laughed. 'That's a talent I never suspected. See you soon. Hey come here. Five stars . . . OK?'

He heard a gasp. Then silence. The silence was going on too long.

'Daisy,' John called from behind the kitchen door. 'Come and help me clear away the plates.'

Top marks for perseverance, sergeant, he thought, as Daisy hurried back with flushed cheeks and shining eyes. She really likes him, but she's far too young to be courting anyone, least of all a Yank.

Daisy went into the dining room. 'Look everyone, here's an invitation to a Christmas dance on the twenty-third. I said we'd all go.'

'Well, you can certainly go with Miro. I'm not sure if I will,' Helen said.

'I was rather hoping you would come with me,' Simon said. 'It will be very informal . . . a get-together, with drinks and dancing.'

'Can you jive, Captain Johnson?' Daisy asked.

'Well, naturally I can. It's all the rage back home.'

'Wow! D'you still go dancing?'

'Sometimes,' he said, trying not to think about Maria.

'Would you teach me to jive?'

'If your mother says it's all right. Is that all right, Helen?'

'Yes, of course.'

'Sure. Can you dance?'

'We had lessons at school. You know foxtrot, waltz, one, two, three, one, two, three . . . that sort of thing.'

'That sort of thing is damned useful, but is that it?'

'Yes. I've never been to a dance.'

'Oh come now, Daisy. What about the hotel in Brixham?' Helen said.

'You danced. I just sat watching.' Daisy looked petulant. 'I didn't dance with anyone.'

'No, that's not true. Your father danced with you.'

'Once. And anyway, he is *no one*.'

'Don't speak like that about your father. He's still your father.'

'He spoke like that about us.'

Helen seemed to shrink into herself. She had no answer.

'Sweet sixteen and you've never been dancing. Now that's a real shame.' Simon looked questioningly at Helen.

'Childhood is so precious. They grow up too quickly, wouldn't you say?'

'Well, I wasn't talking about growing up, I was talking about fun – teenage fun. She only has three years left of being a teenager . . . not much time to pack in a hell of a lot of enjoyment. Forget childhood, that's over around twelve or even before.'

Ignoring Helen's pique, Simon turned to Miro. 'What about you, Miro? Can you dance?'

'Heavens, no.'

'I'll teach you both, then you can practice together.'

Helen decided to leave them to it. She got up and went outside. It was a perfect day for giving the roses a light pruning, she decided. That would take her most of the afternoon. She would clear up the lunch dishes later.

Dad had sensibly fenced off the rose garden. This was a task she loved and it was just what she needed to revive her feelings, but the strains of the dance music bothered her. Simon's subtle criticism had hurt. He didn't understand; the *bobby-socks* cult had not yet reached Britain. British youth had two choices: child or adult, and being in between was tough, but it was all she knew about. She'd never experienced anything else, never thought about anything else. She'd read articles in magazines about youth in America, but that was America. This was Britain.

It was tea time when Simon came to fetch her. He looked happy and his skin had a light sheen to it. It made him look younger. She had no idea how old he was, but she guessed he was in his early forties.

'I didn't mean to offend you. I'm sorry,' he said. 'They want to give you a short demonstration.'

Helen got on with her pruning. 'You didn't offend me at all. What are you talking about?' Why should he have the satisfaction of knowing his words had hurt?

'I guess things are very different here. Back home, teenagers and the teenage years are considered very precious.'

'Well, I guess you don't have much else to worry about.'

She looked round and saw that he was laughing at her. Damn him. There and then she made up her mind to spend what little leisure time she had at the dancing studio in town. She would learn to jive, since it seemed to matter so much. She wasn't going to be a 'has-been' at the Yanks' Christmas dance. Fuck them all, she thought, feeling astounded that she should use such appalling language, even in her thoughts.

Not wishing to disappoint them, she went inside to watch Daisy and Miro dancing and, despite her annoyance, she was impressed.

Twelve

Many weeks had passed since Miro had first met his controller. At the time he had wondered how he could possibly survive his trauma, for he was sick with self-loathing. Nevertheless, on every second Wednesday, throughout October and November, he had cycled to the pillbox and each time he had supplied disinformation that he hoped would confuse Paddy's bosses, keep his parents fed and safe, and guarantee his survival. Paddy seemed satisfied with his work, but at each meeting he was alternatively threatened and bullied to bring more and still more.

After one particularly unjust accusation of laziness, he had protested.

'There's nothing else. How could there be?' He peered into the darkness, unable to see his enemy's face, let alone discern the man's expression, which left him baffled. 'We live in the country. Gramps is retired. My foster mother works hard in a factory, but she has no knowledge of the war effort. My sister goes to school. My friends study hard. Most of their fathers have been called up. Apart from the Yanks, whom I don't know, Mowbray is a village of women. How could anyone know anything that could be of use to you?'

Paddy had hit him hard. The blow had been unexpected and he was caught off guard. It hadn't hurt all that much, but the shock had been devastating. It was the first time anyone had hit him. At that moment he wanted nothing more than to kill Paddy. He had to hold back his natural instinct to go for him. That was when he learned about the dark side of his psyche.

'Don't think I don't know about your morning rides with Captain Johnson,' Paddy snarled. 'Pump him for information.'

What if I kill him? Miro thought. Miro was becoming very tall after an intense growing spell. Since August he had been taking boxing lessons at school. Lately he had a flick knife in his pocket, bartered from a classmate. It was more like a stiletto than a knife and Miro had to part with his stamp collection, but it was worth it. After all, he'd outgrown the hobby, Miro considered.

What if he knifed Paddy in the dark? It would be so easy. His hand tightened around the hilt. He was squatting on the sand, close to the man's ribs. He wouldn't see it coming and no one would know who had knifed him.

But Paddy dead would be no better than Paddy alive – it would be a mistake, Miro decided. The Brits would never know he was involved, but possibly Paddy's controllers might and it would risk his parents' survival. Besides, someone else would take his place.

'Don't argue, boyo. Just do what you're told,' Paddy was saying quietly. 'I would think a nice young man like you would be anxious to help your parents. Shall I tell the camp commandant that you aren't cooperating? That would be tickets for them, Miro. What's it to be? Maybe you don't care enough.'

'Of course I care.' He tried to keep his voice even and give nothing away. Feeling deeply humiliated, he'd blinked hard, fighting his fury which he had managed to keep under control for the past weeks.

Towards the end of December, Paddy announced that he was going away. He would be back early in January and he would contact Miro then. He left him plenty of work to do in the interim. Miro had been given a prodigious task of counting the number of army tents erected in and around Mowbray and checking out the equipment hidden under tarpaulins and dumped in parks and behind the barriers of closed-off roads.

He spent most of his free time during the Christmas holidays on this task and the figures were impressive, but he had no intention of passing on the information. He would divide every figure by five, he decided. Whether or not that would help his conscience, his parents, or even himself he could not say. What if it were a trap? What if all these statistics were known to Paddy?

Free from Paddy for at least two Wednesdays, Miro brightened up. The war news was yet another plus factor. As 1942 drew to a close, the tide of war was turning in the Allies' favour at last: The Red Army's great victory at Stalingrad was almost complete; there were signs of success in the Pacific War: the Japanese were losing badly in Guadalcanal; Japanese troops were trapped in Papua; and the Allied position in the Solomon's was improving daily. British soldiers, too, were still pushing laboriously forward through the jungles of Burma. Lastly, Rommel had been forced to retreat in North Africa. But despite the press cuttings pinned on his wall and the map he pinned on his pegboard, where he could mark the new Allied positions with flags, Miro was suffering from depression, and lately it was because of the GIs' Christmas dance which had been a roaring success for everyone except Miro.

Daisy, who had looked fantastic in her flared, midnight blue skirt with the frilly white blouse and who had relied on Miro for dancing practice every day, ignored him at the party. Instead she teamed up with her young sergeant and danced exclusively with him all evening. His name was Mike Lawson, Miro learned at last. After two rebuttals from Daisy, Miro had retreated to the bar where he consumed several glasses of wine and a Scotch and finally lost his temper listening to the young GIs, who were hardly older than himself, boasting of how the Germans would run like rabbits when they crossed the Channel.

'You don't know what you're talking about, Yanks,' he had said, interrupting their jokes. 'It's a mistake to underestimate the enemy. The Germans are tough and nasty and they fight to the death . . . the closer you get to Germany, the fiercer they'll become. Look at Stalingrad – Germany's Sixth Army was surrounded by Allied forces, their weapons had seized up in sub-zero temperatures, they were wearing summer uniforms, they had no food and they were dying by their hundreds daily of cold, typhus and hunger, but they still carried on fighting.'

'What the heck! We've got a Nazi sympathizer here, boys.' They were all a little drunk when they piled into Miro. It was Simon who saw the incident and hauled him out.

'Don't you think picking on a schoolboy is a little beneath you,' he told the GIs, which put the lid on Miro's humiliation. He was patched up in the camp clinic and went home nursing a black eye.

He tried to explain to Simon at breakfast the following morning. 'All I wanted was to warn them not to underestimate the enemy.'

'Most of these kids have never seen action,' Simon told him. 'They don't know what to expect. Not one of them knows how they will react to extreme danger. What they need is self-confidence, not fearful premonitions. Keep your mouth shut in future.'

That was the only piece of information Simon had ever let slip and it certainly wasn't going to be passed on to Paddy.

As Wednesday, January the thirteenth, drew closer, Miro's fear was like a virus, it fed on his guts and his mind, growing stronger by the day. It invaded his dreams and brought bile to his mouth in his first moment of wakefulness. He was all screwed up, hunched like a soldier under fire. His concentration was severely disabled, his studies suffered and once again Miro became a pariah in the house.

Best to leave him alone, everyone agreed, since he had become
impossibly rude and inattentive. So they let him be, and Miro was
too wrapped up in his own fearful introspection to notice the change.
He had only one defence to cope with life's setbacks, to retreat into
himself and shut out the world. But the world would not let him
be.

The thirteenth was a particularly dark night, which was a good
omen, Miro decided. As he approached the bus shelter adjacent to
the pill box, he switched off his headlight and dismounted. The
beach front was as dark as pitch. He could hear the sea lapping on
the shore, but not a glimmer of reflected light, or a gleam of evanes-
cence penetrated the Stygian darkness. He crept down five stone
steps and set a straight course through the sand to the pill box. So
where was it? Without any wind, the stench was so much worse
and the damp sand saturated his shoes.

'Over here, boyo.' He heard the whisper coming from his right
and slightly behind him. So much for his navigation.

'Whistle or something,' he said.

'Just keep walking.'

Moments later he reached the cement wall. Feeling his way with
his hands, he moved around the corner. 'It's so dark,' he murmured.

'You're not afraid of the dark, are you, Miro? There are thick
clouds, a sea mist and no moon. So what have you got for me?'

'The GI billeted on us spends most of his time in London,' Miro
replied, shaking inwardly. 'When he's around he eats at the camp
and returns to sleep pretty late, but I went to the locksmith and
copied his key, so I'll be able to get in his room when he's out.'

'Good thinking. And the figures?'

'Here.' He drew six sheets of note paper out of his pocket and
handed them over. He was glad of the darkness now for he could
feel his cheeks burning. Paddy put the notes in his pocket.

'Did you bring any pictures?' Miro had chosen bravado as his
best cover, hoping his voice wouldn't crack.

'What sort of pictures?' Paddy teased.

As if the bastard didn't know. 'Proof that my father is alive.'

'That takes time, Miro. You made a deal . . . you agreed to work
for the SS to support your parents. Everything else is extraneous.
You can't expect them to take you seriously with the sort of
information you're bringing in.'

'What do you expect, for God's sake?'

'Make friends with your lodger. Keep your ears open. Particularly for any kind of a scandal. Find something, anything, or they'll have your mum on half-rations until you come up with the news they want. They do that sort of thing . . . just to keep us on our toes.'

Raging inwardly Miro climbed to his feet.

'I'll go then?' he suggested.

'Do better next week. Same time, same place,' Paddy said. 'Let's hear what the Yanks are saying about the invasion. When will you be seventeen?'

'In June.' He was pretty sure Paddy knew that.

'The GIs are not much older than you. If you can't get anything out of the lodger, take one of them riding. Yes, why don't you? Let them know about your Gramps' riding school.'

The thought of Paddy snooping around their house brought another wave of oppressive fear. Trapped though he was, he had no intention of harming any member of his foster family. He loved them all, just as he loved his parents.

'You might as well go if this is all you have.'

'You have three weeks of painstaking research in your pocket. Don't always think the worst,' Miro retorted.

'They always want more.'

The shroud of oppressive blackness had lightened a little. He could see the sand dimly. He trudged back to the steps and stumbled around until he collided with the shelter and found his bike. He switched on his front lamp and wheeled the bike to the road. Soon he was riding into the dim pool of his headlights towards home. He had survived another Wednesday, they were winning the war. One day he would be free.

Thirteen

The NAAFI canteen which Helen ran, together with four other women, bore witness to the empty coffers of a nation whose total resources had been spent on war technology. It had been set up in the corner of a warehouse on the outskirts of New Milton and it boasted three gas burners, two paraffin heaters and several primus stoves in case of gas cuts. There were paraffin lamps hanging around in case of electricity cuts and a paraffin fridge standing alongside a newer electrically-operated one. The walls were painted dark green and posters showing smiling land girls, factory workers and WRENS were plastered over the green. The ceiling was very high and consisted of corrugated iron sheets fastened to girders. It was a dark, draughty, gloomy cavern, but no one working there had time to worry about that.

Helen and Joan, the headmistress of a local school, ran the evening shift on Mondays, Wednesdays and Fridays on a voluntary basis. Usually there were two of them working together, but tonight Helen was alone and for some reason they were unusually busy. Her worn corduroy slacks were spattered with fat, her new woollen blouse looked the worse for wear, which was her own fault, she reasoned, since she had forgotten to bring her clean overall, and she had burned herself several times. Her hair was concealed by a scarf tied like a turban, which was the fashion for women coping with canteen and factory work.

By ten p.m. she was exhausted and her feet burned. A strong smell of sizzling fat on the burner, over-strong coffee and burned toast laid witness to her rush to get through the orders from a never-ending queue of uniformed men and women who were cold and hungry. The floor space was crowded. There were a few troops from the nearby army base, eight Land girls, who had been served and were sitting at a tubular steel table in their khaki and green gear and laughing a lot, plus a crowd of ARP (Air Raid Precaution wardens) in their navy battledresses. They were all over fifty and looked as tired as she was.

'Baked beans and a pork pie, a packet of ten Woodbines and a cup of tea, miss,' said an old man in the uniform of the Home Guard.

She raced to hand him his order. 'Two and sixpence. Next . . . next . . . next . . .'

The room was getting more crowded: several policemen had joined the queue and nearer to the door she saw the navy blue jackets of the AFS (Auxiliary Fire Service).

Joan, a well-built, capable women of fifty with iron grey hair and a ready smile, arrived at half past nine. 'Sorry Helen. We had a school concert,' she apologized. 'I had to be there.'

Helen smiled. 'Don't worry. I guessed it was something urgent. I'll run to the toilet and have a cup of tea. I need a short break. I'm getting careless.'

'You look all in. Busy tonight?'

'Crazy . . . has been ever since I got here.'

At ten p.m. a group of soldiers returning from duty in Southampton walked in. They were grimy and they looked shocked.

'Jesus! You can't believe what it's like, whole streets going down like ninepins . . . the sky's alight with incendiaries, like a fireworks show, only a thousand times better. In next to no time those old houses are bursting into flames.'

Helen nodded, not wishing to remember her own experiences in Southampton.

'Did you hear about the new giant shelter?'

'The one by the civic centre?'

'That's it. It was supposed to be impregnable. Well, a landmine fell clean through the exit. Everyone died of blast. Hundreds of 'em.' When we cleared away the debris to get in, we saw everyone sitting upright in rows, just as if they were alive, but they weren't. Gave me a nasty turn, I don't mind telling you.'

'Knock it off, Mike. You're scaring the ladies half to death.'

'Only because I was right there with my family, night after night for almost a year, while our house was flattened and Daisy's school was burned to the ground,' she muttered to Joan as she rushed to cook his two fried eggs. She overheated the skillet and splattered herself with hot fat. Flames shot up from the burning fat on the gas burner. Her own private blitz.

'Oh God! Mind out!' Joan rushed from the till and rammed the lid on the pan. 'That's what I did to an incendiary that landed in my garden last week. I popped the dustbin lid on it. Worked like a charm,' Joan told her.

'Red or Blue?' The blue exploded, the red merely burned, Helen knew.

'Blue. It made a mess of the lid, but that's all.' Helen wiped over the stove and they were back in business. 'Next . . .'

Simon's feelings for the English had changed considerably since he moved in with the Conroys and he thought about this on the long drive back from London. He tried to analyze his emotions, which were part love and part irritation, but it seemed that he could seldom forget Helen, nor the amazing vision of her standing naked when he gatecrashed her bathroom. He had always known she was lovely, but she had not inspired any physical attraction, perhaps because of those awful clothes she wore. Since then sexual tension was spoiling his sleep and invading his dreams. He had the feeling that she felt the same way, but she had no intention of giving in. Instead they had been scrapping and snarling. He had frequently voiced his criticism of the austere life she lead and the way she had walled up her emotions, the way she neglected to instill joy into her children's lives, and the sad atmosphere in the house.

There was no doubt about her love for her children, but they needed joy as well as love. Daisy's life was very dull compared with that of teenagers in the States and he felt for her. As for Miro, she mollycoddled him. Just look at the fuss Helen had created when he fell off Daunty during a jump. 'How will he ever be a man if you treat him like a girl?' he had snarled at her.

For her part, Helen griped because their fields were occupied and that the church fete could not be held this year because all the available sites were full. Of course, it was his fault that Daunty could not be isolated now that a mare had come on heat. Overall, he reckoned her tension had nothing much to do with these matters, but was caused by her feelings, which she was going to great lengths to deny, along with every other joy in her life.

Simon had to pick up a shipment of valves from Southampton docks on the way back from London and from there he took the route through the New Forest, but as he drove towards Mowbray, a dog fight took place a few miles to the west. German bombers, pursued by Spitfires, were dropping their bombs to lighten their loads as they fled. Alarmed by the proximity of the raid to the canteen where Helen worked, he did a U-turn in the main street and sped back.

By ten-thirty Helen was exhausted. She glanced at her watch. Thank heavens it was nearly closing time. Then she heard the siren.

'We don't get many raids here,' she told the men over her shoulder as she battled with eggs, sausages, baked beans and jam on toast. 'Not much point in bombing fields and woods . . .' Hearing an explosion, she stood listening. It wasn't close, but it was on this side of the forest. She frowned. There was another explosion, nearer this time. A plane was dropping its bombs and it was coming their way. The third bomb was close enough to hear its whistling descent. It was a strangely eerie noise, but rumour had it that if you heard the whistle it wasn't coming for you and that always comforted her. Everyone froze. Hard and fast came the next explosion, much closer this time and three seconds later the third blast fell too close by far. The ground shook, plaster fell from the ceiling and the iron roof rattled.

'Everyone down. Take cover,' one of the ARP men yelled. 'Get away from the stove,' a soldier shouted at Helen. She switched off the taps automatically and fell to the floor, her hands over her ears, eyes tightly shut, tensed up and waiting . . . but for what? A monumental explosion rocked the warehouse and the windows shattered, but Helen could only thank her lucky stars that it had fallen on the other side of the building.

'The bomber's passed over,' she yelled, hanging on to the counter to steady herself as she scrambled to her feet. She couldn't breathe, dust was falling from the ceiling and rising from the floor. Pieces of plaster were floating down like petals in spring. The noise and the blast had felt like physical blows and now she was unsteady, her hands shaking, ears still ringing. It was all she could hear. She walked forward a few steps feeling wooden and unreal.

'I don't feel as if I'm really here,' Joan whispered beside her. She was leaning against the cupboard. 'We were bloody lucky, fucking bastards,' Joan said. Helen giggled. Joan was so controlled. She never swore.

Helen could hardly see across the room. Dust and bits of plaster were floating around her. She grabbed the pan and scooped the sausages into a dish on the warmer. They shouldn't stand in congealing fat like that, makes them tough and oily. She flicked off pieces of plaster with a knife. It was over. No reason to slacken. She looked around. 'Next,' she called.

'Is everyone all right?' an ARP man shouted.

'I've cut myself. Damn glass is everywhere. Got a broom here?'

'The brooms are in that cupboard,' Joan called out. The customers began to clean up fast. Helen wiped the counter, Joan was wiping the stove. Grimy faces surrounded her. There were a few smears of blood from unimportant scratches, someone's nose was bleeding.

'It's nothing. Just pressure from the blast,' he said, holding a handkerchief to his face. Two women from the Rescue Service honed in on him. He was cursing as they made him lie on the floor.

'Bloody fools. You should be in bloody London, then you wouldn't bloody worry about a bloody nosebleed.' Fury held them all in its red hot grip. They wanted to hit back, pummel the bastards who were knocking down their homes, killing and maiming innocent civilians, bankrupting their country. Their suppressed fury came out in strangely violent spurts. A mouse came skittering across the floor, stupid with panic. It was hammered to death in an orgy of rage. A glass broke in a customer's hands, the blood dripped into the sugar and someone swore, not at him, but at the bloody pilot who had only just missed them. They weren't going to show that they'd been scared, but anger was another matter. They were all hunched up and bursting with rage.

'If the pilot had to bale out now, I doubt he'd survive,' Helen whispered to Joan. 'Next.' she called.

When Simon walked in, looking neat and clean and larger than life, Helen's reality retreated even further 'Simon? I must be dreaming?'

'Let's get you out of here,' he said, striding to the back of the counter. He put his arms around her, hugging her. 'I was scared half to death when I heard the explosion. Thank God you're all right. Come on. I'm taking you home.'

'I can't leave now. We don't close until later.'

'The Yanks get all our best girls,' a soldier called. A chorus of cat calls followed. 'Here, miss. I'm available. British-made.'

'You're in shock,' Simon said, ignoring them. 'Your hair's full of plaster, you're covered in dust.' He grabbed her hand. 'Look at your hands . . . you're badly burned.'

'No, no, not badly and it wasn't the blast. It was my careless cooking.'

'You go,' Joan said, looking offended. 'I can cope.'

'Certainly not. We close at eleven and there's another half an hour to go,' she said firmly. 'I have my bicycle here.'

'Don't argue. You're coming with me,' he said firmly.

'Maybe.' She smiled mischievously. 'But only after eleven. You can sit over there.'

'I'll wait in the jeep. It's right outside.' He looked furious as he strode out, but Helen merely shrugged.

'My lodger,' Helen explained to the astonished Joan.

She left at eleven, leaving Joan to lock up. 'Will you call ARP headquarters for new windows, or shall I?' she asked.

'I will,' Joan said.

'Can we give you a lift?'

Joan shook her head. 'It takes me all of five minutes to cycle home.' She was still offended. For Joan, all men were bad news, but the Yanks were the worst.

Her bicycle was in the back of the jeep, Helen noticed.

'How much do they pay you for six hours hard labour? Whatever it is, it's not worth it.' His voice was deeper and gruffer than usual.

'It's voluntary work, Simon. I don't get paid.' She became watchful. She wasn't going to be bossed around by her lodger. She had a stray memory of Eric, arms folded, lips pressed into a tight line, like Simon's were now, as he laid down the law. It had taken all her courage to face up to his temper when she disagreed on anything, however trivial.

Simon was looking shocked. 'Don't you have enough to do, running a family, working in a factory, running a riding school, without this? Let someone else do it.'

'You've missed the point,' she said icily. 'There isn't someone else. We're all doing as much as we can. Tonight . . .' She broke off because it was hard to explain. 'Not just me . . . all of us . . . we were angry . . . we wanted to hit back. We do whatever we can to hit back – packing explosives, helping to run the canteen – it's what keeps us sane. This anger inside me is sometimes hard to bear, it hurts me physically. I get rashes and stiff necks, hay fever and a pain in my shoulder blades. All tension symptoms and it's not caused by fear, but by anger. Sometimes I feel like one of those fabled Valkyries, only warring counts. I've no other emotions left.' She closed her mouth firmly, hoping that this was the end of the matter.

'I think you are mistaken there. Can I kiss you?'

'That would be playing with fire. Please start your jeep. Let's go.'

'What have you got to lose?' he asked, switching on the ignition. 'Eric's run off with someone else. He hasn't seen you for months.'

'How kind of you to remind me.' She glared at him. 'How do you know that?'

'Daisy told me.'

'Why are you always spying on us?'

'Why do you always change the subject?'

She felt infuriated with him. 'Jesus, one should never get involved with a lawyer.'

'Are you involved with me? I see no sign of it, but I'm involved with you. You fill my thoughts most of the time. I have to watch myself. Much against my wishes, I'm intrigued and obsessed by a strange woman who wears darned stockings and ugly clothes and hides her beautiful hair in an ugly bun, hidden under an even uglier turban, and is doing her utter best to hide her innate sexuality and her extraordinary beauty in every way she can.'

Helen laughed harshly. 'I'm much too old for this kind of nonsense,' she said primly. 'Besides, whatever looks I might have are fast fading.'

'Who are you lying to, me or yourself?'

'Oh Simon, you're being unfair. Besides, you're taking advantage of the situation. It seems as if you are one of the family, but of course you are not. We are pushed into close quarters for the war effort and you are using this situation to your own advantage. No good can come of it. You want bed and board with all the trimmings. Well, it's not on.'

'Jesus. You know how to hit below the belt, don't you?'

He put his foot down and for a while they drove too fast through the dark and empty streets. Helen sat in silence, stiff and upright, staring ahead, trying to persuade herself that she had done the right thing, however much she longed for him. So what if he's in a temper? He's spoiled, she decided.

Soon they were passing through a narrow lane with woods on either side.

'Do you cycle through this wood late at night by yourself?' Simon asked.

'Yes, of course. Why not?'

'Don't you get nervous?'

'I love the countryside. It's about the only place where I feel truly safe. Nowadays a house is not safe. We've had two houses destroyed by the blitz and Daisy's school was burned down. There's nothing safe about our lives, so I've given up looking for safety. I'm just moving along, surviving by doing what I can. One day all this will be over and then I'll take stock. But not now. Imagine by-passing the woods because it's dark and scary and then cycling bang into a bomb.'

'So it's dark and scary. Well, that answered my question eventually.'

'Damn all lawyers,' she said with a smile.

Simon parked on the outskirts of the wood in a car park used by picnickers and foresters. Switching off the ignition he sat very still, but she could see how tense he was. 'I know you're in a hurry to get home,' he said, looking unsure of himself for once. 'There's something I want to know so badly.'

'Tch! What is it?'

'You try to pretend that you have no feelings for me, but I happen to know that it's not true.'

'What conceit. What makes you think that?'

'Your body tells me when you're talking to me: your cheeks flush, your eyes brighten, even your nipples harden . . .'

She didn't bother to argue. What was the point? 'So ask your damned question?'

'Can I kiss you?'

'You idiot!' She had expected some heavy soul-searching. Exploding with laughter, she grabbed him by his neck, pulled him towards her and kissed his cheek hard, but when she tried to let go she found she was trapped with his left arm around her back and the other encircling her neck. His lips were on hers, soft and supple, his tongue caressed them. Forked lightning of pure pleasure pierced her body, she had never experienced such exquisite sensations.

She came to eventually to find her knee thrown over his lap and wedged under the steering wheel. One hand was gripping his shoulder, the other was behind his neck. His hand had shifted back and found her breast. She was crying with frustration.

'For God's sake stop. I told you it would be playing with fire.'

'And you were right. At least we both know where we stand. I want you. You want me, so where do we go from here?'

'Home. Please! Right away,' she said, extricating herself from the steering wheel and the hand brake. 'This was a mistake. Blame it on the war and loneliness and of course I've just been dumped. I didn't intend to kiss you.'

'Of course you didn't. I know that. When you're not suffering from shock over the bomb blast, and totally exhausted by hard work, and scared half to death by the woods, you're a very sensible woman who plans her life and gets on with it and never gives in to emotions, or longing, or listens to her heart.' He skidded around the corner and for a while they drove in silence.

'I know I took advantage of the situation, but I really do care,' he said as they turned into the driveway. 'We don't know each other well yet, but I want you to know that I have never before met a woman I admire so much. Add to that, intense physical attraction and you can see that I'm in trouble.'

The moon broke through the clouds. Simon drew her back to him, opening her coat and pushing his hand under her jersey, gently stroking her naked back and her breasts. She lifted one hand and drew his head towards hers, pressing her lips on to his. Then she moved away.

'You must have left a string of broken hearts behind you, Simon. Well, I'm not going to be another notch on your belt. I'm married and I'm still hurting and that's the truth. Eighteen years takes some forgetting. You must try to understand that right now I'm not available.'

'Can't you let go? He has.'

'It's not a case of just letting go. I've been badly hurt. I don't need another hurt and you're merely passing through.'

They sat in silence. She glanced sidelong and saw his pursed lips, narrowed eyes and a deep chasm between his thick eyebrows. He was a man whose passions ran deep and right now he was baffled because he wasn't winning.

I don't care. I have enough problems, she told herself.

She had been meaning to tell him to use the empty bay, next to John's car, but now would not be the best time, he might think half the bedroom would follow.

'I have to be in London tomorrow morning. I'll be away for a few days. Will you be OK?' When he gazed at her he looked so sad.

'Why shouldn't I be? Have a good trip. Goodnight,' she said briefly and hurried inside.

She listened for the sound of his footsteps in the hall, but after a while Simon started the jeep and drove into the next-door camp. Hating herself, she climbed into her lonely bed.

Fourteen

The following morning soon after seven, Simon and his driver left Mowbray for London. It was bitterly cold with a heavy white frost over the fields on either side of the road. On the outskirts of the city they encountered a traditional London smog. Visibility was down to a couple of feet, the smell of oily black soot and grime was overwhelming and disgusting and they were forced to crawl along at five miles an hour. He was going to be late for his appointment with Lieutenant General Walters.

Seething with frustration Simon passed the time by reviewing his problems. First and foremost was Helen. She had got under his skin and he knew that she felt the same way as he did, so why was she wasting their time? These precious months might be all they had. But these were not the sort of thoughts he should be entertaining.

He switched over to the job on hand. His main frustration was that he was losing and it was bugging him. One of the reasons he wasn't getting anywhere was the time that he had to spend in London. Thank God he had finished the classes and with any luck, the men he had picked and trained would be able to cope with any problems that might arise in their areas, which was more than he was doing.

He still had no idea who was spreading disinformation in Mowbray, but he suspected that this person could be living in the house where he was billeted

Of the four suspects in Conway House, he was inclined to cross Daisy off the list. She was unlikely to spread damaging stories about a guy she was sweet on. Helen might be gossiping to friends at the canteen or the explosives factory where she worked, although she didn't seem the type. That left John, whom he planned to investigate. John was a man with a secret. Two or three evenings a week, he crept out of the house at ten p.m. and returned in the early hours of the morning. This was made more difficult for him now that Simon had taken over his former office with the French windows leading to the garden. Lawson had been detailed to follow him wherever he went, but Simon doubted that the culprit was John. He was very English, very bright, a true traditionalist. The most he could be guilty of was gossiping at the pub.

That left Miro. Simon frowned. Time and again his mind veered off Miro. Of course he was a natural target to be coerced into spying for the SS, which was the reason why German foster children of seventeen plus were interned on the Isle of Man, but Miro had been only thirteen when he was sent to Britain. Simon saw something special in the boy, despite his emotional scars. He had witnessed his love of horses and all animals. Miro's affection for his foster family was obvious. He saw adoration in his eyes when he looked at Daisy, love when he gazed at Helen. He had bonded with John and spent his spare time helping him with his chores. He was a boy with his priorities in the right place. Simon had learned early in his career never to ignore his instincts. Most people underestimated their natural born gifts, but Simon took his seriously. He would swear that Miro would never knowingly harm the Allied efforts to win the war.

There was yet another mystery, which concerned the men he had seen going out to the wreck on most calm nights. After bobbing around on the waves for several hours, they would then put in to the beach below the Conroy's house just before dawn. Then they would put out to sea again half an hour later and speed off along the coast in a westerly direction. By morning there were never any footprints, for they had been washed away by the tide. He hoped he'd get to the bottom of this mystery eventually.

Simon's main problem was time...he had to spend more time in Mowbray, exploring the wreck and the surrounding reefs. He badly needed those damned air cylinders for his underwater trials. He had tested them weeks ago and found them ideal. They were ordered and dispatched, but destroyed in a raid on the railways, so now he had to wait for a new consignment.

Simon was late for his appointment. Shivering in the foyer of ETOUSA, he watched the smog infiltrating the building through cracks around the doors and the windows. The smell of soot was worse than before and the temperature was near to freezing. After a short wait, Simon was shown into the functional office of Lieutenant General Walters. He had a new secretary: tall, plain and on the wrong side of forty. Simon tried his best to look relaxed and confident as he waited for the inevitable question: Have you found the Nazi sympathizers yet, Johnson? It didn't come. Strangely Walters had other matters on his mind.

'Sit down, I expect you could do with some coffee. It's on the way.'

'That would be great, sir. How do Londoners manage to drive in this damn smog? We crawled through the city at five miles an hour.'

'It can get worse. Sometimes you can't see your hand in front of your face.'

The coffee arrived and Walters broke off and sat silently waiting until the woman had left the room. 'Help yourself and let's get down to business.' He glanced out of the window. 'I guess I'm here for a couple of years,' he said mournfully. He shook himself like a dog emerging from water, as if shaking off the smog, blitzed buildings, draughts and gloomy vistas.

'I like the way you work, Johnson. My commanders tell me they've introduced any number of your ideas. The mood is improving on both sides.'

'Thank you, sir.'

'We can all learn from our allies, Johnson. I want you to liaise with a certain London organization whose members carry out much the same work as you, but they've been doing it far longer. The Brits are way ahead of us in their campaign of disinformation and deception. Broadly speaking, their aim is to confuse and harass the enemy and to damage their morale while sustaining the morale of the occupied countries. They call this black and white propaganda. Evidently it gets blacker as they get nastier, depending upon just how creative they can get on a daily basis.'

'Sounds as if they enjoy their work,' Simon murmured.

'Don't make any assumptions about them, captain,' Walters went on enthusiastically. 'They consist of some of this country's leading intellectuals. They even operate a few fake radio stations, one of them, *Soldatensender Calais,* is particularly successful in spreading disturbing news among the Germans by portraying the Nazis as corrupt and ridiculous bunglers. They called themselves the Political Warfare Executive (PWE). There are two headquarters, at Woburn Abbey and at the BBC's Bush House.

'The point is, they think they can "both use you and help you". Their words! You'll meet a few of them today, they tell me.' He glanced at his watch. 'A taxi is waiting for you in the car park at the back of this building. No one can beat a London taxi driver in a smog. So, good luck. Johnson. I await your report with interest.'

Thanks to the experienced London cab driver, Simon was on time for his appointment. He was shown into a large room, thick with cigarette smoke, but he could just make out a well-stocked bar at the end of the room. Six civilians were lounging around hugging their drinks.

They stood up as Simon was shown in and introduced, but only first names were used. Later he learned that he was keeping company with a journalist, a government minister, a BBC producer, a professor of mathematics, a lawyer and a copywriter.

'We've managed to procure some rye whisky. I believe you Americans prefer your own poison,' Alf said. 'It's all yours. Help yourself.'

Their ages ranged from thirty to fifty and they seemed a pleasant enough bunch. Simon helped himself to a generous tot of neat whisky and found an easy chair. The usual polite small talk followed on how he liked England and English weather, then they pressed him to have another drink before getting down to business. Simon tried to memorize their names: Alf, wearing a hand-knitted jersey of riotous colours and design, had the rugged, tanned appearance of a foreign correspondent.

'Look here, Simon,' Alf said. 'Congratulations are in order with your white propaganda projects, but you seem to be facing a brick wall in trying to pinpoint the links to your Nazi sympathizers.'

'True,' he admitted cautiously.

It was Dick, short, cultured and expensively dressed, who disagreed. 'Simon hasn't had much time,' he said. A BBC type, Simon guessed. Later he learned that he was right. Dick pushed a dish of cashew nuts towards him. 'We thought we'd knuckle in on your turf. We can be very useful to each other. Why don't you join us from time to time, say for fortnightly meetings? We'll create a few sibs for you, starting today.'

'Sibs?' Simon queried.

'From the Latin *sibilare*, to hiss or to whistle, dear boy. Of course you can make up your own sibs, but you can't go ahead and use them, at least not before you check them with us, and we have to check them with the Executive in the Foreign Office. A free-for-all would lead to chaos. That's why we need this link between your guys and ours. What do you think of this idea?'

'Sounds reasonable,' he answered prudently.

'I assure you, the Executive give a fast reply. There's no question of waiting around, unless research is needed.' It was Josh who had spoken. He looked to be the oldest man present. Pushing sixty, Simon reckoned. Smooth and polished, he had an air of being someone who was often in the public eye.

Simon just nodded. He couldn't think of anything intelligent to add to the conversation.

'This is my brain child, but no one seems to think much of it,' Alf, of the riotous jersey said. 'I suggest that we let it slip, via a sib, that the New Forest has been declared out of bounds for everyone because the Yanks are storing their war technology there, prior to the invasion. Your sib could be broadcast by gossiping at the pub, or a memo left around, or a copy of a letter lying in an unlocked briefcase, anything. Set a trap for whoever it is you suspect and then you wait for Jerry's bombs, or local demonstrations and reports in the press. The point is, this enables you to pinpoint your first link in the chain.'

'It could be a man gossiping in the pub,' Simon said, thinking of John.

'That's right. It's seldom straightforward. Of course, most of our work isn't pinpointing local spies or blabbers, but causing friction in enemy territory. We'd be glad of your help when you have time.'

'Thanks. I'd like to give it a try. I'll keep in touch. To be honest, I don't much care for your New Forest sib. I'm billeted with a family who live nearby.'

'Give it a rest, Andy,' Alf called. 'The idea is OK, but the location isn't. They'd bomb the New Forest to shambles.'

Suddenly they were all arguing, tossing out ideas, tearing them to bits and starting again. Eventually the meeting calmed down, glasses were refilled, the air became smoggier and the atmosphere more relaxed.

'Territorial rights . . . that's always a touchy point,' Simon said in an unexpected breathing space. 'I'm constantly in trouble because there's no available space for the church fete.'

'True. How about farms?' Josh called out.

'No, something nearer to home. Something everyone uses. '

'Beaches,' someone called out .

'For American training.'

'Exactly, damned foreign troops taking our kids' beaches with immediate effect. Nowhere to play or to swim.'

'But it's January,' Dick said. 'Wrong timing.'

'Not necessarily,' Simon argued. 'I see the kids playing football and netball on the beaches all the time.'

'Some of them have been commandeered by the War Office, but others are available for the public. If you were to threaten them all . . . well I think the public would consider this to be totally un-justified,' Josh chimed in.

Andy shrugged. 'It's a daft idea.' He looked a trifle shabby compared to the others. Later Simon learned that he was both titled and rich and he had made his name as a mathematician.

'But what about the after effect,' Simon said. 'How do we get over the fact that none of these beaches are ever commandeered.'

'You mean if the sib works?'

'Well, yes.'

'Well, that's right down your street, Simon. You'd have to use your talents to smooth it over. You're good at that. Right now we want to catch these buggers. I suggest you write a report stating that you endorse the proposal that all beaches along the south of England be roped off for US army training from immediate effect. We'll do that for you now.' Alf got busy on the typewriter drafting the letter. His fingers flew like a typist's over the keys and Simon guessed he must be a reporter of some kind. Moments later Alf got up and walked out. 'I'll get the OK,' he said.

'I like the sibs about the beaches, but that's all so far.'

Ideas bounced backwards and forwards, but to Simon's mind they all seemed to incur hazards for the locals. 'For God's sake, people are killed every night.' Andy argued, until he realized no one agreed with him

'What about a rocket base on an uninhabited island in the Outer Hebrides . . . just to please our Yankee friend,' he suggested as a joke. His idea brought laughs all round.

'Actually I like that.' Josh stood up and poured himself a drink and Simon was impressed with his height and his graceful move-ments. His olive skin, dark eyes and black hair seemed at odds with his accent. Middle-Eastern, but second generation in England, Simon guessed. 'They sure as hell wouldn't like us aiming doodlebugs at Berlin.'

'There's Eilean nan Ron,' Andy put in. 'I've been there.'

'Someone owns that island.'

'A certain duchess. I know her well.'

'OK, let's give it a try.' They all threw in ideas and Alf typed the final memo and gave it to Andy who left the room. He returned ten minutes later with a pleased look on his face. 'It's OK.'

'What did you say to her?'

'I said, "We need to use your island as a decoy. It might get bombed to bits, but if it does we'll have collared another spy." She said. "Why ask? Go ahead, but don't try it in the nesting season." That's exactly what I expected from her.' Andy looked pleased with himself.

'Well then,' Simon tried to smother a yawn. 'One more, just to be on the safe side.'

Lunchtime brought sandwiches of York ham with English mustard and cress, and the meeting progressed, but no one could agree on which to choose out of the dozen or so sibs they had created.

'Remember that idea that Peter had last week,' Alf said. 'We couldn't agree on it, but I felt it had merit. We claimed that most of the German POWs have been turned and had agreed to join our forces. They were going to be trained by the Yanks and eventually drawn into the US fighting forces.'

'It would piss Jerry off, but would they actually bomb their own men?' Alf asked.

'If they were considered to be traitors, the SS would. They might not tell the pilots who or what they were bombing. To date there are two concentration camps in Germany full to overflowing with German students who opened their mouths a bit too wide against the Third Reich.'

'It's a good idea, but not in the New Forest,' Simon said, thinking of Helen in the canteen.

'Then what about Pines? That's an abandoned, pre-war holiday camp not far from Southampton. It's surrounded with fields and you'll be pleased to hear, Simon, that they're not too fertile and there's no livestock on them.' Rob looked pleased with his input.

'Done,' Simon said.

They moved on to find some ideas for their clandestine radio station. Each day, genuine war news was interspersed with damaging sibs. Simon managed to hold his own with the others. The time went quickly because he was enjoying himself. The meeting broke up at four p.m. Simon took a taxi back to his driver who gave him a note from Sergeant June Lucas, the pretty girl he had dated last time.

'How about meeting for dinner tonight? Phone me if you are available.' He phoned, and spent the evening dining and dancing with June, which helped to smooth his ruffled feathers after his rejection in Mowbray.

Fifteen

There were too many secrets in the old redbrick house on the cliff, Simon decided, as he and his team jogged up the steep ascent from the bay. Trying to take his mind off his agony, Simon thought about the family. Despite his efforts to make friends, he felt that he was still very much of an outsider, but Cooper was more of a mystery than the rest of them. A stranger might see an ordinary old man with iron grey hair that almost matched his eyes, a nose that was a trifle too long and too pinched, high cheek bones marred by an aging skin and a strong jaw above a scraggy neck. Closer observation would lead to a number of surprises. John didn't communicate much, but he watched everyone closely and he was very bright indeed. He was an excellent rider, he read the financial and economic journals and he could talk intelligently about any subject you might care to bring up. He was kind to his grand-children and to animals, but he disliked Americans, perhaps because he feared them. But why? Did he have something to hide? Was that why he was so antagonistic?

Simon had decided to pass on the first sib as soon as he could. He was pretty sure that John was not a Nazi sympathizer, but he probably gossiped at the pub. Through John he might be able to trace the Nazi sympathizer, or spy, who had caused so much disruption in Mowbray.

When they reached the lip of the cliff overhanging the bay, Simon said goodnight to his team and jogged back to the house. He showered and changed and found John alone in the lounge. Helen was at the canteen, he assumed, and the kids were probably studying.

'It has turned into a rather pleasant evening. Why don't we walk down to the pub and have a pint,' he said. He had worked out that this was the best way to speak to John without the kids barging in.

'Thought you didn't like our beer.' John looked surprised at the invitation.

'I'm getting used to it, but they might have some rye.'

'OK. I'm a bit fed up with sitting here by myself. Let's go.'

'Where is your favourite pub?' Simon asked as they set off.

'I don't go by myself very often. Occasionally I go with friends to the Red Lion. We might as well go there now. It's the closest and it has managed to maintain a well-stocked bar, although the place is looking tatty lately. It's not their fault. The couple who own it are getting on and they have to do everything themselves since both of their sons joined the navy.'

After that John lapsed into silence. Simon battled to keep the conversation going as they walked along the road. He wondered if he was setting too hard a pace, so he slowed down. The road led steeply downhill and from here they had a completely different view across the bay.

'There it is,' Simon exclaimed. 'Look! D'you see that boat out there?' Once again the launch was zooming towards the wreck. They showed no lights, perhaps because of the blackout, but the moon's reflection had blazed a trail across the dark sea and Simon saw the shape of the motor launch crossing it.

'Have you noticed them going across the bay late at night?' Simon asked. 'It seems to be a regular exercise. I've seen them a few times. Four or five people visit the wreck in the dark. They return just before dawn. I, too, wondered if they were after the valuable cargo that went down with the ship. I called Lloyds, but they were quite certain that their salvage experts would have retrieved the cargo were it still there.'

'I haven't seen them at night, but in daylight they are often out there. There's no mystery involved. They take members of the photographic club out to snap the fish around the wreck.'

'At night?'

'So they say. Perhaps they have underwater flashguns. They held an exhibition in the local studio not long ago. Nothing special . . . in fact, it was appalling – a lot of dark water and shadowy fish out of focus. I believe they have underwater cameras and torches, but the swimmers have to hold their breath, so they can't stay down for long.' They chatted on about the wreck and soon reached the pub.

The pub was shabby, but comfortable and the dozen or so patrons sat hunched over their drinks, gazing at the fire like arsonists worshipping their handiwork. From time to time someone reached forward to take another log from a big copper pot and throw it on the blaze, poking the embers until sparks flew up the chimney.

When they had settled on a table fairly close to the fire, Simon fetched a warm, frothy beer for John, a rye whisky for himself and a plate of heavily salted potato chips, which he hated.

They had hardly sat down before John gave him a long, hard

look and said, 'Well, out with it. Why are we here? What do you want to know so badly that you'll endure my company for the evening?'

'Enjoy sounds better than endure, John. We never have a chance to talk. When I asked you about the bay, I had my reasons,' he ad-libbed.

'Which were?'

Simon shrugged. 'I'm not supposed to say. It's classified, but I suppose it will soon be public knowledge. All beaches are about to become the property of Allied military authorities. No civilians will be able to set foot on a beach until the war ends.'

'So whose idea was this?' John asked quietly.

Simon embarked on the wearisome business of weaving lies in as few words as possible. 'The new regulation concerns all British beaches in the south, from the Thames to Wales.'

Eyes narrowed, John watched Simon sceptically. 'When is this supposed to happen?'

'Within thirty days,' Simon answered.

'What has it got to do with me?'

'Nothing really, I was warning you. You may have to reschedule your early morning rides. D'you think the locals will be up in arms?'

'Some of them might be' John said as if bored by the conversation. 'But most of us have a great deal to put up with. Some have been bombed out and lost almost all they own. They spend their nights in damp shelters in their gardens, most of which flood every winter, and almost every family has relatives in the armed forces. They don't know if they'll ever see them again . . . but the Yanks are here and Poles and Commonwealth forces from all over the world, many of whom have volunteered to come over to help beat the Nazis. I think we would put up with any damn thing that might help the Allies train . . . in other words, help them win the war.'

Christ! He's right! Simon thought. This sib is wide off the mark. Perhaps he had overestimated the PWE guys' expertise.

'I get your point,' he said quietly.

'That's it!'

'I guess so.'

'Well, I want to air a few things, too, since we're here. Let's have this conversation Yankee style, shall we? Don't you guys believe in having it out?'

'Of course,' Simon said, feeling uneasy.

'I know you're after my daughter and I want you to know that

I strenuously disapprove. If you had any morals at all you would not take advantage of your position as our uninvited guest.'

'That's a little harsh,' Simon countered. 'Did you expect me to be unaware of your daughter's beauty?'

'No, but I didn't expect you to move in quite so fast.'

Simon wanted to rebuff the accusation. He had another perfectly valid reason for moving into John's house, but he was unable to voice it. And if he were completely honest he would admit that he was very anxious to get out of that draughty tent on that damned soggy field. The truth was he had been utterly floored by Helen's incredible looks and he had looked forward to seeing her on a daily basis.

He said, 'It's difficult to ignore the appeal of someone so beautiful, but at the same time one is very aware that the person concerned didn't earn it. It is a gift of nature, but Helen herself is as lovely as her looks. That's what really counts, isn't it? She's loyal, brave, kind, resourceful, a wonderful mother, generous and self-sacrificing and plenty more besides, although I must admit, I find her hard to get on with.'

'Plus she's lonely and heartbroken,' John added. 'She married Eric at eighteen. I tried to stop her but she was determined and so was he. He was too old for her, but still youngish, and dashing, life and soul of the party type. What could be more romantic than a commander in the navy. I did my best to stop them from marrying, but I failed. Helen was training to be a dress designer, but she was amazingly successful right from the start. One dress made the front cover of *Vogue*, but after Daisy was born, Eric insisted that she give up her career. He had umpteen dozen affairs and finally he left her with nothing.'

'Apart from a very lovely daughter.'

'Well yes, that goes without saying.' John was sipping his warm, draught bitter and pushing the crisps into his mouth while gazing at the flames in the hearth. 'I'm well aware of the effect Helen's beauty would have on someone like you,' he said quietly. 'My wife, Mia, was very beautiful . . . same eyes, but she had ash blonde hair. She was Danish. I met her on a sales tour to Denmark.'

'Doesn't your own experience tell you something?'

'How d'you mean?'

'You wouldn't give Mia up without a good try. Maybe there are others like you.'

John sat silently glowering at him, so Simon stood up to replenish their drinks.

By the time he returned, John had become even more hostile. 'You're a typical lawyer, Simon. You know all about us, but we don't know a damn thing about you.'

'Well, I can tell you whatever you want to know. Father was a lawyer. He owned a large and successful country firm of solicitors in a town near Seattle. I was supposed to join him, but I wanted to strike out on my own, so I specialized in human rights and joined a Manhattan firm. I moved twice to similar firms in New York and finally became a partner. Then came the Japanese attack on Pearl Harbour, so I joined up. It seemed the right thing to do at the time.'

'Why do I have the impression that you're leaving out all the important parts?'

Simon shrugged.

'Are you married?'

'Yes,' Simon said, sticking strictly to the truth and reasoning that further explanations were unnecessary.

John brightened visibly. Then Simon cottoned on. John didn't want to lose his family by having them marry Americans and leave England. Hence his antipathy.

Munching his chips, John remained gazing at the fire with a far away look in his eyes. Perhaps he was thinking of his late wife. Simon decided not to tell him that his divorce would soon be final. Why spoil his evening?

'I've noticed you down in the bay with a group of GIs. You seem to be in charge of them,' John continued.

'That's right. I'm an underwater diving instructor.'

'Pull the other leg,' John said scathingly. 'Most of the time, you're in London. Strange place for a diving instructor. You never open your mouth without carefully working out exactly what you're going to say, yet you told me about the beaches being closed and made out it was some kind of a secret. Now why did you do that?'

'Well, it is not really a long-term secret, is it? The news will break within thirty days.'

'You had your reasons for telling me and I think I've worked out exactly what that was.'

For a few moments the two men stared at each other. 'It's classified,' Simon said firmly. That was a good stopper to the conversation.

John continued gazing into the fire, as if dreaming, but his keen mind was hard at work. He's no ordinary soldier, not even for a captain, he said to himself. The guys seem to treat him with a great deal of respect. He's always moving around England, visiting other camps and he spends half his time in London. Why? John suddenly remembered reading somewhere that the pick of the lawyers who had volunteered were being drafted into military intelligence. Furthermore he had told John that he felt the cold after six months in South America. Yet this evening he claimed to have joined up right after Pearl Harbour. There are no US troops in Argentina, which meant that he was working undercover for military intelligence.

John felt pleased with his deduction. They seemed to have run out of conversation, so they eyed each other malevolently for a while, before opting to walk home.

'By the way,' John said, as they reached Conroy House. 'I was in intelligence in the last war, so we have something in common after all. I must tell you that I was a damn sight more sly than you are. Perhaps you should stick to scuba diving. I won't be passing on your sib for you. It's too bloody silly for words, but don't worry. I won't interfere with whatever it is you are up to.'

One down, three to go, Simon comforted himself as he fought to recover his composure.

Sixteen

Mowbray sat huddled beside the sea, shrouded in total blackout, but even this had its compensations, John Cooper thought, as he slid the bolts across the stable doors and walked slowly back to the house. Without the multitude of lights of prewar days the stars seemed brighter, lighting his way across the cobbled yard to the back door. En-route he enjoyed the evanescent gleams of phosphorescence on the sea which brought back memories of midnight summer romancing down in their secluded bay when he and Mia returned to England. His wife had never felt the cold and he had suffered in silence. Those were the days. He breathed in deeply, enjoying the peaceful night and the scent of ozone which he loved.

An owl screeched, a dog barked from the next street and he could hear the sound of a distant aircraft. Not one of ours surely, and more than one, he realized with a jolt of unease. He stood listening, watching the eastern horizon, wondering if the enemy bombers were fleeing the spitfires or simply running off course. The siren's sudden, monotonous dirge sent him sprinting to the back door that led into the scullery. Closing it behind him, he pulled the heavy curtain across the door before switching on the light. The house was in darkness, but he could hear the radio in the living room. 'Dick Barton, special agent in No Place to Hide,' he heard the announcer's macabre voice. This was the kids' favourite programme, so where were they?

'Where is everyone?' he shouted.

'In here. Don't put the light on,' Helen called.

Daisy was half out of the window with Miro close beside her, as usual. Helen stood by the closed window staring at the sky, frowning. She was deeply afraid of the raids and not without reason. She had never told him this, but he knew from the way she bit her bottom lip and played with her fingers, trying to knit them together over and over again.

The light was off so that the family could hang out of the window letting icy blasts into their warm room. 'It's three degrees outside. It will soon be the same in here,' he grumbled.

Daisy turned from the window. 'Enemy bombers,' she called out. 'That's strange. What are they doing here?'

'They might be our bombers setting out for their nightly raid. I bet you can't tell the difference,' John said.

'Of course I can. There's no mistaking the sound. Enemy bombers make a deep low-pitched rumble in stops and starts. Our planes have a lighter, steadier drone.'

'You should know,' he acknowledged. John would never forgive Eric for dragging his daughter and her children to every blitz area. They should have been here, or in Wales at the very least. Just look at Helen twisting her fingers into knots. God knows how she had survived the Dover shelling and the time bomb on their house, followed by the Plymouth and Southampton blitzes. When he'd gathered them up and brought them home, they'd possessed little more than what they stood up in, but they were alive and that was all that counted.

'Come inside and shut the window, Daisy please, before we freeze to death,' Helen called. 'You two should get under the stairs and hurry up. The planes are getting too close.'

'And you, Mum?' Daisy sounded nervous.

'Yes, all right. I'll look around first.'

'There's nothing to bomb here,' John said.

John joined Helen at the window. The planes were moving closer, but several fighter aircraft were zooming into the attack. By now the sky was lit by searchlights swinging from side to side, criss-crossing as the gunners searched for their targets. A searchlight caught a plane in its beam and immediately hung in there. It looked more like an iridescent silver moth zooming around a lamp. More beams raced across the sky to pinpoint the moth, who was trying its best to evade the searchlights. Puffs of exploded shells hung in the beams. A sudden flare showed the moth's demise. As the enemy plane spiraled to the ground the searchlights resumed their swinging search.

'One down. I think it crashed into the New Forest. They're way off course if they're after the docks,' John said, pulling down the blackout blinds and drawing the heavily-lined curtains.

A mattress, pillows, blankets, a milk churn of fresh water, biscuits and paper cups were kept under the stairs and replenished daily. In summer, they went to their Anderson shelter which was dug into the garden, but it flooded every winter. Knees hunched up, the family sat in a row, leaning against their pillows which were placed against the wall, listening to the shriek of shells and the drone of heavily laden enemy bombers circling overhead. The rat-a-tat-tat of ack-ack guns and a few exploding bombs sounded muffled and distant.

'Sounds like they're bombing the New Forest. The trees deaden the sound. It must be a mistake,' John muttered. 'Perhaps they're lost.'

Miro's anger burned like acid in his chest. He couldn't stand to sit a moment longer. He muttered, 'I'm going to check the stables,' and scrambled to his feet, running to the front door and slamming it behind him. The sky was alight with thousands of burning incendiaries falling to earth. It was beautiful, macabre and deadly. Most were red, but some were blue. The blue ones carried explosives, he knew, while the red ones merely set light to whatever was flammable, and most of Southampton was, he remembered. So was this old house. There was a hissing sound as one landed nearby. 'Where's a spade?' he muttered. He ran to the shed, but he couldn't see a thing. Fumbling along the row of hanging tools in total darkness, he felt for the spade, hauled it off the hook and ran back to shovel earth over the incendiary. It sizzled and went out. Another two landed nearby. Miro upturned the dustbin on one of them, and piled earth on the other. But what about the roof? He wouldn't see the blaze from ground level. The house would burn down before they knew what was happening. One of the attic windows led out on to a ledge, he knew, and from there he could climb up and put out any small blaze with a fire extinguisher. Grabbing a torch and the fire extinguisher from the scullery, he raced up four flights to the attic. As he had thought, it was simple to get out on to the roof, and so far there were no firebombs.

He sat there and watched the show. If you weren't afraid of who would die and whether or not the house was going to be bombed, this was a show to rival all others, far better than any fireworks.

They used to have great displays back home. He remembered when the news first came of Germany's right to accede Sudetenland, right after the Munich Conference. The celebrations had gone on for days: fireworks, singing, marches, all night dancing, his friends dizzy with beer and joy, his parents staying alone at home, wondering what it would mean for them. Miro had sat at the attic window obsessed with a feeling of isolation. He didn't seem to belong anywhere. Funnily enough he no longer felt isolated and Daisy had a great deal to do with that. She was always there in the back of his mind.

He could smell smoke. Searching for its probable location, he quickly assured himself that it was not the roof that was burning.

Yet something was. A horse let out a high-pitched whinny of fear, more like a scream. Climbing around the ledge to the back of the house Miro saw that the stables had received a direct hit from an incendiary.

Spasms of fear pierced his stomach, but then he saw John racing across the cobbled yard. He was flinging open the stable doors and coaxing the mares out into the yard, giving each one a smack on the rump to make it gallop away in the dark. Miro wanted to go down and help, but the planes were circling overhead and incendiaries were falling around. One might land on the roof. He'd better stay. He could see Gramps running around with a torch. At that moment he saw a dull glow. An incendiary had landed on the roof of the communal stable closest to the army camp. Daunty was the only horse there. He was taken there at night to keep him as far from the mares as possible. The door lay open, but the horse was locked in his stall at the very end and judging by the high-pitched screams it was mad with fright.

'The roof,' he yelled. 'Gramps! The stable roof's alight. Get Daunty out.'

Could Gramps cope? He'd better go down. He scrambled through the window and leaped down the stairs. 'The stable roof is burning,' he yelled, as he passed. Gramps was right behind him, followed by Helen and Daisy. So who had let out the horses? As Miro raced across the yard, he could hear Daunty bucking and screaming as he lashed his hooves at the walls.

Unable to catch up, John was shouting at him, 'Leave him, Miro. He'll kill you. Get the hosepipe.'

Miro ran into the stable. Blinded by smoke he began to choke.

'Get out of here,' someone called. 'Get out of the way fast.' An American accent.

Miro threw himself into a stall as the stallion reared over him. He heard a crash of splintering wood as it bucked and kicked the wall with his hooves. A whip cracked twice, then horse and rider swept through the stable door into the yard.

Coughing and retching, Miro stumbled after them. He leaned against the wall, gasping for air, watching Daunty showing his famous temper. Mad with fright, he leaped high, all four hooves off the ground, landed, bucked and reared, then plunged his head between his front feet and tossed his hind legs high, but the rider hung in there as if glued to his back.

'Daunty! Calm down, Daunty,' Daisy said, slowly approaching.

'Get back, Daisy. Get away,' the rider shouted. When Miro heard him call her name, he understood exactly who he was, the very same GI she had stayed with all evening at the Christmas ball. So he was still around. Trembling with rage, he watched Daunty try every trick he knew to unseat his strange rider and his heart went out to the frantic stallion. But what about the stable? For God's sake, how long had he stood here like a lunatic while the fire took hold? Moments later he was running around the corner, a ladder over his shoulder, a sack in his hands to beat out the flames.

Daisy felt her fury rising as she watched Mike bring the frenzied stallion under control, until he ceased fighting and stood still, shuddering violently. She resented Mike's extraordinary maleness and strength and his need to win against a poor beast twice his size which was scared out of its wits. He could have jumped off and left Daunty to race around the garden and slowly recover his cool, but he had to win. Just as he had wanted to win on that rainy day when he brought her home. She ran to the store and fetched a towel to rub the horse down. 'Get off him, then,' she snapped, noticing that he was barefooted and wearing only shorts and a shirt.

Mike, who had expected some favourable comments on his performance, was overcome with dismay. He dismounted and stood watching her rubbing down the horse, speaking softly to him.

'It's all right, Daunty. Miro's putting out the fire. You're safe. You'll go back in your old stable tonight. What a fighter! What a stallion!'

It should be him she was concerned about. 'Be careful. He might panic again,' Mike warned her.

'He's thoroughly beaten. You took care of that,' she muttered, cold and angry. Neither of them noticed that the planes had fled out to sea until the All-Clear siren sounded.

Mike stroked the shuddering beast, wondering what he had done wrong.

'That horse is too damned dangerous. We should have got rid of him months ago,' John called from behind Mike. 'That was a most amazing performance, young man. Well done and thank you. I'm John Cooper. You seem to know my granddaughter.'

'Yes, sir. She was at the dance,' he muttered, relieved to have got out of that without lying.

'It's Dad's horse, so there's no way we could have "got rid of him",' Daisy snapped.

A group of GIs were running into the yard with searchlights and fire hydrants and Mike realized that only a few minutes had passed, yet it had seemed so much longer.

'Remember the blackout. Better put those lights out,' Mrs Conroy called.

'Sorry, ma'am.' The searchlight went off and the torches came out.

'My God! That was unbelievable. Well done. Who are you?' She asked Mike. 'And who are these men?'

'Sergeant Mike Lawson, ma'am, from the camp . . . my friends are helping out. We're used to horses, so we came over to give you a hand, but they had to fetch the fire equipment.'

'Thank goodness you came! It was like a rodeo performance. I've never seen anything like it. Thank you, again.'

'My pleasure, ma'am. Back home we have rodeos about once a month. I usually take part when I've got the time. That's a great stallion. I've noticed our captain riding him.'

'You can ride him if you'd like to. I can see you're a superb rider.'

'I sure would like to, ma'am. I miss my horse.'

'Well then. Captain Johnson likes to ride him in the mornings if he's around. So check with him for the timing. Daunty could do with more exercise. Your captain is billeted here.'

'Yes, I know that, ma'am.'

'Come inside and have a drink. Invite your friends, please do.'

'That would be great, but we'd better make sure that there are no more fires first. I'll see you after that. See you later, Daisy,' he called.

She ignored him and Mike bit his lip. She was a strange girl. He didn't want to get involved in yet another fight. He was in with the mother which was a step in the right direction, but why couldn't Daisy give way and be a bit friendly? She was acting as if he had started the blaze. He stood still, feeling perplexed and wondering what he could say to make things right. Just look at her now, her lovely eyes blazing with anger.

'What is it with you?' he asked, walking towards her. 'What's wrong this time?'

'You wouldn't understand, so I won't waste my breath.'

'Try me.'

Mike caught sight of Miro who was clearly eavesdropping. He was standing by the piles of earth with a spade, but doing very little. He gestured in his direction.

'Why don't you leave that until it's light, Miro.' Daisy called.

'The fire's out,' he said sullenly.

'Miro,' he heard John call. 'Can you get up there to assess the damage? We'll use asbestos for a new roof in case the bastards drop a few more of their damned incendiaries.'

Miro disappeared around the corner leaving them alone.

'You're high and mighty for a schoolgirl,' Mike said softly.

'I've finished school. I told you at the dance.'

'Your mother has invited us in for drinks. Is that all right with you? Or would you rather I went?'

'If Mum invited you, then you must go,' she said, evading the question.

'See you soon.' She wasn't easy, but he liked her a lot. What was it his mother had drummed into him? 'Don't go for looks, Mike, my boy. Find yourself a good woman and you'll lead a happy life.'

That was all very well, but Mike knew when he was beaten, and Daisy had the beating of him. She provoked his ire and his desire. He wanted to be her adoring slave, but on his terms. He felt the need to show his male power, but she was determined to ignore all that he had on offer which wasn't much since he was far away from home, and in uniform, without his ranch, his horse or his car, or any damned thing that seemed to provide a reassuring part of his personality. Here he was hardly better than a number. So what if he'd hung in there slightly longer than necessary. He was trying to show her who he was, who he would be, that he was strong enough to look after her, and now she was provoked into fury. Women were too damned weird for words, he decided, as he sauntered off to find her mother.

Once in the house, Helen was immersed in gloom. She had difficulty coming to terms with the reality of war, but her fears were hidden as safely as her handgun and bullets, which she had bought when they feared an invasion. Raids were rare around this area, but she had not lived through three blitzes unscathed. Something had changed deep inside her. She only became aware of this altered perspective during the Southampton raids. Every evening she had taken the children to the new public shelter in the centre of town, which was claimed to be indestructible, although it was wrecked now, she reminded herself with a spasm of fear. With their flask of tea, bottles of water, sleeping bags and sandwiches, they would settle themselves along the wall, as near as possible to the exit in order to leave quickly at dawn. From here the noise was deafening.

One night, on a particularly heavy blitz, when the shelter rocked with blasts and the noise was unbearable, she had tried to pray for their survival, but she found that she could not. Whatever she had once believed in had entirely vanished. There was nothing, but herself. And what was she really? An intelligent primate. Everything else was a lie. When she saw people praying she was overcome with compassion for them. They existed by some fluke of nature and that was that.

The doorbell was ringing, thank heavens. She'd had enough of her morbid introspection. The GIs trooped in as polite and sweet as one could wish. They had one drink each, made it last, talked about their impressions of England and then left. Well brought up, helpful boys, but so young. The thought of them going to war was terrible. As for Mike, she could see what an asset he would be to the riding school. He'd already offered to shoe their horses, and she had quickly accepted what with the blacksmith having been recently called up.

Mike found Daisy in the stables. A lantern hung on the wall and for a moment he stood there unnoticed, entranced by the scene. She was standing beside Daunty, stroking his neck and talking softly to him. Mike walked down the aisle, leaned over the barrier and said, 'Hi,' softly. There was no answer. How lovely she was, but somehow frail looking, yet she was a strong girl. Perhaps it was her nose, a pinched, small European nose sloping to a full mouth. Her blue eyes looked so serious and secretive and when he spoke she looked down, so that her long lashes brushed her pale cheeks.

She'll still be beautiful when she's old, he thought. Her bone struc-ture is fine and delicate and I shall look at her and remember how she looked when she was sulking in the stables. He noted the dull flush of temper scarcely concealed, the virginal lips pursed. Those candid eyes, which were so expressive, told him that he was absolutely in the dog house. He wanted to explain how he felt about her, how he had wanted to impress her by showing her who he really was and a little of his background, but shyness blunted his wits.

'There's a place in the village where they teach you to dance your sort of dancing . . . old fashioned and boring. I've had a few lessons although I felt a fool,' he said.

One side of her mouth twisted into a lurking smile, but a frown still hovered between her thick, pale brows. 'Oh, lessons, is it?' Then she giggled.

Mike frowned. For two pins he'd leave, but he knew he didn't want to. 'Do you want me to leave?' he asked moodily.

'Suit yourself.'

'Tch! You'd better come out. It's not safe there. The horse is still uptight. Look how he's showing the whites of his eyes.'

'He doesn't like you. He's frightened of you and no wonder. He was fine until you came.'

'Hey, Daunty, I just saved your life, you ungrateful hack.'

Daisy stood up and dragged the sack of straw towards the door.

'For God's sake keep away from his back hooves.'

'You seem to think horses are your enemy. Daunty loves me. I'm only coming out because Daunty doesn't want you in his stable. Oh, Mike,' she said with a sudden change of heart. 'You didn't have to show off so. You could have left him to calm down by himself. Why did you have to beat him into a state of total submission?'

'I guess I wanted to show off to you.'

'I'd be more impressed with kindness. Daunty lost face.'

'Well, he's not Japanese, is he? So he needn't worry.'

She smiled despite herself. 'I'm glad you're taking lessons. What are you learning . . . the waltz?' She began to circle around in the aisle between the stalls. The mares were watching her and whinnying. 'They all want to dance,' she said.

He caught her hands and pulled her close to him and kissed her quickly on the lips. He felt embarrassed by his passion. He was sure she would feel it, so he stepped back and swirled her round in the sawdust, singing, *'Daisy, Daisy, give me your answer, do . . .'*

He pulled her closer, which caught her off balance, but he held her up, hugging her close against him. The top of her head reached his chin, so he tilted her face back and bent over to press his lips upon hers.

'Oh,' she gasped, pulling her face away. Suddenly she felt feverishly hot.

'You're my girl, Daisy,' he said hoarsely, feeling as flustered as she. He caught hold of her tighter and crushed her against his chest.

'You're hurting,' she said, but now she was acutely aware of his body pressed against hers. Stubble scratched her forehead, and the sheer bulk of him took her breath away. She slid her arms round his waist, hugging him closer, feeling the muscled back and hips hard against hers. Something strange was growing and pressing against her.

'Oh Mike,' she whispered. 'Go away. Leave me alone. I can't stand this feeling.'

Mike was feverishly exploring her breasts in clumsy, hurried move‐
ments. He tugged at her sweater and slid his hand under her bra,
pushing it up.

Suddenly they heard footsteps on cobbles. Daisy was overcome
with shame. She thrust him roughly away and pulled down her
jersey.

'Daisy . . . Daisy?'

It was Miro calling her. Gramps echoed him.

'Oh God! Hide. Just stay out of sight.'

She fled out of the door. Mike stood up and switched off the
lantern. He heard the stable door bolt being slid across, footsteps
faded and then he was alone.

'Oh shit!' he muttered.

It took him half an hour to painstakingly ease back the bolt using
a nail file pushed through the crack. The house was in darkness as
he crept across the yard and vaulted over the fence.

Seventeen

The underwater engineering course was scheduled to start on the first of March, but the first class was delayed by gale force winds from the Arctic buffeting the oceans on both sides of Britain, resulting in a mighty collision of currents off the coast of southern England. Breakers smashed against boulders, mounted the sea walls and drenched the flats and hotels along the sea front. The storm lasted for ten days and then the wind fell and Simon awoke to a glorious winter morning and a calm sea.

They needed two launches to propel the divers and their gear to the wreck, but soon they were bobbing on the calm sea, staring down at the dark shadow fifteen feet beneath them. Simon scanned the sky anxiously. Clouds were gathering as if from nowhere as a cold front moved in. The sea turned from turquoise to navy with frothy white spray tipping every wave. He felt anxious and undecided whether or not to go ahead.

Recently, Simon's class had grown in numbers. He had established fifteen scuba diving teams in the various camps around the coast. Every team had a leader who joined them in Mowbray for each new course of instruction. When they returned they passed on the training, but they were not as skilled as his own guys.

'Be back on board in fifteen minutes,' he told the guys. 'Keep an eye on your watches.'

The scuba divers were keen to get down and get on with their class. They adjusted their gear, strapped on the ungainly tanks and the additional weights they needed, checked the spotlights strapped around their heads, and strapped their knives to their shins before tumbling backwards into the sea.

Twenty-two men sank out of sight around the wreck and Simon followed them, leaving one man on each boat. They stayed in pairs, each man communicating with his buddy every few minutes while watching the instructor patch a hole. On the second dive, they would do it themselves. A sudden strong backwash sent the guys swirling off into deeper water. They hung on to the reef, watching the backwash swirling the seaweed out to sea.

Simon wondered if he should recall the guys, but after that one strong wave, the sea remained calm. Seven minutes into the lecture, the wreck gave a long shudder and slipped at least two feet to star-board blocking the main gaping hole completely. Now he could see that the ship was swinging like a pendulum, impaled on rocks, but not held tightly enough to remain stable in strong tides. He felt uneasy, but he did not know why. After a few minutes, he decided to go by his instinct and evacuate the class. He gave the signal and the students adjusted their alternators and rose slowly towards the boats. His guys looked pretty embarrassed at their boss's decision to quit.

'Sorry, but I have a feeling something's wrong,' Simon explained to them. 'Is everyone back? Check each boat please,' he called out.

'Sir,' a voice called from the next boat. 'Mike Lawson is still down there. Has anyone seen him?'

'Get a fresh tank on,' Simon said to his second-best student, as he exchanged his used tank for another. 'Where was he last seen?'

'Sitting right next to me, sir. We were at the extreme right of the semi-circle, closest to the wreck. He chose that place. I didn't notice him leave.'

Simon's stomach lurched. 'Was he your buddy?'

'Yes, sir.'

There was no time for recriminations right now. 'Let's go. He's got six minutes left,' he told his buddy. 'The wreck shifted so the main hole is now against the reef. He could be trapped inside, or even squashed between the rock and the hold. I've been down there often. I know another way into the hold. It's very dark so stick close to me.'

Twenty feet below, Mike was clambering over the debris in the hold, kicking his feet to frighten the eels and crabs, but with each step he stirred up a big black cloud of sediment that obscured his vision. The spotlight seemed to lessen visibility because the light reflected on the debris. It was like walking in a narrow tube of light and beyond was only darkness. If there were another way up to daylight, he wouldn't see it like this. He switched off the beam and stared around trying to see a glimmer of light in the Stygian blackness, but he could not see his hand in front of his face. He tried to push his way through a mass of debris, but it seemed to keep pace with him. He knew that there must be another way out, but he had only five minutes to find it. The wind was strengthening, the wreck shuddered and swayed as wave after wave smashed against it. There was a clamour of grinding and cracking, huge floating objects swirled around, threatening to pulverize him. Another glance at his watch showed that he had only four minutes of safe air left. He made another attempt to swim towards the stern where he might find another hole, or even the hatch to the deck.

'Keep going,' he muttered. 'There has to be a way out.' Reality was receding, but a minute later he thought he saw two lights moving in unison far ahead of him, in another part of the hold. He switched his spotlight on and off, on and off. Praying that he wasn't hallucinating, he forced his way towards the lights. Suddenly they altered direction – they were zooming towards him. He was saved and his relief was so great he gulped great mouthfuls of air. Now his head was hammering, his body felt limp and exhausted, his movements were shaky and he was only dimly aware of being propelled to the surface. Moments later he was hanging on to the side of the boat gasping.

It had been a near disaster, Simon thought grimly as the boats sped back to the shore, surfing on the waves. He had been so close to losing Mike. The weather had worsened, so Simon called it a day and summoned the men to an impromptu lecture in the canteen where he tried to instill in them the vital, life-saving system of working in pairs – the buddy system – and keeping an eye on each other.

Later he called Mike to a meeting in the canteen. 'You of all people, Mike. I could have you court-martialled for this. What the fuck did you think you were doing, crawling into the hold alone? Disobeying orders! You know the rules. And what about the demo you were missing?'

'I've been doing that sort of thing often enough, sir. Dad and I had to repair our bridges underwater . . . I wanted to look around. Then the wave came and the wreck shifted, blocking my exit.'

'But why?'

'Sir, Daisy feels that her father is dead. She claims that when she last saw him, which was on her birthday in June last year, he told her he was intending to explore the wreck and find out what the big attraction was for the so-called photographers. She is sure he would have contacted her, were he alive.'

'You were looking for his corpse?'

'Yes, sir.'

'Why didn't you tell me?'

'I guess I thought it sounded a bit fanciful, sir.'

On Sunday morning the family were gathered around the breakfast table for scrambled eggs, from their own fowls, and bacon supplied by Simon, when they heard the echo of a loudspeaker from the bay below.

'What on earth . . .?' Helen began.

'Rabble-rousing, that's all,' Miro said. 'A crowd of rowdy youths scrambled across the rocks and some of them came in by sea. They are marching up and down with home-made placards reading:"Yanks, keep off our beaches." I think that is their only message.'

John's eyes were drawn to Simon. 'I didn't mention it,' John said, glaring at him. 'I thought it was too bloody silly for words.'

'Yes, you said so,' Simon said quietly.

'What is? What's going on?' Helen asked.

'It's nothing serious,' Simon said. 'By the way, does anyone know any other way to reach the bay, other than by boat, or the path from the camp?'

'I do,' Miro said. 'It's a long haul, but I noticed months ago that someone – well, it must be more than one person – had cleared a path through the boulders at the western end of the bay. It's only visible at low tide.'

'It's not low tide now,' Simon said, glancing at his watch.

'They arrived by dinghies with outboard motors,' Miro said.'There are more demos along the coast towards Claremont.'

'How do you know, Miro?' John asked.

'I called a friend who lives that way. As a matter of fact, they've been whipping up support around the market at Claremont, handing out leaflets, that sort of thing. They asked me to join them . . . well, all of us . . . you know, boys in my class. We meet there for coffee sometimes. None of us went.'

'I'd better organize guards to stop them from coming up to the camp . . . or to you.' He pushed two rashers of bacon between two pieces of toast and stood up. 'See you guys.' He walked out of the house and then turned and walked back again.

'It's a lovely day out of the wind,' he announced from the doorway. 'Warm for late April.'

'We noticed,' Daisy said, laughing at him.

'Why don't we go for lunch at the Mowbray Heights, a family outing. Come on, let's go. It's my treat.'

'Perhaps you could pick us up from church . . .?' Helen began.

'Oh Mum. Why can't we skip church?'

Helen shrugged.

'How about you, Miro?' Simon asked.

'It's a great idea.'

'So it all hangs on you, John. All or nothing.' Helen was smiling happily.

'I look forward to it,' John said.

Lunch went well. John decided to unwind and told them stories about some of the intelligence bungles he'd been involved in. When Simon went to the window to watch the demonstrators, John followed him. 'They're just kids, roped in by professional trouble-makers and you can bet they're being paid to rustle up this demo. It might be worth your while to find out just who organized this nonsense. You may find it's connected to the boats that visit the wreck at night.'

'Just what I was thinking, John.'

'You've been training there for two weeks, you are probably preventing them from doing whatever it is they were doing.'

'Or maybe they're afraid of what we might find there. It's something that's been bugging me. I've searched around the reef and the wreck a few times. I haven't found anything yet, but visibility is poor. It's a rough corner and surf hits the reef and churns up the sand. Why the hell would they think that a few kids waving placards would prevent us from training?'

'I have an idea that certain people want to get you away from the wreck on a temporary basis,' John said. 'I'd take care if I were you.'

'Yes, you're right. Thanks.' Simon had given up suspecting John after hearing that he was in British intelligence in the last war. He'd checked that out and it was true. Mike had reported that John's nightly excursions were to Alice Bronson, his mistress, who owned and ran a sweet shop in Claremont.

The following night there was no moon and the sky was overcast. It was so dark Simon could hardly distinguish the sea from sky. He was keeping watch from the folly. Around midnight he saw dim gleams of light coming from around the wreck and he guessed that club members were once again out there. His gear was set up and ready, hidden in box in the bushes halfway down the cliff path. It took only moments to don his rubber suit and the tank and shortly afterwards he was wading into the water.

He was taken by surprise by a blow which struck him across his head and shoulders and probably would have killed him if it weren't that the iron bar collided with the air tank strapped on his back. He fell forward into the surf and for a brief moment he panicked, knowing that he would be unable to get up quickly enough with his heavy encumbrance. His wits returned fast and he pulled back the clip that released his harness leaving him free. His assailant, who had been wading back to the shore leaving him to drown, turned fast, but not fast enough. Simon's right fist lashed out at his assailant's head. He ducked, but Simon's momentum sent his shoulder crashing into the man's chest. They fell with flailing arms and legs into the yielding wet sand.

Simon caught the thick, wrestler's neck between his hands and squeezed. His attacker knew the score, Simon realized. He knew he was fighting for his life against a man trained in unarmed combat, but he knew the right moves, too. They were wrestling in waterlogged, shifting sand and their feet could get no purchase. Desperately the man grabbed a handful of sand and flung it into Simon's face. Simon grabbed him around the neck until he was gasping for breath, his eyes bulging, his face turning blue, but they skidded on a wet rock and fell. Rising to his feet, Simon saw that his attacker had a knife in his hand. He raised his arm a split second too late and the knife cut him across the shoulder. Reeling back, he lost his balance and fell forward on to the sand as his attacker leaped forward and hit him hard with an iron bar. Simon grunted, but felt no pain. He caught hold of his boot and flung the huge body sidelong into the surf. They were both down, but Simon was stronger and fitter. Tire him out, he thought, then go in for the kill. His attacker was snorting and bellowing like a tired old bull and making mistakes. Suddenly he charged, head down, arms threshing. Simon feinted to the side, brought up his foot and sent him hurtling into the sea. He threw himself over him, shifting his full weight on the back of his head, holding his face underwater until he was only semi-conscious and his struggles were more feeble. He was unconscious when Simon pulled him out of the sea. He shoved him into the harness and bound his hands behind him. Dragging him into the bushes, he secured the harness to a tree. Falling about with exhaustion, he forced himself to hurry up the path to the camp. He sent the guard to wake the boys in the nearest tent and send them down to fetch up the unconscious man.

By two a.m., his assailant was locked in the police station, telling McGuire all he wanted to know. When the so-called photographers arrived back at their mooring at the Claremont fishing harbour, they found a squad of police waiting for them.

Eighteen

Helen woke from a light sleep to hear unusual sounds coming from the camp, voices raised, vehicles moving, running footsteps. She got out of bed shivering with cold and fear. It was happening! The invasion had begun; the GIs were leaving and within hours they would be crossing the Channel to face God knows what hell. It seemed to take forever to feel her way across the room and fumble with the blackout. She nearly tore it in her agitation. The lawn was white with a late frost. Looking up she saw that the clouds were clearing. She could see patches of stars. As she flung open the window and leaned out in order to see the camp, the cold air shocked her into mental alertness.

They were not leaving . . . not yet, but something was wrong. Several GIs were up and dressed, a crowd of MPs stood around their vehicles and lights were shining in the medical tent. Someone was hurt. Someone else was being 'assisted' to the back of a police van by half a dozen MPs. They pushed him in and the van took off. There was no sign of Simon. Perhaps he was sleeping downstairs. Glancing at her watch she saw that it was past two a.m.

She closed the window, but left the blackout open and went back to bed, but not to sleep. She was remembering Simon and the way he had kissed her in the car on the night of the blitz. Guilt had drowned her need, but Simon had not understood. Since then he had been very correct, very polite, and very remote. He had removed himself to another dimension where he could remain inviolate and untouchable. He would never come back, she feared. Why was she so obsessed with the rightness of things? Or was she paying Simon back for Eric's crimes? She shivered and felt a sudden revulsion for herself and the life she had created. Why couldn't she reach out for love? Why was she so afraid? She should have grabbed any joy coming her way, however ephemeral. They were at war, once he was gone she might never see him again.

But Eric might return. What if he did? This was her father's house, there was no law that said she had to have him back. She had enough grounds for divorce however long it took.

An hour later, she heard a jeep turning into their gate. It must be Simon. The door opened and she heard three men walk in. She got out of bed and opened her door, to listen to their voices. They were half-supporting Simon to his room.

'Be quiet . . . careful . . .we don't want to wake the household.' Simon's voice.

She caught her breath. Something was wrong with Simon. Stepping forward, she gripped the banisters and looked down. A tall man stood silhouetted in the doorway. His mop of blue-black hair shone in the passage light. Of course, it was Mike Lawson. Simon had mentioned that Lawson was his PA. There was a third man with them.

'Sure you'll be all right, sir?' she heard Lawson say.

Simon muttered something that she could not hear, followed by soft laughter. The boys left.

Helen stood worrying and shivering. Why did they have to help him home? What had happened to him? Was it Simon who she'd seen being treated by the medics? Anxious and indecisive, she listened, but heard nothing. Finally she crept downstairs. Simon's door was unlocked. She opened it and paused in the doorway.

'What's wrong with you?' she whispered. Light flooded the room and suddenly she was on guard, aware that she was wearing only her nightdress. Propped up on his elbow with the blankets around him, Simon looked perfectly normal. She was overcome with embarrassment. His dark eyes were glinting with laughter. His lips, too, were curving into a grin, more on one side than the other, while one eyebrow slowly rose, wrinkling his brow

'I'm so sorry to barge in, I was afraid you'd had an accident and I couldn't sleep for worrying. I heard Mike and another man bring you home. Why was that?'

'Perhaps I was drunk.'

'No, not you.'

'And you can't sleep for worrying. Doesn't that tell you something?' He watched her critically and she flushed.

'As long as you're all right.' She turned to leave, but paused, feeling the need to explain further.

'But I'm not.' He tried to sit up and the blankets fell back revealing the bandage around his torso. His shoulder was heavily bound with pads around it, but the blood was oozing through. When he pushed back the blankets and swung his legs to the floor, she saw that he was naked. But why was his ankle bound so tightly?

She gasped, 'What happened? How bad is it?'

'Very bad. I'm freezing. Come and warm me, Helen.'

'Tell me what happened and cover yourself. Do you always sleep naked?'

'Yes, don't you?'

'No.'

'I'll change all that when we're together.'

Her face was burning. 'Tell me what happened?'

'Don't worry. It was worth it. It brought you here.' He was smiling as he attempted to stand, but fell back. 'Ouch.'

She reached forward to steady him. 'Simon . . . tell me.'

'We had a fight. I won, but it doesn't feel like that right now.' He caught her wrist, but when she pulled back, he gasped. 'Don't do that. It hurts too much.'

'Then let go.'

'No. Come to bed.'

'Dear God!' she wailed. 'Will you let go before I pull my hand and hurt you again?'

'No. How cold you are . . . icy,' he murmured, suddenly serious. He let go of her hand and tried to sit up straight. 'Can you help me?' She leaned over him and pushed him forward, pulling the pillows straight to prop him up and saw the cuts and bruises on his back. 'Oh my God. You've been in a fight. Why?'

'I wanted to find out why several men in a boat go out to the wreck on dark nights without showing any lights. I was convinced something illicit was going on.'

'Eric said much the same to me before he left.' Helen's words sounded alarm bells, but Simon didn't respond.

'I intended to swim out there, but they'd left a guard on the beach. He came up behind me when I wasn't looking. Criminal carelessness.'

'Did you catch sight of him?'

'Not really. It was too dark.'

'So you've no idea who it was?'

'He's in the police station so they'll soon find out. We had a fight. I won . . . eventually.'

'Oh my God.' Her eyes were brimming over with salty tears.

'All these tears. Why? Is it my fault? I'm so sorry.' He smoothed her cheeks with his thumbs and pushed her hair off her face.

Helen fumbled in her pocket and blew her nose on a handkerchief.

'Come on, hop in. What have you got to lose?'

She gazed inquiringly at him and saw the love in his eyes. Pulling off her nightdress, she slipped into bed beside him.

'This is not right for you and it's not right for me. God knows how it will end.'

Morning light! Helen stirred sleepily and turned on her back. The memory of their brief hours together flooded into her mind and she smiled softly. They had made love, despite his wounds, and slept entwined, and later begun all over again. It was as if . . . as if . . .? How could she explain even to herself? It was as if he loved her. He had been so tender and so skillful, like a man who had been away from home for far too long. He couldn't get enough of her. No one had ever done the things that he had done and she had reciprocated with as much ardour as he. Her body felt pleasantly used, complete, glowing in every place, with a dull ache around her thighs.

She was too relaxed to stir, but when she reached out and found that he had gone, she felt regretful. She lay back on the pillow and closed her eyes. Then she heard gurgling in the kitchen. It sounded like the coffee percolator, muted clicks of cups and teaspoons placed on saucers. He appeared in the doorway holding a tray with his right hand.

She scrambled out of bed to grab the tray and became aware that she was naked. Her nightdress lay on the floor. What did it matter? She smiled at him. 'You made coffee. That's amazing, but now you must stay in bed. I'll bring your meals in here.'

'What's amazing about it?'

'You only have one arm.'

'That's temporary, Helen.'

He was scanning her quizzically. She had the feeling that she should comment on his amazing virility. 'I'm afraid I let my hair down. It's been a long time.' It sounded like a cliché and she flushed.

'That was good sex. The best.' He stirred her coffee and passed it to her.

'Helen, I'm crazy about you. I want to marry you as soon as you're free.'

'Let's not kid ourselves,' she began, in a harsh voice. 'Divorce takes years in Britain. Last night was an accident that should never have happened. I was caught off-guard. I don't intend to let this happen again.'

'I'll remember you as you were last night, softly seeking, shy and giving, a different woman altogether. What has life done to you, my sweet Helen?'

He put down his cup and leaned forward to kiss her forehead.

Forgetting about their one night stand wasn't quite as easy as Helen had expected. She coped in daylight hours, for her mind was as well-schooled as a Lipizzaner horse. Admittedly her body rebelled, but she tamed it with cold showers. It was the nights she dreaded, for then she was badly let down by her sneaky subconscious which opened the door to *him* the moment she shut her eyes. She tried every possible cure: a stiff drink before bed, sleeping pills, even tranquilizers, but nothing worked. In her dreams, *he* devised the most pleasurable activities to wile away the night. At dawn she would wake, spread-eagled on the bed, with damp thighs and a smile on her lips.

Stupid to pine, she reasoned. He'll leave soon and I might not hear from him again. She didn't need two disasters in her life.

Nineteen

On a calm day in May, Simon took his underwater team for their pre-dawn dive to master advanced sabotage skills under the wreck. He set out through the chill mist with Mike and a team of six good swimmers from Mike's water polo team, two of whom were experienced in handling explosives, plus twelve visiting GIs from other divisions. The sea was like a metal sheet, calm, grey and deceptive. A cold wind started from the north-west, driving a fine drizzle as they reached a spot above the wreck which they had marked with a buoy. It was low tide and a remnant of the wreck still protruded from the surface, although it was breaking up fast due to the recent storms. The guys donned their gear, gave the thumbs up sign, gripped the mouthpieces in their teeth and tumbled backwards into the sea, leaving only two men to guard the boats. Simon, who was never warm enough, shivered at the prospect of icy water filling his rubber suit. He gritted his teeth and followed them.

Leaving the class gathered around the wreck, Simon approached the gaping hole in the stern. He was loathe to enter, but with Helen's words in mind, he knew he must. He pushed one leg through the jagged hole and moved into the pitch dark hold.

As he put his foot down, something thick and alive squirmed under his foot. He waited for the bite, which didn't come. When the sediment cleared he saw dozens of eels wriggling amongst the debris. The hold filled him with loathing, but a glance at his watch told him he had better get on with it. After a complete search of the hull, he glanced at his watch again. Time to surface! His team were bobbing up around him and making for the boat.

'Everyone OK?' he asked, after a quick head count.

'Irwin cut his hand, but it's not serious,' his buddy said.

'OK! Take a look, Mike.'

'Couple of stitches when we get back to base, but I reckon we can finish the lesson,' Mike said.

'You're in charge. I'm circling the wreck within a fifty metre radius. I'll mainly focus on the reef.' While he spoke he was unbuckling his harness to fit a new tank in. 'I'm looking for signs of the original cargo of copper from Zaire,' he lied. He changed tanks, gave them the thumbs up sign and fell backwards over the side, floating gently down. From the wreck, he swam southwards, following the line of the reef. A sudden surge in the current washed him off his feet and flung him against the nearest rocks. He hung on against the swirling water and marvelled when the sun broke through the mist. Now he could see the fish swimming past. A crab scuttled across the sandy surface into the reef. Watching it, Simon caught sight of a piece of chain, like heavy anchor chain, almost obscured by seaweed. He dived head first on to it and tried to haul it up, but it was so heavy it could be anchored to the sea bed. He felt his way along it, at times having to squeeze between the rocks, moving southwards. The chain appeared to be laid in a straight line amongst the rocks that formed the reef. Swimming a couple of feet above the chain, with his searchlight trained on to it, he followed it into deeper water.

The tide was coming in, the backwash took him off course frequently, but he kept going. Thoughts of narcosis were uppermost in his mind, but then the tallest reef of all loomed ahead of him. It was at least a hundred metres from the wreck, but this was probably the rock that had holed the hull. The sea calmed for a few seconds and once again he saw the chain half submerged in the sand. He circled the reef which was rectangular, consisting of four rocky outcrops stretching over fifty metres of sandy sea bottom. There was no sign of the chain, so it must end in the reef. He'd probably find an anchor and nothing else, Simon guessed as he picked up the trail again.

At first the going was reasonably good. There was a heavy swell starting up and numerous swirling eddies and choppy side currents buffeted him against the rocks, but he was a strong swimmer and he kept moving forward, pushing himself to go harder and faster to beat the damned twenty-minute deadline. A sudden lurch sent him hard against a rock that was solid and still. He lay still, hanging on, waiting for the backwash to still. Switching on his lamp, he swung the powerful beam into the shadows between the rocks. He was in a narrow channel and between the rocks, secured by chains, he saw dozens of boxes. They were laid in a line all the way down the reef, but he did not have enough air left to find out how many were stowed there. Something else brought a thrill of physical horror even before his mind had worked out what it was. He was lying on a corpse and the head lay only inches from his face.

He longed to rocket to the surface, but he had to examine the corpse first and he was running out of air, his movements had become slow and sluggish. Whoever it was had been wearing some kind of breathing apparatus, but the air had been switched off and it hung from one strap, the other was sliced through. His flippers were still on his feet, but there was a jagged tear in his rubber suit just below his right shoulder blade. He wondered just how much of a fight he had managed put up with his air switched off. He was still wearing his goggles which had partially protected his eyes. The rest of his face was swollen, grey-white and eaten by the fish. He had been wearing a body suit, which left his arms and legs bare, and here, too, the flesh was swollen and half-eaten. Simon unfastened his watch and his knife for the police.

Only then could he rise, taking it slow and pausing for a while halfway up. He surfaced, pushed off his mask and found that he was at least a hundred yards from the boats. Switching his spotlight on and off, he trod water until a boat reached him.

'Jesus, Simon,' Mike said, forgetting protocol. 'I was scared shitless. We didn't know where to start searching. Get in fast.'

'No, hang on. Pass me one of the buoys. I need a long line. There's a corpse right below us and dozens of boxes. It could be the corpse you were searching for, plus a portion of the missing cargo. The body is weighed down by chains. It's no accidental death, believe me, but we'll have to leave it until we fetch a body bag. Not a word about this until the body is identified,' he warned. He secured the buoy and climbed into the boat.

'I should have come with you,' Mike said.

An hour later, Simon drove to see McGuire, taking the watch and knife, and an offer to retrieve the corpse after photographing it, which was gratefully accepted. McGuire accompanied him back to the house to speak to Helen.

Daisy, who had been eavesdropping outside the door, rushed into the room and flung herself onto the couch, sobbing. 'I knew it. I knew all the time. I told Mike to find him . . . and he did. It's best to know the truth, but I knew that Dad would never have gone away without letting me know.'

Helen officially identified the watch and the knife with a cool composure, although she turned very white and went upstairs afterwards, locking herself in her room for the rest of the day, until John went up and spoke to her. Simon never knew what he said, but

Helen joined the family for supper looking calm, but pale and even more beautiful. She made it very clear that she did not want to talk about Eric ever again. But it was not over yet.

Two days later, early in the morning, the police came to tell Helen that Eric's body had been in the water for about seven months. Until then he had been living in an exclusive Edinburgh hotel with his pregnant companion under the assumed names of Mr and Mrs Laruelle, which was his secretary's family name. She had not known that he was going to Mowbray, and the Edinburgh police had not realized that Eric Conroy and her supposed husband were one and the same. Simon guessed that Eric had come to Dorset to see Daisy and to investigate the wreck for possible salvage rights.

Helen simply shrugged, got on her bicycle and left for work. Yet Simon sensed that she was still in turmoil. He noticed little things: she would forget what she was doing, leave the stove on and burn the food, all kinds of memory lapses which told him that she was under a great deal of strain.

'Helen, listen, your family needs you. Pull yourself together,' Simon told her days later. 'All this introspection is doing you no good and it's harming the family. I know you're grieving, but try to put it aside.'

'I'm not grieving. That's my problem, but at least my adultery was never adultery, since I was a widow, not a wife. Eric is the cheat, not I. His precious mistress was sent to Scotland for safety, while we endured three blitzes.'

'So all this gloom can end now?' he asked gently.

'You don't understand,' she whispered. 'It's not that . . . not that at all.'

'Then what is it?'

'Why are we here? What's it all about? One brief burst of life . . . well, it's simply not enough. To know . . . to feel . . . to love . . . *to be*. And after all that – nothing? Is it possible? Yet I don't believe in anything.'

Mere words would never help her, Simon sensed. She had enough of them every Sunday morning.

DI Rob McGuire, local police chief and now his friend, was the perfect companion for his escape strategy. The man was unassuming, straight talking, moral and trustworthy. So when they met once a week in a pub called *Ducks and Drakes,* overlooking a pebbled river with reeds and willows, they talked of pre-war matters like fishing, women, sport and how to get enough sleep, faced with their work loads. It was the first day of spring, and McGuire told him how his tulip bulbs were being dug up and eaten by badgers. He didn't grudge them their meal, but his wife was putting out bread and peanuts, hoping to save the rest of their spring bulbs. McGuire was a man Simon admired. He should have retired two years back, but he had agreed to stay on until the war's end to free younger men for the armed forces. He had taken the place of two men, he worked all hours and he'd aged more than he should have since Simon met him a mere seven months ago. His grey hair had turned almost white, but his eyes remained youthful and discerning.

They ate an excellent meal of trout, salad, new potatoes and minty, home-grown peas followed by a piquant apple pie, and it was only over coffee that they turned reluctantly to the job on hand.

'It's like this, Simon,' Rob began. 'The beach demonstration was created by this gang of misfits in order to play for time. They wanted to keep you and your guys off the beach for a few more weeks while they salvaged, or should I say pilfered, the rest of the copper, which they had moved to the furthest reefs. Until you came along, they were making a fortune taking a little at a time and selling it to the black market. There are four charges involved, including murder, so they'll be put away for a long time. One of them might be hanged.'

'When can we get the body back?' Simon appealed to the policeman. 'Helen is very depressed nowadays. A funeral might bring some sort of closure to a very unhappy period of her life.'

'Very soon,' McGuire told him.

So that left only Miro, Simon thought gloomily. He drove back to camp feeling depressed. How do you harden your heart against a boy of sixteen whom you trust and admire? Miro was kind and loyal, a boy of deep passions. He loved his foster family and proved this daily in so many ways. He spoke six languages, scored brilliantly in his exams, played soccer in his school team and he was a good swimmer. Simon felt that he was creating a bond with the boy.

Nevertheless, it was time to set a few traps around his room and as he had feared, Miro fell into most of them, leaving his finger-prints on the door handle, the desk and the lock of his briefcase, neglecting to put his papers back in the correct order and breaking the slender thread on his drawers and suitcases. Perhaps he thought being a spy was a cinch, particularly with Simon being out for hours and days at a time. It was time to trap him, but they hang spies in England, Simon reminded himself. This month Miro would turn seventeen and he was unlikely to be shown much mercy in wartime. Perhaps he should investigate his background a little more thoroughly. He would start with Helen, so he waited for the right opportunity to bring up the subject.

A perfect spring day had turned into a balmy evening. Helen had the night off from the canteen. She had put on some make-up and dressed attractively and Simon wondered if she were getting over her depression. They were sitting in the garden drinking sundowners which Simon had created and which he was rather proud of. Daisy decided to go for a walk down to the sea, but when Miro suggested he should accompany her she looked embarrassed and said she had arranged to meet a friend. Miro looked sulky and went up to his room.

'He's jealous,' Simon said, wondering if he should have mentioned it.

'Is it that obvious? I was hoping no one else had noticed. They have always been very close. Daisy sees him as her brother, but of course he isn't. I call him my foster son, but the truth is we're merely looking after him until the war ends.'

'Just how tough was it for him?'

'I'll never forget seeing him for the first time. He'd only been in the camp for a few months, but he was so skinny. You could see he'd been starved. He was frightened, too. The Nazis made sure that the kids' journey was humiliating and terrifying. They travelled in sealed compartments, food was limited and Miro had only the clothes he stood up in. Not even a coat. He travelled to Britain in a shirt and short trousers.

'He was handed to me at the station without ceremony or safe-guards or any idea of whether he would be properly looked after. I couldn't even reassure him, because he didn't understand me. He was ill. I called the doctor and he spent the next two weeks in bed. Daisy was wonderful. Within ten minutes of his arrival she found out that he could speak French. She was learning French at school so they could communicate a little. She spent most of her spare time with him, teaching him English.' Helen smiled sadly at Simon.

'After he recovered, I used to feel embarrassed taking him shopping, because people used to stop me in the street and say how thin he was. One woman even threatened to report me to social welfare.'

She chattered on, but Simon was having his own thoughts. What proof do we have that he really is Miroslav Levy, he wondered. The SS could have sent one of their own as an impostor. How could he possibly check on this? He turned his attention back to Helen.

'We had a few problems at first, but as you can see, it turned out well,' she was saying.

'What kind of problems? I mean, you're all so close now. How did this happen?'

'Oh, nothing much.'

'What were you remembering?' Simon asked.

'He used to hide food in his room, but he soon got over that nonsense,' she answered evasively.

'And after that?'

'After that what? Nothing! We were a family. He worked hard at school, his English improved in leaps and bounds. He feels like my son. We feel like a normal family.'

'But who sent him? How did he get out of the camp?'

'Kindertransport,' she said briefly. 'That's enough of your questions. Let's listen to the news.'

The news was exciting. The Tunisian Campaign was over. All enemy resistance had ceased, the Allies had taken 250,000 prisoners of war and they were now the masters of the North African shores.

'How about I cook the supper?' Simon said. 'I heard the news this morning and I brought champagne to celebrate. It's in the fridge. You stay and listen.'

Twenty

'Kindertransport,' Helen had said. So that was where he would begin. The organization was a complete mystery to Simon, but after a day spent on the telephone those involved had become akin to saints in his estimation. Slowly a strange story was unfolding. In 1938, a young English stockbroker, who wished to remain anonymous, travelled to Prague to help a friend working at an Adult Help Centre. Shortly after his arrival, he realized that there was no organization to save those children whose parents had been taken to the camps, so he stayed on, at his own expense, to help the children. He contacted the Refugee Children's Movement (RCM) in London and asked them to find foster homes and the financial backing they would need, plus Government approval for the wholesale evacuation of children imperiled by the German advance. Because of the ferocity of the pre-war German persecution of the Jews, the British Jewish Refugee Committee appealed to Parliament to admit as many children as they could rescue from genocide, up to the age of seventeen. The government insisted upon a fifty pound bond being guaranteed for each child to assure their ultimate resettlement, but they put no restriction upon the number of children who could be brought to England. The bonds were guaranteed by the Jewish Committee and a Quaker organization and within weeks the clerk was organizing the departure of trainloads of children from Prague.

The rumour of the 'Englishman of Wenceslas Square', which was where his hotel was situated, quickly spread and hundreds of Czech parents tried desperately to get their children on his list. He personally organized the evacuation of 669 children from Prague. Among them was Miroslav Levy, who was on the very last successful transport. A ninth train, with 250 children, was supposed to leave Prague station on September the third, but that was the day war was declared on Germany and the train was not allowed to leave the station. The children were never heard of again.

This heroic man's story was only part of the evacuation. Altogether, ten thousand children were brought to Britain with the cooperation and finance of Jewish, Christian and Quaker groups.

From a member of the PWE, Simon obtained a letter of

introduction to one of the organizers, a woman, Marion Boyd, who had been a nurse at the time and was retired. Simon explained that he needed information about the background of Miroslav Levy.

Mrs Boyd lived in Wimbledon in a bungalow almost hidden by tall oaks. She was heavy-set and strong, with iron grey hair cut short and for a moment, as he shook hands at the gate, he thought she had sent her husband to fetch him.

'How is Miro? Is he happy in his new home?' They had moved into her office and they were sitting on either side of a massive old desk.

'Yes, very happy,' Simon told her, 'but I need details of his background. Exactly how did he come to be put on your list? In other words, why did they let him out of the concentration camp? I would also like to see a photograph of him. Presumably your files contain passport pictures of the children concerned.'

Boyd's face registered her alarm. 'What has he done? Why are you investigating him?'

'No, nothing, but he will soon be seventeen, and many refugees are interned on the Isle of Man. He would prefer to continue with his studies. I need to know why the Germans let him leave the camp.'

'Surely you realize that even SS guards can be compassionate toward children, Captain Johnson. Don't you agree?'

No, Simon thought, but he merely nodded. He had no wish to antagonize the nurse so he changed the subject.

'I wonder if I could see Miro Levy's file?'

'I am most reluctant to reveal such private details. Why this interest in the boy from you, an American military man?'

'I admire you for your loyalty to your children, but of course your objections were predictable. I brought this letter of authority from the Foreign Office,' he said quietly.

'Very well,' Boyd said, after a brief glance at it. 'I'll fetch the file.'

While she was absent, her maid brought coffee and biscuits. Mindful of the rationing, Simon left the biscuits but drank the coffee. When Boyd returned, five minutes later, she looked flushed and angry.

'I understand your fears,' she began, 'but think of what this young man has been through.'

'It's my job,' Simon told her. No longer able to keep the flood of guilt at bay, Simon wished with all his heart that he was wrong. After all, Miro was only a boy of thirteen when he arrived. Yet instinctively he had always known there was something wrong. Miro was too concealed. He kept a tight lid on his feelings. He was watchful and cautious and he never let down his guard. Besides, he was systematically searching Simon's room.

'I know what you're thinking,' Boyd said. 'You're wondering if he really is Miroslav Levy. When you go through his file you'll learn that Miro was a very talented musician. He twice played solo with the Prague State Orchestra. Have you heard him play the clarinet?'

'As far as I know he has not mentioned music since he arrived in England.'

'Well then. You have an easy task,' she said.

Finding a good clarinet and some Van Doren reeds, which Simon had been advised were the best, was no problem in London, but how could he prevent Miro from realizing that he was checking on him? He couldn't, he decided.

It was bright and sunny when Simon arrived back the following day at noon, but he was feeling depressed. He had never hated his work as much as when he placed two provocative sibs from PWE into his briefcase and left it unlocked on his desk. He went to the kitchen to announce his intention of catching some fish around the wreck. Adding: 'I'll be at least an hour,' in case there was any doubt about this. Miro was sitting at the kitchen table helping Daisy shell peas.

Miro watched Simon leave and shortly afterwards saw him row out to the wreck in the small dinghy he had purchased for the family to mess around in. The peas were just about finished when Daisy announced that she was going to make an apple pie. Lately she was going through a period of domesticity and normally he would grumble, but it fell in with his plans. 'Suit yourself,' he said. 'I have better things to do.'

He ran up two fights of stairs and peered out of the attic window. Helen was helping John saddle the mares for her training class in the afternoon. He could see Simon sitting in the dinghy, which was bobbing over the waves. Daisy was absorbed with God knows what dreams of marriage and kids. She was practising making pies for a future family. He fought off a wave of depression and went into Simon's room. He listened to the mournful gulls and the sound of children's voices singing hymns in the church hall down the road and then he got to work. There was a memo written to Simon from his commanding officer stating that the Anglo-American installation of a rocket base at Eilean nan Ron, an island in the Outer Hebrides, was to be guarded equally by English and American troops. 'This base will be capable of sending rockets with atomic warheads as far as Berlin. The 29th Infantry has been picked to send a squad of fifty men, all of whom should be proficient in underwater construction, sabotage and unarmed combat. Pick your men and start training soonest. Our squad must be ready by mid-July.'

A wave of elation passed through Miro. So that's what Simon's men were doing night after night in the bay. There was no chance of Paddy seeing this one. The rockets could bring a quick end to the war and then perhaps he would find his parents. Miro put the memo carefully on the table and rifled through the rest of the file.

'Two thousand German prisoners-of-war have been turned and have volunteered to join American forces in the forthcoming invasion,' he read in a memo from ETOUSA headquarters to Captain Rose at the Mowbray camp. 'They are being housed in a prewar holiday camp called Pines in a farming area not far from the New Forest. Most of them are highly trained troops,' he read, 'but some have volunteered for underwater training and Simon should visit Pines at his earliest convenience and organize the classes.'

There was nothing else of value. Two thousand German POWs seemed like an excellent target for enemy bombers. He would have to change the venues, transfer the rocket station to the Pines and deliver the message verbally. Paddy could take it or leave it.

Lately Paddy's demands for more information were alarming him. It was always accompanied by threats to his parents. Finding news that satisfied him, while not actually harming the war effort, was becoming increasingly difficult. He was frightened most of the time, but he never forgot his mission: to send enough information to make his parents' board and lodging seem worthwhile to the SS. Simon's proximity, plus his careless handling of classified news, was a gift.

Ten minutes later Simon was bobbing gently over the waves, holding his rod in one hand, a book in the other, while leaning back on a lilo he'd brought along. It was a lovely Sunday morning early in May. The air sparkled, the sea was calm, reflecting the blue sky and fluffy clouds hung around the horizon. There was only one thing missing and that was Helen. 'Give her time,' he muttered.

By eleven he had a bucketful of codling and mackerel. He took the fish home and sat beside the stable tap scraping and gutting the fish until Helen came to find him. She managed a smile, which was a change.

'That will do nicely for supper. Plenty for everyone. Well done. Fish and chips and salad. How's that?'

'Just right.' He hated lying. The British penchant for chips with their fish was an on-going irritation to Simon, but anything that made Helen cheerful was OK with him right now.

'I'm going to shower. Where's Miro?' he asked when he found Daisy alone in the kitchen, busy making a pie for dessert.

'He popped out to see a friend.'

You bet he did, Simon told himself with an ache. He went to his room to check the briefcase. This time, apart from a thin thread which had been snapped in his briefcase, there was nothing to show that anything had been touched. His onerous duty now was to wait for Miro to be trapped.

It was noon, but it was almost dark. The frenzied wind sent low clouds racing across the sky, tore the petals off the late spring flowers and flung fistfuls of icy rain in the faces of the mourners. The stately procession following behind Eric's coffin were blown into disarray as women clutched their hats and skirts, umbrellas turned upside down and coats flapped like wings. The mourners gathered around the newly dug grave as the Reverend Thomas recited the prayer for the dead, 'Ashes to ashes . . .'

Holding her wreath, Helen was gripped by sadness. She had loved Eric for seventeen years, but now he was dead, horribly murdered, but it was hard to find the tears to cry for him. Daisy was dry-eyed, too. In a way it was a relief for Daisy to know the truth. The funeral should bring closure to the agony of not knowing. I am Mrs Helen Conroy, she told herself. I shall bear my widowhood bravely and resolutely. I loved my husband until he abandoned us. From now on I shall continue to be the sensible, hardworking Helen Conroy.

But she was not. Not any more. She was a stranger who quivered and shook at the sight of Simon, whose stomach churned when she heard his voice. At night she was filled with longing to be close to him, to touch him. For the first time Helen realized that her quick, incisive mind, her intellect, which she had always relied upon, was just a small part of her: a precarious minority rule over the emotional mass that made up the rest of her being. But not for long. She would force her body to obey her mind. She would not give in to lust.

At that moment a sudden gust blew up the coat of the woman standing opposite. Her hat blew off and as she reached for it she dropped her bouquet into the grave. 'To my beloved Eric,' Helen read. Looking up she hardly recognized Eric's pretty young secretary. Her hair hung limp around her face, her eyes were swollen from weeping and her breasts were leaking milk on to her dress. She must have travelled from Scotland for the funeral.

Helen stared at the woman with morbid fascination. She closed her eyes and tried to shut out the image of Eric's blue eyes gleaming with pride as he told her of his love for his pregnant secretary, and how she made him feel young and alive. How she had hated this woman, but now she felt sorry for her. All her hatred had slipped away. She clenched her fists and hung on to her composure.

Why had she come here? she wondered. Grieving for Eric was futile. He wasn't hers. Had he ever really loved her? Could he love anyone, other than himself? For the first time she saw him as he really was: narcissistic and neurotic. He had deceived this young woman, just as he had deceived her when she was only eighteen and he was thirty. Why grieve? It was time to start again.

'I'm going to work,' she told Miro, handing him her wreath. 'I should never have come. Look after Daisy. I'll see you later.'

'Are you sure you'll be all right?' His brown eyes were filled with caring as they linked with hers.

'Of course.'

She turned from the grave feeling as if a heavy burden had slipped from her shoulders.

Twenty-One

It was mid-June and a glorious summer day. Simon had the afternoon free and he and Helen were wandering through the wood looking for mushrooms. Hands in his pockets, Simon was hunched forward as if searching the ground, but he wasn't; he was miles way, Helen knew, and his thoughts bothered him.

'Whatever it is you are doing, I know it's good, because you are a good person. You must stop worrying so much. Please believe me.'

He turned looking puzzled and shocked, as if he thought she had read his mind.

'Tell me, Helen, do you believe that the end justifies the means?'

'Depends. I mean . . . sending a handful of men to their deaths in order to save a city . . . well, I suppose so, in wartime, if the end means saving vastly more people than you destroy, then yes. One strives towards . . .' For a moment she was lost for words. 'What do we strive for? Goodness? People? Love?'

'But what if we're striving to destroy an evil thing that has come amongst us and in so doing we destroy the very people that we love.'

'Perhaps the people destined to be destroyed should have a say in the matter . . . what if they volunteer for this dangerous mission?'

Instinctively she knew that Simon was heroic. He carried a torch, but for whom, or what, she had not discovered. His mind was all too often lost in another world.

'What are you thinking about?' she asked.

'Nothing.'

'Hardly anyone can think of nothing. That's a very difficult thing to do. Believe me, I've tried. I'm no good at meditating. You were working something out . . . or plotting your next move. Tell me about it.'

'You think enough for both of us. I'm just coasting along.'

He was up to something, but knowing Simon it could not be anything bad. She was as sure of Simon as she was of herself. What he needed, she decided, was love. We both need love, she thought. She reached out and took hold of his hand.

Simon glanced at her and she read the surprise in his eyes. She flushed.

'It's almost a month since the funeral,' she said. 'I wish . . .'

'Yes,' he said softly. 'Go on,'

'I wish to write off the past. I need closure and a new start. I wish I could mourn for longer. In fact, I wish I could have mourned, but I never did. I was in shock admittedly, but whatever I once felt had entirely gone.'

'You've been punishing yourself for far too long. It was never your fault.' They were walking through a copse of silver birch. As they followed the meandering path around a thicket of brambles and hawthorn, they found themselves in an open glade, and there was the folly squatting beside the cliff edge in all its oriental splendour.

'Jesus! It's bad enough from the bay, but from this angle it's a monstrosity. Did John build it?'

'No, his father. Owning a folly was all the rage in those days.'

'I didn't realize we had been walking in a semi-circle, or that we were so close to the cliffs. Did you?'

She flushed. 'Well, of course I know the woods very well. I played here all my childhood. I used to think that this was my own private house.'

He glanced at her suspiciously and then he laughed. 'So we haven't stumbled upon the folly by mistake. We've been making for it via a circuitous route and I've been duped, thinking that we needed the mushrooms.'

She ignored his gibe. 'It's bound to be full of spiders and dust.' Opening the door, she stepped inside.

'Someone's been cleaning up around here. What a devious woman you are. How long have you been planning this seduction scenario?'

'Couple of weeks I suppose, but we keep it clean anyway.'

'Lucky me.' He took her into his arms. 'I've been longing for the chance to show you just how much I can love you on a day-to-day basis.' He bent down and brushed his lips over her shoulder and became suffused with longing.

Helen sensed that his body was awakening with more than just an urge for sex. Much more. He ached to feel joy again, as she did, and to feel close to each other, to have the right to make love and to plan for the future. Her love would always be safe with him.

Time is a voyeur with an eye for the dramatic. Beguiled by pleasure or pain, it cannot tear itself away, but hangs around bolt-eyed, spiraling that one moment into a timeless zone. Or so it seemed to Helen.

Friends noticed Helen's sparkling eyes and glowing cheeks, but no one suspected a lover. As a GI billeted upon them, and there were so many, Simon's presence was taken for granted.

Mornings, they met up while riding to the beach. Some evenings he brought a bottle of wine to share while they watched the sun set behind the furthest bay along the coast, which they could see from the folly. They enjoyed the same music and art so they often met up at concerts and occasionally the theatre. Simon often passed by the canteen around eleven when Helen locked up. Then they would toss her bicycle into the back and drive home together. All these seemingly accidental meetings kept idle tongues at bay, or so they imagined.

If Simon was home late, he would creep in, shed his clothes and climb softly into bed; but she was a light sleeper, when she felt his naked body against hers she would catch hold of him and pull him close, wrapping her arms around his neck and pushing her lips on to his. She liked to sleep in Simon's room because it was downstairs and away from the children. But that was not the only reason. Simon had a single bed and so they lay very close, turning in unison, sharing their breath and their warmth. Even their heartbeats seemed synchronized.

This is not me, she told herself. What is happening to me?

The summer was ripening along with the plums and apples in the orchard, it rained most days and the gardens were muddy and damp, but Helen saw the beauty of the morning mist drifting amongst the trees, and noticed how the branches of the silver birches glistened against a backdrop of purple skies. She collected chestnuts and roasted them on the stove for the family, made blackberry pie, baked milk tart, rice puddings and recipes she learned from her mother. There was always mulled wine and supper warming on the stove, however late Simon was.

She loved him, and those who were close to her said nothing, because they loved her. She sang in the car, hummed as she worked, smiled at everyone and saw beauty in commonplace objects.

She gloated over her prize. How did she get so lucky? Her life had been spent waiting for him to appear. Her body was not her own. It was shared. Simon set his seal upon her flesh: a bite mark on her neck, a bruised nipple, swollen lips. She was beginning to look as if a piranha swam in her bed. She took to wearing darker lipstick and scarves.

British troops were having it easy for the time being, so Helen couldn't understand why her friend May from the factory was being so remote and curt, replying in monosyllables and seemingly in a world of her own.

'May, what's wrong?' Helen asked her one morning whilst they were taking a break in the canteen.

'Nothing, really. I'm just a bit depressed, for no good reason. '

'But why? We're winning the war . . . slowly, but surely.'

'Yes, but Reg is in the Eighth Army. I guess he'll be in the thick of the fight again. He can't be lucky forever. Every time I see the postman my stomach turns. He's endured thirteen months of fighting in the desert. He hasn't got nine lives. I just feel that it's too much.'

'Where is Reg now?'

'In the Eighth Army. That's all I know.' A sudden cold front seemed to have penetrated the factory.

'I'm sure he'll be all right, May. You mustn't anticipate the worst that could happen. You're not psychic. Be positive.' Helen said. 'Most of our soldiers will come home.' May nodded and tried to smile, but Helen read sadness in her hunched, slender shoulders. Cycling home she remembered how full of fun May used to be. She'd kept them all laughing with her jokes and stories. Maybe her separation from Reg had been much too long. If so, she wasn't any different to most other women in England. Their husbands were seldom home on leave and then only for short periods. She, too, would suffer when the troops invaded France. Helen could not help admiring May's courage, but there were dark shadows under her eyes and her skin looked drab.

By contrast, Helen was so happy she felt guilty and scared. Nothing lasts, she reminded herself.

'Do you love me?' Simon asked one morning.

'I don't know. I haven't thought about it,' she answered evasively.

The question remained in her head like a tune you can't stop humming. She loved his lips, so soft, sensitive and expressive, she was his harmonica, emitting sighs and gasps in place of melodies. She loved his shoulders, muscled yet comfortable, where her head lay, and the salty taste of his skin. Exploring his body with her mind obsessed her when she cycled to work. She loved the musky smell of him after sex, and the way his expression softened with caring when he looked at her. So many different kinds of love, focused on every part of his being.

Was that love?

★ ★ ★

The following week May called to tell her the news: the dreaded telegram had arrived. Reg had been killed in a road accident. She would be absent on sick leave for a week, she explained. Helen sent flowers and gifts, and called daily. She longed to be May's friend outside the factory, but May resisted all her advances.

'Give up Helen. You can't mix oil and water,' May said finally. 'Different income, different backgrounds, different tastes . . . it wouldn't work.'

'You're so wrong, May. This war and the American occupation will put paid to class divisions in England.'

'It'll take more than the Yanks to do that,' May said. Her call terminated with an impersonal click.

Damn you, May, Helen fumed to herself. How can England ever become a strong and united nation, if we can't throw off divisions of class that are straight-jacketing all of us, even in wartime?

Twenty-Two

Simon had been persuading Helen that the children deserved more fun, and he was right. The more she thought about it, the more determined she became that Daisy and Miro should have a great birthday party. Miro's and Daisy's seventeenth birthdays were seven days apart, on the sixteenth and twenty-third of June, so Helen decided to hold a joint party this year and it would take place on Saturday, the nineteenth.

Everyone was determined to make the party a success. Simon privately hired a GI three-piece band, the family room was emptied and French chalk was rubbed on to the floorboards. The dividing doors into the lounge were thrown open and the Welsh dresser was turned into a bar. Miro invited fifteen school friends and Mike wanted to bring along three friends, so Daisy had to find enough girls to even up the numbers. Finally she had four girls too many, so Mike invited another four GIs.

The five of them pulled together to plan the buffet supper. They had their own eggs, plenty of fish that Simon had caught and garden vegetables in abundance. Simon made pickled fried fish. Helen exchanged five pullets for a turkey and stuffed and roasted it. Simon persuaded the proprietor of his favourite restaurant to sell him a huge dish of lasagne, and he ordered several large cakes and plenty of coffee, while Mike mysteriously acquired several crates of cider and beer. John opened up his cellar and it was amazing what they found there.

Their first guests arrived just after seven and by eight the house was rocking to the heady beat of jiving. The girls shrieked as they were whirled around, skirts and petticoats flared. The GIs were all good dancers.

At nine, the dining-room doors were opened and there were gasps all around at Daisy's and Helen's amazingly artistic arrangements of the food and the flowers. Simon said a few words on Anglo-American relationships, which set them all laughing and he then presented Daisy with an emerald pendant and Miro with a clarinet.

'Hope you like it, Miro,' Simon said as he handed him the long, thin box.

This was a nervous time for Simon. He watched Miro's face, trying to discern his thoughts from his expression, but the boy kept his face rigidly impassive. He could have been at the waxworks for all the emotion he showed. *Come on, Miro. Look scared, or pleased, or melancholy. Any damn thing.* Miro was slowly opening the brown paper, folding it carefully and placing it on a side table. Come on, Miro, Simon agonized. The boy opened the box and withdrew the clarinet, and almost without thinking ran his hand over it, stroking it. Then his eyes met Simon's and the two remained locked in a moment that seemed to last forever.

'Thank you, Simon,' Miro said distinctly, as if standing on a stage. 'What an extravagant gift. I will treasure it.'

'And play it, I hope,' Simon replied.

Against the clamour of his school friends: 'Yes, come on Miro . . . Bet you can't play a note . . . Can you really play that thing?' Miro's eyes remained locked with Simon's. What were they saying? Simon wondered if he were imagining a touch of hauteur, or was it merely a memory of who Miro once was? There was sadness in the set of his mouth and in his eyes. Then Daisy rushed between them and the spell was broken.

Miro was well aware that Simon was watching him carefully. What did he expect to see: shock or sadness? He had learned to control his expression in the camp. To show even a glimpse of the hatred and disgust he had felt for the guards could have led to an immediate execution. He felt he was teetering on the very edge of disaster. His mind raced over the practical details of the gift. Simon knew he could play the clarinet. No one in England knew. He'd kept his past to himself. It belonged with his parents and their home in Volary. Naturally the Kindertransport organization had a file on him, and all the other children they had rescued. His few concerts were probably mentioned in his file, which meant that Simon had been checking out his past. Why would that be? Perhaps he thought he was an impostor. Either way it showed that Simon suspected him. He had known for some time that Simon was an intelligence agent. That would account for his close friendship with DI McGuire and the constant stream of classified information he received. There had been a huge fuss over that foolish attempted rape story and it was Simon who had calmed the locals, who were up in arms at the time. Once again he made an effort to pull himself together.

'Dearest Miro, you never *mentioned* a musical background. Can you really play the oboe?'

Miro turned his attention to Daisy. 'It's a clarinet, Daisy. Yes, I have played, but that was long ago, another lifetime, another me.'

The room was silent suddenly and Mike's voice seemed louder than it should have been. 'You have to practice daily, Daisy. I expect Miro has almost forgotten how to play.'

But Miro didn't want to be rescued by his rival. He launched into 'In the mood', and the guys in the band were sufficiently impressed to join in. The music was joyous, but Miro was far from being so.

He came to the end of his piece and bowed at the applause. It was a beautiful clarinet – it must have cost Simon a packet. The sound was mellow and strong and exactly right. It was a thing of joy.

Helen was crying, he saw. Why was that? She put her arm around him. 'All this time, Miro, and you never said a word. Why make a secret out of such a wonderful gift?'

Daisy was pleading for more, but he shrugged and went back to run the bar. It was his turn. Suddenly he knew exactly why Simon had left his briefcase unlocked, although it contained two top secret messages. The revelation was like an electric shock through his body. Simon was playing cat and mouse with him. Obviously there was no rocket base in the Outer Hebrides and Miro had moved this fictitious rocket to the Pines holiday camp. But what if the information went all the way to the Nazi hierarchy? What if they bombed the area? Could Simon have done all this planning by himself? There must be others involved. They were waiting to see if he had passed on the information. If Pines were bombed, he would be arrested and hanged.

All the while Daisy was helping with snacks, dancing with friends and introducing her guests to each other, Mike could not take his eyes off her. She was only four days off seventeen, yet she had blossomed into a lovely young woman. She was wearing a halter-neck blue dress with a tight bodice that flared into a full, ankle-length skirt. The blue matched her eyes and showed off her flawless white skin and sexy shoulders. Her ash blonde hair was tied in a pony tail with a sparkling blue clip. He had never seen anyone as lovely as Daisy, but he knew that although her looks had been the initial attraction, he had fallen in love with the real person . . . his Daisy, who could find beauty everywhere and in anything, who loved animals with a passion, rode like a demon, painted divinely and who, for some ridiculous reason, was sweet on him.

Mike had let his friends dance with Daisy from time to time, not wishing to alarm her mother, or antagonize her possessive brother, who watched her like a coyote on a rabbit. He had to look out for Captain Johnson, too. He knew that their commander had suggested that he should stay away from Daisy after the attempted rape furore. There she was, gazing over the shoulder of the guy she was dancing with, sending him messages with her eyes and shrugging to show the absurdity of their dilemma.

'Care to dance?' he asked casually, because she was standing beside her grandfather.

Daisy could not help laughing at him. Everyone knew they were together.

'Sure! Hang on a sec. Do you like to jive?' she asked, entering into the spirit of their play-acting. She signalled the band for something faster.

Moments later she was whirled over his shoulder, under his arm, twirling and jiving, skirt flaring, petticoats showing, while the guests moved back and formed a circle, clapping in time to the music.

Daisy was shrieking with laughter as Mike caught her and threw her and spun her and caught her. She knew all the moves. She'd become an expert dancer under his tuition.

'Listen,' Mike whispered, when the dance ended. 'When your friends leave, say you're tired and you're going to bed. I'll be in Daunty's stable.'

'I can't wait, but you won't leave yet, will you?'

'Of course not.'

Helen came in with some snacks and saw at a glance what was what. Until that moment she'd had no idea they were seeing each other regularly, but Daisy's prowess at jiving told quite another story. Apart from the outrides with Gramps and Miro, they must be meeting at the Palais. She looked towards the bar at John, who was collecting empties and shrugged, as if to show their helplessness in the face of young love. John raised his hands in a Gaelic gesture as he shrugged back. What was done couldn't be undone by the look of things. Only Miro's eyes burned with helpless rage and pain. He turned away as if unable to bear the sight of them.

Helen followed John into the kitchen to help wash the glasses. 'He's a nice young man,' she said placatingly. 'And a wonderful rider. Let's not forget that it is I who invited him here.'

'Aren't you worried?'

'No. I trust both of them and I like him.'

Most of the guests went home at one a.m. and shortly afterwards Mike's buddies announced that they would leave, after a couple of hints from Mike. Mike sauntered off to the stables and fell asleep in the straw, glad to find that Daisy had left a blanket over the partition. He woke to feel her snuggling down beside him.

Daisy was still a virgin and Mike intended that she should stay that way for the duration of the war, while he wasn't around to look after her, but they were both hot-blooded and imaginative, and their caresses satisfied both of them.

'Will we have a happy ending?' Daisy asked Mike that night as she lay in his arms. 'Will you keep safe for me?'

'Of course I will, and I'll take you home. You'll love the ranch. I have such dreams. My favourite is of you in the paddock, training a horse with our kids hanging over the corral. Of course, they all look like you.'

'I want a son who looks like you.'

'Oh darling. If only the darned war would end.'

'My dearest love.'

'What do you keep besides cattle and horses? Mike . . . are you asleep . . .?'

She snuggled closer and fell asleep beside him.

Cocky crowed, and Mike woke and sat up with a start. 'Wake up, Daisy,' he said urgently. He jumped up fast as panic gripped him. 'Daisy. Come on, Daisy.' He caught hold of her hand. 'We've overslept. It's almost dawn.'

'Gramps!' they whispered together as heavy footsteps approached from the house. 'Let's hide under the straw,' she whispered.

'You could hide. I'll tell him I drank too much, so I sat here to cool off and fell asleep. How will you get back to the house?'

'Dunno,' she said.

Gramps' footsteps echoed as he crossed the yard to the feed store on their side. Then there was silence as he walked inside.

'Quick!' she said, grabbing Mike's hand.

They fled. Mike leaped over the fence to the camp while Daisy raced through the open scullery door. Gramps saw them both and dropped the buckets he was carrying. The oats spilled over the cobbles and he swore angrily as he tried to sweep them into a pile with his hands. It wasn't the oats he was swearing at, but the Yanks, who were too cocksure of themselves, swaggering and brash, like that bloody horse the bugger liked so much. He stopped short, scowling, as he remembered the joke he'd laughed at in the pub last night. It was about a new brand of knickers: 'One Yank and they're off', but he no longer felt like laughing.

Twenty-Three

For the next two weeks Miro hardly slept or ate. At times he was in a state of denial, refusing to believe that Simon was trying to trap him, for the man remained as friendly and easy-going as always, even on their morning rides. At other times Miro would sink into a state of terror and plan how he would kill himself when they came for him. He was afraid to sleep because when he did his nightmare returned and it was always the same.

He is handcuffed and weak with fright. Half-supported by a policeman on either side, he is escorted to the place of execution. A priest is intoning prayers, but he longs to recite the prayer that must be on the lips of all Jews who are about to die: 'Hear, Oh Israel! The Lord our God, the Lord is One. And thou shalt love the Lord thy God, with all thy heart, and with all thy soul, and with all thy might.'

Miro's mouth is frozen and he cannot utter a word. They put a hood over his head, the noose is placed around his neck. He waits. The floor beneath his feet swings away. He falls . . . and wakes. This is not a nightmare, but a premonition, he realizes.

For Miro, two weeks of hell followed the party. Helen chided him daily for neglecting such talent. He must practice . . . and practice. Thank heavens they did not know that he also played the piano. That would upset Daisy. Much as he loved her, he had to admit that her great talent was art, not music. She strummed through her practice pieces like she battered their tough meat: thoroughly, painstakingly and glad to get the job done.

Usually, in the pre-dawn of summer, Miro would creep out to the summerhouse in the woods to practice his scales. It was the only way to keep his fearful thoughts at bay. It was amazing how his fingers still remembered their drill, although he had blocked music out of his mind.

He began to play a piece he learned a few months before they moved to Prague. He made a few mistakes and played a few bars over and over, but before long the music was flowing as freely as his daydreams. He was back with his family in Volary. The silk curtains rustled in the breeze, a cockerel crowed in the distance and Mama crept downstairs in her dressing gown and slippers, trying not to disturb him, but anxious to let the dog out. He smelled her perfume as she passed his open door. Was Mama still alive? Would she last out the war? Tears rolled down his cheeks as he played. Mama was so beautiful. Even in the camp snapshot you could recognize her delicate bone structure and her large, velvety eyes. Once her hair had been a rich and vibrant titian, but in the picture Paddy had given him it was white.

Miro had no foolish fancies that the war would soon be over, as many others had, but he knew that they would be victorious eventually. Germany was surrounded by Allies and if the troops succeeded in fighting their way up the heavily defended European beaches nothing would stop their advance from all sides.

Miro followed the war news assiduously. Last week had been a bonanza when Germany's Ruhr Valley munitions factories were put out of operation by an air attack on six dams. Using nineteen Lancaster bombers equipped with bouncing bombs, the pilots succeeded in sending their bombs bouncing along the surface of the water to destroy the well-protected dam wall overlooking the Ruhr and Weser Valleys in the heartland of Germany, flooding the entire area.

The coming invasion was the big question mark. To fail would put the Allied plan back for a year or two. Would his parents last that long? Who would feed them in their last days of incarceration? Would they be abandoned? Or would the guards open the gates as they left? And if they were freed would local civilians feed them?

Miro often imagined himself part of the British fighting forces. He would arrive in a Challenger tank and break down the gates and the barbed wire, to the cheers of the inmates who would surge around him. Then he would stride through the camp and find his parents. This was his favourite daydream.

Lately he spent more time daydreaming because reality was unendurable. He liked to remember the first nights of the concerts he and Mama attended. Mama always looked beautiful with her hair piled up over her head and held in place with diamond clips. She would wear a long satin dress, and a black cloak of embroidered velvet. She had always refused to wear furs. The truth was, Mama loved all animals and trees and flowers. Every summer she took him tramping through the woods around the Upper Vltava with their cameras and haversacks.

Sometimes Helen did that, too. Last summer they had packed sandwiches, water and flasks of coffee and cycled to Corfe Castle to explore the surrounding woods. He loved the English country-side; it was not dramatic like the woods and lakes around the Upper Vltava, but it was beautiful in a quiet way, with subtle pastel shades and exquisite cloud formations. Where would he live after the war? This wasn't his country and he wasn't English, Miro told himself time and again, so why did he feel that it was?

Darkness cloaked the earth, under a brilliant starry sky, but in the east came a glimmer of grey. Simon, who was toiling up the steep slope after a four-hour night diving session, heard the strains of a clarinet coming from the folly. A shrill note of startling clarity pierced the air. As if in answer a blackbird began its song to herald the dawn. As more birds chirped their morning chorus the air reverberated with their noisy song. Grey turned to rose, while the subtle chords of a clarinet mingled with birdsong. Then there was only birdsong.

He quickened his pace as he and the team lugged their gear up the steep slope.

'When will the road be fit for jeeps, Mike?' he asked.

'Give or take another few days, sir, depending upon the weather.'

'Did you hear that clarinettist? It was Miro. He's pretty good.'

'Sounded weird to me.'

'That's because you're a Philistine. He was playing Nielsen's 'Clarinet Concerto', if I'm not mistaken. It's a tough piece,' he said with satisfaction. Simon reached the top first and leaned against the Cooper's fence post. 'You go on. I'll stay here for a rest.'

When the others reached the camp, Simon followed the winding path to the summer house. 'Hi! That was brilliant. Money well spent.'

'How did you find out that I used to play the clarinet?' Miro challenged him.

'From Kindertransport. I went to see them and they showed me your file.'

'Why's that?'

'Routine? Any one of you could be a plant. If you were, you would be moved to the Isle of Man now that you've reached seventeen. You must know that. But no one could imitate a decade of training, to say nothing of the talent it takes to play that piece.'

The relief on the boy's face was obvious, but transient.

Simon went on his way wondering if he was delaying too long with his plan. But no, he decided. He had to wait for proof. Only German bombers would satisfy those PWE pundits.

*　　*　　*

Captain Rose had no love of the Brits. Not that he knew any personally, but he'd come into contact with workers and contractors, the police and British army officers in the past eight months since they arrived. He found them introverted, cold and odd. You never could tell what they were thinking, particularly since they said very little. What the hell did they think his boys were supposed to do with themselves? he wondered, remembering that silly business with the people who owned the fields they occupied. It was over two weeks since Cooper first voiced his complaint. Rose had been hoping that the entire matter would be forgotten, but now the man was waiting to see him. Damn!

Mike Lawson had volunteered to fight the Germans within days of America coming into the war, leaving his father to run their large ranch single-handed. Now he was stuck here – wasting time, as they all were – and for God knows how long, until the Brits decided it was safe to move into Europe. In Captain Rose's view they should have gotten straight over. Now he had to try to keep the men happy for up to another year, according to the latest prediction. It was absurd and ridiculous. He had a bunch of first-class boys in his camp – brave, tough, disciplined and aggressive – which was all Rose wanted from his men. Lawson excelled with all four of these virtues. His men needed their breaks from Army life. The regimentation and loss of individuality infuriated everyone. Facilities here were pathetic. Back home they had sports, movies and games. In Britain, the lack of radios, phonographs, magazines and baseball equipment was a constant complaint, plus the BBC's dominance of the airwaves. The difficulties of importing American newspapers, magazines and movies, meant that many GIs felt alienated from their culture. Back home the guys were likely to write letters home, listen to the radio, read magazines, or see a movie, whereas men stationed in England were drinking beer, playing cards or dating girls. Most of them complained of trouble in finding anything interesting to do on their free evenings.

The lack of responsibility, which army life encouraged, led to irresponsibility. Worst of all was the 'maleness' of their lives. Most of them – missing their wives and girlfriends overseas – cried out for female companionship, and to make matters worse the English women found Yanks attractive and desirable. They were only too happy to supply sympathy, companionship and help in relaxing. His guys deserved what little they got. At some time in the future they'd be required to risk their lives to win the war and some of them would never see their homes again.

All this went through his mind as he glanced again at Cooper's complaint that he had recently discovered that Mike Lawson and his granddaughter, Daisy, had spent the night together in the stables.

She could have said no, Captain Rose thought to himself. I don't suppose she was kidnapped. 'Send him in,' he told his sergeant.

Cooper was looking particularly frosty-faced. He said, 'It is over two weeks since I brought this matter to your attention, but there appears to be absolutely no progress on your part.'

'I quite understand your concern, sir. Pressure of work has been holding up our decision. I'll look into the matter immediately.'

'You must surely be aware that he has been forbidden to see Daisy, since that fuss about the attempted rape last September.'

Rose vaguely remembered something of the kind. He excused himself and went outside to get his clerk to find the file. So the boy had already been warned off her, he discovered. 'How old is your granddaughter at present?' he asked, when he returned. He tried to disguise his relief at hearing that she had passed seventeen.

'I don't think you understand,' Cooper retorted in his staid English accent. 'These two fancy themselves to be in love, but my grand-daughter is too young to make a permanent commitment, so I'd prefer Lawson to be transferred elsewhere.'

'What about your granddaughter . . . couldn't she be sent else-where?'

'Daisy has won a scholarship to study art in London, but my daughter, that is Daisy's mother, decided to keep her at home for a year, feeling that she was too young to cope with living alone in London.'

Captain Rose stood up. 'I'm sorry this incident arose. Personally I wanted to keep my boys and the locals at arm's length, but our commanders, in their wisdom, decided that Anglo-American friend-ship is the order of the day. Such a strategy leads to the kind of complaint you have indicated. I believe you've invited him to your home many times. However, I'll transfer Lawson. Good day to you, sir.' There was fury in his eyes as he contemplated Cooper.

Cooper looked relieved as he walked out of his office, but the captain did not share his optimism. In his opinion, Lawson would have something to say about this, and so would Simon Johnson. Best to get in first. He called his sergeant.

'I want you to transfer Sergeant Mike Lawson before the month is out.'

'Where to, sir?'

'Send him round the coast to teach scuba diving and underwater sabotage. Start him off at whichever camp is furthest away from here.'

'But sir, he leads the underwater team, in fact he's doing most of the training nowadays and there's a polo match coming up.'

Rose ignored him.

'How can he teach without equipment, sir?'

'Find out what he needs and then see to it.'

'Yes, sir.'

Twenty-Four

A few weeks after Miro delivered the news about the construction of a rocket base at the site of the prewar holiday camp, he woke to the sound of the air-raid siren. He came out on to the landing and saw Helen emerge from Simon's room. He smiled to himself. He was about to call out to her, but then he realized that she would be embarrassed, so he remained on the landing, leaning over the banister, wondering if the bombs were coming their way. Simon came out to join her, tying the cord of his dressing gown.

'My! You look respectable,' she teased. 'Should we wake the children?'

'No.' Simon replied. 'Let them sleep . . . at least for the moment. The bombers appear to be passing over the New Forest towards the coast.'

'How can you be sure? There's nothing there for them to target.'

'Let's say it's an informed guess.'

'No. Let's rather tell the truth.' Now she sounded irritable.

They were speaking in undertones, yet Miro could hear every word. For the first time he realized that the hall and landing were like a whispering gallery.

'I don't understand why they are coming this way? We might be in danger. I had better wake the children.'

'No, wait a minute,' Simon said. 'I'm pretty sure they're going to Pines.' He sounded satisfied.

'If you mean that old holiday camp? It's been abandoned since war began.'

'I suspect that's their target. Our searchlights and the guns will be waiting for them.'

'How do you know this?' Helen asked.

'I don't know, but I was warned that it might happen. It's classified, so don't ask. They should drop their bombs any minute and make off across the Channel.'

The blitz began, incendiaries were dropping, lighting the eastern horizon with a ruddy glow, searchlights crisscrossed the sky in their endless search, four enemy bombers spiralled down, engines screaming, to erupt in a massive explosion.

Miro was hardly aware of the action. He was gripping the banisters and trembling violently. Daisy came out of her room, fastening the belt of her dressing gown. She linked arms with him.

'My word, you're shaking like a leaf,' she said.

'I'm freezing,' Miro lied.

'Sh!' Helen said quietly. 'Here come the children. We'll talk later.'

'I have to leave for London at once, Helen. I don't know when I'll be back, but I hope later today.'

Of course he had to go, Miro realized. Simon now knew exactly who had passed on the message. His legs seemed to have turned to rubber as he stumbled into the bathroom. He felt unreal, as if he were watching himself from a great distance. Wave after wave of nausea was rising from his gorge. He was too shocked to think straight. He had felt like this once before, nearly four years ago, but right now it seemed as if it happened only seconds ago. He collapsed on the cold floor tiles, his head in his hands, unable to prevent himself from reliving the trauma.

They had been locked in a cattle truck all day, but the train only left Prague in the late afternoon. It progressed with constant stops and starts and long waits, but they were given no food or water and they were all suffering. Miro was wedged in the corner, holding his hand over his mouth and nose to try to stop himself from throwing up. The smell worsened. Children were crying and they were all terrified. Later that night the metal door opened with a crash and they were greeted with loud shouts, blinding searchlights and ferocious dogs.

'Be quick! Get out,' the guards shouted.

People were crying out, 'What's happening? Where are we?' Pushed from behind, some of them tumbled to the platform, hurting themselves, but they scrambled to their feet to avoid the blows. The guards were carrying *schlags* and hitting out at anyone in reach. His father grabbed Miro's arm and tried to shield him from the blows. They were marched through mud and pouring rain to God knows where. Miro and his father remained close together, afraid that they might be separated. Two hours later they reached the concentration camp called Dachau. They had heard the rumours. Drenched, exhausted and scared, they passed through a large gate with tall towers on each side manned by two guards with machine guns and a rotating searchlight which dazzled them. They kept going until they reached a large shed, but then they were separated. Men to the left, women and children to the right.

Hanging behind, Miro had a last glimpse of his father being pushed into a shed. Then he followed the line of women and children.

'Undress, be quick,' the guards shouted. They were told to hang their clothes on the rails. Everyone was handed a piece of soap and they stumbled naked into a large square room with rows of shower roses in the ceiling. The doors closed and they waited, tense and scared. No one could guess what fate awaited them. Rumours abounded, but no one knew anything for sure, except one terrible truth: you never heard from anyone after they were taken away.

A strange thought came to him: is this the end of the nightmare? Mothers were clasping their children to them. Suddenly, unbelievably, warm water drenched them. After the filthy cattle trucks they were able to get clean. They were herded into another room and handed striped prison pyjamas. Then Miro was marched to the children's sector. He didn't see his father again, nor his clothes or shoes. God knows who owned the clothes he was given to wear when he was sent to Prague, or whether he was alive or dead.

But now he wasn't in the camp. He was lying on the bathroom floor feeling confused. This nightmare would pass. It was over. He was safe in England. Then he remembered: his life had unfolded into a new reality, far worse than before. He had added guilt to his fear and misery and he faced the prospect of being hanged.

Had Simon laid a trap? If so, he had fallen into it. But it was the fate of his parents that tormented Miro the most. They would be executed. Terezin was supposed to be a model ghetto, set up specifically for Red Cross inspections. They never saw the fear and the dread engendered by the sight of hundreds of people being shifted out daily on the cattle trucks. They all wanted to believe they would be able to remain in Terezin and be relatively safe. Now his parents would live out the nightmare of the cattle trucks again, but for them it would be real.

Why don't I kill Paddy and then kill myself?

The thought was inviting. He knew exactly where Helen kept her gun and he knew he could kill him. But how would that help his parents? There must be another way. Think! Think! But he couldn't get control of his mind. He forced himself to wash his face, stumble downstairs and rejoin the family. Daisy looked relieved to see him. 'You look awful. Do you feel any better?' she asked, gazing at him solicitously.

'Yes, thanks.' He shook off her arm.

By now John was awake and standing in the kitchen. 'That's it,' he said. 'The show's over. Back to bed you two.'

Miro lay on his bed trying to make a plan. It seemed to him that there was no way out. The only way to prevent Paddy from telling his controllers there was no rocket base at Pines was to kill him.

Simon arrived at PWE headquarters at four thirty a.m. Once there it took all his tact and guile to persuade the night staff to call the gang to Bush House. It was short notice and he wondered if they would come, but by six they were all present.

They were chuffed by Simon's success. There had been no casualties at Pines, they told him, because the caretaker and his dog had been moved elsewhere. 'Just in case,' Alf explained. Four enemy bombers had been shot down and Jerry had wasted a fortune. They had several more sibs ready to pass on to Simon's mole.

'No. I can't take them. Listen to me.' Simon had to convince them. 'I don't believe that my contact is grabbing everything he can lay his hands on and delivering it to his controller. He's being selective. That could be dangerous for our plans. He's a loose cannon. Let's take last night. Ten formations of enemy bombers pulverized the abandoned camp, yet we have not yet provoked a response to the news that a highly evolved rocket, with warheads capable of blasting five acres to smithereens, is nearing completion in the Outer Hebrides. Why not? Because he didn't pass on that information as it was given to him.'

'But they bombed Pines, old boy,' Rob said.

'And with such ferocity . . . ten formations of bombers . . . to wipe out two thousand turned POWs. For God's sake be realistic,' he shouted in exasperation.

'I must admit we have queries about this from the Foreign Office,' Dick admitted. 'They smell a rat.'

'I think it's time you came clean with us, Simon,' Alf said. 'Who is this suspected spy and why does he have to produce the goods for his masters? And why is he messing around with the sibs?'

Simon had known that he would have to reveal Miro's identity sooner or later. Perhaps now was the right time. 'He's just a boy and they have his parents in one of their ghastly camps. What could be more compelling than trying to keep your mother alive? I don't suppose there will ever be a raid on Eilean nan Ron, because he didn't pass on that sib. And why? Because he didn't want to damage the war effort.'

'We should arrest him,' Dick said quietly.

'I'm prepared to compromise. I'll bring him in, but I need your support to keep him out of prison and to convince him that we are on his side. That's why you need to put out a broadcast.' He glanced at his watch. This was taking too long and it would soon be too late. 'Put out a news release stating that Pines was under military surveillance, and that some vital, top secret construction was taking place. If you do that, we'll have a grateful, clever boy and, even more important, his Nazi masters will be so pleased with him because they won't know that they have been duped. This will provide him with the means of keeping his parents alive while saving his soul. Plus, we'll have an outlet for all our disinformation.'

They began arguing amongst themselves.

'How can we employ a boy of seventeen?' Rob asked.

'If he's old enough to be interned, he's old enough to be useful.' That was Alf, who seemed to be on his side.

'Why wasn't he?'

'He was only thirteen when they released him from the camp to the Kindertransport organization,' Simon replied.

'Surely someone should have suspected that there was reason behind their unlikely philanthropy?'

'His father is a talented Czech composer. The boy was an accomplished clarinettist, having twice played solo at Prague's concert hall. That was the reason given for letting him go.'

'He should be sent to the Isle of Man. It's not that bad. I went there to check up. They'd definitely let him practice the clarinet as much as he likes.' Dick said.

'You're missing the point – he spies to keep his parents alive and that is why he can be extraordinarily useful to us.'

'This makes sense,' Alf said. 'I vote we give it a go.'

'Bring him to us,' Rob said. 'We have experts who'll do the debriefing. You can't get involved.'

'How long will it take?'

'A week . . . a month . . . six months. All depends.'

'It seems we're agreed. Over to you, Alf,' Dick said.

Alf was typing while he composed the brief. 'At two a.m. this morning, ten waves of German bombers inflicted heavy damage on the southern coast of England, around an area known as The Pines. Six months ago . . .'

Breakfast was being wheeled in on a trolley and laid out on a

table. Simon reckoned that his job was done and he could enjoy a
good breakfast.

At half past six, Miro washed and went downstairs. Helen had the
coffee percolating and breakfast was ready. He sat down at the table
wondering how he could force himself to eat. John turned on the
radio for the seven o'clock news.

'Just in time,' he said, as a voice emerged from the static.

'. . . the Home Service of the BBC. Here are the news headlines,
read by Alvar Lidell. Just before dawn this morning, ten waves of
German bombers inflicted heavy damage on the southern coast,
around an area known as The Pines. Six months ago the land was
bought by the government to build a secret military installation,
rumoured to be a rocket station. Local villagers state that both
American and British troops have been seen patrolling the area,
which is out of bounds to civilians. Whatever the purpose of the
construction, the site has been razed to the ground by enemy
bombers, four of whom were shot down during the raid. In Parliament
yesterday . . .'

Miro felt paralysed with uncertainly. Had he made a mistake? The
rocket base was in the Outer Hebrides, only he had changed it.
What the hell was going on? He'd been duped. But why? Had he
been responsible for destroying the best chance the Allies had for a
quick end to the war?

Miro got up and left the room. Running upstairs, he locked his
bedroom door, shifted his chest of drawers and pulled up the loose
floorboard. He took out his notes and read through them. There
was no mistake. The memos to Simon had stated that the rocket
base was being constructed in the Outer Hebrides. The old holiday
camp was where the German POWs were being housed. He felt as
if he were going mad. Running downstairs, he reached for his duffel
coat and ran to his bicycle. Moments later he was pedalling towards
Pines.

The morning sun rose ruddy in a clear sky. By eight, the sun's
heat had warmed the earth, releasing the scent of damp grass and
wild herbs. A sharp tang of ozone was rising from the sea, but Miro
had no eyes for the beauty of the morning. He searched in vain for
signs of the military and eventually settled for two ARP men trying
to straighten a broken sign which read: 'Pines Holiday Camp, closed
for the duration'.

'Were they all killed?' he wanted to know.

'Who's that then, young lad?' one of them said.

'The German POWs.'

'You've got noises, young man. I'd go home and rest if I were you. There's nowt here but old huts and one main dance hall. The rubble's over there, but you aren't allowed in. The land has been for sale for this past twelve months. Who would want it now? Off you go then.'

So Miro investigated the adjoining wood. Soon he was perched on the tallest pine tree, scanning the demolished camp with John's binoculars, which he had borrowed for the occasion.

He took a last look to satisfy himself that there was no rubble, no barbed wires, just craters with scattered broken masonry, and splintered wood as far as you could see. He felt strangely disorientated as he climbed down the tree.

Helen was talking on the telephone when Miro reached home. 'But darling, we don't have enough coupons for a lamb roast. Be reasonable. Tell you what, get a chicken from Mrs Smith. Tell her I'll send her a parachute.' So Daisy was out shopping. He could see John mucking out the stables.

Miro crept upstairs to Helen's room, turned the door handle quietly and stepped inside. There was a vague smell of lavender, perhaps from the little muslin bags Helen filled to go into her drawers. He knew exactly where she kept her gun because Daisy had shown it to him. It was in the bottom drawer under her petticoats. He didn't feel bad about stealing it. Helen no longer needed it. She had acquired it early in 1940 in order to be able to fight the Germans should they invade Britain. Eric was in Iran at the time. All threat of invasion was over and she should have handed it to the police, like everyone else, but she had hung on to hers.

Miro's hands were shaking as he took the gun and a box of six bullets, which was all that he would need. He shut the drawer, took a deep breath and opened the door. Fortunately Helen was still on the telephone. He crept downstairs, waved to Helen and left via the back door. It was much too early to meet Paddy, but he could not risk staying at home since Helen might discover that her gun was missing. He would hang around the beach, he decided. He set off on his bike.

He was calmer now, and a great many puzzling facts were fitting together like a jigsaw puzzle presenting a picture that he didn't want to see. It was right there, always had been, but he had not bothered to look the facts straight in the face. He'd stupidly believed that Simon was not investigating him. What were those reassuring words Simon had uttered when he came across him practising in the folly: 'Any one of you Kindertransport children could be a plant. If you were, you would have been moved to the Isle of Man by now, since you've reached seventeen. But no one could imitate a decade of hard training, to say nothing of your talent.'

Flattery and reassurance had smothered his common sense and he had continued to rifle through Simon's work for something innocuous that Paddy might consider useful. And Simon, as if to show that he trusted him, had been just as friendly and helpful as ever, leaving his door unlocked, his bin full of crumpled, classified memos and his briefcase open on his desk. Miro shuddered. He couldn't think straight, but he knew what he had to do.

Twenty-Five

Simon returned home from London late that evening. At first the house seemed empty. Then he saw that the door of his room lay open.

'Helen!'

Hurrying to the doorway he saw her standing at the window. Her back was turned to him and for an insane moment his spirits soared and he imagined that she wanted to make love. He had a stray memory of Helen sitting astride him, as she had been two nights ago, her mouth swollen with passion, her eyes half-closed.

Helen turned abruptly and her expression dispelled all such foolish dreams.

'Helen what's wrong?'

'I don't know. I don't know what's happening. Miro has gone and he's taken my gun. Something is going on and I know that you are involved. Get him back, Simon. I'm telling you now . . . I want him back here unharmed and I don't want the police to hear about the gun. Don't call them.' She stepped forward and gripped his shoulders hard. 'Safe and unharmed, do you hear me? Do that for me.'

He's not a child, Simon wanted to tell her, but now was not the right time. 'I'll do my best. Where's John?'

'He's out looking, too.'

Moments later Simon was speeding out of the driveway in his jeep. He glanced at his watch. It was ten p.m., that curious time of the evening when headlights are swallowed by the gloom and visibility is down to a few metres. His team had been keeping an eye on Miro for the past few weeks. They knew where he met his controller and where his controller lived. They also knew his name, which was Brannigan, and his shop, and they had been following him for weeks. So far he had led them to three other spies in his network. The PWE didn't want him picked up yet. He was too valuable where he was.

Miro always met Brannigan between eleven and midnight on summer evenings when twilight lingered, but Simon didn't have much time. He called his PA.

'I need backup fast. Send some of the team to the main Mowbray roads from London and Claremont. Call me at once if Brannigan passes in his van or his car. I may need you to go after him, so be quick and have a motorbike at each point.' It was unlikely that Paddy had changed the meeting place. He'd just have to hope for the best.

Why would Miro want the gun? To kill himself? Or to kill his controller? Both, Simon reckoned. If Miro realized that the game was up he would be very frightened. Frightened boys are dangerous, both to themselves and to others. Simon pressed his foot on the accelerator.

Miro listened to the gentle splashing of the waves and smelled the seaweed and shellfish exposed by the low tide. A slight breeze from the sea brought a tang of ozone. It was colder than he had realized and he shivered. Gulls were crying from the neighbouring rooftops and he heard the occasional car drive by. Once a couple walked past the pillbox. Lovers perhaps. He heard the throb of a fishing boat returning to harbour half a mile down the coast and later he heard voices raised in the parking square behind the beach. He tried to concentrate on these familiar sounds and not to think of what he was about to do. It was over for him, and his parents, but he was determined that Paddy would die, too, because he was the enemy and he had to be put out of the way. God knows how many others were caught in his web.

Half an hour later, Miro heard a jeep pull up. The engine started up again and the driver moved a hundred yards along the road before parking. Footsteps came softly along the pavement and down the wooden steps to the beach. Someone was creeping towards the pillbox. It was Simon, Miro decided. Helen had discovered that her gun was missing and Simon had come looking for him. So he knew where they met. He wondered what more Simon could possibly know. He had underestimated him. They might have been watching him for weeks. The footsteps paused outside the pillbox and he heard a rustle of fabric as Simon squatted by the entrance.

Miro tightened his grip on the gun.

'I know you're in there, Miro. You shouldn't leave your footprints all over the damn place. When you work for me you'll have to do better than that.'

Miro shivered. He wasn't going to be fooled that easily.

'Come out. I know exactly what that place is like. Fetid air, sand sodden with urine, so come out before you catch something. I promised Helen I'd bring you back safe and sound.'

Don't bring Helen into this, he longed to say, but he decided to remain silent.

'It must have been hell having to choose between working for the SS and letting your parents die. You thought you were locked between two evil choices, but you were wrong, there is another way . . . a way out for you and your family. I was waiting for the right opportunity to tell you. As a double agent you would be very useful to us, and you'll be able to satisfy these creeps sufficiently to keep your parents alive. I'm coming in, Miro. We have to talk. We don't have all night. Brannigan usually gets here around ten thirty to eleven.'

'I don't believe you, Simon.'

'So far twenty-three spies have been caught in Britain. Nineteen of them have been turned and are working for the Allies. Four Nazi zealots have been hanged. It's standard procedure.'

Was he merely one of them? Simon's words hurt. 'Keep out,' he said softly. 'I have a gun, it's loaded and I'll see you clearly silhouetted against the sand. I have something to do tonight and if you try to stop me I'll shoot you.'

'I don't think you'll do anything of the sort,' Simon whispered. 'We're friends. I'm coming in. Please don't shoot Brannigan. We need him to pass on our disinformation.'

'Don't . . .' Miro said loudly. 'Don't come any closer.'

The dim light darkened as Simon blocked the exit.

Miro put the gun down. Simon was right. He couldn't shoot him.

'Give me the gun, Miro. Is it loaded?'

'Yes. The safety catch is on.'

He handed it to Simon, who ejected the bullets and put the gun and the bullets in his coat pocket. 'Came out of the ark by the look of things. It's a good thing Helen never used it. She might have blown her hand off.'

'How long have you known?' Miro asked.

'I suspected you ever since I arrived here . . . even before then. There had to be a reason why they let you out of the camp. They aren't philanthropic, as far as I know. Have you any proof that your parents are alive?'

'They send me snaps from time to time.'

'Did you hear the news this morning?'

'Just the news . . . is that it? Yes, I heard it. How did you guess that I'd transferred the rocket station?'

'I knew you wouldn't reveal a rocket station to those bastards, but from the enemy's viewpoint, the exercise was far too costly merely to annihilate POWs who had turned traitor.

'Listen Miro,' Simon continued, 'surely the news bulletin proves that I'm backing you? It was broadcast to save your ass. Come on, Miro. Let's get back to the jeep. I have four teams looking out for Brannigan. They'll contact me on the radio when he's on the way, but you never know. He might even walk here.'

'I can't leave. I have to deliver some information and you know why. When I come empty-handed they cut back their food.'

Simon swore. 'What have you got?'

'Nothing much. Your memo about the Yanks stockpiling masses of equipment in the New Forest, but I changed that to Dartmoor.'

'The Foreign Office has to check all the info we pass on. They call them s' s, from the Latin—'

'I know,' Miro said.

'Then you should know that you can't change them around to suit yourself. Give it to me. It will be more useful later. Meantime you can tell him that a twelve-man team, set up by me, has learned the rudiments of underwater sabotage and that we are ready for a night raid on Calais to inspect the defences. Oh yes, and there's something else. Tell him the Brits are sending financial aid to the anti-Hitler movement inside Germany. Tell him it's almost a million strong. That should wipe the smile off his ugly face.'

'Why should I want to tell him about the sabotage?'

'You won't be giving him anything that's factual.'

'So what happens next?'

Simon exhaled with relief. It was over.

'I'll take you to London to meet the real agents – not amateurs like me. You'll have to put up with a gruelling interrogation lasting days, or weeks. After that comes specialized training which takes a couple of weeks . . . probably longer. Tell Paddy that you are being sent away for a month's musical study with a family friend who lives near Canterbury. We want him to believe you when you tell him about the vast array of US technical equipment being stacked all over Kent. You'll be sent to a school in Kent to learn the things you'll need.'

'And then?'

'Life will carry on much as it is now, except . . . and I must be honest here . . . it will be more dangerous for you, because you might get caught. Of course you'll get paid.'

'But after the war . . . I'll face the music?'

'No. If you're smart you'll be able to put yourself through university with what you will have saved. Take care. We're with you, Miro. All of us. See you later.'

'What about your footsteps?'

Simon swore. 'Good thinking.' He scuffed them with his jacket. The sand was dry and it worked.

Paddy arrived at eleven p.m. and found Miro squatting on the ledge outside the pillbox. He told him what he had supposedly overheard Simon telling John. Paddy seemed satisfied.

'Not bad, Miro, not bad at all. In fact, well done! Your mum will get caviar, my boy.'

Miro hoped that Paddy couldn't see the fury in his eyes. Was he really human? Hell was too good for him.

Paddy seemed pleased when he heard about his holiday. He wanted an update on US equipment stashed around Kent and details of additional troops arriving. 'We need some juicy gossip, Miro. Everyone's too pally around this area. How about the black market? That's a fertile area. See what you can find out.'

Miro said goodbye and cycled home, but something was different tonight – what was it? He paused some distance down the road and stood still, scenting the air, listening and feeling the vibes. It was well after dark, but some birds were still singing and there were rustlings in the grassy ditch beside the road. He smelled honeysuckle and privet in bloom, and the strong scent of tobacco flowers from a neighbouring garden. But what was new? Then it came to him. He had lost that spooky feeling, a sense that someone was targeting a spot between his shoulder blades. He felt as if he'd shed a heavy load. The penny dropped at last: they must have been following him for weeks, but tonight no one was targeting him. He was completely alone and it felt great. Jumping on his bike, he sped home.

Miro endured Helen's tears and hugs and reprimands and insisted that he had only borrowed the gun to shoot a badly maimed rabbit caught in a trap.

Later, in bed, he wept because at last he was able to live with himself. He wept for his parents, too, who had encountered only hatred, and for himself, because he had found only love which he was sure he had never deserved, and he wept for Helen, who would worry about him for the rest of the war, and Simon, who he knew loved him, too, and he wept for every Jew who had ever been abused. Finally he wept for all humanity because now he knew that people were filled with love, but sometimes that love was smothered and suffocated, through no fault of their own until they lost faith in themselves and forgot who they really were. Mainly he wept with relief.

Twenty-Six

As Mike drove towards the village centre on Sunday morning he had an impulse to turn back to camp. He had planned this stolen day to give him a chance to explain to Daisy what had happened, but he could hardly face her. It was his fault for falling asleep. He understood Gramps and knew where he stood with him. The old man wanted to keep his family in England, but he'd been sneaky and underhand in going to their company commander. Captain Rose was determined that 'his boys' would not marry foreign women and he'd taken Cooper's side without bothering about the emotional repercussions, although he'd had the nerve to lecture Mike at length on doing the right thing by 'this young lady'. Mike guessed that Daisy could do better for herself, perhaps living on a ranch was not ideal for a talented artist, but she wouldn't find anyone who loved her more than he did.

It was early September and the day was perfect, warm and sunny without a cloud in sight. He was driving past farmlands, with occasional stone cottages set between the fields and before him the morning sun shimmered on the dew-damp road. This year's lambs were fat and glossy and almost fully grown and the wheat was ripening, as strong and healthy as you like. He swerved to miss a partridge racing across the road. A good place for farming, he thought, but he'd rather be home. Daisy and he would build their own house right next to Pa's, or maybe down across the river beyond the willows. It was nice there, with ducks in the dam and trees all around. He began to plan the house and almost before he knew it, he was pulling up at the bus stop.

There was Daisy, looking so pretty in her blue floral frock, with a white leather belt and her hair piled up on top of her head, a straw purse flung over her shoulder.

He waved and Daisy ran towards him, cheeks flushing, eyes sparkling, her fine blonde hair loose and bouncy. He hurried around the jeep to help her in and she pounced on him, but he fended her off. 'Whoa there! Hang on . . . let's get out of the village first.'

As soon as they were out of sight of the village, Mike pulled up on a grassy verge to kiss her. Her thighs were warm against his. 'It's real nice here,' he said, feeling down in the mouth at having to leave.

'What's the matter with you?' Daisy asked. 'You're different . . . you even kissed differently and you're making an effort to talk. You never have to make an effort. What's got into you?'

'No, nothing.' Perhaps he should tell her now and get it off his chest.

Daisy snuggled hard against him and he stirred uncomfortably, remembering what her Gramps had said, 'I don't want to see you here again, at least not until the war is over. When the war's over you can do what you like, by which time Daisy will be old enough to know her own mind.'

She brushed her lips against his cheek. His frustration hurt. Something stronger than him needed to impale her under him, take her far away and guard her forever. *Oh, Jesus! I don't know how to handle this. I never felt like this. I need to get out of here.*

He said, 'Let's get out of the jeep and walk a bit.'

'All right.'

There was a gap in the hawthorn hedge. Mike held back the branches and helped her through. He took off his coat and laid it on the grass.

'But we're going sailing, aren't we?' She looked anxious.

'Of course. I just thought we might sit here and talk for a while.'

She flung her arms around his neck and snuggled up close, but Mike was reluctant to start again. He'd come here to spill the beans and she wouldn't like it, but with Daisy pressing against him he could hardly bear the frustration. It was too painful.

'Ease off, Daisy. I just can't trust myself. I'm worried about you. We've gone about as far as we can go without "doing it". If we were to make love and I got killed and you got pregnant . . . Hell! It doesn't bear thinking about. No more petting. Truly. If I survive the war, I'll be back for you, you can count on that.'

He'd intended to tell her that this was goodbye, but he didn't have the guts, so he stood up, feeling foolish and chicken-hearted.

'You *will* survive, dearest darling Mike. You *must,* for me.'

'One last kiss,' she said, grabbing him and pushing her mouth towards his, but he didn't respond, so she hung around his neck. Legs dangling, she tried to reach his lips. She fell back rubbing her arms. 'You are a spoilsport today,' she grumbled.

'Let's make the most of the day. Come on. Race you back to the car.'

As they bumped along the uneven country road, they were equally awkward and tongue-tied, each engrossed with their own worries.

Mike had booked a flat-bottomed boat at Sandbanks Yacht Club and he hoped they would enjoy a day fooling around Poole Harbour. He had a hamper hidden under his parka in the stern. They would find a great place to picnic and he would tell her afterwards.

All the way to Sandbanks, he felt unbelievably awful, his throat so swollen he could hardly swallow. His lips were parched and his eyes burned, but men don't cry, so of course it was hay fever.

Why was Mike acting so strangely? What had he meant by 'we have this day'? She could see that he wasn't intending to tell her, but why spoil the treat by sulking. It was a lazy, somnolent morning, hot, but not unpleasantly so. They sailed for a while and then Mike pulled the boat up on the banks of Brownsea Island, which was private property, but there was no one around. They sat on the sandy shore and listened to the water splashing over the sand and the drone of insects. A blackbird was singing in a wild peach tree. They had little to say to each other. When Mike reached out and put his arm around Daisy, she felt happy beyond anything she could remember. She sat breathless, watching a cormorant diving in and out of the water.

'This is the happiest day of my life,' Daisy said eventually. She smiled at him and he felt entranced by her and pulled her roughly towards him, crushing her against his chest. But he kept his hands to himself and Daisy wondered why he had changed so much. It became hotter and the sea water gurgled invitingly.

'Let's . . .' they both began.

They had been naked together before, but always at night. Never in broad daylight and never in the sunshine. Daisy looked around nervously. 'I should have brought my bathing costume.'

'Nonsense. I've seen all of you, bit by bit.'

'But not all together,' she said.

Mike jumped up and took off his shirt and trousers. When he kicked off his pants and stood naked, Daisy gasped. She had never taken in the whole of him. He was lovely. His suntanned body rippled and shone, but his buttocks were pure white. When he turned she saw that he wanted her so much, and she him.

'Cold water is what I need . . . and fast,' he muttered. He waded into the water and soon he set off in a fast crawl. Daisy went behind a rock and thought about it. Shall I? she asked herself wistfully. 'No.' she said firmly. But for some strange reason she was removing her clothes piece by piece. The breeze caressed her skin, the sun soaked in and she had the strangest feeling that this was so familiar, yet she had never done this before. She set off after Mike, and soon they were swimming side by side. He was her man. She felt so strongly that they had always been together, but were separated by some accident of birth. The afternoon flashed past and suddenly it was time to go.

The silence on the drive home was louder than any words.

'What is it?' she said eventually. 'You have to tell me what's wrong.'

'I shouldn't have fallen asleep. I should never have let Gramps catch us out like that. He said I was being selfish. That if I survive the war I can come back here and start something serious with you, but meantime I should get lost.'

'Who cares what he said. He's very old-fashioned. It's my life . . . and your life. Not his life.' Indignation surged, bringing a purple flush to her cheeks. 'Silly old fool,' she added.

'Unfortunately, that's not all, Daisy.' Mike braked and pulled into the verge. He switched off the engine, took out a pen and wrote his number on her wrist. 'There you are,' he said, trying to make a joke of it. 'Labelled and purchased. Mine forever.' He tried out a smile, but it didn't work too well. 'Promise me to learn the number by heart. Look, here.' He took an envelope out of his pocket. 'I wrote it out, too, so put it in your purse and keep it safe. If I'm suddenly gone, at any time, for any reason, you can write to US Military Headquarters and put my name and number on the envelope. I'll get your letter wherever I am, I promise you.'

She knew he was trying to be light-hearted. Everyone knew that the troops would face a sudden, overnight, mass evacuation to a secret port of embarkation prior to the invasion, but not yet.

'The invasion is months away,' she said. 'Everyone says so. Even the newspapers.'

'Of course it is, but keep it safe, Daisy. You see, your grandfather complained to our commander, Captain Rose.' Mike's words were blurted out before he could stop himself. He wasn't sticking to his plan.

'I don't believe you.'

'D'you think I'd lie to you? I got hauled up before Rose and forbidden to see you again. I'm to be transferred at once. I stole today by pretending I had a mission for Captain Johnson. It helps to have two bosses. I wanted us to have one last day together.'

'This can't be true.' She was glaring at him with wide, hostile eyes, her chest heaving. 'Gramps would never, never do that.'

'Don't blame him too much. I reckon he's scared of losing you both . . . that is, you and your mum, to American husbands.'

'Mum!' She giggled. 'That's crazy. Mum's too old. But Mike, this is the absolute limit. We don't have to do what they say. We can lie. Say you're not seeing me. Pretend I'm someone else.' Even while she was arguing with him, she knew it was no good. There was a pain in her chest that hurt and her eyes were burning. She had to hit out at someone and she would, but not Mike. 'So what can we do?'

'It's too late. I'm under orders and I'm being transferred. This is the army, it's not like civilian life. Surely you understand.'

'I understand that you're prepared to take this lying down.' But she would be strong for both of them, she decided.

'That's not fair, Daisy. It would take more than an hour to explain how the army works and how Rose views fraternization. Meanwhile, I can be sent wherever he likes.'

'They can all go to hell.' She hammered her fists on his chest. 'What are we going to do?'

'Don't fret so. When the war's over we'll be married, that's if you still want me.'

'Kiss me. Just kiss me. It's now I'm worried about. I won't allow this to happen. I won't let them win. We can't waste what little time we have. This is the twentieth century and we're not Romeo and Juliet.'

He folded her in his arms and they hung on to each other. Neither of them saw the military police vehicle speeding towards them until it drew up beside them, blocking the narrow road. Two military police sergeants stepped out.

'Sonovabitch,' Mike muttered.

'Are you Sergeant Mike Lawson?' Mike nodded. 'OK. Get out of the car and put your hands on the bonnet.'

Daisy sat in shocked silence as Mike got out of the car. An MP stepped out holding handcuffs. 'You don't need them,' Mike said. 'I'm not going anywhere. We were saying goodbye.'

Daisy shivered, part humiliation to see her hero so browbeaten, and part suppressed anger. Mike had volunteered, but she had not. Her life was not going to be run by the US army. Come to that, not by Gramps either. She used every bit of self-control she could muster to sit still and bide her time.

Mike was bundled into the back of the vehicle. Before she could even call out to him, the vehicle took off at speed, leaving Daisy with the second MP, who was getting into the driving seat.

'Whereabouts do you live, ma'am?' he asked coldly. 'I'll take you home.'

'Next door to your camp. What will happen to Mike?'

'Nothing much if you don't want to lay charges. He's being transferred.'

'Why should I lay charges. He's done nothing wrong. We love each other.'

He smiled, but said nothing until they drew up at her front gate. 'This it?'

'Yes,' she said angrily. She longed to hit out at him, but he wasn't the culprit.

'Hi darling, did you have a nice day?' Helen approached smiling from the kitchen, but froze with alarm when she saw Daisy's expression. 'What's happened? What is it? Are you hurt?'

'Very hurt, Mum. Gramps reported Mike and me to his commanding officer and he's being transferred away from here. They were out looking for us and they picked us up on the road as we were driving back. I was driven home by a military policeman. They behaved as if we were criminals. All because we overslept in the stable after the party, but nothing happened, Mum.' It took all her will power not to burst into tears. She longed to throw herself into her mother's arms, but she sensed that she had to grow up fast or she would lose Mike.

'I'm not taking this lying down, Mum. This is not the Victorian age and Gramps is not my guardian. He'll regret this and so will you.'

'Calm down, Daisy. Dad is out. We'll sort it out in the morning.'

Daisy raced upstairs, bathed and locked herself in the bedroom. She didn't answer when her mother called her down for supper. She wasn't hungry. Besides, she was too busy packing. She could only take as much as she could hold in a knapsack on her back and a smallish suitcase which she would tie on the back of her bicycle.

'Goodbye forever' she wrote on a notepad which she left on her table when she woke in the morning. She would miss Miro . . . and her home . . . and the horses . . . and especially Mum, but she intended to lead her own life, so this was the way it had to be.

Twenty-Seven

Daisy had noticed the sign on a farm gate the day she and Mike had driven towards Corfe Castle after her birthday. It had read:

Land Girls needed. Good food and accommodation provided. Apply within to Leslie Bates.

Hoping that the notice was still there, Daisy arrived on her bicycle at eight o'clock, her suitcase precariously strapped on the wobbly pannier over the back wheel. She paused outside the gate and worried about what she was doing. Mum would be devastated, but how else could Daisy assert her independence? She would never forget the look on Mike's face when the MPs marched him away. Gramps had gone too far.

She pushed open the gate and walked up the gravel driveway. As she approached, she read: Land Girls' Hostel typed on a sheet of paper and pinned to the door. I've come to the right place, she thought.

Leslie Bates, who ran the hostel, was a middle-aged woman, with brassy blonde hair, dark skin and a cheery smile. Everything about her seemed to be in excess: her costume jewellery, her smile, her make-up, her breasts and more than anything else the compassion that oozed out of her. Daisy was taken under her wing, given a man-sized breakfast, with real eggs, bacon and chips, and a heart-to-heart talk while she ate.

'Some men can be real sods, love. These farmers are a tough lot and their wives are no better. They'd work you to death as soon as look at you, so unless there's an emergency you'll work regular hours: from eight thirty until five thirty. If there are cows to be milked you simply adjust the hours to fit. Nine hours is the maximum. Any longer and you'll come and see me. If any of the lads try it on, tell me and I'll be after telling them where they get off. Now, let's get you kitted up. You'll be a temp until you're registered. I'll help you fill in your form tonight. As a matter of fact I have an emergency. An old lady nearby, who lives alone, has broken her leg and she needs help to look after her goats. Have you ever milked a goat?'

Daisy shook her head.

'Or a cow?'

'No.'

'Tch! One of my girls will be here soon. I'll send her with you to show you how it's done.'

Two hours later, dressed in the green and khaki uniform of a land girl, with a peaked cap and sensible shoes, Daisy was learning to milk a goat at Mrs Jenkins' farm. She was a 'temp' until she was properly accepted by the authorities, but who cared, all the farmers were crying out for help, registered or not.

Mrs Jenkins supplemented her income by selling goats' cheese to the local co-op. Some of it went under the counter, too, Daisy learned. The job entailed feeding and milking almost a hundred goats, cleaning out their sheds, scrubbing the dairy and making the cheese. It was fun, except for the old billy goat who butted her into the mud if she didn't watch out.

Daisy was working three miles from Sandbanks' ferry, which was roughly sixteen miles from home and she was enjoying herself. She was freer than she had been in her life and she was earning her keep which gave her huge satisfaction. She had a large room to herself. It was clean and bright, freshly whitewashed, with a raffia mat on the wooden floor and pictures of land girls at work on the walls. There was a wardrobe and a chest of drawers, but since she had only brought one change of clothes and a little extra under-wear, she did not need much space. Admittedly the room contained two extra single beds, but right now there were only six girls for the hostel's six rooms.

On her first day off Daisy wrote to Mike, but before long she began to worry that her letter had gone astray, or Mike had decided to end their relationship, or maybe they had sent him back to the States. As the days passed and she did not receive a reply, her depression worsened. How would she ever find him? She missed her mother, and Miro, and she knew that she should have stayed at home. At least Mike could find her there, if he ever wanted to. Life had become a burden and when Billy butted her into the hay, instead of laughing she cried.

Daisy had gone and Helen was livid. Her fury was mainly directed at John, but Daisy was also at fault. How could she be so selfish and headstrong? Imagine writing 'goodbye forever' to her own mother? It was an undeserved slap in the face, as if the past seventeen years counted for nothing. Then Helen's mood would change to one of acute anxiety. Where was she? How was she surviving? All would be forgiven if she would only come home.

Simon realized that he must try to persuade Daisy to return, but first he must find her, and his best chance was via Mike Lawson.

From Captain Rose he learned that Lawson had been sent to a Devon camp. He used his contacts to persuade Rose to bring him back as soon as he completed his training course in Brixham. A call to Lawson made him feel more confident.

'If I know Daisy she'll be here just as soon as she finds out where I am,' Lawson said. 'When I see her I'll persuade her to call her mother.'

Next, Simon had to find a convincing reason for Miro to be absent from home for the next four to six weeks. The PWE came up with the answer, with the connivance of Professor Frederick Joshua Pemberton who, when he wasn't engaged in counter espionage, coached gifted musicians. The professor, otherwise known as Uncle Fred was one of the founding members of the intelligence organization that preceded the PWE, but he was also a composer of some note, and it was rumoured that he took in talented pupils to make ends meet. He would provide Miro's alibi for the month.

'But are you sure you want to go?' Helen asked Miro. She had the strangest feeling that she was missing out on most of the facts.

'More than I've ever wanted anything,' Miro assured her. Then he added: 'Whatever you're thinking, you're probably right, Helen, but please leave this to me. It's very important to me.'

He didn't even notice that he called her Helen instead of Mum, but Helen did. He, too, is growing away from me, she thought sadly. He's almost a man.

'Don't worry,' John said when she voiced her concern. 'They always come back. Miro will . . . Daisy will . . . just like you did. Can you imagine how I felt when you married Eric at eighteen?'

As Simon's prodigy, Miro's recruitment was conducted by personnel from both the British PWE and the American MO (The Morale Operations Branch of G2). It took place in a safe house within a mile of PWE headquarters. The so-called 'discussions' were scheduled to take five days. They consisted of non-stop interrogations for fourteen hours a day.

The room was brilliantly lit with spotlights, each of which were trained on Miro, so he could not see much more than dark shapes behind the lights. Every night, when the questions were over, Simon looked in on Miro in his bare room, bringing him fruit and treats from Helen, chocolate from the canteen and anything else he had requested. This was the fourth evening and although Miro was pale, he showed no signs of strain or distress.

'How's Helen?' he wanted to know.

'Naturally she's sad and lonely because she is missing you and Daisy. She tried to find the address of the professor, but it's a safely guarded secret to all but a few. She wanted to thank him for having you and bring you both some gifts . . . mainly food, I believe.'

'She was checking up on us,' Miro said.

Simon wished he could remove that smiling mask from Miro's face and find out what was going on behind it. He should be looking exhausted and depressed. Instead he was withdrawn, but otherwise unchanged.

By now the PWE had an excellent record of Miro's progress through kindergarten, junior school and his eventual graduation to high school in Sudetenland. While they had no access to reports or his teachers' views, via the Jewish Union they obtained an assessment of the boy's abilities compiled by Rabbi Isaac Rabinowitz, who had coached him for his Bar Mitzvah.

'A brilliant intellect, but sadly uncommitted to Judaism,' the rabbi had written. 'None of his close friends are Jewish, but he scores in Hebrew studies because of a good memory and a traditional Jewish background. Miro prefers soccer to music practice, but again he attains high marks because of his talent. He spends too much time at parties with his school friends. Uncommitted. Speaks Yiddish, Hebrew, French, Czech and German fluently.' At the bottom of the report he had written: 'God knows what he could do if he actually tried.'

Simon went over his file with him. 'You've scored, Miro,' he told him. 'Your staunch refusal to pass on any information that in your view might be damaging to the Allied cause has brought you safely through this mess. I trust you, and so do the members of the PWE. What I'm going to tell you now is classified. Listen carefully: deception is destined to play a major role in the Allied campaign to invade the Continent. Basically, the job is to mislead the Germans into believing that Pas de Calais will be the site of the coming invasion. Eisenhower's staff have created a mythical 1st Army Group, with an order of battle larger than that of Montgomery's 21st Group. The phantom force will be based near Dover, just across the Channel from the supposed target; construction crews are building dummy installations of plywood and canvas and filling the space with inflated tanks and vehicles. Plus, a vast armada of rubber landing craft is being placed in the Thames River estuary, where German reconnaissance aircraft will be sure to spot it. General Patton, the American general the Germans respect the most, is to command this phantom army.'

Only the slightest inclination of his head showed that Miro was taking this in. Simon wished he would be more outgoing.

'Supplying information on the progress of Patton's force will be our immediate task. We shall be small cogs in a vast network of intelligence agents whose job is to signal to German analysts that a major military organization is in fact functioning. I am being supposedly transferred to the phantom army, so I shall spend more time in London, which I have to do in any event, in order for you to filch my information when I return. I shall carelessly tell Helen of these Allied plans. You will listen in to our fictitious conversations via a hole drilled into the back of your wardrobe and through the intervening wall. You got that?'

Miro nodded.

'Improvise a bit, Miro. You might even ask Brannigan if he thinks this is a good idea. Heavy aerial bombardment of Calais will back up the ploy. Prior to the invasion, Allied airmen will drop more bombs on the Pas de Calais than any   e else in France.'

'Wow! What else can I say,' Miro said, with a lurking smile.

'I'll see you tomorrow, Miro. Hold tight. It's almost over.'

'No, wait a minute, Simon. The worst of this is being so cut off. What's the latest war news?'

'Most of it is good. Allied tanks moved into Naples a couple of days ago; the Corsicans have turfed the Germans out of Corsica; Italian partisans are fighting the Germans, and the Red Army has cut off 150,000 German troops in the Crimea, plus the bulk of the Seventeenth Army. Allied air forces have stepped up bombing raids on Germany and countless wounded troops are being saved by a new wonder drug called penicillin.

'That's all I can remember. See you tomorrow. Goodnight, Miro.'

I am being taken apart and rebuilt, Miro told himself. I am learning to be useful, to be more of a man, to throw off whatever remains of my millstone of guilt. He felt depressed at the prospect of another long, lonely night and he missed his home desperately, but Miro had no intention of letting Simon know about his weaknesses.

It was dark by seven p.m., so he faced twelve hours of loneliness, with only a dim electric bulb hanging from the high ceiling, which was hardly adequate to read the many military textbooks Simon had brought him.

Tomorrow would be the fifth and last day of Miro's interrogation, Simon had been told, so he arrived in the morning to witness the proceedings. Josh, of PWE, was discussing Miro's relationship with his controller as Simon walked in and took a seat at the back of the room.

'Surely you knew that you should have reported this man to the authorities.' Josh leafed back through the pages. 'Just how many items have you given Brannigan?'

'At least one a week, sometimes more, over a thirteen-month period.'

'And you claim that during this time you gave him nothing relevant that could help the German war effort.'

'Every piece of information is listed in detail, in the file. You've read the file.'

Simon stirred uncomfortably, but Josh carried on.

'Do you regret giving him any one of them?'

'Yes. All of them.'

'And specifically?'

'Well, maybe the one about the American equipment stashed around the streets. I estimated it all to the best of my ability and then I divided by five and gave him the figures. I reckoned they must know that the Yanks could not invade without this equipment, but still . . . maybe they didn't know the true extent of it.'

The day dragged on. Simon was considering creeping out and then Dave took over from Josh and moved to another tack. He picked up a file and read from it.

'I suppose you know that on September 9, 1941, the Parliament of so-called "independent" Slovakia, a Nazi puppet regime, ratified the *Jewish Codex* that stripped Slovakia's Jews of all their civil rights. The government press boasted that the *Codex* was even more severe than the Nazis' Nuremburg Laws. The full expulsion of Slovakia's Jews to the camps began in March 1942. The fascist Slovak leaders were so impatient to be rid of the Jews that they paid the Nazis DM 500 for every Jew that the Nazis deported. Slovakia was the only Nazi satellite regime that paid cash to expedite the expulsion of its Jews. How does that make you feel, Miro?'

'Are you asking me that? Don't you understand how I felt and how I feel?'

'I'm asking you . . . yes.'

'When I was still in Prague, I felt second class. No . . . worse . . . let's say tenth class. I saw the posters going up. I remember one read: "No Jew is ever going to be a parasite on the flesh of the Slovak Nation." I longed to be anything but Jewish. Tension gripped me . . . and guilt because I was a Jew, and of course fear about what would happen to me and my parents. I wondered why we had nowhere to go, no country of our own. To be honest, until that time we had been patriotic Czechs. Later, after I was sent to England, I felt quite differently. No longer a Czech, but a Jew.' For a moment he fell silent. Then he said, 'I want you to understand that Helen, my foster mother, gave me back my self-respect and taught me to like myself. When the war ends, I hope to get involved with others in creating a Jewish Homeland, but for that I need to study law. Helen has offered to sponsor me, but I don't want to take advantage of her. She's not rich. I hope to save enough myself.'

'And how do you feel about your boyhood friends now?' Josh asked.

'I miss them sometimes in moments of nostalgia. They were all right. Full of fun and derring-do. Later they were brainwashed. I don't blame them. I blame the Nazis.'

'Yet after this, you still signed up to spy for the Third Reich. Why was that?'

'Have you ever seen a young woman garroted?' Miro asked. 'I was taken to watch one woman dragged out to the garroting machine. She was beautiful, a recent arrival, not yet gaunt and hollow-eyed. She screamed piteously as they dragged her across the yard. I don't want to describe what happened next. I expect you have guessed why I was taken to watch this execution: it was the fate they had planned for my mother if I refused to help them – or so our Gypsy supervisor told me.'

Dave interrupted Miro. 'Terezin concentration camp was created to cover up the Nazi's treatment of the Jews. A high proportion of artists and intellectuals are incarcerated there. A recent Red Cross inspection found Terezin to be a "model ghetto". Are you saying that this is not true?'

'It has to be a cover up. What the Red Cross wouldn't have seen was starvation and disease, but worst of all was the constant dread of being transported to camps that were far worse. When I was in

Dachau there were rumours of mass deaths – we never knew for sure. We all wanted to believe that we would be safe.'

'So how do you feel about spying for the enemy of your people?'

'How do you think I feel? Of the two alternatives the other was so much worse. How could I abandon my parents?'

'And what do you think your parents would say about your decision?'

'They would tell me to leave them to die, to always remember that I am a Jew.

'I remember what my father said when we arrived at the camp. He knew that we would be separated. He said, "Hang on to good-ness, Miro. There's always a choice, you see. Choose the moral path and never forget that you are a Jew."'

'So you chose the immoral path and you forgot that you were a Jew. You betrayed your race.'

'Not race, please, religion,' Miro objected. 'Or you could call Judaism a culture. Other than that, yes, I agree with you. But I made that choice because I love my parents. I wish you had known my mother as she used to be: gracious, cultured, beautiful and kind. She had so many friends, nearly all of them were musicians and she loved to entertain. So I decided that it was worth being a traitor, even at the risk of losing my soul, if there was a chance of keeping her alive. I thought about it and I made my choice. I don't regret it for a moment.'

'Yet you didn't play the game with the Nazis, either. You betrayed them as well.'

Miro was smiling. 'Nothing like enough. I wanted to kill them all. I would have killed Paddy, but Simon stopped me.'

'Thank God! Well, Miro, we're offering you a third choice . . . to be a double agent, undertake some vital work for us and keep your parents alive at the same time. This is a chance to redeem yourself, but make no mistake, it will be dangerous and you will have to be very smart indeed not to be caught by your controller. I don't want to deceive you. Paddy will kill you if he finds out you are betraying him, make no mistake. That's one of the reasons why we're sending you to a special training camp in the north where you will learn a great many things you might need, such as unarmed combat.'

'OK, Simon. This is where you take over,' Dave said, looking over his shoulder. 'He's all yours.'

'Welcome to MO, Miro.'

'Which is what exactly?' Tears of relief were threatening to shame Miro. He blinked hard. 'Could the damn lights go off? My eyes hurt.'

'Not so much of the "damn" Miro.' Simon looked over his shoulder. 'Could we have the lights switched off?'

Sudden darkness left Miro blinking and unable to see, but he could hear.

'The Morale Operations Branch of G2 is part of US military intelligence. MO is cooperating with British Intelligence in this all out effort to fox the enemy. We practice covert strategic and tactical morale operations based on deception and subversion. In plain language this means that we attempt to break ιe enemies' morale, also confuse them so that they cannot make ιhe right decisions. We're a late starter to the intelligence forces. Basically, from the US point of view, this group is only a few months old. MO output is unofficial, disclaimed by Federal Authorities and it is usually covertly disseminated to make it appear to be of enemy origin. You will continue to work with me and you will pass on whatever disinformation is given to you − solely by me, for the time being − and from now on you don't have to make your own alterations because what we give you will be just what we want them to believe. Everything will have been passed by the Foreign Office.'

'By the way, Miro,' Alf cut in. 'How did you change the messages to make them real enough to fox Paddy?'

'I retyped the memos on Helen's typewriter − she thought it was school work.' Miro glanced apologetically at Simon. 'Then I stuck my message on to Simon's memo and photographed it. As I mentioned, Paddy gave me a camera. This made the operation much simpler.'

'Are you old enough to drink, Miro?'

He grinned. 'Officially or unofficially? Well, either way I'd like a lemonade, if you have such a thing. I'm dying of thirst.'

He was introduced to the PWE guys by Simon. Dick shook hands with him. 'Your languages are going to come in handy,' he said. 'Particularly for our broadcasting stations. Just how good is your German?'

'As good as my Czech. Sudetenland was mainly German speaking, but there's a strong local accent.'

'I'll send you some tapes, via Simon. Shed the accent. We'll probably need you − and many others like you − when we move into Berlin.'

Miro leaned back in his chair, sipping his lemonade and hoping that at last he was going to get into the fight against the Nazis. He indulged himself in his favourite dream, but just when the tank reached the gates of Terezin, Simon broke into his daydream as he said, 'Finish your drink, Miro. We have to get moving.'

Twenty-Eight

Daisy was depressed. Leslie noticed and spoke to the other land girls, but no one could find out what was wrong. Big shadows appeared under her eyes and she tackled her work listlessly. Daisy was badly shaken. She loved Mike passionately, but he had not replied to her letter.

One morning, just before breakfast, Leslie handed her a letter which had just arrived. One glance told her it was from Mike. She fled to her room to read it in private.

> Dearest Daisy,
> I tried to call you at home. Finally I got through to John who told me that you'd left home and no one knows where you are. He said your mother is worried and depressed. She's a great lady, Daisy, so please call her. I'm sure a call from you would transport her to heaven, just as your letter did me. Remember that our letters are censored and we can't give any vital facts away, such as where I am.
>
> Don't expect a romantic letter, since so many others will read it, but my feelings for you remain constant, as I told you in the stables and at our last meeting. I was transferred here later that same evening.
>
> It's very pretty here. They have dances at the hotel on the cliff top, but I couldn't bear to go without you. I think about you most of the time and I remember you telling me that when you turned sixteen, you and your mother joined your father for a short holiday, because he was working away from home. I think of this often and I dream of meeting you by chance, as I walk along the beach, which I like to do on my afternoon off, which is usually a Wednesday. Guess what! Yesterday I picked up a few pieces of coal wedged between the rocks. There is a wreck here, they tell me.

Daisy threw down the letter in a rage. What a lot of nonsense! Why couldn't he write something sensible? Who cares if Mike found coal on the beach. But wait a minute . . . coal! Dad was in Brixham to refloat a tramp steamer full of coal, holed by six direct hits. The family stayed with him for the summer holidays *in a hotel on the cliff top*. 'He's there,' she shouted. 'Mike's right there!' She danced around the room, round and round, until she was so dizzy she collapsed on the bed. Suddenly she felt sad. They'd had a lovely holiday and now Dad was gone forever. He had succeeded in salvaging the boat, but on the very day when it was due to be towed to Southampton, enemy bombers came and blew it to bits. The much needed coal was scattered all over the place.

She hugged her letter and sat on the bed, laughing and crying at the same time. 'I will be walking along the beach on Wednesday afternoon if I have to kill to get there,' she promised Mike solemnly.

Daisy sang to the goats as she milked them, and she talked to the pigs as she fed them and cuddled the cat and gave him some cream – which wasn't allowed – and never grumbled when Mrs Jenkins asked her to sweep the floor and make her a pot of tea and some egg sandwiches, which strictly speaking wasn't allowed, since she wasn't a char. Nothing could dampen her spirits, she was as happy as a skylark, rising up and up, from one euphoric state to the next, bursting with joy.

'My, you must be in love,' Leslie said, when Daisy arrived at the hostel, having cycled three miles in the pouring rain. 'Look at you, drenched, but smiling. It's that letter you got, I'll be bound. I'm going to run you a hot bath. We'll forget about the five-inch rule for once. You have a good soak or you'll be down with pneumonia. There's a nice beef curry for supper, so don't be late.'

Asking for a five-day holiday turned out to be more difficult than she had thought. Mrs Jenkins was alone and they had to find a replacement before she could leave, but then a young land girl complained that the farmer's son where she worked was hitting on her, so she took over Daisy's job at short notice.

'Don't be late back. Five days . . . that's all,' Leslie begged her.

So here she was, sauntering along the water's edge at Brixham, just as she'd dreamed, wearing her rolled-up corduroy slacks and a thick, hand-knitted jersey under her duffel coat. She had arrived on the previous evening and found a room in a boarding house offering bed and breakfast, just around the corner from the sea. She had bought a sandwich and a lemonade for supper and shivered madly as she undressed, but whether this was from the cold lino, or the decor, she couldn't say. Photographs of troops in the Boer War hung above her bed and around the walls were pictures of Victorian ladies clutching flowers, with pale swains on their knees before them. The entire catastrophe was set against ghastly mauve and green wall-paper.

Ugh! It was a pleasure to switch off the light and leap into bed. The linen was fresh and clean and smelled of Persil, but the blackout curtains wavered in the breeze letting in stray beams of moonlight reflected from the corrugated iron roof jutting out below her window. Pale and spectral, they lit the ceiling, making weird patterns and then moving pictures. She saw strange pictures of troops in the Boer War with their horse-drawn guns, and then came the Tommies floundering in the mud of the Great War, and then there was Mike, crossing the Channel and fighting his way across the beach which had become the front line and she was there, too, running before him, clutching a basket to gather up the mines.

The north wind strengthened during the night and clouds piled up on the northern horizon. Daisy set out at two p.m., thoroughly chilled. The sky was dark and purple-looking and the beach and promenade were deserted.

I must look like an idiot, she thought as she walked on to the beach. They'll have to amputate my toes. There was no sign of Mike. What if he didn't come? What if he'd been sent somewhere else?

Mike was worrying as he sat on the bus. He'd been summoned to see the captain just as he was leaving, He wanted to know how his scuba diving training was progressing. 'It seems they want you back at Mowbray camp,' he told Mike, 'but I insisted that you finish this training course.'

'About a week should see me through it, sir,' he'd said, cutting off a couple of days. The guys would have to work that much harder.

They weren't as liberal with their jeeps as Captain Rose had been and he'd stood at the bus stop for half an hour before a bus came. It was only four stops. He could have walked there faster and he wished he had.

They reached the beach stop at last. As he quit the bus, he saw that the beach was deserted, but right at the end a woman was crossing the road. Could that be Daisy? Huddled in a duffel coat with the hood pulled over her head, it was hard to tell. He set off at a fast sprint, dashed across the road and was just in time to see her turn the corner, but when he got there she had vanished. He paced the street forlornly, wondering if she had gone into one of the tatty shops along the pavement, but then he saw Daisy emerging from a cafe, holding a chocolate bar.

He crept up behind her, but she spun around.

'Oh, Mike . . . I thought you weren't coming.' She burst into tears, grabbed him and dropped the chocolate.

'Even if I'm late, I'll always keep my word. Don't worry so much. I've good news . . . the captain called me in just as I was leaving. I'm to be sent back to Mowbray. Captain Johnson has been pulling strings.'

'Wow! That's great,' she said, stooping to retrieve her chocolate.

He pulled her up. 'Leave it, Daisy. The gutter's mucky. I saw a fish restaurant just around the corner. I'm pretty hungry myself,' he lied. 'Let's go.'

It wasn't bad there, clean, but cramped, but at this time of the day they were the only customers. He plied her with questions about where she worked and where she slept, was she getting enough to eat and was she lonely? She answered between mouthfuls of plaice and chips with mushy peas.

'Why aren't you eating?' she wanted to know. Mike forced himself to eat at least a part of his second lunch while she told him about Mrs Jenkins and her goats.

She had five days leave, he heard, and then she was going back to the hostel.

'You must know that your mum is desperately missing you. Miro is away studying music with some nutty professor for a month and she's all alone, apart from Gramps. Simon knows you've come here to see me. I told him. He has kept in touch with me since you left home . . . for Helen's sake.'

He paused to pick at his overcooked chips.

'Look here, Daisy. I want you to go home. I've been desperately worried about you. I couldn't tell them where you were, because I didn't know, but I guessed you'd write. It was such a relief to get your letter, but I wish you hadn't done that, Daisy. It wasn't right. You overreacted.'

'Gramps had no right—'

'Of course he did,' he interrupted her. 'I'd do the same if we had daughters your age. Simon persuaded him to withdraw his complaint, and Helen has explained to Captain Rose that I was a friend of the family and that they need me to shoe the horses.'

'Wow! She did that? I'm amazed. She must like you a lot.'

'No, she did it to get you home.'

'Oh my goodness. Of course it wasn't Mum's fault, but I wish they'd stop treating me like a child.'

'Then don't act like a child.'

Daisy felt insulted. How could he say that? 'Stop nagging me. All you've done is blame me. You're spoiling our holiday. Aren't you glad to see me?'

'Yes, of course, but I want you to call Helen. You're so lucky to have a mother like Helen. She's so supportive. I envy you.'

Remembering that Mike's mother had died when he was young, Daisy was overcome with compassion. She reached out to hold his hand. 'All right I'll phone Mum. Let's not fight.'

They walked back towards her boarding house where there was a pay phone. Daisy was strangely silent, not sulking, nothing like that. Her arm was linked with his, but he realized she'd seen another side of him.

'I didn't know you could be so hard,' she complained.

'I'm not hard. I'm pressing for what I believe is best for you because I love you. I'm going away and it might take a couple of years or more to beat the Germans and the Japs. I might even be killed.'

'Don't . . . Please . . . Don't say such awful things.' She looked horrified.

'Let's face facts, Daisy. Some of us will die, but most of us will live. I don't want to worry about you when I'm in the thick of a battle. If you love me you'll go home.'

'Otherwise what?' she challenged him.

'Otherwise nothing. I'm not threatening you, I'm just telling you. Go home! I'll be there. We'll have fun, like we used to.'

'You want me to leave, just when I got here?'

He sighed, still undecided. 'What are you going to do here all day while I'm training? I can only get off on Wednesday afternoons. We've almost had a full Wednesday.'

'So why did you ask me to come?'

'Because I needed to persuade you to go home.'

'This is where I booked in.' She paused in front of a gaunt building in need of a coat of paint.

'Good. Now let's phone your Mum.'

★ ★ ★

Helen had been waiting all day for a call from her daughter. Mike
had told her they would phone on Wednesday, but it was five o'clock
and dark. Brixham was a place she detested. The hotel on the cliff
was where she had first learned about Eric's affair . . . Luckily, the
telephone rang, rescuing her from bitter memories.

She heard Mike's voice saying, 'Hi, Helen, hold on,' and then:
'Mum, it's Daisy.'

'Darling. I've missed you. When are you coming home?'

'I'm in Brixham. Do you remember we were here—'

'I remember,' Helen said, interrupting her.

'I've just met Mike. We had lunch. He's going back to Mowbray
in a week's time.'

'Is that so, Daisy.' Helen had decided not to mention that she had
spoken to Mike twice by telephone and that Simon had pulled
strings to get him back.

'Look, Mum, I'm sorry you've been upset, but you should have
known I'd be all right.'

Like you were when you ran off to London to find your grandmother, Helen thought, but all she said was: 'I miss you, darling.'

'You have to understand that Mike and I are getting married as
soon as the war ends.'

Remembering how much she had loved Eric, and how she had
fought her parents to marry him, she shivered inwardly and told
herself that she must end the rift fast because the time might come
when her daughter needed her.

'Well, let's hope that doesn't take too long,' Helen said. 'When
will you be back?'

'Actually, Mum, I have a room of my own at a Land Army hostel.
It's pretty nice and I can't let them down. I'll have to give a long
notice.'

'Can't you cycle to work every morning?'

'I suppose I could come home for weekends.'

'Or be transferred to a farm that's nearer to home. I'm sure you'll
manage, dear, since Mike will be here, although I don't understand
why you're so determined to give up your career.'

'But Mum, I'm not giving up anything. How could you think
that? Whatever time is left before the invasion, I'll spend with Mike.
Then I'll take up the scholarship.'

'Meantime, come home I need you.'

Feeling obscurely blackmailed, Daisy agreed. 'D'you want to say
hello to Mike?'

'Yes, of course. Mike. It might be better not to tell her that we've spoken on the telephone or she'll think we're conspiring against her. She's seems to be very much on the defensive.'

'Exactly. See you soon, Helen.'

'Mike.'

'Yes.'

'I trust you to look after her. You know what I mean.'

'Yes. Of course.'

She said goodbye and replaced the receiver.

They were walking arm-in-arm along the moonlit, empty street. They could hear singing coming from the pub on the corner. A hungry cat rifling through a bin, yowled and fled as they approached. Not a night to be alone in that cold and ugly boarding house, Daisy decided.

'You must stay the night,' she whispered.

'Oh Daisy, God knows I'd like to, but we must be careful.'

'Then stay for a little while.'

They were halfway up the stairs when Mrs Browning, Daisy's landlady, caught sight of them. 'Where do you two think you are going then?'

'Up to my room,' Daisy said.

'Oh no you don't. This is a respectable house. No men in your room, young lady. Whatever next.' She turned on Mike, looking furious. 'You should be ashamed of yourself, young man. I don't allow any going's on in this house.'

Daisy's face was crimson, but Mike thought it was funny. 'She resembles a rat,' he whispered. 'Those teeth sloping back. She's absolutely terrible. Paint her for me, against her horrible wallpaper.'

'All right I will . . . when I get home.' She giggled. Life was so much better when Mike was around. She knew she'd always be laughing, even when things went wrong. He had a knack of seeing the funny side of life. He was dependable and kind, and loyal and she would never love anyone as she loved him. They had a few precious months, or weeks. No one knew for sure. They must make the most of the time they had left.

They said goodnight formally on the top step of the rooming house. 'Go to bed, young lady,' Mike whispered.

'No, not right now. I want to walk around the corner with you.'

★   ★   ★

Arm in arm, they walked along the pavement, their footsteps making sharp, metallic clicks on the frozen pavement. 'This way,' she urged him, tugging at his arm. 'Do you see that shed?'

'Yes, but what's special about it?'

'That's my window right above. Even I could climb up there. We could pretend we were back in the stables. Please Mike. I came all this way. I don't want to be alone. That room depresses me.'

'Oh, I don't know.' It was what he wanted more than anything, but not here and not now. Daisy's eyes were filling with tears.

'We'll have to wait until the rat lady goes to bed,' he said.

Mike waited a while. He walked down to the pub and back again, enjoying the scent of ozone which reminded him of holidays by the sea back home with his dad. He took off his shoes and climbed on to the roof of the shed, feeling prey to curiously mixed feelings: part guilt, part desire. Mainly he felt uneasy. Daisy was such a child and she wasn't thinking of the consequences. What if she found herself pregnant and he was fighting somewhere in Europe. He'd be unlikely to get leave to marry her.

He thought about the stories they had all heard about English girls being real pushovers, but Daisy wasn't like that. She was just like the girls back home and her grandpa, John Cooper, had been acting just like dads back home. He was glad of their long, chaste friendship.

He had curiously mixed emotions about Daisy. He regarded her artistic talent with awe. He'd seen some of her paintings and they were really great, but apart from her extraordinary talent she was such a child. She should never have left home, but he knew how much she loved him. Just as much as he loved her. She had unlocked feelings he never knew existed. He wanted to guard her, protect her, take her home and look after her forever. This damn war made all that impossible, which was why he felt so unsure of himself.

He reached the window which was slightly open, pushed it up and climbed into her room. A vague scent of toothpaste, perfume and talcum powder rose from the bed. How beautiful she looked lying there softly lit by reflected moonlight. One arm was flung over the pillow, the eiderdown was disarranged, revealing one perfect breast. Her mouth was open showing a glint of white teeth, long lashes fanned her cheeks, her hair was damp and tousled and she was warm and highly desirable. He would love nothing more than to climb in beside her. But then what?

He thought of Helen who trusted him. Was he free to love Daisy when he might be killed over there? He pulled the duvet up around her neck and stepped through the window.

He was sliding down the roof of the shed when Daisy called, 'Come back. Mike . . . *please.*'

It sounded like real anguish. He sighed and climbed back in again.

Twenty-Nine

Miro's training at spy school was like nothing he could ever have imagined: a place staffed by cranky adventurers who were paid and housed in order to further their craziness. One afternoon in late November, Miro saw one of their instructors go down and nearly drown in a midget submarine in the duck pond behind the house, amongst the golden carp and water reeds. He was dragged up, in the nick of time, fronds of weeds trailing over his shoulder and several litres of murky water pouring from his blue lips. 'Not quite watertight yet,' he gasped, when he could speak.

The unarmed combat instructor, who lived on brown rice and sat cross-legged in the corner of the floor to eat, could be seen most evenings, weather permitting, meditating on the lawn, but he knew his craft and Miro was black and blue for most of his month there. These were two of the many weird men who ran the school. They taught him to drill, to fight dirty, and to live off the land, and a variety of ways to turn ordinary items like cutlery, pens and garden spades into lethal weapons.

Miro was training with four other Czechs, all crazed with ambition to get home and kill every German they saw. This restored Miro's faith in his countrymen. After ten days, the unknown men who ran the camp decided that Miro was more English than Czech and transferred him to a group of upper class graduates who seemed to think that all Jews needed pulling down a peg or two. Miro tried to keep his sense of humour and eventually they became buddies, perhaps because of their mutual hatred of their instructors who demanded perfection. Miro scored at languages, speaking German and Czech like a native, they told him, which of course he was.

After three weeks at the combat camp came the demolition school, located in a former farmhouse near Inverness. Miro exploded mock-ups of railway lines, bridges, interior machinery and stable walls a foot thick. Then it was time to move on to the parachute course, which was more complicated than necessary because of the large amount of gear he had to carry. Miro was becoming fit and tough and his shoulders broadened. Despite the late season he was sunburned with blond streaks in his light brown hair which was making him anxious. Could he look like this after five weeks of playing the clarinet, he asked himself? Mainly he worried about the family. Hitler's so-called first 'reprisal weapon', known as the doodlebug, was menacing Southern England. This pilotless, jet-propelled aircraft was capable of travelling at 400 mph and carried nearly a ton of high explosives.

Whenever he could, Miro borrowed a bike or cadged a lift to look around. All coastal areas were banned to visitors and US troops were camped on every pavement and corner of spare land. Military exercises were taking place in every available space and villagers were becoming used to hundreds of parachutists dropping around them, while heavily-laden gliders swooped low overhead as troops practised over and again for the big day.

And where would his duty lie, Miro often wondered? When Simon joined the invasion armada, his job as a courier of disinformation would be over. Would he join Simon? Could he, as a Czech, become part of the US fighting forces? He decided to work on Simon. This was what he wanted above all else. Miro sweated it out, wishing he could do his bit.

Then, towards the end of the month Simon telephoned in the middle of an unarmed combat lesson.

'OK. This is it. I need you in a hurry. Get on the six a.m. train to Whitstable,' he said. 'Pick up your ticket at Information. You'll be met by Uncle Fred . . . an old friend of the family and you'll spend the day with him. I'll collect you the following morning.'

Miro boarded the train, which was two hours late, and after an uneventful journey was met by a bearded stranger who put one arm around his shoulders and said, 'My dear Miro, it's great to have you back again, and looking so well. You must have grown a foot since I last saw you.'

Miro, who was becoming used to the wonderland he inhabited nowadays merely smiled, shook hands and said, 'It's great to see you, Uncle Fred.'

They drove due east and half an hour later 'Uncle Fred' pulled up before a graceful, red brick home, with a windswept garden full of leaves, dead chrysanthemums and little else. Miro sensed that Fred lived alone here, but he was wrong, for a red setter bounded out and made straight for them, scattering his ecstatic welcome over the two of them. 'Clearly Rosa remembers you,' Fred said.

Miro smiled as he stroked Rosa. Was she an agent, too, he laughed
to himself, or was she trained to love everyone?

They hurried inside. Uncle Fred showed him around the house
beginning with the music conservatory at the back and next the
kitchen, where Miro had often made hot chocolate at midnight
because he had difficulty sleeping, he was told. Fred made a great
show of explaining where everything was kept, and the idiosyn-
crasies of the hot-water system and how to get a hot bath if the
water was switched off. After that he was asked to study the various
certificates on the wall in the music room. Uncle Fred, otherwise
known as Professor Pemberton, was a composer of some note. He
was also one of the founder members of PWE, but Miro only knew
this because Simon had told him. He toured the house, saw the
bedrooms, examined the room he had slept in for a month and then
joined the professor downstairs.

'Now Miro, you are spending the night here in order to remember
the sound of things that go bump in the night, and to learn what
time the milkman comes, and when the birds return to the dam at
the bottom of the garden, and how ashamed Rosa is when she is
caught swimming after them. Basically we lived on home grown
vegetables, eggs and chicken from our own flock plus our meagre
meat ration, which you must know all about by now.'

He had a strange way of talking: streams of information poured
out in his soft, high-pitched voice, followed by long silences while
he smiled to himself, as if at some secret joke, or maybe he was just
a little bit loopy, Miro pondered.

'Let's get to work. Sit down, Miro. We have only twelve hours
in which to cover the work we would have done in the month that
your controller must believe you spent here. So, for starters, let's have
coffee. Why don't you make the coffee. I've shown you where everything is. Next we shall have to borrow the tuition your father gave
you, using the pieces he chose. I'm sorry if it revives sad memories,
but it is the only way we can get through an extraordinary amount
of work that you *must* have in your head. Music is everything here.
During your stay, we seldom thought of anything else.'

'And Sunday?'

'Sunday, too. I try to give clients their money's worth. Now sit
here and breathe in the atmosphere and remember the pieces your
father taught you to play in the six months leading up to the German
occupation of Sudetenland. Remember what he said when he was
annoyed with you, and when he was unfair, and when he praised

you, and transpose me for him in your memory bank. Visualize this. Don't forget to write down the pieces.' He slid a notebook and a pen across the desk. 'We'll go through some of them. Whatever we have time for . . . maybe we'll manage a couple of lessons.'

'How did I wash my clothes?' Miro asked. 'And what about shopping?'

'Good thinking, Miro. Mrs Lo comes in for an a few hours, three times a week. You'll see her shortly. Perhaps she could have done your shopping. I mean, what would you need . . . toothpaste perhaps?'

Miro forced his mind back to uncharted, dangerous territory where no one should go, scenes that hurt beyond measure: Father persuading him to use music as his escape when the word anti-Semitism entered their lives; Father refusing to listen to his wife's fears and her pleas that they should leave Czechoslovakia; Father's sobs when Mama was taken away. Looking back, it seemed that every tragic moment had been played out to a backdrop of music, with or without lessons. He visualized their tragedy, set to Mozart and Beethoven, and then he did it all again, but Papa had grown taller and broader and his eyes were grey, and so was his hair, yet the stubble on his cheeks was reddish brown and when he spoke, it was with a sudden rush of words followed by a bemused silence. Papa's words, but Uncle Fred said them. So when he brought Miro a cup of coffee and some biscuits, Miro shouted at him in Czech, 'You were so full of denial. You should have listened to Mama!' And then he apologized.

'I forgot to tell you that you must think these thoughts in English,' Fred said quietly. 'Not Czech, or Yiddish or whatever you were speaking. Your superb talent for languages could be your downfall, Miro. Watch it!'

Amazingly, it worked. The professor seemed to have plucked some conversations from Miro's memory, for when they played out the lessons, it could have been his father talking. By the time Simon fetched him at ten the following morning he had a month of new memories in his head and he could trot them out at will, as Simon learned in the car when they were driving to London.

Returning to the safe house brought an unwelcome surge of memories. It was just as cold. Rain was still pelting the windows, and it was too dark to read. As before, the lights only switched on after dusk, an absurd economy Miro detested in England's grey days. He liked his cold weather served with bright sunshine, skiing weather, and the rain should fall in thick sheets of water that pulverized the soil and reduced visibility to almost nil. These grey days served no useful purpose. They were like his thoughts, depressing and a complete waste of time.

What on earth was Simon doing? Miro had been sitting here for at least ten minutes, blindfolded, feeling chilled and listening to clicks and expletives. From the sound of things, Simon had suffered several small electric shocks.

'Why don't you let me help you, Simon.'

'No, it's OK.'

'Then switch off the power.'

'It's done. Shut up and listen, Junior. Try to follow my directions. Paddy wants more and still more information. His masters are leaning on him, so he leans on you. You get the bright idea of making a hole in the back of your wardrobe and another through the wall immediately behind the hole in your wardrobe. You've been very careful, lifting a small section of wallpaper in Helen's room and sticking it back over the hole. God, how I hate wallpaper. So where was I?'

'I think you had me squatting in the wardrobe listening to Helen's snores.'

'Does she snore?'

'How should I know? I haven't drilled the hole yet,' he said, bolstering the illusion that no one knew Simon and Helen slept together.

'OK, from now on I shall be giving you a great deal of information that we want Paddy to send back to his masters. He would never believe that you have gleaned all this by yourself, but you might get away with this by saying that I blab to Helen every night when we are in bed together.'

'And if I don't get away with it?'

'Then it's curtains for you, Miro, unless you tell me in time, in which case I'll get you out and deal with Brannigan. Are you a virgin, Miro?'

'What's that got to do with—'

'Just answer. It's important. And tell the truth.'

'Yes.'

'Any near misses?'

'No. I really don't have—'

'It's all right, kid. That's what I assumed. Your sexual education is about to begin. You can't see. You're sitting in the wardrobe, in pitch darkness, but you can hear. And this is what you will hear . . . if this damn recorder works, that is. There was something wrong with the plug, but I've fixed it. This is a prewar, French, blue movie. You only get the soundtrack. God knows why the guys had it here. Memorize the sounds. I'll be back in ten minutes.'

Whispers of endearments, gasps and groans, panting, more whispers . . . their voices sounded so young and so ridiculously chaste. What makes two young people do this for a living? Perhaps they were students in dire need of pocket money. They seemed so near . . . right beside him, and he had the strangest feeling that he was participating. He could feel the heat of her body, and the bare skin under his wandering hands. He was getting a hard-on and he thanked heavens that Simon had left the room.

He pulled himself together and wondered about his ignorance. His state of virginity caused him deep humiliation, but he was shy. Other than Daisy, he seldom had a chance to meet girls, except Daisy's friends, who he'd decided were out of bounds. He still loved Daisy, but the pain was lessening. The blue movie was in French and it had a story of sorts about a young and beautiful girl of sixteen who was orphaned during the Crimean War.

To his shame, he fell asleep.

He woke when Simon came back and switched off. 'You got the picture?'

'Unfortunately not, but I got the soundtrack.'

'That's what I meant, clever stick. OK, take off your blindfold.'

Miro pushed the scarf up with difficulty, and slid it off his head.

'Now listen. You have been at the movies with Daisy and Mike. Mike returns to his camp. Helen has waited up for you. Daisy makes you coffee from the US stores with which I keep you well supplied. You go to bed, but you're not going to sleep for a while. Instead, you make yourself comfortable on a blanket in the wardrobe, pushing the clothes to one side and putting the duffel coat around your shoulders. The central heating switches off at ten. Remember? You have a torch and I gave you some new batteries. By the way, here's the torch. You have a pencil and notebook. You jot down what you hear. And this is what you are going to hear on your very first night back, which is tomorrow night. OK?'

'I'm with you.'

'Helen complains that I spend too much time in Dover. This is in between the sighs and kisses that you've been listening to. I tell her that it can't be helped. I explain rather pompously that the Brits simply don't have the know-how to do the job themselves. They have excellent deep sea divers, but scuba divers can do most of the work quicker and we're all in a hurry. I'm in a hurry, too, but Helen prevaricates and persists in questioning me. I tell her it's classified, so she withholds sex, complaining that I don't trust her, or love her. Finally I give in and tell her a little more, which is that British and US forces are combining their technical skills to lay a pipeline for petrol right across the Channel, from Dover to Calais, so that all Allied vehicles will be able to refill on the other side, once they have secured a beachhead. You got that?'

'Loud and clear.'

'The pipeline is being laid by specially converted barges, but the first hundred yards of the pipe consists of a different kind of material which is more flexible, but also more delicate so it has to be carefully checked every inch of the way: joints and joins must be carefully inspected, reefs must be avoided, and the pipe must be laid within twelve months, in time for the invasion. OK, you got that?'

'Absolutely,' Miro said.

'I guess they explained to you at school, that if Paddy or his masters were to realize that you had given them deliberate disinformation, it would enable them to sort out what it is we are trying to hide, and this could cost the lives of hundreds of thousands of young soldiers.'

'Yes, I know,' Miro said.

'Well then. We're going to have a drink over at Bush House with some of the guys you've already met and then it's home in time for supper. I believe that Helen is planning a great reunion, because Daisy is arriving home today, too.'

He glanced shrewdly at Miro. 'Don't give yourself away . . . not by your manner, nor your new found self-confidence, nor our friendship. You must be the same introverted, cynical Miro with the chip on his shoulder. The same goes for your future meetings with Paddy. From now on, every second of every minute, night and day, you must be on your guard, watching what you say and what you do.'

So what's new? Miro said, but silently to himself, so that Simon would not hear.

Thirty

The house seemed like an empty shell with the children away. Helen was lonely and filled with vague misgivings. Had anything happened to any of them? Normally she would stifle her fears, but with the doodlebug, as Hitler's rocket was called, you could never be sure. Only one had exploded in their district so far, probably because it was off-course, but in London and the surrounding roads there had been loads of hits.

John was often grumpy and tense. She sensed that he felt guilty for driving Daisy away. He'd come close to apologizing once or twice, but it wasn't all his fault, she reckoned. Daisy was headstrong and willful. She might be the splitting image of Mia, but there was a lot of Eric in her, too. She went to extraordinary lengths to get her own way. But how could she criticize her talented daughter when she was missing her so much?

She heard her father's footsteps on the driveway. He came into the kitchen nursing a bulky carrier bag.

'I'm glad you're back, Dad. What have you got there?' As she leaned over the table she smelled liquor on his breath. 'You've been down at the pub.'

'You're damn right. I've been chatting up the barmaid, and look what I have here.' He lovingly unwrapped five bottles of French claret.

'You're a genius, or should I say a gigolo? Young or old, you know how to charm them.'

'Hey, steady on there. I paid for the wine in hard cash, not in kind.'

She laughed. 'It's perfect. Just what we need. Thank you, Dad.'

'It's a peace offering,' he said.

'And gratefully accepted. Miro and Simon are on the way back from London, but Miro called from a cafe to let me know they'd be late. I've been expecting Mike and Daisy for the past hour.'

'I think I can hear them,' John said. Helen followed her father to the porch and shivered as her condensed breath drifted away.

'Mum . . . Mum . . .' Daisy ran up the driveway and flung her arms around Helen. 'We had to walk from the station . . . of course, the train was delayed. I'm so sorry, Mum. We intended to call one of Mike's friends to fetch us, but the station phone is out of order.'

'Say hello to Gramps,' Helen whispered.

'Hello, Gramps.'

'I'm glad you're back, Daisy,' he muttered grudgingly.

Mike joined them. 'Hi there, Gramps,' he began with a friendly smile holding out his hand.

John scowled at him, but took his hand. 'You can call me Gramps if and when you marry my granddaughter. Meantime I'm Mr Cooper, or sir. Take your pick, young man.'

Flushing, Mike fought down a surge of irritation and followed Helen to the kitchen. 'I'm quite handy in the kitchen. What can I do to help, Mrs Conroy.'

'Oh for goodness sake call me Helen, like you always do,' she said. 'Everything's ready and in the warmer, but we're still waiting for Simon and Miro.' She smiled at him. 'I want to thank you for persuading Daisy to come home.'

'She wanted to come home,' he retorted.

'I'm sure she did. I have no doubt that she regretted her hasty action, but she would not have come, nor would she have phoned me without quite an effort on your part. You seem to have influence. I hope things work out for you both.'

Mike felt touched by Helen's friendly welcome. As far as he was concerned, Helen could do no wrong. He had warmed to her at their very first meeting. He hardly remembered his own mother, just vague memories of eyes as blue as Helen's and a smile as warm as hers. He was quite ready to adopt Daisy's family as his own, but her grandfather's snub had wounded him.

'I don't think Mr Cooper will ever accept me.' Mike sensed that he could confide in Helen.

'He's become a bit grumpy and I think it's part of growing old. He's frightened that we will go away and leave him alone. Of course we wouldn't do that. Age is a strange thing, Mike. It's like putting on another outfit, like you put on your GI uniform, so everyone takes you for a soldier, but of course you're really a farmer and goodness knows what else besides, and so it is with an *old* appearance.'

'Surely one feels old. Here, let me do that.' He took the cloth out of her hands and began to dry the saucepans.

'I don't think so, Mike, but I'll let you know one day. I think you still feel the same person, but everyone says you're old and when you look in the mirror you are shocked to see that you *look old* and maybe you get scared and grumpy, but you know underneath you're the same person you always were.'

'He probably thinks that I'm shooting a line with Daisy, but I know we're going to marry one day and I know we'll be happy. The moment I saw her I knew. He doesn't understand.'

'Perhaps he understands only too well. That's why he's scared. Go and make friends with John. Ask him about Mia, or the Great War, or even the Home Guard.'

Mike chose Mia, and in no time at all John Cooper had produced the sherry and he was drifting into the distant past, talking as if it happened only yesterday, with tears in his eyes and a far away smile on his lips.

Daisy came running downstairs in her prettiest skirt and blouse, with a brand new ring on her finger that she was dying to show off.

'Look, Mum.' She waved her hand at Helen.

'It's beautiful, Daisy. Congratulations, darling.' She kissed her daughter and turned away quickly to hide her expression, but Daisy noticed.

'Don't be sad, Mum. You'll love Mike. When you get to know him you'll realize how lucky I am.'

'I'm sure I will, Daisy. Just don't give up your career.'

'But I'm not giving up anything. Who said I was? Oh Mum . . . silly Mum!' She put her arms around her mother and hugged her hard. 'I'm sticking around while Mike is still in England. Then I'll take up my scholarship. I can be a painter in Denver. Why not?'

'And if Mike wanted you to give up your career?'

'But he doesn't and he never would. You don't understand him at all.'

'Well, give me time,' Helen said.

'Dinner smells divine. What is it?'

'Roast mutton.'

'But how on earth did you manage that?'

'May's daughter is training to be a model. She only eats fish and vegetables, so May swopped a month's meat coupons for my clothing coupons. She needs to dress well and we need to eat. It made sense.'

'If you carry on like this, Mum, you'll be walking around in rags.'

The moment they heard the jeep pull up, they raced out of the house.

'Miro, you're grown huge,' Daisy called out, running to hug him.

214 *Madge Swindells*

'Not really.' He grinned at her, shook Mike's hand, hugged Gramps and handed a package to Helen. 'A present,' he whispered as he kissed her on both cheeks. 'From Canterbury.'

'Come in all of you. Dinner's ready, but let's have a drink first.' Simon gave Helen a formal kiss on the cheek, but something about the way he looked at her caught Daisy's attention.

'Smells great,' he said.

'Dad dug up the vegetables and washed them and peeled the potatoes. We don't give him enough credit.'

'Do we have any sparkling wine, John?'

'Do we have an occasion?'

'Mike and Daisy are engaged.'

John bit his lip and went off to the cellar, but no one noticed his disappointment. They were too busy congratulating Daisy and Mike.

'Great to see you again, Mike.' Simon clapped him on the shoulder. 'Did you finish the job?'

'Yes. Fortunately I found a stack of engineers who are also good swimmers down at the Brixham camp. They enjoyed the training. We should write a manual on your method.'

'Would you all please go into the lounge,' Helen called. 'You're in my way.'

Daisy had turned her attention to Miro. He was different. His eyes glowed, his habitual stoop, that had kept the family nagging him for the past three years, had miraculously gone. He stood tall and he looked happy. Could a month spent playing the clarinet really do that for him? She had never thought that Miro was a musician at heart, despite his talent. He wasn't that committed. It was his intellect, not his talent, that drove him.

She jumped to the sound of a cork popping. Gramps had opened a bottle of champagne, Mum was carrying in a tray of glasses, suddenly the family were toasting their engagement. Daisy felt quite emotional – it was kindness, not weakness that had brought about this sudden change of heart.

Dinner passed too quickly. They all had stories to tell of their experiences during the past month or so. Only Miro was strangely silent. The penny dropped after dinner when they were sitting in the lounge.

'So what about a recital, Miro?' Daisy suggested. 'You were great before, so now you must be marvellous. Please play for us.'

The family echoed her plea.

'No. Not now,' Miro said.

'Oh, please.' Daisy persisted.

'You know how I hate performing, Daisy. I feel like a circus animal, it's totally not me. My father used to make me do it and I hated it.'

'But that's what musicians do, isn't it?' She frowned at him, longing to understand. 'You perform. What's the point of trying for a place at a college of music if you don't want to perform? Or are you aiming to be a composer? Even composers conduct their own music.'

It was then that Miro looked to Simon for help. It was an instantaneous gesture, and as quickly withdrawn, but Simon saw and came to his assistance.

'I guess there's a difference to being a member of a large orchestra and standing up alone after a couple of glasses of wine.'

'More than a couple, I fear,' Miro agreed.

Everyone laughed and Simon came up with a funny story about a skiing escapade when he was under the influence to try and take the attention off Miro.

Daisy sat silently wondering about Miro's amazing transformation. He'd only been away for a few weeks. She sensed that she had hit on something deep and hidden, something that no one must know. Was Miro working for Simon? The more she thought about it the more likely it seemed. Since when could playing the clarinet make you stronger, taller, suntanned and fit? Perhaps it was only she who could see that Miro had left as a loser and returned a month later as a winner.

The family was irrevocably changed. Mum laughed more than she used to. She had been quite browbeaten by her father. Now she was more assertive and less inclined to do what she felt was expected of her. Simon was good for her, Daisy decided. Simon himself seemed part of the family. When the American occupation was over, life in England would never be the same again. She felt so sure of this. But Gramps would still be Gramps. Nothing would ever change him, she reckoned. It was a comforting thought and after Mike had gone back to the camp, she spent a while with her grandfather, talking about his youth and the pottery and the way things once were.

Thirty-One

It was mid-December. The talking and the learning were over and now was the time for action — a time of danger. Miro approached the bus station, padlocked his bike to the post and crept towards the steps. There stood the pillbox: gross, ugly and twice as large as life, silhouetted against the moonlit sea.

Miro swallowed hard and tried to pluck up the courage to walk towards it. Paddy was lurking somewhere there. Paddy believed that he had been sent to study music for a month, but he had returned suntanned, muscled and fit. But after all, it was midnight and very dark, Miro assured himself. Paddy might also wonder why he had not been interned, since he had turned seventeen.

Something was moving. The great lake of shadow that surrounded the pillbox had stretched and flowed into another shape and it was silently coming his way. Miro's fear was becoming physical. It felt as if his hair was standing up on end all over his back and shoulders and down his arms, prickling and tingling, a sensation he had never before experienced. Paddy was walking towards him with a heavy tread. His huge shoulders were hunched, his head jutted forward and Miro could sense the menace in the man.

'Hi,' Miro said shakily.

'Well, if it isn't Miro himself, back in the land of the living, after a month spent playing the clarinet.' His voice brought twinges to Miro's stomach.

'Not all the time.' Miro gave a casual laugh that sounded too high-pitched, even to him. 'Uncle Fred is a bit past it. Four hours tuition a day was his maximum. I spent the rest of the time enjoying myself.'

'Doing what exactly?' he growled.

'A lot of roaming around to see what's going on.'

'Glad you tried to make yourself useful. What else?'

'I joined a gym, a Christmas present from Uncle Fred. He has a dam and I swam a lot. Got a bit suntanned despite the season.'

'Why are you making excuses for yourself . . . are you guilty of something?'

Miro swore inwardly. 'I got a bit of flack from Helen. She thought I hadn't been studying enough, but she got over it.'

'So what have you got for me?' Paddy leaned closer and Miro almost gagged on the stench of tobacco and stale sweat.

'Well, nothing really. Nothing much, that is. I saw a huge build-up of forces and equipment all around the south east. It's chaotic. The coast has become one massive armed camp. All coastal areas are banned to visitors . . . but I'm sure you know that . . . and US troops are camped on every pavement and corner of spare land.'

'And what are the Yanks doing with themselves?'

'Training, I suppose. Military exercises are taking place in almost every village. Troops are being moved in every day. You should see Dover harbour. It's jam-packed. Troop carriers are lying off-shore all around the south east, waiting their turn to unload.'

'How did you see all this?' Paddy asked.

'It wasn't a problem. If you have relatives, or you're staying in the restricted area, as I was, there are no problems. From the cliff tops you can see everything. It used to be all cows, now it's planes, tanks, lorries and troops . . . all under canvas.'

His words poured out impulsively. It was not exactly what Simon had told him to say. But Simon was wrong. He felt this instinctively. To come back from holiday and have everything off pat would be a mistake.

'I only got back the night before last,' he said. 'But listen. Things have changed while I was away. Daisy got engaged to a Yank.'

'To that fellow she met last year?'

'You've got a good memory,' Miro said.

'They came in useful, didn't they?' He laughed and once again Miro shivered.

'I guess so. My foster mum seems to be having it off with the lodger.'

'The scuba diving instructor?'

'Yes. They think no one knows, but he goes creeping into her room when we're supposed to be asleep. I can hear their voices vaguely. They talk a lot. I'm in the next room, but I can't hear what they're saying.'

'So what do you think they talk about?' Paddy sounded tense. Miro could sense his excitement. Good, a bullseye!

'Dunno . . . can't hear . . . sometimes I catch the odd word.'

'Been listening in, have you? Dirty little bugger. Listening to the sexy bits.'

'I would never have expected Helen . . .' Miro's voice tailed off.

'Ah, but you should always suspect women because they're devious. Try putting a glass against the wall and your ear against the glass. It sometimes amplifies the sound.'

'The problem is there's a ruddy great wardrobe on their side.'

'Built in, is it?'

'No, a big, old-fashioned oak thing. Helen doesn't like it, but she has no idea what to do with it. I had another idea. How about I make a hole through the wall, behind the wardrobe and hang a picture or a poster on my side to cover up? Or I could move my wardrobe to cover the hole and sit inside it.'

'Good idea. Tell you what? I'll lend you an electric drill. I've got one in the van. Come up to the bus station and wait there a minute.' The two went side by side to the bus station where Miro sat on a seat to wait. He heard Paddy's footsteps fading, and then the sound of the van being unlocked, and the footsteps approaching again.

Paddy suspected him. He could hear it in his voice. Miro mopped his forehead with his handkerchief. He was sweating with fright. Thank God it was dark. Paddy moved swiftly to Miro's side and caught him by the upper arm, pulling him off balance. Miro let his arm go slack so he wouldn't feel the muscle. 'Putting on a bit of weight, aren't you Miro?'

'Is there a law against it?'

He switched on his torch, blinding Miro. 'Why are you sweating, boyo? You never used to give a damn. Now you're scared. Why is that?'

'I don't like standing here waiting to get caught. What if one of the Yanks passes and sees me? They could tell Simon. And why are you shining a torch on my face so anyone can recognize me? What the hell's got into you?'

The torch went off and Paddy grunted his approval. 'Are you looking for a job, Miro?'

'No.'

'What then?'

'I'm studying to become a clarinettist. I have a place at a London college for next year.'

'Why not this year?'

'I have to think about my parents. I told them I didn't feel ready yet.'

'OK, you're right. See you on Wednesday. Try not to be so late next time.'

'Now I've left school, I can't pretend to be helping friends with their homework. I've lost my alibi.'

'Try the cinema, or invent a girlfriend. Any damn thing.'

'Yes, all right,' Miro said, feeling glad to get away.

Simon quizzed him the next morning when they went for an early morning ride down to the bay. 'How did it go?'

'Better than I had expected.'

'Why? What were you expecting?'

'Trouble. I've changed. According to Daisy I'm taller, stronger, suntanned and more self assured. I no longer stoop. They knocked that out of me in the first couple of days of drilling, so I was scared he'd pick up on all that . . . and he did. I'm pretty sure it went all right finally. I told him what I'd seen around the south east, but I held back on the news you told me to give him.'

'Why was that, Miro? There's plenty more where that came from,' Simon said.

'It was too much too soon. He's a shrewd bastard. I was supposed to be listening through the wall but these old houses are built substantially. It didn't feel right.'

'The room is partitioned and the connecting wall is made of wood.'

'Yes, I know, but to have it all worked out pat so soon after I returned. It seemed dangerous. I'm sure he would have suspected me. As it is, I told him I'd find a way to listen in and he lent me a drill.'

'Did he? That's great. I like that. I think we'll have to make that hole in John's wall, Miro. The house is often empty. Paddy could break in to check up on you. It's life and death for him.'

'I'm going on Wednesday evening to give back the drill and any information I've overheard, so that's when I'll give him the info about the pipeline.'

'Good and I may find something else for you by then. You did the right thing, Miro. Always obey your instinct, or your sixth sense. That's a major rule in our work. I should have thought it out more carefully. Come on, let's go.'

They had reached the beach. Miro felt light-headed as they galloped over the sand dunes. It was a sunny, winter's morning and in no time Miro and his horse were in a lather. Things were going well for him. He'd flung off his guilt and moved on. All he had to do now was keep Paddy happy and not let him suspect that he was a double agent. He reckoned the war would be over in a year, or a little more. If only his parents could survive until then.

'I'd love to have a swim,' Miro said, watching the sea sparkling in the sun.

'Go on then. I'll take the horses to the spring.'

Miro stripped down to his underpants and ran down the beach to the sea, running and splashing until the water reached his thighs. Then he surged forward in a fast crawl to circle the old wreck before hypothermia set in, returning through the breaking surf, diving under a massive roller and fighting the backwash that caught at him. There was one nasty moment when the sea dragged him back and rolled him over the sand, but he fought and won and coasted in on a metre high roller, fired with exhilaration. His mouth and eyes stung with salt and his skin tingled and glowed.

They returned along the steep, zigzag path which the troops had dug out and resurfaced until it could take a convoy of trucks if necessary. Reaching the cliff top they paused and looked back at the sea shimmering below. 'Jesus! It's almost eight,' Simon exclaimed as he glanced at his watch. 'Come on. Race you back.'

Miro grimaced. None of the mares could beat Daunty, but he loved to try. He set off at a gallop and Simon followed.

'Can a Czech national join the US army, Simon?' Miro asked. He was rubbing down his horse and trying to look unconcerned. 'I'd sure like to be in your team. I'm good with languages. I could be useful. You know how I long to get into the war.'

'I've been thinking much the same thing, so I'll try my best,' Simon promised. 'But I can't promise to succeed. PWE want you for the radio station they are setting up on the German border, as and when we get there. Let's see what transpires.'

Despite his optimism, Miro was almost rigid with fear when Wednesday night came and he had to cycle to his controller's rendezvous. Paddy had caught a bad flu, which was gratifying. His voice was hoarse, he coughed and sneezed repeatedly and complained about a sore throat and earache.

Handing back the drill, Miro told him about the hole he had made at the back of Helen's wardrobe and how he had covered it on his side with his peg board.

Paddy examined his drill. 'This is new and it hasn't been used,' he said, looking grim.

Simon had decided that it was useless for the job because the wall was made of wood, a recent partition, they found, so Miro borrowed a brace and bit from Gramps' toolbox.

'It wasn't. Evidently the room was partitioned with wooden panels years ago. I took a brace and bit out of Gramps' tool box and did it when they were at church on Sunday morning.'

Paddy scowled at him. 'OK,' he said thoughtfully, as if turning the whole matter over in his mind. 'Good boy. Now, what have you got for me?'

It's so easy to slip up, Miro was thinking. And if he lost out, it would probably be over something as insignificant as Paddy's drill.

'Listen to this . . .' He tried to hide his fear and sound enthusiastic. 'Simon came creeping up at one a.m. Helen was asleep, but she woke. There was a bit of love stuff, but basically Helen seemed peeved. She complained that Simon spends too much time in Dover. He tried so soft soap her with kissing her and that sort of thing. He told her how lovely she was looking at dinner, but she wasn't satisfied. She wanted to know what was going on. I think she thought he might have another girl there. This went on for a long time, but she wouldn't give in and finally Simon said, "It's classified." She replied, "Then I'm going to sleep." '

'That's how women operate,' Paddy growled.

'So Simon said, "We and the Brits are combining our skills to lay a pipeline for petrol right across the Channel, from Dover to Calais, so that Allied vehicles will be able to refill on the other side as soon as they have secured the beaches." Then he explained that they needed scuba divers because things snarl up all the time: the joints have to be inspected regularly, reefs have to be blown up, and the pipe must be finished within twelve months in time for the invasion.' Miro paused.

'That's it?' Paddy questioned.

'Sure. But wait a minute. There's something else. That was Sunday night.' Was he overdoing the info, Miro wondered? Paddy should be thrilled at the news . . . unless he was still suspicious.

'On Monday night, Simon told Helen that the invasion would not be before August. There's a delay because they have to wait for landing craft. There aren't enough. Simon and Helen are going on a short holiday at the beginning of July. I didn't write that down because I knew I would remember.'

He offered Paddy the notebook. 'Look here, shall I tear the pages out? I can't afford another notebook.'

'Let's have a look at it.' Paddy flipped through the remainder of the empty pages, tore out Miro's notes and handed the rest back.

'There you are, Miro. You've done well. Our masters will be very pleased and this will affect your parents, you can be sure of that.'

'I haven't had a picture for some time,' Miro said. 'I'd like one soon.'

'Don't you trust me, boyo?'

'I trust you, but I don't trust the camp guards.'

'I'd feel the same in your shoes. Fair enough. I'll send on your request. By the way, I'm going away for a month. I'll see you on the last Wednesday of January. Make sure you don't get lax while I'm away. I'll expect something riveting.' Inexplicably, he squeezed Miro's shoulder. 'You've done well, boyo. I'll leave first today. Wait five minutes before you go.'

Miro waited impatiently, the beach was pale and empty under a half moon. The sea murmured on the sand in small, quiet waves, pillboxes stood in rows along the beach, barbed wire prevented swimmers from entering the sea. This was one of those heavily fortified beaches once considered ideal for invading forces. Ancient history, Miro considered. He wished that it could all be cleared away. Just like he longed for the war to be over. But then Simon and Mike would be gone and maybe Daisy, too. And what about his parents? Would they be free? Had they survived?

As he trudged up the beach in the loose sand, his shoes making a grating sound, he blew his nose and spat and tried to get the taste out of his mouth and the stench out of his nostrils. Was it the pillbox or Paddy, he wondered?

Thirty-Two

Rumours of a party to be given by the combined US camps around Mowbray on New Year's Eve caused a wave of excitement in Mowbray. It was to be held in a five-star hotel, the Mowbray Heights, built on a cliff top overlooking the bay. The party would see out the rainswept December and welcome in a brand new year. By the time the year was over they'd be well on the way to victory, or so everyone believed.

Lately no one talks of anything else, Helen mused as she cycled into Mowbray to do her Christmas shopping. Over five hundred guests were expected, which was most of the village; the best looking girls were scrambling for invitations and dressmakers were working all hours running up ball gowns from dyed parachute silk. The band would consist mainly of GIs stationed around the village, but a few local musicians had been invited to give solo performances, one of whom was Miro Levy who would play 'String of Pearls'.

Helen had spent the last ten days making a fashionable dress for Daisy and at the fitting, for the first time, she noticed her daughter's plumper breasts.

'Heavens, you're getting busty, Daisy? Are they feeding you too well on the farm?'

'I guess so, Mum. All that butter and cream on our bread and jam.'

On the night of nights, John's car made a rare appearance. Helen, Miro and Daisy, who were waiting in the car, tried to contain their impatience as Gramps spent a long time going through his pockets for the house keys. At last he locked the door, turned and stepped down from the porch. Hunched and frowning, he hobbled towards them, as if walking on marbles. He sighed as he stooped and ducked his head into the car, sending the scent of moth balls, aftershave and tobacco over them. He twisted around and let gravity take over, falling backwards into the seat with a grunt and a curse as he bumped his knee on the steering wheel. No one had wanted John to drive. He had insisted, but they controlled their irritation because they loved him.

They proceeded at a funeral pace as John peered short-sightedly through the windscreen. Blackout restrictions were lax because there were no longer raids over England. Doodlebugs passed over Dorset occasionally, but only when they were off-course. Emerging from the trees, they saw that the cliff was blazing with multicoloured lights. Soon they heard snatches of music carried by the wind.

Feet tapping, fingers clenched together, Daisy's face was bright with anticipation. She knew she looked superb, despite Mum's grumbling. Her skin had never looked so fresh and clear, her eyes were wide and sparkling, her dress could have been on the front page of *Vogue*. Even Miro had said so, yet he seemed so quiet and introverted lately. Most times you can't get a word out of him, Daisy thought to herself. Look at him now, the silly clot, face all screwed up with nervousness, you'd think the world was coming to an end, but he was only playing the clarinet, when all was said and done.

Music was far from Miro's thoughts. He could not shake off his fear. Paddy would be back soon and he sensed coming disaster. He had no facts to back up his fears — it was just a strange feeling of foreboding and however much he tried he could not shake it off.

Daisy squeezed his hand. 'Don't worry, Miro. No one can play like you. You'll stun them, just you wait and see.'

Nearing the gates they saw that the entrance was blocked by military police checking the tickets. When they caught sight of them, they saluted smartly and waved them through. 'Go ahead, sir. Have a good time, ma'am . . . and you Miss Daisy,' they said.

'I feel like royalty,' Helen said, smiling to herself.

At the hotel entrance, night burst into day. 'Wow!' Daisy gasped. It was four years since Daisy had seen lights blazing at night and she was fired with excitement. John stepped out of the car and handed the keys to a GI doing duty as a parking attendant. The soldiers helped the women out of the car and a tsunami of sound and light engulfed them and swept them into the entrance hall, where flashlights dazzled them. The GIs whistled under their breath while the attendants took their coats.

Mike was waiting. He shook hands with Helen and John, clapped Miro on the shoulder and grabbed Daisy. 'Get lost, you guys,' Mike told his buddies and led Daisy on to the dance floor. They were playing 'Moon Love'. The two danced so well together and the band was superb. Helen stood watching them for a few minutes. The music changed, the ballroom was filled with jiving couples, but Helen had to admit that Daisy and Mike were the best. It was thrilling to watch them. The jiving ended and a GI threesome sang one of the latest hits, 'Moonlight Becomes You'. They sang well. Groups of pretty young girls were standing around waiting for one of the shy Yanks to ask them to dance.

Helen was impressed. She knew so many of the guests and since there was no sign of Simon, she made her way towards the bar, stopping every few seconds to greet someone she knew. Weaving through the crowd while looking for someone to dance with, Helen caught snatches of conversation:

'They say they're leaving this month. '

'The weather's too bad, so don't believe it.'

'I've heard we're short of landing craft.'

'A U-boat has been seen in the Channel.'

'They're expecting millions of casualties.'

'You can't believe all you hear.'

May buttonholed her. She looked quite different: petite and glamorous with make-up on and a lovely dress instead of their usual uniform of thick, navy dungarees. She was holding a glass and a bottle of champagne and looked happy. 'Hi, Helen, grab a glass and let me fill it for you. One of my daughters is going steady with one of the Yanks, hence this invitation.'

'I'll fetch a gin and tonic, May. I'm not fond of champagne, although I'll have a glass at midnight to see the New Year in.'

'I guess the guy who's billeted on you gave you the invitations,' May asked, her bright eyes alight with curiosity.

'Well, they have our fields. Fair's fair,' Helen murmured.

'You never talk about him. What's he like? Is he here?'

Helen shrugged. 'He's . . . he's just like any one of them. I expect he's here.' She tried her best to look non-committal, but then she felt two hands clutching her shoulders.

'Hi darling,' Simon said. He wrapped one arm around her waist. 'I've been looking all over for you. You look lovely. Come and dance. Excuse us,' he said to May. 'I've been longing to dance with my date.'

Helen laughed at May's astonishment.

'You're a dark horse,' May called after her.

Arms around each other they swayed to a foxtrot. The band was superb. Then she realized that Miro was playing 'Perfidia'.

'Simon . . . it's Miro. He's really great.' They stood still watching him.

'He's a real pro,' Simon said.

They applauded and listened proudly to the audience's whistles and stamping. After a few words from the band leader, Miro stepped forward again and the band played 'Moonlight Serenade'.

'I need to talk to you,' Simon said, when the dance was over. 'Let's move to the terrace where it's quieter.' Leading her to the heated terrace, he found a seat for her and went in search of one for himself. 'Hang on to this, while I get us some drinks.'

'It's like this, Helen,' he said when he returned. 'I want to know how you'd feel about marrying me.' He grinned self-consciously.

'I love you with all my heart.' She smiled, wondering why he needed this reassurance. 'And all the rest of me, of course.'

'Enough to marry me . . . now . . . before we go? And it could be any time? A week . . . a month . . . No one knows for sure.'

'I can't leave my family until they are all settled.'

'We wouldn't be able to move to the States until after the war.'

'It's not a case of love, Simon, but of duty. I can't leave my kids and I can't abandon John. Most of his antipathy towards you is because he doesn't want to lose his family and be left alone. He's been very good to us. Why should I abandon him now . . . in his old age? He's pushing eighty.'

'You could persuade him to sell the house and fields and join us in the States.'

'I have to consider Miro and Daisy, too. I need to see them settled before I leave England.'

Simon looked upset, so she took hold of his hands. 'You will never know how much I long to say yes, Simon, but I can't allow Daisy to feel that she's getting in the way of my happiness. She has a home with her mother and I aim to keep it that way until she flies the nest. The same applies to Miro. He's like my son. If I were to marry you now, Daisy and Miro would know I'm waiting to leave for America. They'd feel pressurized and even homeless.' She gazed appealingly at him. 'I've been a good mother. I've put a lot into it. I don't want to ruin it now.' Simon was gazing out of the window. There was an ominous silence. 'Surely you understand. I need to wait until the kids are older and settled with jobs and their own homes.'

'They seemed like my kids, too,' he said quietly.

They danced for a while, but it wasn't quite the same anymore. When one of the GIs needed to talk to Simon, she went looking for John. She found him sitting alone in an easy chair tucked around the corner of the bar. Unbelievably he was having a snooze. Compassion surged.

'Ah! There you are. Did you hear Miro playing solo, Dad?'

'I certainly did and I was impressed. The boy has enormous talent. He should be studying music. Perhaps we've failed him.'

'Right now he wants nothing more than to get into a fighting unit. Well, I can't say I blame him. Stay there, Dad. I'm bringing someone to talk to you.'

May was dancing with her daughter. 'Do me a favour, May. Come and talk to my father. He's a bit older than you, but he's a good dancer . . . or he was.'

She left them together and the next time she saw them, they were doing the Charleston with a small circle of admirers gathered around them. John, smiling for once, with crimson cheeks and shining eyes, seemed to have shed a couple of decades.

Daisy, who was jiving flamboyantly, but expertly to 'Chattanooga Choo Choo', suddenly felt thirsty and dizzy. Her back hurt and she felt tearful and fretful. 'I'm tired,' she complained.

'Well, that's a first. I thought you never got tired.' Mike scanned her face and saw how pale she had become with deep shadows under her eyes. 'Let's get some food for you. How about a coke first?'

'I would absolutely hate a coke right now,' Daisy said vehemently, surprising herself. 'I'd like a glass of cold milk . . . really cold. Yes, that's what I'd like. And I'd like it now. I'm truly desperate.'

Mike saw a flash of petulance in her mouth, but moments later her mood had changed. 'Jesus, Mike. Try and get that milk fast. And a piece of bread with butter on it. That will make me feel OK. Just a slice of nice brown bread. Not the rubbish we've been getting nowadays.'

'I'll get it myself, hon. Just sit tight there.'

Mike grabbed a waiter and paid him to show him the way to the kitchen to get her snack fast. The waiter was Polish, he'd come over to join the war only to find that his heart was faulty. 'How far gone is she?' he asked.

'What do you mean?' Mike knew what he meant, but shock had turned him into an idiot.

'Your wife. She is pregnant, yes?'

'I don't know,' Mike said.

'*Mazel tov!*' The waiter smiled knowingly.

Mike's blood ran cold as he considered his predicament. Daisy was too young to marry and he was about to fight his way through Europe. He wouldn't be there to help her. Her family would be furious and she would bear the brunt of their contempt. Their leaving could be anytime now. Everyone knew that they would get very little notice. What would she do? What could he do? He'd been so careful to pull out in time since they'd started making love. Surely it wasn't possible. No, of course not. Daisy would have told him.

Moments later he hurried back to her, the waiter following, with the milk and the bread and butter on a tray. He glanced approvingly at Daisy. 'Lucky you,' he whispered. Lucky wasn't the word Mike would have chosen at that moment.

Daisy gobbled it all and sighed because she would have liked more. He tried to tempt her with the buffet supper, but she would have none of it.

'Daisy,' he whispered, when they were sitting on the glass-enclosed terrace watching the moonlight shining on the rippling sea. 'When was your last period?'

'Why do you ask that?' She felt irritated. First Mum, now Mike. There was nothing wrong. She couldn't be pregnant. Things like that didn't happen to girls like her. She'd only been having periods for two years. She was a late starter and they were never regular. She was just late and that was all.

'We seem to have been making love on and off ever since Brixham. I don't remember you having a period since then.'

'It's just late, that's all. I find the whole business absolutely yucky. D'you mind if we don't talk about it.'

'We must talk about it. We share everything, don't we?'

'Oh Mike. I missed a period, but so what. I've never been regular and I've missed periods before. Forget it. I don't want to talk about it ever again. We always take care, don't we?'

Icy shivers ran through him. Shocked and helpless, he no longer felt like dancing, or eating, or anything. He just wanted to know, so he could make a plan.

'Let's dance,' she said.

'No, you look so pale, you should rest.'

'Oh . . . how ridiculous. I suppose you'll be brooding over this forever.'

Shouldn't you be? he thought.

'I'm going to ask someone to dance with me. I feel like dancing,' she said moodily.

'OK. Come on then.' They were playing 'South of the Border' and Mike took hold of Daisy and propelled her slowly round the ballroom. She was certainly changed: moody, emotional and difficult and she looked pale and drawn, although she had been fine when they arrived.

'Ouch!' she said. 'You're not concentrating. You stood on my foot.'

'Would you marry me, Daisy?' he replied.

'I thought we'd already settled that. After the war I'll join you in Denver and we'll get married.'

'But would you marry me now?'

'Yes, of course, if we could, but I'm only seventeen.'

'I'll think of something,' he said.

John was enjoying himself. May and he had danced for two hours, eaten their way through prawns, chicken and trifle and told each other their life stories. Now she was leaving with her daughter and her daughter's GI boyfriend. John linked arms with her and kissed her on the cheek.

'Listen May, I don't know how you'd feel about seeing me again, for supper, or a film . . . anything you'd like.'

'What would Helen think of that?' she asked.

'I'm sure she'd be delighted. After all, she introduced us.'

'Then I'd like that. I've been very lonely since Reg died.'

He beamed as he waved them goodbye. When Helen found him sitting by the bar she couldn't help noticing that he looked much happier.

'How d'you feel after all your dancing, Dad?'

'Delighted! You've been keeping an eye on me, have you?'

'Spellbound actually. I had no idea you had all that energy.'

'Well, now you know. May's quite a girl. A good sport and fun to be with.'

'Yes, I like her, too,' Helen said.

Helen, on the other hand, was feeling tired and despondent. It's like a bloody orgy, she thought, gazing moodily at the bar and the buffet. There had been so much revelry and laughter, and the guests, stuffed with food and dizzy with champagne, had sweated and writhed their way through the latest dance steps, all desperate to pack as much fun as they could into the time left, but no one knew just when the Yanks would go. A thrill of fear touched her as she thought of Simon fighting his way up the beaches against the

Germans' massed defences. She shuddered, blinked and rushed to the cloakroom to bathe her eyes.

The party came to an end all too soon, but from then on, as the days passed, it seemed to Helen that time had speeded up. It wasn't just Helen who felt like this. Everyone was complaining. Almost half of Mowbray was involved with someone in the armed forces.

Who would live? Who would die? These were the unspoken questions that were never voiced, but for women in love, the questions were always with them.

Helen began to think about God. She always went to church on Sunday mornings, but it was for the children's sake. She had lost her faith somewhere in the Southampton blitz, or perhaps it had begun long before in Dover, or when the young nun at Daisy's school was trapped in the chapel during the blitz and burned to death. All she knew was that no one was up there looking out for anyone. Nevertheless she prayed for the survival of every one of her loved ones and others whom she barely knew. What else could she do?

Thirty-Three

The weather was changing; the bitter cold of January had given way to windy days that were mainly grey. Living under canvas was always a pain, but the damp cold of an English winter made it so much worse. Mike began to notice new fears surfacing amongst his friends: first and foremost the fear of change. The young men knew that they were to be propelled into an unkind world. Perhaps because they dreaded leaving, the days were whizzing by faster and faster, leading them into the unknown. They might as well be going to another planet for all their beliefs and traditions would help them. The hitherto sacred concept of the sanctity of human life would no longer apply. They were about to become pawns: dispensable, disposable, disabled or deceased. What was a thousand lives lost, weighed against achieving long-term objectives? Life as they knew it was ending for the foreseeable future. This truth was beginning to slide into the guys' consciousness, just as England's cold humidity was seeping into their bones, making their joints ache. So they hid their fears, but they were always there, lurking around corners, waiting to catch them in their weaker moments, just like the aches in their joints.

Mike had other worries and they were not of his personal survival, but of Daisy's future. In spare moments he would count the weeks that had passed since Daisy could remember having a period. She wasn't sure, she didn't keep a record, what a bore it all was. Was it really possible that she could be so unconcerned about her altered state? Mike wondered. Perhaps it was a ploy to stop him from worrying. Yet she worried about her paintings. When she couldn't get them just as she wanted, all hell broke loose.

From the many calculations he had made, he reckoned she had conceived around about the end of November, in Brixham, when he'd climbed up that slippery corrugated iron roof to spend the night in her room. At the time, he'd felt as pleased as if he'd climbed Everest. So in mid-December she missed a period for the first time and in mid-January she missed it again. So she was six weeks gone. Early days. Anything could happen, according to a couple of married sergeants he had consulted. But nothing happened and in mid-February she missed her third period. It was time to get moving.

Mike had been doing some research, aided and abetted by his closest pals. In England, anyone under twenty-one needed their parents' permission to marry. Under the circumstances, Helen might very well give in, but Daisy refused to tell anyone about her pregnancy until they were married, and even after then no one should know until it showed, she vowed. He tried to talk her round, but she would not give in.

From an expensive visit to a local lawyer in Claremont, he learned that different laws held sway in Scotland. They could marry there from sixteen years on and all they needed were their birth certificates. A day to drive there, a day to drive back, two nights at a hotel, separated in the first one, together in the second, and a day to get married. Mike put in for three days leave at the end of February, but leave was refused. He appealed on compassionate grounds, but Captain Rose was adamant. 'All leave is cancelled for the foreseeable future. We have no idea when we're moving and when we do we won't get much notice,' he told Mike.

Mike's stomach clenched. So soon! When he got over his fright he wondered how Daisy would cope as an unmarried mother.

'I wouldn't care. Not a jot,' she told him that evening. 'We'll marry when you get back.'

'If I get back,' Mike muttered, when he was alone. Lately all their training was about coming in fast on landing craft in the face of enemy fire; wading through deep water carrying their gear; and moving from cover to cover to get out of the defenders' range. This was where sergeants came in useful. They had to get their men off the beach as fast as they could. The quicker they moved, the more men they saved. No one considered they could save them all, but Mike kept this to himself.

Everybody was scared and so was he, but no one talked about it. They quaked inwardly, but hid their fears. Watching his pals, Mike realized that this was true. He loved the guys and he wished he could blow away all their insecurity. They were young and had never been in a battle and his heart went out to them. The more he worried about them, the more his fears for himself evaporated. He was amazed by this strange transformation, but while his fears for his safety lessened, his fear for Daisy grew stronger every day.

Finally he went to Simon and told him why he needed leave: that his girl was pregnant, and there was nothing they could do about that. 'It wasn't planned, sir. I tried to be careful. I slipped up badly, but we aim to get married right after the war.'

'Let's get one thing straight, Lawson. Are we talking about Daisy?'

'I can't tell you, sir. She doesn't want me to.'

'Does her mother know?'

'She won't tell anyone until we're married.'

'It'll break Helen's heart and as for John . . . he'll never forgive you. His major fear is that the women in his life will marry Yanks and he'll lose out. I guess marriage is your best plan. What about your parents? Have you told them?'

'My mother died of cancer when I was a teenager. There's just my dad. He knows about Daisy and he approves. I own half the shares of our ranch and we do all right. If Daisy can take to ranching we'll be fine.'

'And if she can't?'

'I've promised her I'll try farming in England. I have a degree in agriculture.'

'Yes, I know. OK, I'll do my best, but you two must fly both ways. I need someone to demonstrate a new design of underwater diving equipment in Inverness. I'll try to swing it so that you go instead of me. No promises, but I'll see what I can do. You must leave and come back the same day. I'll throw in Daisy's airfare.'

'Why, sir? Why should you do that?'

'That's my business, so don't ask.'

'Yes, sir. Thank you, sir.'

After that he received a curt note from Captain Johnson. It said simply: 'March 30. Get organized with the bookings. Good luck.'

Daisy was stunned when Mike calmly announced that they would be married in Inverness the following week. He had written to Inverness Magistrate's Court to obtain the licence and he had booked their flights. When he explained about the total ban on all leave and the demonstration he must give on a new alternator, Daisy hugged him. 'You're a genius,' she said. 'I always knew you were.' Mike felt bad about stealing the Captain's thunder, but since he'd been told to leave Simon out of it, he endured her adoration as best he could.

Daisy could not help remembering what might have been when she stood in the plain room in Inverness Magistrates Court, for the simple ceremony, which lasted for five minutes, with two clerks as witnesses. Her mother had always planned a white wedding with a guest list running to a thousand, but it was best not to think about what might have been, she decided, as she pledged her life to Mike.

After their marriage ceremony, they drove in a hired car to a hotel
overlooking Loch Ness, where Mike had arranged to meet a group
of GIs who were trained in scuba diving. Leaving Daisy in the lounge
with coffee and biscuits, Mike met his team at the reception desk and
they walked down to the water's edge shouldering the gear.

Daisy watched him leave and then made her way to the public telephone to call her mother. Twice she picked up the receiver, only to
replace it. She felt truly embarrassed. Mum would be furious, but she
would also be worried. Daisy had crept out of the house at five that
morning, leaving a note for her mother which read, simply: 'Gone to
get married in Scotland. Back tonight. Love, Daisy.' Despite her bravado,
she was deeply ashamed at being pregnant and unmarried.

But she was married, she reminded herself. It seemed unbelievable, despite the two rings on her finger. Mrs Lawson. Mrs Daisy
Lawson. Murmuring the words a few times made her feel a trifle
braver. Until recently she had been in a state of denial about her
pregnancy, but now she allowed herself to consider the baby that
was growing inside her. Or perhaps it was all a mistake. There must
be other reasons for missing periods, morning sickness and putting
on weight, but Mike said there weren't. She shivered as she thought
about Mum. Gramps would be furious, but this had nothing to do
with him. But what about her mother? She loved her so much and
she wanted to look good in her eyes. Mum adored her and had
always been a good mother. Daisy was spoiled, she knew that, and
she knew, too, that she had been particularly hateful to Mum when
Dad disappeared.

Losing her courage, Daisy sank into a chair beside the telephone
and covered her face with her hands.

At that moment, Helen, too, was trying to hold back her tears as
she told Simon about her daughter's note. She looked shrivelled and
red-eyed and he guessed that the note had hit her hard – or was it
the rejection?

'How could Daisy do this to me?' she wailed.

'What else could she do since she's pregnant?'

'Pregnant!' She was so astonished, she stood staring at Simon with
her mouth open.

'Well, I don't know,' he hastily corrected himself. 'It's what I
assumed. It's a little over three months since she followed Mike to
Brixham. I noticed she's getting plump. Didn't you?'

'Well, yes, but I didn't . . .' Helen's voice tailed off. 'You don't understand how we feel about these things. One expects nicely brought up girls to remain virgins until they marry. It's simply not acceptable not to obey the rules.'

'Did you?'

'Of course.'

'It's the same in the States, but don't you think that things change in wartime? She was living with the land girls for a while. They probably influenced her, too. Anyway, she's almost eighteen.'

'Seventeen and a half. It doesn't matter what age she is, it's simply unacceptable.'

'I suppose that's why she was too scared to tell you.'

'Scared of me?'

'Of course. You seem to be hidebound in tradition and social mores. Daisy's an artist. She's a little bit different.'

'Is that what you think?'

'Yes.' He said firmly. 'Do your friends feel as you do?'

'Of course.'

'Then why don't you have another ceremony here?'

'Because you can't marry under eighteen.'

'But she's married by now. It wouldn't be illegal to bless the marriage. How about I pop down to see your local vicar and if he won't play ball, our chaplain sure as hell will. Get a nice wedding dress and have a reception. I would, if I were you. It would launch them nicely and keep local tongues from wagging. Something great for both of them to look back on.'

'Well, I don't know . . .' Helen frowned out of the window, not able to look at Simon.

'Nothing can be changed, so you might as well accept it graciously, as Daisy did when Eric walked out on you.'

She gasped and was about to retort, but changed her mind. 'She could wear my wedding dress. It's lovely. I have it packed in a trunk upstairs in the attic.'

'Well then! I can organize the reception.'

'Certainly not. We'll have it at the Mowbray Heights and John and I will organize it, but you will be our first invited guest. You can double as her father.'

'I'd be honoured.'

The telephone rang at that moment. Helen answered it, longing to hear Daisy's voice, but it was a voice she didn't recognize.

'Is that Mrs Helen Conroy?'

'Yes it is.'

'I have a Mrs Daisy Lawson on the line. Here she is.'

'Mum?'

'Daisy, darling. Congratulations. Hurry home. I'm missing you already.' Helen bit her lip and hung on to her cool.

'Mum, I'm sorry.' Daisy sounded tearful.

'How are you getting back?'

'By plane, Mum. We're being flown to Edinburgh by a US shuttle flight and we have our return tickets for the shuttle from Edinburgh to Croydon. Mike left the jeep there.'

'But why Inverness? Most folks who elope opt for the closest town across the border, which is Gretna Green.'

'Well, we had to get here somehow. Mike couldn't get leave. All leave has been cancelled. So he managed to be chosen to take up and demonstrate some new underwater diving equipment. It's a bit hush-hush. I shouldn't have told you that.'

'Never mind, darling. I didn't hear. Just make sure you don't miss the plane. See you later. You can stay here with Mike since you're a married woman now. That's if he can leave his base, of course. I've been planning a white wedding ceremony for you, just to bless your marriage. We'll have a reception at the hotel, if you like. It would please me so much.'

'Oh Mum.' Daisy burst into tears.

'Please don't cry on your wedding day. See you soon, Daisy. I love you. Take care.' Helen replaced the receiver.

'A scuba diving demo?' She glared accusingly at Simon.

'We're due to leave any time for the invasion. Mike might be killed. We're expecting heavy casualties. Better a widow than an unmarried mother.'

'Oh my God! Don't say that. Let's pray that they have a long and happy life together in Denver,' she said sternly. 'But thank you, Simon. Just one thing . . . why didn't you tell me?'

'Mike was sworn to secrecy. Daisy has no idea that he had to wangle this through me and I feel that it's better that she doesn't find out. She insisted that she would tell you after she was married, but all leave is cancelled, so they couldn't get to Scotland. It was a no go situation.'

'Thank you, Simon. You have planned a very neat solution to a very tricky problem.'

Helen lost no time in organizing the church and reception, because no one knew for sure exactly when the bridegroom would be gone.

A traditional wedding with the wider family was out of the question. Helen's and Eric's family were spread all over Britain and due to travel restrictions to the South of England, they were unable to attend, although invitations were sent to everyone. Mike's buddies and Helen's friends from the canteen and the armaments factory, and Daisy's and Miro's school friends and several of John's old buddies, filled the church to overflowing. The reception began at eight and went on until after midnight. Later they played the latest hits and the mood became sentimental. Clasped in Mike's arms, dancing to the mellow strains of 'Moonlight Serenade', Daisy thought her heart would burst with happiness.

Thirty-Four

The PWE, government agents and Simon had agreed that the spy, Brannigan, alias Paddy, had outlived his usefulness and was to be arrested as soon as he showed up in Claremont, but he did not return from his trip to Ireland. Since the end of January, Miro had been waiting in the pillbox every Wednesday night, but Brannigan had gone to ground. MI5 agents were watching his home, his shop, his usual haunts and his friends, but there had been no sign of him. Only his boat had quietly disappeared from its mooring at the beginning of March.

Simon knew that Miro was in danger and he worried about the boy most of the time. Miro had done a wonderful job. It was time to pull him in, but PWE and MI5 wanted him left just where he was.

'But why?' Simon exploded at a PWE meeting when yet another month had passed.

'You're thinking with your heart, not your head, Simon. Brannigan's attitude towards Miro will show us whether or not he's learned about our massive scam. If he or his controllers suspect Miro, they'll attempt to kill him and then we'll know. If they carry on as usual, it's OK. Hundreds of thousands of lives are at stake. Surely you can see where our priorities lie?'

'I'll pull him in myself,' Simon retorted in a fit of anguish.

'Miro knows the score. He won't agree. Our scam is at stake and so are his parents.'

They were right, as Simon found out shortly afterwards, when he tried to talk Miro into throwing in the towel. Simon had to endure his guilt as best he could.

On a cold morning early in May, Miro showered, dressed and went outside to fetch the mail from the gate, which was his morning chore. A note, delivered by hand in a plain envelope addressed to M. Levy, was lying in the letterbox amongst the letters and bills. It read: 'Be at the car park at Claremont fishing harbour at 10 p.m., Tuesday night.' A wave of fear shot through him, leaving him weak-kneed and gasping for air. Pulling himself together, Miro sauntered back to the house.

'How does the bastard know that it's me who collects the mail?' Miro asked Simon, who was sitting at the breakfast table. 'Has he been here watching the house, or perhaps there are more of them.'

'Right on both counts. You can be sure of that,' Simon said quietly, indicating with his thumb that Helen was in the scullery. He held his hand out for the note and thrust it in his pocket. 'I'll speak to you tonight. Meantime forget about this,' he murmured.

Brannigan's note created a few moments of absolute pleasure to the PWE agents when Simon arrived and passed it round. The spy had served his purpose. Further disinformation might prejudice their scam. Now he had to be picked up, interrogated and put out of harm's way. It was considered vital that they arrest him to find out whether or not he knew the info he'd been passing on was suspect. Hundreds of thousands of lives were at stake.

'Let Miro meet him and give them some time together. Miro must deduce whether or not he knows he's been fooled. Miro is the only chance we have,' Alf said. 'We could pick him up in Claremont when he comes to meet the boy.'

'So we're offering Miro as a live sacrifice,' Simon said angrily.

'Not if you have a better idea.'

There wasn't a better idea, as Simon knew.

It was decided that Miro should meet Brannigan, but their agents would keep tabs on him, giving Miro enough time to deduce whether or not his cover was blown. They would then attempt to rescue him.

Simon didn't like the plan, but being the boy's friend was not a reason for vetoing it – not when soldiers only a year older than him were about to invade the European mainland and die in their thousands.

That night he found Miro alone in the stables and told him the plan. 'Listen carefully. What we need to know is whether or not Paddy has learned that the info we've been feeding him about the invasion was *disinformation*. You're very sensitive – very perceptive – but you don't always trust your instinct. You should. You'll be able to deduce his mood pretty quickly. Then get out, no matter where you are. I suspect he'll lure you on to his boat. In my room I have a couple of distress rockets. They're new and small. They'd fit into your trouser pocket, so if he tries to search you, jump overboard! These things are waterproof. Wherever you are, all you have to do is press the button. The flare will lead us to you.'

'Thanks. Have you got anything for me to give him if he comes?'

'Tell him we've trained three thousand so-called ghost-killers. These are highly trained hand-to-hand combat experts armed with silent automatic rifles and daggers. They are about to infiltrate German coastal defences from behind. They will strike when Patton's troops, together with the British 12th Army, invade Calais. Got that?'

'Sure.'

'I don't like this, Miro. He knows he's in danger. Why else would he go to ground and abandon his home and his shop? What we don't know is how much he knows. Either way you're in great danger.'

'Not necessarily,' Miro said. 'I could be your innocent dupe.'

Suddenly he was appealing to the boy. 'Is there any reason why he should suspect you? Go back over every visit.'

'I was suntanned and fit. Perhaps too fit for a month of music lessons. I can't think of anything else.'

'What were the last words he said to you before he took off?'

'He wanted to know the number of troop carriers lying off the south-east coast. He asked me to try to find out the date of the invasion. He was his normal, blustering, threatening self. I should give it a go. I have the answers he wants to hear.'

'Perhaps it's time to call it quits?' Simon faced the dilemma every agent-runner fears. He was sending someone he loved into mortal danger. 'No one can force you to do this, Miro. You're not in the army yet. He'll come for you in his boat and he'll invite you on board. How could you refuse to go? Then he'll probably try to kill you . . . that's if he's in the know. If he's not, he might consider it safer to kill you anyway.'

The forceful way Simon said this, and the fear in his voice, sent Miro into panic mode. For a moment he just wanted to run, but he forced himself to consider the odds. They were not in favour of letting him save his life. If the enemy knew about the scam, then he must inform the PWE. To run now would destroy all that he had done, for it would lead to the certain death of his parents and the loss of hundreds of soldiers.

'Nothing has changed for me . . . I'm going. End of story,' Miro said.

'Remember this: if you die, your parents die, too, so try to keep alive.'

Miro laughed. 'I surely will.'

'Get out at the first sign of trouble. Don't wait to be sure. Don't try to kill him. He's a trained fighter and he's stronger than you.

We'll take care that he never sends off his messages just as soon as you set off the rockets.'

The sky was overcast and there was no moon. It was a coal black, sullen night, disturbingly so, for a storm was threatening. Miro had to flick his torch on in order to padlock his bike to the railings. He walked along the quay, inspecting the boats that were moored alongside. Paddy's boat was not there and Miro felt ashamed of his relief. He exhaled silently.

'That bike of yours will probably be stolen,' he heard from right behind him.

He stood very still. If he tells me to put the bike on a boat then it's tickets for me, he told himself. Clearly the bastard has another boat. Strangely Miro's fears had entirely evaporated. 'Put it on the deck. It won't come to any harm there.'

How had he got so close, so soundlessly. 'Which is your boat?'

'Right here, boyo. We're going for a trip. You've done a good job, Miro. It's time you met a pal of mine. He's got a couple of pictures for you. Your reward. We can't meet in Claremont . . . it's not safe.' As he spoke, Paddy was looking away. Then he shot him a glance as hard as flint.

The bastard's lying, Miro decided. He went along with the plan only because he couldn't get out of it without revealing who and what he really was. Besides, Simon needed the information.

'I have a few plans for you, Miro,' Paddy said, as he went into the cabin. 'Cast off, then.'

Miro threw the rope on to the wharf. The boat shuddered into a deep throbbing from the powerful engines and swung out towards the harbour entrance, aiming for dead centre between the red and green lights. Miro loved boats and the sea. The gentle rise and fall over the waves lulled him into a sense of false security, but he remained alert, clutching the gunwale. About five miles out to sea it became much colder and Miro zipped up his anorak and shivered inside it. 'Let's talk,' Paddy called poking his head out of the wheelhouse. 'Come in here, Miro. It's cold out there.'

Miro tottered towards him. 'I feel terrible . . . sort of dizzy and I'm about to throw up. I can't help myself.'

'Then stay on deck.' Paddy pulled a sou'wester over his jersey and joined him.

'Got anything for me?'

'Not much.' He repeated what Simon had told him and gave him the information he had asked for when they last met. Clutching his stomach he crouched on the deck and leaned over the rail as if he would vomit.

'That's it?'

'Yes.'

'How come you get so much top material?' Paddy asked.

'You know how. Listening in to Helen and Simon.'

'He knows a hell of a lot for a diving teacher.'

Miro shrugged. 'I feel terrible. How should I know where he gets it from?'

Paddy moved towards him in silent strides. He was holding an automatic and it was pointing at a spot between his eyes. So this is it, Miro thought as he turned ice cold. Time had slowed, but his thoughts were speeding up. He seemed to see everything remarkably clearly. He was still alive. There was a reason why. Paddy didn't bring him here merely to kill him. He wanted to know something. He could sense the hatred coming out of him in waves. He sympathized. He felt the same way about Paddy, he longed to see him dead, but if he tried out his newly-learned combat skills he might find that Paddy had learned the same routine. He stayed where he was and kept his mouth shut.

In a menacing tone, Paddy said, 'I hate to think what punishment the guards will think up for your parents when I tell them what a load of codswallop you've been giving me.'

'I listened to Simon and I told you what he said. Night after night. D'you think I would prejudice my parents' survival?'

'There's still a chance for your parents. Tell me truthfully now how much of the information you gave me came from Captain Johnson and how much from your own observation?'

Was that it? Miro wondered. 'I don't understand. Why do you think Johnson's conversations to Helen were all bullshit? Why should he bullshit her? He never knew that I was listening in. I'll swear to that.'

'OK. Now work out which bits he told you and which bits you overheard.'

'But why? It's impossible. I've been working for you for over a year and a half.'

Paddy lashed out with his foot and caught Miro on his cheek. His head snapped back against the rail. He leaned over the bulwark and pretended to retch. Should he try to slither out now? No, the boat had powerful engines. What he needed was a good, hard leap from the deck to get far enough away from the pull of the engine. He was searching round for every store of energy his body possessed. Groaning, he pushed himself to a sitting position.

'Everything I saw in Kent came from me. I told you what I saw. It's everywhere. Anyone who lives there can see it all. Why don't you trust me?'

'Not you, boyo, but him.'

'I don't understand,' he said wearily. 'I've done a good job, haven't I?' Lolling back, he waited for Paddy to be off-guard.

'While you were supposedly honing your skills on the clarinet, I was in Dublin seeing my old mates again. They had a scrapbook of mug shots with names and records of their past achievements. Your pal, the scuba diving instructor, spent six months in Argentina before arriving in England. He wasn't a scuba diving trainer then, he was a disbarred lawyer scrounging for any odd job available, but that was just his cover, like the diving lark. The bastard is a military spy and because of him five agents were identified. The CIA moved in and bugged their radios. It was a disaster. Eventually they all died in various so-called accidents.'

'I didn't know,' Miro said. 'I'd never do anything to endanger my parents.'

'You little turd. If I'm going to die, you will, too.' Paddy's left hand took hold of a chain from the deck. He swung it round as he slowly stalked towards him, keeping the gun pointed at his forehead. His foot collided with Miro's bike, which had slipped towards them with the boat's momentum. He swore. Losing his temper, Paddy turned to kick the bike overboard.

Miro had a split-second to act, he reckoned. He dived from the deck, head first into the sea, and kicked his way down, out of reach of the bullets that were probably peppering the surface, clamping his mouth shut to stop himself from gasping at the icy water. It was so dark. He could not tell if he were sinking or rising. He had lost all sense of direction. He swam as hard as he could, but was he moving away from the boat or towards it? Then he saw a circle of light on the surface of the water about ten metres behind him and he swam in the opposite direction until he felt that his lungs would burst. He surfaced, trying not to splash. The searchlight was moving round the boat which was only thirty metres away. Taking several deep breaths, he dived again.

The next time he surfaced he saw Paddy silhouetted against the spotlight. He was leaning over the bows. His footsteps seemed unnaturally loud over the wind and the waves. Perhaps he was imagining the sounds. Miro kept moving away from the boat, taking mouthfuls of water when a wave flapped into his face. The searchlight continued circling slowly around in every direction as Paddy searched for him.

Ten minutes later, Paddy gave up. With a powerful surge, the boat leaped forward, leaving evanescent gleams of phosphorescence in its wake. The sound faded away. Now all he could hear was the roar of waves which seemed to come from all directions. There was no sign of land, not a blink of light anywhere. Praying that Simon was looking out for him, Miro fumbled for a distress rocket, held it up while he trod water. Moments later it was shooting into the sky. He suspected that seeing the flare, Paddy might return to kill him, but he was passing out with cold and no longer able to think straight.

Thirty-Five

Miro was almost unconscious with hypothermia by the time he heard the powerful engines of a motor torpedo boat planing towards him. How would they see him in the dark, choppy water? He had to set off the second rocket fast, but his fingers would not obey his brain. They wobbled and shook . . . Oh God! The boat was almost on him. Then the flare rocketed into the sky, although he was never sure how he had managed to set it off. The thunder of the MTB's engines became a purr, a searchlight scanned the surface of the sea, it was moving closer, but he hadn't the strength to wave.

Simon saw him first. 'There he is! Careful. Get him in,' he yelled. Miro was hauled up over the side by two strong marines.

Despite his studied calm, Simon looked frightened. 'Everything's all right. You're safe. Easy does it. Are you wounded . . . or injured?'

'Bloody cold, that's all,' Miro said, his smile still unavailable through frozen lips.

'I need to ask you this, so pull yourself together and think. Does Brannigan suspect that the info he received is a load of bull?'

'He doesn't know . . . just suspects . . . he's hoping for the best.' He took a deep breath and tried to pull himself together. Easy does it, he told himself. 'He's found out . . . in Eire . . . that you're an agent, but . . . the stuff I got from you, wasn't meant for me.' He paused to get his breath back and rub his lips, which were frozen. 'It was what you told Helen.'

'Here!' Simon took a flask of brandy from his pocket and held it to his lips.

Miro gulped it down and choked. Once he'd got his breath back, the fiery warmth was definitely helpful. 'He believes my eyewitness accounts. He's not sure enough of his doubts about the rest to pass them on to his superiors . . . and he's deeply afraid that they might kill him if he does. I'm sure of his fear . . . I could smell it.'

Simon relaxed visibly. 'Get down in the cabin. Get your gear off . . . fast . . . everything. There's a pile of clothes on the table. You'll be a GI for while. Be sure to put on the parka,' he told him. 'You'll soon warm up.'

Miro hung on to Simon as he tried to move into the cabin. To put a foot down as the boat swung up was hazardous. Simon poured a mug of coffee from a Thermos, spilling some on the floor, and splashed a little brandy into it. 'Here . . . drink this first. Don't swill it this time.'

Simon went back outside. Miro found it difficult to change his clothes. The boat was surging forward at maximum speed, huge waves rolled implacably towards them, smashing into the bows with sickening force. One moment the boat was poised on a mountain of water and a moment later they were plunging down into a deep green trough, landing with a smack that seemed it would smash the boat. Miro hung on with one hand and dressed with the other. Somehow he managed to do it, then he collapsed on a bunk and lay in a strange half-asleep, half-awake state, hanging on tightly.

Perhaps he slept. He wasn't sure, but he woke to a massive explosion. The port holes turned red. Miro thought they had been blown up. He crawled out on to the deck, expecting to find himself back in the sea, but dead ahead was Paddy's boat blazing and upended. Momentarily it hung poised, then slid, hissing and steaming, into the sea. Huge bubbles of air churned the surface and then there was nothing but the waves. It was as if the boat had never existed.

'A good ending to a bad day,' Simon said.

'Where's Paddy?' Miro asked.

Simon shrugged. 'Like a good captain, he went down with his boat.'

'I wouldn't count on that. He thought I had, too. He can easily swim under the spotlights. I did.'

'Listen, Miro, the boat exploded. We torpedoed it. He must have been carrying a good deal of extra petrol stashed in the hold because it all caught at once. Add to that, we're five miles from the nearest land.'

'And he would never know which way to go, not on a night like this. That was my problem. Listen Simon. Your cover is gone. Paddy went to Eire for a month and while there he was given proof that you are in Military Intelligence. They have your picture in a file of Allied agents. I assume that's why he went into hiding. He must have realized you would track him down. He told me you were responsible for the deaths of five Nazi sympathizers in Buenos Aires.'

'You've done a good job, Miro. We'll publicize your death and send you somewhere safe. How would you like to go to the States?'

'No. How can I? How would that help my parents?'

Simon swore under his breath. 'I'd like to see you safely away from here. Paddy wasn't alone, Miro. Whoever his controllers were, they'll come looking for you, either to recruit you, or to kill you. You're not out of danger yet.'

'I'll see it through,' Miro said.

Simon looked upset. 'Well then . . . for now it's over. Let's go home.'

A day later, Miro read of Paddy's death in the local rag.

> May 2, 1944.
>
> Poole Coastguards announce that they have given up the search for the skipper of the Pride of Shannon fishing boat, which sailed out of Claremont Harbour on the evening of May 1, and capsized five miles offshore. Wreckage was spotted several miles off the coast the following morning. A salvage officer, Ian Wren, who examined the wreckage, stated that a mine was reported in the area three days ago, but a local minesweeper had been unable to locate it.
>
> The vessel was owned by Sean Brannigan, a locksmith of Claremont, near Christchurch. He was believed to have been sailing alone. Members of the Lifeboat Association confirmed that it is unlikely anyone could survive for more than a few hours given the temperature of the sea and wind velocity. A neighbour, Mrs Lucy Brown, stated that Brannigan always fished alone. He was a generous man who supplied his neighbours with fish from time to time.

It was a stressful May as the world held its breath. British harbours were congested. The Allied air forces were opening the way for the attack by waging massive bombing campaigns in Germany and France. In France, members of the French resistance cut railroad tracks, sabotaged locomotives and targeted supply trains. Allied aircraft bombed roads, bridges and rail junctions to prevent the Germans from moving reinforcements towards the invasion beaches. To confuse enemy intelligence, the attacks occurred along the entire length of the Channel coast.

For Miro, tension lurked – the nerve-racking tension of waiting. He held it at bay with hard work as his stressful days sped by. A soldier in waiting, Miro checked out strangers, hostile glances, people loitering with nothing to do, suspicious remarks from unknown faces, the grocer's delivery boy, a new milkman, a younger than usual ARP man checking the blackout, a woman canvassing carpet cleaning. In wartime? Pull the other leg, he thought, but he never set eyes on any of them again.

He tried not to invite suspicion from the family, particularly Helen, by combining all his roles: a schoolboy swotting for university entry exams, a part-time cook, Helen's son, John's stable hand, an athlete in training, Simon's spy. In the privacy of his bedroom, he did hours of press-ups, he jogged along the beach and cliffs for miles, caught up on his German and French and gave clarinet tuition for pocket money. He told himself he was preparing for his eighteenth birthday in June, when at last he would be old enough to join Simon's group. The truth was, he was waiting for Paddy's controller to contact him . . . or kill him. Surely they had to know by now that the masses of information Paddy had obtained was suspect.

Later that month, a young man from Portugal came by in a hired car and stopped to look at the horses. His name was Raul Nobre. He was fascinated by Daunty and asked if he could look around the stables. He spent a while telling Miro about the horses his family bred on their ranch, fifty miles from Lisbon. He was the marketing manager in Britain for his family's business which manufactured high quality shoes. He hadn't been home for four years and he was homesick. In particular, he missed the horses. Finally he decided to stay an extra week in order to take early morning rides with Miro.

He talked a lot about shoes, and Miro, who had never been interested in footwear, listened, but had little to say. He liked Raul, who was an excellent rider, and they both enjoyed the early morning canters to the beach.

As he was leaving on the first morning, Raul thrust a envelope into his hand. 'A little gift,' he said.

'Oh no, that's not necessary,' Miro exclaimed, handing it back. Raul had paid for his ride in advance.

'No, keep it. It's not cash. It's something you will value,' Raul said. 'Before I leave, maybe you could find something for me.'

Miro puzzled about that. What could he mean?

It was only after Miro had rubbed down the horses and fed them, that he opened the envelope. For a few seconds he was in shock, for he was gazing at a small photograph of his father. His hair was white and he was thinner, but otherwise he looked the same.

He was playing a violin, or pretending to, and wearing the prison's regulation striped pyjamas.

Nerves jangling, Miro waited for Raul to arrive the following morning. The two of them cantered down to the beach. Raul stripped down to his underpants. 'Come on, Miro,' he called. 'Race you to the wreck.'

This is it, Miro decided, but he went anyway, reminding himself of his combat lessons as he tried to beat him, and succeeded.

'Why did you bring a picture of my father, but not of my mother?' he asked when they were sitting on a rock near the water's edge.

Raul shrugged. 'I don't know, Miro, and I have no way of finding out. I simply obey orders. So, my friend, what have you got for me?'

'Very little,' Miro said truthfully. 'I waited at the pillbox every Wednesday . . . that's where we used to meet, but Paddy didn't return from Ireland. Do you know why?'

'No.' Raul was lying, but he looked so sincere. 'Like you, I assume he decided to remain in Ireland. Now what's your story? How did you get all this information? Paddy was excelling because of you. Did you know that?'

'Listen, Raul. I feel I should set the record straight. I have no love of the Nazis. I'm a Jew. These people have my parents in a camp. You know that. You brought the picture of my father and you were right, that picture is very precious to me. I was arrested with my father and I, too, was in Dachau, but in the children's sector. It was terrible. One day, they took me to see an execution by garroting. I still have nightmares about it. Later, an SS official offered me the chance to support my parents by spying for them. I agreed and we made a pact: I would work for the Third Reich and they would give my parents special treatment. I love them dearly and I would never do anything to put them in peril. I have worked hard to keep them alive and I will continue to do so.'

'Anyone would,' Raul said sympathetically, placing his arm around Miro's shoulders.

'I was upset when Paddy disappeared. I wondered if our pact had come to an end. It was Paddy's idea to make a connecting hole in the wall between my bedroom and Helen's. We have a GI billeted with us. He seems to know what's going on and he tells Helen at night before they go to sleep. That's where most of my news originates.'

'Oh Miro, my clever friend. These are hard times. I'm in a similar situation to you, but I can't give you the details. Nothing has changed except that Paddy disappeared. So what have you heard?'

'Not much,' Miro said archly. 'The GI—'

'Captain Johnson,' Raul interrupted.

'That's him. I heard him tell Helen that when the Allies invade Calais they plan to send a diversionary force to Normandy, to lure Germans away from the main attack area. I've known this for some weeks, but I didn't know what to do with the information.'

'Don't worry. It's not too late. Do you know the date of the invasion?'

'No. I don't think anyone does yet. A lot depends upon the weather. To be honest, I gave up listening after Paddy stopped coming,' he said.

Raul shrugged. 'Who can blame you. It's difficult for me to stay away from my headquarters, but I'll come down for a ride every two weeks.'

'Let's go back,' Miro said, hoping that his agitation was not visible.

The horses were eager to get home. They kept breaking into a trot, but Raul wanted to walk. 'There seem to be hundreds of thousands of Americans around this area,' he said.

'The south-east is full, too. This is a transit area,' Miro said. 'Or so Mike told me.'

'Who's Mike?'

'My sister's husband. He said they move the guys east as soon as they find room for them.'

'So why does he stay?'

'He's part of the transit camp. Something to do with the underwater training here.'

'Ah. I understand. Well let's go.'

And that was that. Miro reported every word to Simon when he returned from London later that evening. They were meeting in an empty stable, where they would not be overheard. 'Do you know where he was staying?' Simon asked.

'Not for sure, but I checked out the car parks of all the hotels here. At night his hired car was parked at the Mowbray Heights.'

'Good for you. They'll have his address. Can you describe him?'

'Six foot, very slender, an upturned nose, large brown eyes that are slightly tilted, prominent cheek bones, jet black hair, straight, and a lock that keeps falling over his forehead, just like Hitler. He's very elegant, good-looking, with a wide friendly smile and great teeth. He looks more like a male model than a Nazi agent.'

'That's the trouble. There's no stereotype for this kind of work. He'll be back, I'm afraid.'

'Have you any more news for me? Oh, by the way, I gave him the sib about the diversionary force approaching Normandy.'

'Excellent. There won't be any more, Miro. We're closing down this operation. You are about to be arrested for spying and you can't tell anyone that it's fiction. Not even Helen. It will take place in the next few days. Raul will be arrested, too. All the real spies have been dealt with long since . . . well, all that we know about. Now we're going to pull in the "turned" agents. We have nineteen genuine double agents. They, too, have to be arrested so that the Germans will never suspect them, even after the war.'

'And where will we be taken?' For once, Miro could not hide his feelings. He felt disappointed and suspicious.

'They'll go to camps on the Isle of Man for the duration of the war. You, on the other hand, will get a new name and personality and you'll be trained to join the US army and ultimately my outfit. You'll be able to see Helen and the family only after Terezen is freed, which could take a while. In the meantime no one must know, for your parents' sake, apart from the obvious reasons.'

'Helen will be devastated.'

'True, but I can't think of any other way to keep suspicion off you, so that your parents remain safe until the camps are freed. Can you?'

Miro sat down and thought for a while. 'No,' he said eventually. 'It's a good plan.'

'The family will get some very nasty flack from friends and neighbours.'

'Helen will move heaven and earth to get me released.'

'She'll be wasting her time because you will be in Scotland. I had to pull strings to swing this.'

'Thanks. It's what I want, but I'm worried about the family. What if we tell them in secret?'

'The less anyone knows, the safer your parents are likely to be.'

It took a while for Miro to realize that he was free of his burden. Slowly his anxiety slipped away. The next few days were the most carefree he could ever remember. Each morning he could be seen in shorts, rushing down the zigzag path, doing press-ups in the wet sand, jogging until he was drenched with sweat, then diving into the cold water and setting off in a brisk crawl. It was hard to be happy. He had to work at it, and always in the background was the thought of his parents suffering in the camp, and Helen's grief and shame when he was arrested as a spy.

Thirty-Six

They were dining at the Mowbray Heights Hotel, amongst the elegant, candlelit tables, double-thick woollen carpets and wall-to-wall satin drapes. The head waiter bowed from the shoulders up as he laid the menu reverently before them.

'How the heck does he achieve that manner of obsequious arrogance?' Mike asked Daisy.

'Sh! It's his job. Now stop teasing me. Tell me why we are here.'

'We're celebrating,' Mike said mysteriously. 'You must remember this night.'

'It's lovely. But why? You have to tell me. I insist.'

'Our son is six months old,' he told her.

'He might be a she.'

'He's a he. I know it.'

'Oh, you silly. We don't know *when* it happened.'

'I do. It was the night I climbed up on your roc I heard his panting as he raced his siblings to the target.'

She giggled, but she wasn't going to be put off by Mike's silly stories. There had to be a reason they were here, but Mike stuck to his excuse. He seemed to be so homesick. He described his family's ranch in great detail: the cattle, the horses, cats and dogs, the chipmunks and the birds, all of which he loved so much. Then the surrounding hills and valleys and finally he got on to the rivers, while Daisy ate her way through soup, entree, fish, curry and ice cream.

Her appetite had become gargantuan. It filled her with dismay, even though she knew she was eating for two. She was big for six months. The doctor wanted to put her on a diet, but she had resisted.

'Listen,' Mike said. 'I've just received photographs of the ranch from Pa. I brought them along to show you.' He undid the briefcase he'd been carrying all evening with the excuse of doing some studying at home.

'It looks lovely,' she said, smiling softly, humouring him, as he produced shot after shot. 'But Mike, what if I don't like Denver?'

His face fell, but manfully he found the right words. 'Then we'll come right back here and I'll have a shot at farming in England.

I'm getting to like this country. It's different, but it has a lot to commend it.'

'Such as?'

' It's . . . comfortable.' He managed to find a word that suited him at last. 'This is my father. He's over the moon about the coming baby and our marriage. I sent pictures of you. He thinks I'm the luckiest man in the world.' He passed her another picture. She saw a tall thin man with a shock of white hair and a wide smile. He looked a lot like Mike, she thought. A large, hairy dog sat beside him. There was a certain resemblance here, too, she thought.

'Really? How sweet of him.'

Daisy's mind was obsessed with time, not ranches. How long had they got? How many nights? Everyone knew that Britain was stretched to bursting point. There were rumoured to be one and a half million American troops in England, plus British, Canadian, French and Polish divisions, along with hundreds of thousands of service troops. Mike had told her that more than sixteen million tons of supplies were stored in England. She knew for a fact that hundreds of thousands of jeeps, trucks and half-tracks, tanks and artillery pieces were crammed into every park, field, street and even back gardens. Depots to house all these men and their supplies were mushrooming across the English countryside. The fields of Somerset and Cornwall were armouries for the vast stores of bombs and artillery shells that would be needed. She found that out in her brief period as a land girl. But what was Mike talking about now?

'I've set up a trust in case anything happens to me, Daisy. Half the ranch will be yours, and on your death it will go to our son.'

'Please don't talk like that. Please, Mike. You're spoiling the evening.'

'I don't want to upset you, but Daisy let's be sensible. One of these days I'll be gone and it will be too late to talk. I own half the shares in the ranch, my lawyer holds them and I have arranged everything with him. The shares will be held in trust for you and my son. The lawyer's address is here in this envelope. All my savings come to you and if anything happens to me, I want you to use the money to finish your studies, just as soon as our child is old enough to be left with Helen.'

'Oh, Mike. Please be positive. You are coming back safe and sound. You will. I know you will.'

'Of course I will. I just want to get this over with, so please listen.' He sounded so stern. 'Everything is here in this briefcase. Keep it somewhere safe. Do you have a safe?'

'Gramps has a big one.'

'Ask him to put it inside. You'll need my birth certificate, which is here, too. You'll have to go to the American Embassy by yourself to register the birth of our child as an American citizen. Do not neglect that, Daisy. I won't be here to help you. Promise?'

Casually, without warning, the realization came to her: *it's now!* So this was it . . . the reason for their celebration . . . their last night together. She should have guessed from his expression and from the way he was talking. What sort of a fool was she? Besides, look at his face. He was pale, his eyes were half closed, his lips set in a taut line. Behind the tough man lurked an oversensitive boy, she had learned. All his rodeo riding, his water polo, his unarmed combat and underwater fighting were Mike's efforts to drive that boy clean out of existence. She hoped he would never succeed. She loved him just the way he was.

'Mike . . . promise me . . . promise you'll keep safe. I need you.'

Tears were coming. Damn! However hard she tried she couldn't hold them back. She got up and went to the bathroom and cried there briefly, perched on the lavatory seat. Then she bathed her eyes with cold water, reapplied some powder and lipstick and returned to their table.

Sleepy with rich food and too much champagne, Mike drove her home. They crept in, but Simon and Helen were still in the lounge. Helen came out to the hall and gazed long and hard at Mike as if she wanted to say something, but then she said, 'Good night', and went back into the lounge.

Mum knows, too, Daisy saw. Suffused with a sense of apathy, Daisy could hardly get upstairs. She was too sleepy to undress. She sank into her armchair and closed her eyes.

Mike returned from the bathroom and found her asleep in the chair. Daisy was one of life's decorative assets. Even pale and over-wrought, with deep shadows under her eyes, she was still incredibly lovely. He had been snared by her looks, but then he was a prosperous rancher and he knew he could afford her. Lately he wondered if ranching would suit Daisy. She was used to a different kind of life. How would she take to the loneliness? But she loved all wildlife and particularly their horses and perhaps she would be happy. There were other ways to earn a living, he told himself.

She looked exhausted. The baby was taking all her energy. Mike longed with all his heart to stay and look after her. He had not yet told her that this was their last night. He could not think how he was going to do this. He stripped off his clothes, folded them and placed them on the bedside chair.

Watching Mike through half-closed eyes, Daisy considered how magnificent he looked. She should have painted him just as he was this evening: suntanned, and much tougher and stronger than when they met. He was a boy then, now he was a man. He'll go on looking better as he gets older, she knew. Watching him always made the blood surge through her body. So he was leaving. She wouldn't let on that she knew. She didn't want her sadness to worry him, or spoil their last night together.

He looked up and saw her watching him and a look of infinite tenderness made his eyes glow, while his sensuous mouth turned up at the corners in a grin.

'I thought you were asleep. Come to bed? Or are you sitting there all night?'

The next moment she was grabbed off her feet and pressed against his body. She felt the leanness of him. He was like steel. She ran her hands over his back. Then she forgot about sadness and thought only of the feel of his skin against hers and how much she wanted him.

He undressed her and crouched beside her and ran his lips over her shoulders, gently moving down to the curve of her breasts and her thickening belly. She groaned softly and dug her nails into his shoulder. She sat astride him, which, Mike had been told, was the only safe way to make love. She looked debauched and boisterous. His preconceived notions of women and sex were fast disappearing.

'Are you sure it's all right . . . safe for the baby? We don't have to make love. Come and lie down next to me.'

She laughed, compelling him to participate as she slid her body backwards and forwards. She looked abandoned and vitally female. Her breasts were full and erect, thrusting forward aggressively, bouncing with the force of her passion. 'Now,' she commanded. 'Now!'

Later Mike got up and tiptoed to the bathroom for a shower. When he returned, she was sleeping and he cursed himself for being a coward. He should have told her. He dressed and crouched beside the bed, holding her hand, but the walls seemed to be pressing in on him, the ceiling lowering like ancient horror movies he'd seen as a kid. Mike detested the blackout and the dim lights and the need to keep the windows covered all the time. It made him feel claustrophobic. He threw back the curtains, pulled up the blackout blinds and leaned out of the window taking deep breaths until he felt calmer. Despite their exhaustive training, the thought of being shot at still seemed like a macabre joke. This time tomorrow . . . or the next day . . .

He knelt beside the bed and hung on to Daisy's hand. Unbelievably, he dozed off. When he woke he glanced at his watch and sighed with relief. Eleven p.m. He must be back within the hour.

Fumbling for his wife's hand, he rested his head on her stomach. He could sense a movement. Entranced, he felt a strong thrust against his face. Their baby was kicking him. There it was again, an aimed kick, bang in the middle of his cheek. *He wants me off there. The little bastard wants his mother to himself.* Perhaps he'd been squashing him. He lifted himself off her stomach, but placed his hand there instead and waited. There it came again. A strong, well-aimed kick.

Mike felt humble and deeply moved. Intuitively he knew that he was no longer captain of his ship. It was as if his son's lunge at life had thrust deep into his soul and he was contaminated with caring, an incurable disease, he sensed. Daisy's as yet, unnamed child, had kicked his way into his heart. He stroked her swollen belly and whispered, 'I'll try to get back to you, kid. We're gonna need each other. There's a hell of a lot I'll have to teach you. You'll be the best rancher in Texas. Just you wait!' he murmured.

Thirty-Seven

Mowbray, June 4, 1944.

Midnight was almost upon them. To Simon it spelled his coming doom. They had made love and it was unsatisfactory. They both knew this, but neither of them cared to comment. Helen blamed it on the tension that hung around them like a London smog. She could not remember any time since they'd met when they had nothing to say to each other. She knew that Simon blamed her for not marrying him.

Why is she so difficult? Simon was thinking. She should realize that he needed more reassurance. A long separation faced both of them. He watched her lying on the bed in her silk nightgown made from a discarded parachute. She had a flare for designing clothes and this was one of her best. She had drunk some wine and so had he. She looked dreamy and highly desirable and he wished that his libido would return, but he knew that it would not.

'Why are you sitting over there?' She propped herself up on one elbow. 'Why do I have the feeling that you have already left?'

'Don't ask.' He got up and sat on the side of the bed and reached for her hand.

'You've changed, Simon. You never forgave me, did you?'

Simon stared at her without answering and for a while they sat without speaking.

'No answer?' she persisted. 'Is it over?'

'Is it? You tell me.'

'I said "no" to your proposal because of family commitments. You can't weigh love against responsibility.'

'I don't seem to figure in your scheme of things at all.'

'Yet here we are in bed together. Doesn't that tell you something? Would I go to bed with someone I didn't love? Nothing has changed. I will be here when you return . . . waiting for you. I promise.' She sat up and put her arms around his waist and tried to pull him back into bed, but he resisted.

'I wish you had said that long ago.'

'I did. So why do you look so gloomy?'

How could he tell her what he was thinking: that he and Mike and all the rest of the 29th who had shared the camp next door were to be the first ashore on Omaha beach. God knows if any of them would survive. The odds were against it. These were the thoughts that soldiers anguished over, but never talked about. Thank God the men didn't know, but the sergeants knew . . . Mike knew.

'You are so capable of sealing yourself off from the rest of us,' she said sullenly.

'Us?'

'I know so little about you, but you know all there is to know about us . . . that is the family.'

'What can I tell you? My education is typically middle-class, American style. You wouldn't understand much about my work. It would bore you. I volunteered to join a fighting unit and I was disappointed, but now that I know I'll be landing with the rest of the guys, I feel uneasy. In other words I'm all talk.'

'On the contrary. You never talk about yourself.'

'My ex-wife used to say that I erect invisible barriers.'

'I can't get the hang of you ever having been married. It's seems strange, such a large area of your life that I know nothing about. You have this ability to switch off. One minute you are my Simon, someone I love and trust, someone I know so well I can read your thoughts. Then you become someone else. Someone who keeps secrets.'

'It's a protective mechanism. Nothing more than that.'

'What do you have to protect yourself from, Simon?'

'Reality, perhaps. The reality of being me, Simon Johnson, heir to the Johnson fortune. I don't like to talk about that. It's dogged me since my earliest days. Housemaids who were kinder to me than to my cousin who lived with us, teachers who never punished the son of their main benefactor, and so on. As soon as I qualified I got out on my own, but the reality of being a Johnson, dogged my marriage, too. My ex-wife's name is Gloria and she is an actress, or was. I thought I loved her, but now I know that it wasn't love, only lust. I didn't know what love was. You taught me that . . . watching you, feeling for you, sharing your problems and finally loving you.'

Helen smiled enigmatically, not wanting to interrupt him.

'We were both whoring. She wanted to share my family's wealth and I wanted to show off her beauty. The marriage didn't work out. To me she seemed vain, self-obsessed and an opportunist. She said I was tight-fisted and insular. End of story.'

'There's something I need to say, too, Simon. I want you to know that you and yours brought hope and fun along with your parachutes, coffee and extra rations. We've all caught some of your get-up-and-go attitude. I'm not just talking about our family, but all of England. I had lost the ability to feel joy. I felt that there was nothing left for me. Now I know there's a whole new life waiting. I never thought I'd love again, but I fell in love with you. Dearest Simon. I can't wait for you to come back when the war ends. Then I will marry you, if you still want me.'

Suddenly everything was all right again. 'Come,' she said pulling him down on to the bed. Desire surged through his blood, his fears fled and he succumbed to passion.

Time was running short. He got up and showered and dressed and sat on the bed beside Helen. 'I can't wait to get back to you. I might get leave, but when the war ends I'll be retained longer than most. I'm bound to get involved in searching for Nazi criminals. They'll go to ground all over Europe.'

'You are an intelligence agent, aren't you?'

He watched her without answering but his eyes glowed with compassion.

'You can't tell me, I understand, but I know that you are.'

'Miro's very late,' Simon said, glancing at his watch and frowning. 'He's usually back much earlier.'

'He came back early. He said he had some work to do. He must have gone to sleep.'

'Without supper?'

'Yes.'

'I feel like an omelette. Would you like one?'

'No thanks, but I'll make it.'

'Let me. I need something to do.'

So Simon busied himself in the kitchen. He made toast and beat half a dozen eggs and then he went upstairs to wake Miro. 'Get dressed, Miro. It's time,' he said quietly. 'Be sure to take your duffel coat and a change of underwear. You'll probably need a book to read. You have a long train journey ahead. I'm making an omelette and toast. Don't be long. There isn't much time left for eating.'

At exactly half past two a convoy of three cars arrived at the front door. The first one was a police car, followed by military police and some plain clothes civilians. They knocked loudly. Helen grabbed her dressing gown and hurried to answer the door.

'I'm sorry to disturb you, madam, we're here to see Miroslav Levy.'

'I'm here,' she heard him call from behind her.

A police officer stepped forward. He said, 'Miroslav Levy? You are suspected of passing information to enemies of the state. I'm arresting you under Defence Regulation 18b of the Emergency Powers Act, of 1939. You will be detained by the police for the fore-seeable future.'

Helen gave a sudden high-pitched cry. 'No. You can't.' She grabbed Miro and hung on to him. 'He's not a spy. He's just a schoolboy. He's my son. What has he to do with spying? You've got the wrong person.'

Miro hugged her. 'Sh! I'll be all right,' he whispered.

Helen turned and saw John. She shook his arm. 'Stop them. He's not a spy. Do something, Dad. Say something.' Tears were running down her cheeks. She saw Simon behind her. 'Tell them . . . it's a mistake,' she begged. Why was he keeping so quiet?

The police hustled Miro out of the door and into the car as press photographers leaped from another car. By now, reporters were running up the driveway. Their flash guns lit the scene as the police car sped past them and turned the corner. It was over so quickly.

Simon stepped forward and spoke to the press. 'We've suspected Miroslav Levy for some time. Several other Nazi spies have been arrested in the past few hours. This arrest finalizes a year-long inves-tigation into a dangerous spy network.'

The press yelled questions at Simon, but he declined to answer them and eventually they drove away.

A hush fell over the porch. Simon saw Helen standing in the hall as if unable to take a step forward.

'Listen to me, Helen,' he said urgently 'You can't know what's going on. How could you? Trust me, Helen . . . Things are not as they seem. I wish I could tell you more.'

His voice went on and on while Helen listened to his excuses, but she was more attuned to the sounds of the camp breaking up, canvas flapping in the wind like sails unfurling, whistles, curses, hammering, wood splintering, lorries starting up and stopping, the occasional motorbike racing in and then out.

How pleasant it would be to allow herself to believe that every-thing was going to be as Simon said. Time would turn backwards

and Miro would reappear, with the apologetic police officer trying
to explain his mistake. Did Simon say that? Maybe not, but that was
the general drift of his conversation. She dragged herself back to
face reality.

'You are a liar and a cheat, Simon. You pretended to love me, but
you came here to trap my son.'

'I can't explain. There's no time and anyway it's classified, Helen,
but *everything's* going to be all right.'

That old cliché again. He was waiting for her reply, but she felt
so unreal, quite unable to get to grips with the here and now.

Simon had packed earlier and he was ready to go. He picked up
his gear and paused at the front door.

'I have to leave now, Helen. For God's sake . . . if you love me,
trust me. Miro is going to be fine. For the last time I beg you to
believe in me. I love you and that goes for your family. I would
never harm any one of you.'

'But Miro *is* my family.' She walked inside and slammed the door.
Her courage gone, she flopped on to the bench and buried her face
in her hands.

'Are you sure, Helen?' John asked, watching his daughter fight
for her composure.

'Dad! What are we going to do?'

'We'll get Miro back. He's only a boy and I still have a lot of
friends up in London. We'll petition Parliament, go to the press,
raise such a stink they'll be glad to let him go.'

'Do you really believe that?'

'Of course. I know how much you love Simon, Helen. Go and
tell him so. Don't throw your future happiness away.'

She shook her head. 'I'll get over Simon just as I got over Eric.
I can never forgive him and I could never trust him. Never again.
It's over.'

Sleep evaded Helen as she sat in the lounge staring at the wall, but
seeing Simon in her mind's eye. Every sweet memory she had treas-
ured made Simon's betrayal more hurtful. She dragged them out,
one by one: Simon galloping Daunty along the beach, racing her
to the wharf, sponging her back in the shower, bringing her breakfast in bed when she had the flu, teaching Daisy to jive; there were
so many precious memories to be consigned to the rubbish bin, or
trash can, as he would correct her. Oh God! She would have no
more of him.

Eventually she tried to work out her best tactics to free Miro. She would get a top lawyer, petition Parliament, visit old friends in influential positions, but she had difficulty concentrating. There was so much rumbling going on: heavy lorries were trundling over the grass and out of the gates. Even the walls were vibrating, but Helen would not think about this.

She turned her mind to remembering Miro when he first arrived: scared, but trying to hide this, proud, determined to hang on to his dignity, trying not to accept the new clothes she bought him when his own trousers were at half-mast. He'd insisted on working to pay for his keep, so they taught him to groom the horses and bath the dog, and John taught him to catch fish for the table. Gradually he'd relaxed and became one of the family. How pleased he was when he finally mastered English and rocketed to the top of his class. She had taught him to ride, to jump and to school his horse. He was a willing pupil and he did everything so well.

And now this! Damn Simon! If he were spying, it could only be to help his parents in that awful camp, and what could a mere schoolboy know? He'd done no harm. She stood up and paced the lounge as her fury boiled and bubbled over. Finally she heard John coming downstairs. He must have slept for a while.

'Are you all right?' he wanted to know. He opened the curtains and pulled up the blinds.

'Good God! It's morning.'

'And you have sat here all night.'

She shrugged. 'What was left of it.'

'Let's look on the bright side,' John said. 'The horses have their fields back.'

'But will we get our garden back in shape?'

'Come on, Helen. Don't be like that. It will be fun. Where's your famous optimism?' John pressed his fingers into her shoulder before leaving the room. She heard the front door open and his footsteps on the gravel. 'Will you take a look at this,' she heard Dad calling. Helen followed him, wishing he'd leave her alone.

'There's absolutely nothing left. No rubbish, no discarded equipment. Our fields are quite empty. Unbelievable organization!' John was fingering the fence, looking for snags or holes, but there were none. He put his arm around his daughter in a rare moment of physical affection; they were not a tactile family. 'He'll be back,' John whispered so softly Helen wasn't sure that he had said it. 'I'll make coffee.' Leaving her there, he walked back to the house.

'There must be something left,' she wailed to the silent field. 'An empty bottle, a pencil stub. Good God, they might never have been here.' Ashen-faced, she walked the full length of the fence looking for something . . . anything. She heard John calling from the kitchen. He emerged from the scullery door waving an envelope.

'Look here! Miro left you a letter.'

She took hold of the envelope, but her hands were shaking so much she had trouble opening it.

'Give it here.' John slid open the top with his penknife and handed it back

'Read and burn' was written across the top of the page.

'Oh Miro . . . Miro!' Now she was laughing and crying at the same time.

> My dearest foster Mum
> Thank you for five years of happiness I never deserved. No one is allowed to tell you what is happening for many reasons: one is national security, another – the vital one for me – is to safeguard my parents, but I know that if I don't tell you a little you'll be up in London causing a stink. You'll also be sad. So please be assured that by the time you make the coffee, I shall be training for the US army. Miro Levy is no more, for the time being. He is supposedly languishing in prison. I have a new identity now. My story is not a very honourable one. When my parents and I were taken to Dachau Camp, I was told that I could save their lives by spying for the SS. I had two choices, but I wanted them to stay alive so I made the selfish choice. Soon afterwards I was put on a train and you know the rest. I thought that I would have to live with my guilt and shame until the war ended, but then Simon came and it didn't take long for him to work out my situation. Do you remember the night I stole your gun? I realized that Simon was on to me and I decided to kill my controller before killing myself. Simon came after me and offered me a third choice, one that enabled me to keep my parents alive, to work for the Allies and to be proud of myself, too. I jumped at the chance and became an agent for British Intelligence, passing on dis-information to my controller. I am to be arrested tomorrow morning. It is important that my arrest is authentic, in case there are any spies still at large, but by noon I shall be just another GI in training. I hope to join Simon's outfit later.

People in high places have bent the rules for me and the deal was conditional on Simon's silence − even to you. Hence this letter.

Until my parents are released I cannot come home, but I think of you as my mother and I know you think of me as your son. I pray that my parents have survived and that they will be able to lead normal lives after their ordeal.

With all my love and all my thanks. Miro. P.S. Burn this now.

Helen burned the letter in the stove. 'He's all right,' was all she would say to John.

'We'll get a good deal of flak from the villagers and possibly our friends, so be prepared,' John told her.

Helen wasn't listening as realization hit home. 'Oh my God . . . Dad . . . help me. What have I done? I must find Simon. Give me your car keys. Be quick, Dad.' How could she have been so wrong? She should have trusted the man she loved and she intended to tell him so.

Thirty-Eight

With her foot flat down on the accelerator, Helen raced to the main road and skidded to a halt as she nearly collided with the troop carriers that were entirely blocking the road.

An MP standing by the roadside, walked towards her. 'Steady on, ma'am. This road is closed to civilians. Only army vehicles allowed. Sorry.'

'So how can I reach the main road to Southampton?'

'You can't. Only army personnel today and maybe tomorrow. Sorry, ma'am.'

'Please . . .' she said. She had never begged before. 'I have to see Captain Johnson. Reconnaissance, 29th Infantry Division. It's vital. He left about two a.m.'

He gave her a quizzical look. 'He could be anywhere. Even if I let you into the convoy, which I can't, you wouldn't be able to catch up. It's like this all the way to the various ports. All the roads are blocked . . . have been since midnight. You can guess why. Take a good look and go home.'

The lorries were full of troops who whistled and called out. They were on a high, keeping up their spirits as they rolled towards the Channel crossing and the front line.

Heedless of the danger of oncoming traffic, Helen reversed back up the road and into the driveway. She had to tell Simon that she had been so wrong and that she loved him. Then she thought: why don't I try? The convoy is slow, ten miles an hour at the most, with frequent stops. I can do twenty, if I really try. Weeping tears of frustration she reached the house, abandoned Dad's car and grabbed her bicycle.

Racing along the narrow walkways, pavements and cycle tracks towards the main highway to Southampton she recalled every cruel remark and shameful phrase she had hurled at Simon in her anger and grief at Miro's arrest. She made good timing, stopping now and then to call out, 'Have you seen any sign of the Reconnaissance Division of the 29th Infantry from Mowbray?'

'Up ahead, ma'am,' they called back. Then one or two would yell, 'Good luck.'

An hour later she was feeling exhausted and there was still no sign of them. How could she give up? If she did, Simon would never know how much she loved him and how sorry she was. She tried to smother her regrets as she cycled on for another hour. She knew she could do better. She began to pedal harder, her bike bumping over the rough grassy verges.

The convoy of troop carriers went on and on. There was no end to it, but she pedalled as hard as she could. The road was uphill and tough going. She should have a rest, she decided. Sometimes one had to give up, if only temporarily. She felt strangely apathetic. She longed to stop and lie uncaring on the grass. But at that moment she reached the crest of the hill and this cheered her. She free-wheeled down the steep slope, making up lost time, faster and faster, while the wind whipped her face and her vision clouded with tears.

'I'll make it,' she muttered. 'I can't be that far behind.'

Unaware that she was approaching another T-junction, she braked too late and too hard and skidded head-on into a stationary lorry. The crash somersaulted her into a ditch, but she knew nothing of this.

The convoy halted. Two medics pulled her out of the ditch and agreed to stay with her until an RAF helicopter arrived to airlift her to hospital.

Helen regained consciousness at four that afternoon. She tried to move, but it was too much of an effort. Her left arm was attached to a tube that hung from a bottle overhead. Her right shoulder was in plaster. Her body felt heavy, but that was only natural, she thought, since she had just returned to it. Or had she? She might have been dreaming, but it seemed to Helen that she had been elsewhere, although she had remained in this room. All she knew for sure was that her consciousness had surged out of her body; she didn't need her body after all. She became part of the room, the walls, the insects, everything . . . even the jug of water at the foot of the bed and the tiny spider spinning a web in the corner of the picture rail. She remembered watching herself lying prone on the bed and wondering how she got there. Most of all she remembered the overwhelming love, like a living force, that was everywhere and she had been part of it, too. How strange. Now she was back inside Helen Conroy, which seemed like a prison. Salty tears ran down her cheeks. She heard footsteps and moments later a nurse was bending over her.

'So you're awake. That's good. I'll call the doctor.'

Helen closed her eyes and dozed until she heard a man's voice.

'Wake up Mrs Conroy.' She opened her eyes and saw a man bending over her. His skin was very dark against his white coat.

'How do you know my name?'

'You woke and told us when we were resetting your dislocated shoulder.'

'I don't remember.'

'That's perfectly normal.'

'I've been watching you all from a dizzy height . . . somewhere up there,' she said.

He laughed.

'Aren't you astounded?'

'No. Why should I be? I'm a Hindu. What else did you encounter?'

'Love. A sort of living love . . . like a force and it's part of everything and I was part of it all. It was beautiful, but it's hard to explain.'

'Good! That will help you in the months ahead. Don't let go of the memory.'

'I can't move my feet.'

'You injured your back. According to the medics you were doing over forty when you smashed into a lorry.'

'Will I be able to walk again?'

'The prognosis amongst the doctors is no. However, I usually put my faith in that force you encountered. In my business I see miracles happening all the time.'

'Thank you.'

'Drink this,' he said, gesturing the nurse to come closer. 'You need to sleep now.'

It was an anxious day for Daisy and John. With the roads completely blocked, there was little the police could do to find Helen, although a district police helicopter had searched the roads for a lone cyclist en route to Southampton. The US army had reported a smash between a cyclist and a troop carrier, but they would have to wait until the hospital contacted them before they knew the woman's name.

Daisy had slept through the press onslaught, but John explained what had happened, and assured her that Miro was all right. They would have to be strong and ignore the press reports. Later that day the doctor called John to tell him about the accident. 'The collision caused concussion, a dislocated shoulder, numerous bruises and a fractured spine,' he said. 'Mrs Conroy may never walk again. We've made her as comfortable as we can, but she will be here for at least two weeks. She's at Ringwood Hospital in Casualty, but we'll be moving her to the Fracture Department later today.'

John kept the bad news about Helen's spinal injury to himself, but since the roads were still blocked, they were unable to go by car or by train to Ringwood. The two of them coped with the house and the horses. John called all the employment agencies he could think of to search for a housekeeper with some nursing experience. Daisy cooked and moped and tried to look cheerful for Gramps' sake. By nine p.m. they were sitting side by side listening to the news.

'As dawn broke this morning,' the announcer began, 'nine battleships, twenty-three cruisers, one hundred and four destroyers and seventy-one large landing craft of various descriptions, as well as troop transports, mine sweepers and merchantmen – in all, almost five thousand ships of every type – the largest armada ever assembled, stood off the Normandy coast. The entire horizon, between Caen and Vierville-sur-Mer was filled with the invasion armada, rank after relentless rank, ten lanes wide and twenty miles across. The naval bombardment began at 05.50, detonating large German minefields and destroying blockhouses and artillery positions.'

As the news of the invasion unfolded they were both stunned into silence, imagining the scene, but it was the news of the 29th Infantry that held Daisy 's special attention and that came towards the end of the bulletin.

'On Omaha beach, the invading GIs encountered the worst conditions of the entire battle,' the announcer read. 'High seas swamped many landing craft during the ten-mile run from the mother ships to shore and consequently those survivors who reached the beach were seasick and wobbling. Over half of the dual-drive amphibious tanks capsized, strong winds and currents pushed many of the landing craft away from their targets into areas where their maps were useless and supporting fire from friendly ships was totally lacking. Most of the landing craft that survived were grounded on sandbars fifty to a hundred yards from the surf's edge. Troops had to wade ashore carrying all their equipment through water that was often neck deep, and many were picked off by enemy machine guns. Only one-third of the attackers reached dry land during the first hour of the invasion.

'Conditions were near-inferno on Omaha. The beach was a tangle of obstructions: concrete cones, slanted poles, logs with mines lashed to their tips and steel rails welded together and set into the beach at angles designed to stave in the bottoms of landing craft. Even worse, the Germans had guns along a line of cliffs, four miles long and 150 feet in height, running parallel to the length of the landing zone. Enemy mortar and artillery batteries, unscathed by Allied fire, poured destruction upon the attackers. Allied rocket ships responded, but from extreme range and when their missiles fell short they hit the troops on the beach. Despite these setbacks, GI riflemen succeeded in opening six complete gaps. Casualties for the engineering task force ran to 40 percent of the men in the first half-hour of the attack.

'As the invaders reorganized, Allied destroyers moved close to shore. Risking grounding and point-blank fire from the enemy batteries, they raked the cliff with their guns. More and more landing craft pushed their way to the beach, bringing new troops, heavy weapons, radios and ammunition. Inch by inch the invaders moved forward, up through the bluffs and on to the flatland above. By nightfall, two thousand, five hundred men had been lost at Omaha.

'All the Normandy beaches were a shambles of burning and disabled vehicles, but one hundred thousand men were ashore, the first of the millions who would follow, and almost all of the coastal villages located inland were in Allied hands.'

Daisy prayed that Mike and Simon had survived. She tried to keep calm, for her baby's sake, but her fears for Mike's safety drowned every rational thought. She took refuge in hard work.

Bitter days followed. Helen returned from hospital in a wheelchair. Her legs were numb, but the pain in her back was sometimes agonizing. For Daisy's sake she tried to be cheerful. Daisy was large for seven months and feeling clumsy and heavy. John closed down the stables and found good homes for the horses, keeping Daunty only to please Daisy. He hired a housekeeper, a Polish refugee, called Ada Govlovsky, who coped magnificently with all the chores, but hardly spoke English. She was a blonde, middle-aged woman of fifty-two, who looked ten years younger than her age. Tall and slender, she had an air of elegance about her. Helen, who had nothing better to do than to sit around watching people, admired her sense of humour and her talent at cooking, but Ada kept to herself and never confided details of her past. She lived in the village and arrived sharp at seven each morning in time to make breakfast. She was always smiling, and as her English quickly improved she became a valuable addition to the family. May became a regular visitor as she tried to cheer Helen. She brought her books and chocolate and news from the factory.

Six weeks after the invasion, Daisy received a letter from Mike in which he poured out his love and his longing to be with her and urged her to take care of herself. He was trying to get compassionate leave for when the baby was born, but he doubted he would succeed. She must write as soon as she knew the probable date. 'Simon sends his love to everyone,' he added in a postscript.

Another letter came in the same post. It was from Captain Rose. He wrote that the landing on Omaha Beach was a near-disaster which was averted only by the courage of our Allied soldiers and sailors. 'There were many heroes on Omaha that morning,' he went on. 'One of them was Sergeant Mike Lawson, who waded back into the sea time and again to recover vital radios they needed and guide the men through the debris. Later he found a safe route off the beach and returned several times to guide his men and others to the top of the plateau. He has been awarded the Medal of Honour and promoted to the rank of lieutenant. It is an honour to have your husband, Lieutenant Michael Lawson, in my division.'

Daisy carried her letters around at all times and read the commendation to everyone she met. Helen never grew tired of having it read to her, although she knew it by heart already.

The time had come to write the letter that Helen had been putting off for so long. She might as well face up to it, she decided.

My dearest Simon,
Every night we follow the news and pray for you all. The company's heroic actions on Omaha beach on D-Day were truly inspiring.

I am sorry for our last fight, which I have regretted ever since. You were quite right, I was wrong and I should have trusted you and realized that you had worked out a solution for Miro's dilemma, as you solved all our problems when they occurred.

You changed our lives, and brought hope and joy and a newfound optimism.

The truth is I loved you dearly, but that was then, and this is now. I have decided that I do not wish to marry again, nor to leave England, nor even this house. John will need looking after as time goes by. I am busy with the horses and happy

with the way things are. I think it's best if we don't see each
other again or write. So this is goodbye.

I pray you will keep safe until the end of the war and I
wish you all the success in the world to rebuild your career
when you reach home. Dearest Simon, my two years
spent with you will always be my happiest memories.

With thanks and my warmest regards,
Helen

Helen agonized for days over the ending of her letter. Should she
write 'with love'? If she did would Simon come looking for her?
He might, so love was out. 'Warmest regards' would do the job
adequately.

She sealed it, addressed the envelope and May took it to the post
when she went to the village to buy their groceries.

'He won't come now, May,' she told her friend later. 'He is proud,
far too proud to try to force himself upon someone who has thrown
him over. I'm determined that he will never see me in a wheelchair. I love him too much to let him be saddled with a crippled
wife. This is how it must be.'

Thirty-Nine

Once again she had dreamed of him.

Helen had fought and fought to be free of Simon and his world all through those bitter months following her accident. She had to put her love aside in order to live. And she had done well, if you were to judge her progress by other people's views. John's, for instance. He had nurtured her through her bad times, encouraged her to study for a psychology degree, so that eventually she would earn her living as a child psychologist. He converted his former office into an office for her, so she could run an employment exchange for ex-servicemen; it had worked, too. And it was her father who had encouraged her to go for an operation, which, the specialists assured her, had only a twenty percent chance of fusing her spine and restoring feeling to her legs. It had been successful, although the pain had been excessive for months afterwards. She could walk with the aid of a stick and with time, patience and practice she should improve, the doctors told her.

But deep inside she was losing. What extraordinary trauma bound her to Simon? Through dark days in the wheelchair, and her recovery, and the painful business of learning to walk again, and starting her business, she had consciously put away all thoughts of him. She forced herself to accept that Simon had no place in her life. The GIs were gone, the war was recently over, Britain was learning to stand on her own feet and pay back her debts and so was she.

Yet, as the months passed, the bond grew stronger. When she looked out of the open door and saw the first spring blossom bursting from the almond tree, she would turn to tell Simon and feel shocked that he was not there. And so it went with all those daily sounds and smells and images. The click of tea spoons and the scent of steaming coffee would bring him into her room carrying two mugs. He would stand there smiling and say, 'That was good sex.' But she fought back. She would close her eyes and will his unwanted image to spiral away into outer space. Sometimes this worked well enough to see her through an entire day.

On the whole she had coped well enough. Miro had managed to get leave and come home at least once every two months, if only for a day, but she had longed to see Daisy again. Mike had left the army right after V.E. day, eighteen months ago, his demobilization hastened by a bullet in the knee. Despite his wounds, he had flown back to England on crutches to collect his wife and son, not forgetting his horse, and flown them all back to Denver. Their leaving had been hasty, but they had promised Helen and John to return for a long family reunion when Mike was completely recovered . . . and so they had, arriving two weeks ago for a long stay.

Tonight was the big family reunion party and tomorrow morning Paul Eric Lawson would be christened at the grand age of two years and three months.

Helen could see how happy Mike and Daisy were. Mike was a great husband and father and Daisy had never been so contented. It was a shame that Mike's father had not been able to come, but one of them had to look after the ranch.

Miro had arrived two days ago, bringing Irwin, his father, with him. Sadly his mother had died in the camp only days before the prisoners were released. Helen's office had been turned into a bedroom for Irwin, whom she knew well. He had become a good friend, visiting Helen once or twice a day when she was in hospital in London.

Helen dressed and went downstairs. Daisy was sitting at the kitchen table, frowning as she put the finishing touches to the icing on Paul's christening cake. She was lavishing as much care on the decorations as she gave to her paintings. Most of the characters from Paul's books adorned the icing: Mickey Mouse, the Wizard of Oz, Pluto, Bambi and others Helen had never heard of, each one made by her daughter. Helen had not seen a such a magnificent cake since pre-war days. It was only possible because Daisy had brought most of the ingredients with her. Food was still rationed in Britain and the bread looked even dingier. It was not the U-boats, but a lack of foreign cash that was keeping them short of food. Long, hard years lay ahead.

Suddenly she was glad that Daisy was living in the States. That was one good result of the so-called American Occupation, but there were many others, although it was hard to tell if it were the war, or the American influence that had brought about so much change.

Stealthily and unseen, the sweet semen of Yankee culture had splattered Britain and their fertile country had stirred, opened its thighs and sighed contentedly.

'What are you thinking about, Mum? You look so far away,' Daisy asked.

'I was thinking about how much we have all changed.'

'And Miro most of all,' Daisy retorted. 'He's really dishy. Have you seen his girlfriend yet?'

'Not yet,' Helen said. 'I'm longing to meet her. Where's Mike?'

'He's taken Paul to the airport to fetch his friend.'

'The friend who is going to be godfather?'

'Yes.'

'Do I know him?'

'I think you've met him,' Daisy answered. 'They'll be back quite soon. Mum, why don't you put on something pretty . . . *please.*'

'I don't bother about pretty anymore.'

'For me, Mum. I want to show you off back home. Mike's going to take photographs. You look wonderful. You don't look a day over thirty. Did you know that? I'm sure you'll marry again.'

'Don't be silly. No one looks at someone who's crippled. Besides, I would never be able to . . .' She broke off. Now was not the time to remember Simon.

'But you can walk now.'

'Only slowly and with a stick.'

'But it's a miracle, don't you think so?'

'Yes. I do . . . and I hope I will continue to improve.'

'Do you ever think about Simon?'

'That's forbidden territory, Daisy. I try to keep my mind on my studies.'

'OK. Sorry.'

Daisy got up, rinsed her hands under the tap, and hugged Helen. 'I think you're wonderful, Mum. You're the best mother in the world. I remember you had such a pretty blouse . . . thin Swiss cotton in blue and violet. Do you still have it?'

'Yes, would you like to have it?'

'No, Mum. I want you to wear it. And let your hair down. These pictures will be all I have . . . since you won't give in and come to live with us.' She sighed dramatically.

'I'll come for holidays,' Helen promised. 'Are you lonely, Daisy?'

'No. I have lots of friends, but I miss you, Mum.'

'I miss you, too, but that's life, endless growth and change. If you want me at my best for the photograph I'll have to go and wash my hair. See you later.'

While she was washing and drying her hair, she heard Irwin practicing with the new violin Miro had bought him, the price had put the boy in hock for years. Irwin was to play tonight at the party, together with Miro and the small band they had hired.

He switched to 'String of Pearls' and foolishly Helen allowed herself to listen and muse, but too many memories came with the melody. Please stop, she wanted to call down to him, but how could she? Instead she switched on the radio.

All at once a fearful suspicion came to mind, sending her into panic mode. Just who was this friend who would be Paul's god-father? She wasn't sure . . . she didn't know . . . so why was she so fearful? She hadn't felt like this since the air raids and her fear would not go away. It felt as if doom lurked just around the corner, waiting to demolish her world. She heard Daisy running a bath, so she dressed hastily and crept down to the kitchen.

The catering staff were bringing in boxes of food and Ada was keeping an eye on them. 'Ada, please . . . I need to get out. I'm going for a walk. Make excuses for me. If anyone asks, tell them I felt like some fresh air.'

'Where shall I say you've gone?'

'Anywhere . . . any place. Make up something. I want to be alone.'

Seeking out the flat, safe ground, Helen crossed the garden to the woods, hoping that no one saw her from the windows. She had not been here for a very long time. The path was overgrown with brambles and clumps of wild parsley. Blackthorn and hawthorn trees formed impenetrable barriers. She had to make detours and push the branches out of her way, scattering squirrels and birds. A fox stood astride the path ahead of her, as if in shock, before fleeing. She kept going, feeling dazed and confused, so at first she did not recognize the folly, for it was half-covered with ivy.

Negotiating the slippery stone step up to the door, she pushed hard and it opened with creaks and groans to a room that was thick with dust and bird droppings. Several starlings bolted through a hole in the roof. What a mess! The old cane chair was still there. She thumped it on the floor to shake off the dust, and pulled it to the doorway so she could sit in it for a while and pull herself together.

The sea was turquoise and calm and she could hear the waves lapping on the shore. Panic receded as the sun warmed her. Now she could get to grips with the cause of her fear.

Who exactly was the friend that Mike was fetching and why had they waited so long for him to get leave? Who could be that import-ant to them both? Why did Daisy care what she wore, or how she looked? Taking photographs was not an adequate excuse since they had both taken dozens of snaps since they arrived. Could it be Simon? What if he were married? How could she bear the pain?

If I loved him I would want him to be happy, she told herself. Love is not selfish, not real love. Did I expect him to go through life a bachelor just because of a wartime affair? So why was her stomach churning?

She should go back, but she knew that she could not. She tried to recall Mike's many friends, but why would any of them be coming from Nuremberg? The wind was coming up, gulls were circling and crying below. Helen shivered, but remained gazing out to sea, feeling quite incapable of moving or going home.

She was distracted by the sound of branches cracking, footsteps were approaching. She saw a flash of khaki through the branches, black hair burnished by sunlight, a loping walk, arms swinging – every expression and every mood was deeply loved. Look at him now, brow furrowed, lips pressed together, the way he had always looked when there was something tough he had to face up to. Simon squatted on the step beside her and glared at the sea. He was steeling himself to say something, but he looked so fierce and so very determined.

Whatever it is, I'll take it on the chin, she promised herself. No more running away. She forced a smile and bravely waited for the verdict.